I0662147

Happily Ever Austen

EMBER

ELLEN MINT

Ember
ISBN # 978-1-80250-576-4
©Copyright Ellen Mint 2023
Cover Art by Erin Dameron-Hill ©Copyright October 2023
Interior text design by Claire Siemaszkiewicz
Totally Bound Publishing

This is a work of fiction. All characters, places and events are from the author's imagination and should not be confused with fact. Any resemblance to persons, living or dead, events or places is purely coincidental.

All rights reserved. No part of this publication may be reproduced in any material form, whether by printing, photocopying, scanning or otherwise without the written permission of the publisher, Totally Bound Publishing.

Applications should be addressed in the first instance, in writing, to Totally Bound Publishing. Unauthorised or restricted acts in relation to this publication may result in civil proceedings and/or criminal prosecution.

The author and illustrator have asserted their respective rights under the Copyright Designs and Patents Acts 1988 (as amended) to be identified as the author of this book and illustrator of the artwork.

Published in 2023 by Totally Bound Publishing, United Kingdom.

No part of this book may be reproduced, scanned, or distributed in any printed or electronic form without permission. Please do not participate in or encourage piracy of copyrighted materials in violation of the authors' rights. Purchase only authorised copies.

Totally Bound Publishing is an imprint of Totally Entwined Group Limited.

If you purchased this book without a cover you should be aware that this book is stolen property. It was reported as "unsold and destroyed" to the publisher and neither the author nor the publisher has received any payment for this "stripped book".

EMBER

Dedication

My TEG journey began with Pride & Pancakes. I had no idea back in 2019 that I'd eventually publish fifteen books and counting with them. Thank you to my awesome editors for believing in me and polishing up my brain goo into a diamond. To my extraordinary readers kind enough to leave reviews on all of my books. And to you for taking a chance on this book. Once more into the HEA.

Chapter One

"I'm Ember Woodhouse, and I've been blessed with beauty, intelligence and a blissful life." Ember jumped in her chair, her arm extended so the gold and diamond bangles nearly snagged the mike. Steadying her chair, she looked to the shadow behind the massive lights. "How was that?"

"Good. Do you want to mention your father?"

"Oh, how could I forget?" Ember flicked her freshly tipped nails against her forehead, doing her best to not smear her makeup. "The Woodhouse name isn't traffic stopping. I mean, we don't have a yacht and there's only the one summer home. We're not *rich*, merely well off."

"Uh-huh." The producer—who'd taken Ember under her wing—rolled her hand for more.

Narrowing her eyes, Ember could just make out the producer with a hand pressed to the side of her headphones while staring at a tablet. "Why don't you tell us why you tried out for this show?"

Again?

The second she felt her smile dipping, she cranked it to eleven, then lowered it to an eight. The last thing she wanted was to come across as insincere. "Well, I'm pleased as punch to be on *Constructing Love*, the only DIY and romance show."

"Yeah, that's... That's fine." Producer Sam scooted forward in her chair, knocking into the three-hundred-watt light that'd been beaming directly into Ember's eyes for the last twenty minutes. "But why pick this show? Is it because your family made their money in lumber? And please answer by including the question."

Smiling to show off her new veneers, Ember straightened her back. "While my daddy's lumber has gone into some of the most famous buildings around the world, that isn't why I signed up."

She'd thought her family connections would be a detriment. Actual construction workers were cut within the first three episodes over seventy-eight percent of the time. The last thing Ember wanted was to come off as a ringer — they got the villain cut every time.

Sloping her shoulder down, she let her gaze wander past the hanging screens keeping her penned in. Behind the camera, a tree branch shook. The red and yellow leaves danced, threatening to tumble right in front of the shot.

"I'm here for love," Ember said in a soft voice.

The producer sighed and jabbed a stylus at her tablet. "Isn't everyone?"

"Not for me," Ember interrupted, causing the woman to look up in surprise.

"Why not?"

Sweat beaded on Ember's brow and she nipped her lip. "Under the tutelage of Miss Shandy — a respected life coach — I am on a sabbatical from sex."

The cameraman behind the black lens snickered. "What the shit's that mean?"

Smiling without a care, Ember declared, "Instead of falling in love, I intend to be this season's matchmaker."

Sam leaned back. "That's a lofty claim. We've only had one successful matchmaker reach the final two."

"I can do it. I recently returned from the beautiful wedding of my sorority sister Anne whom I set up with her future beau. Their love was destined in the stars, but they would have never met were it not for me."

Producer Sam twitched her lip as if she were about to laugh, but Ember was dead serious. "Excellent. Well, why don't you close this interview out by saying, oh, I don't know? 'I'll craft buildings and make matches on *Constructing Love'*."

Were they going to give her the first bumper? Ember raised her shoulders and steadied her back. Lifting her chin, she opened her mouth while still smiling. "I'll cra —"

A massive beam swung from behind, knocking out the PVC pipe holding up the background screen. The entire structure collapsed, revealing the parking lot of an abandoned Home Depot behind them. Ember's heart leaped into her throat. She jerked in the chair, narrowly avoiding the metal beam smacking her in the forehead.

"Damn it!" Producer Sam berated the two guys who were staring at the destruction as if it was someone else's problem. "Will you watch where the fuck you're going? We don't have time to reset all of this. If we don't get them into the woods tonight, she'll have my head. You hear me?"

Two burly men in sagging construction belts bent over and delicately picked up the fallen purple silk. "Sorry," the largest muttered while slipping it into place.

"Okay." The producer ran her hands back through her hair, tugging down the ponytail as she slammed her butt into her chair. "Do the line again."

* * * *

"What's the point?"

The producer below the ball cap splashed with the logo for *Constructing Love* flashed his teeth. No doubt he thought it a soothing smile, but the fact that only his top lip moved gave him away. He glanced behind to another gaggle of harried but silent watchers, then focused on the man in the hot seat.

"Mr. Knightley... Can I call you Booker?"

He answered by shrugging, his long legs bent wide to fit in the short chair.

"We need you to introduce yourself to the cameras, so America can get to know and love you."

Booker dropped his hard arm cross and glared directly into the dark, uncaring eye of the camera. "I suspect much of America formed an opinion of me the moment I sat down." He stopped and looked behind himself to the paler screen glowing like a nuclear explosion from the massive lights. "Assuming they can even see me."

"Of course they can," his producer said before leaning back in the chair. No doubt he wasn't supposed to overhear him whisper, "Gary, check the exposure. What? Well, get a few lights over there. Sorry about that. We've had a few setbacks as of late."

The scattered gaffers hustled over a huge light, its legs snagging on a cord. They kept pulling, dragging the set of monitors and the producer watching it with. His producer, a far too friendly man named Ash, reached over as if to pat Booker on the knee.

Booker shifted his legs before he could touch him. "When will we be arriving at the construction site?" he asked.

"Excited to get to work?" Ash didn't answer Booker's question. "Ah, says here you've done some work. Anything official?"

Booker glanced to the tablet crammed full of white lies just sparkling enough to be true. "No," he said and the producer kept staring as if he needed more. "I helped my grandmother build a shed once."

"That's so kind of you. Why don't you tell me about her?"

"She's dead." Mr. Knightley's tone dropped to the parking lot cement.

"Oh, well, that... We don't have that down here. Why don't we have that here?" Ash leaned back, furiously whispering with what looked like a fifteen-year-old girl holding ten clipboards. She squirmed at the attention and kept offering up excuses Ash wouldn't take. He looked about to fire her on the spot.

"It happened recently," Mr. Knightly interrupted, drawing the producer's attention and forced smile. "And I'd prefer to not discuss it."

"Of course, of course. We'll be nothing but respectful of your wishes."

Indeed.

Ash fiddled with his tablet for so long Booker began to wonder if this waste of time was over. He slid forward in the chair and reached for the mike they'd wired up under his Henley.

"You're the oldest person we've had on the show."

Booker froze, his fingers wound in the cord, and he stared at the producer, who then tapped a cardboard circle above the camera. Sighing, Booker looked to that instead. "I find that surprising."

"The closest was Mac from season five at thirty-two. You've got him beat by four years. Are you at all concerned how that will affect your showing in the competition?"

"Most people can swing a hammer well into their forties. I'll be fine."

"Ah, but what about—?"

"Wrap this up!" a voice shouted from beyond the camera lights. Booker raised a hand over his eyes to try to see, when the assistant tapped him on the shoulder and told him to keep his face visible.

His producer complained to what was probably the lead on this farce, "But I haven't gotten anything usable."

A woman with the LA-standard pinched face that looked both thirty and fifty at the same time clamped a hand onto Ash's shoulder and glared over at Booker. "We don't have time, the sun's dropping. We've got to get to the next location."

"He hasn't even introduced himself," Ash sounded panicky, as if the lack of a cheesy line from Booker would spell the end of his career.

The woman glanced once more at Mr. Knightley sitting primly in his seat and turned away. "He's a premiere. Don't worry about it. Mr....Kingly?" She finally looked at Booker like he was a person and not a piece of the set.

"Knightley."

"Sure. Could you please get in the limo? We have a schedule to keep. And you, get your ass to the site.

Sam's riding with the contestants, and I need a producer before arrival."

Nodding madly, Ash sprinted to his feet, only for his head to jerk back. The headphones pinned to his ears were still plugged in. The woman in charge watched with minor interest as Ash swung backward and crashed into his foldable chair. "Mr. Knightley?" she said, pointing behind him.

Booker got to his feet and tugged on the mike, ready to be rid of the tether. The assistant once again caught his hands and pleaded in a whisper for him to keep it on. If not, then he'd be going home early.

Sighing, he let go, leaving the cursed thing on. Not that it was going to get much from him. In the distance of the parking lot idled a white stretch limo that glinted in the fading sunlight from a recent wash. He didn't care about the glitz or the fame. Nothing mattered to Booker except the work. Stick it out until he could get to the site, put up with this stupid competition and all of this trouble would be over at last.

Play the damn game.

His brother's parting words rang in his head. Casting a glance over his shoulder, Booker glared at the camera and said, "I'm Booker Knightley, and I'm here to win. There? Happy?"

"Uh, we weren't rolling, so... Do you want to do it again?" the assistant asked.

"No."

Chapter Two

Ember scrunched her knees tighter. The limo's mood lighting danced against her dress' sequins. The air was heavy with excitement and the smell of eleven strangers' breath. One of the men in a hand-me-down suit that looked like it'd been "borrowed" from Uncle Zeke before he went in the ground nervously chewed on his cuticles. But even he was dashing compared to the last entrant into the limo.

The man stared around the cozy accommodations for barely five seconds before groaning. With a beleaguered sigh, he plopped his ass down right beside Ember, then stretched his tattered jean legs wider, forcing her to slide into her neighbor. Sequins ground against chiffon and, as Ember tried to push her way back, one of them had to give.

"I'm sorry!" A squeak like a sneezy mouse broke from beside her. Ember ran a finger down her dress, expecting to feel her control top, but it was the cute little girl whose dress had torn. Her freckled cheeks drooped into a frown as she kept pressing the ripped seam back together, only for it to fall apart.

"Allow me." They weren't allowed to bring anything more than a small clutch holding the bare essentials—and no electronics—but she had just the thing. "A little needle and thread should fix that right up. Could you hold your breath?"

"I think so," the girl said before sucking air in like she was about to dive into the deepest swimming hole.

Ember got to work fast, stitching up the tear while doing her best to not poke the girl. Lucky for her, the dress was a size too big on her willowy frame. She was nearly drowning in pink silk, which wouldn't do for the competition.

"Thank you. I'm...I'm so nervous. I've never been on camera before. I mean, aside from my school's play, but that was only for the library and I don't think anyone's ever seen that. Sorry. I'm babbling."

"Not at all." Ember smiled to herself as she slipped in the last stitch. "It's adorable."

"Really? Most people tell me to close my trap before the flies get in. I'm, uh, I'm Harriet."

Had she already found her diamond in the rough? Harriet was pure country-fried southern charm with a touch of innocence that'd make any man's head spin around. *She's perfect.*

"I'm Ember," she said, holding out her hand. Harriet nervously slapped her palm and Ember laughed.

"Let's get this party started!" the only man in a real Armani suit yelled, then leaped up. Blond and blue-eyed, with the kind of face one expected to find below a football helmet or above a bow tie, he could be a ticket right to the finals.

"Mr. Churchill, will you please sit down?" Sam the producer yelled from the floor. With every seat taken, she was forced to lie at their feet, all the girls twisting to keep from accidentally kicking her. The men didn't seem to care.

"Logan. I'm Logan. Hi, hi," Mr. Churchill said before his gaze landed on Ember. "Hello." His voice rumbled as he plopped into his seat, both arms resting across the backs of the women at his side.

"Save the introductions for the cameras," Sam ordered. "Remember, if it doesn't happen in front of the camera..."

"It doesn't happen," a half-dozen of the people chimed in. They'd gone through a damn near bootcamp to prepare, being tasked to remember cues, how to find the best angles, avoiding cursing, never mentioning brands and dressing properly. Ember's gaze darted to the man at her right, his thigh pressing into her knee.

No suit, not a jacket, not even an untucked button-up shirt. Heck, he couldn't even bother with a polo — as uncouth as that was. No, the fairly handsome ebony man who was far too old for this wore a stained Henley with the sleeves rolled up and a pair of jeans he'd probably yanked from the rag bin. It was pathetic.

The engine started and everyone began to cheer. As the limo lurched off to their next destination, Ember tried to keep from slipping against the man. But despite how hard she dug into the seat by the power of her yoga-honed buttocks, she couldn't fight gravity. Every seat bounced, causing Ember to yelp as she flew into the air, then crashed onto the lap of the underdressed man. His arm wrapped around her shoulders, seeming to catch her...or keep her in place.

Flustered, Ember pushed him away and tried to elegantly slide back to her seat without ruining her dress. Five scarlet sequins glittered in her hand. "Damn it."

The man leaned over, caught her exasperation and snorted. "So what? Don't tell me you're the type to get bent out of shape for breaking a nail."

Not about to rise to the bait, Ember slipped the sequins into her purse and tried to ignore him.

"A little superglue should fix 'em right up. Maybe staple them back on?"

"Staple? Staple!" Ember scoffed, spinning in her seat to glare at him. He'd been hiding in the shadows, but as their tinted windows rolled past neon signs, his eyes lit up — a tempestuous sloe black that almost caused her to gasp. "You do not staple a Dior dress together."

"I don't see why not. It should hold in a pinch." He folded his hands behind his head and sat back with the smug smile of a cat that had knocked a priceless vase off of the table.

Ember kept turning in place, struggling to keep her ass on the seat, her feet from clomping on Sam and her eyes on the infuriating man. "Tell me something, Mr...."

"Knightley."

"Can you expect to handle building entire rooms when you misunderstand simple instructions?"

He shook from his daydreaming stance and glared at her. "Excuse me?"

"You were told to dress elegantly, yet this is the wardrobe you settled on." Ember couldn't hide her disgust if she'd wanted to.

Mr. Knightley tugged on the Henley, revealing a small white stain just above his right pec. "I dressed for the job. Hammers and saws don't need to be impressed with tuxes and ballgowns."

Oh, that impudence! Ember flung her hands out and spun in her seat. She'd have stomped to the other side of the room to shoot him the stink eye all night if they weren't trapped in the limo. Instead, she was forced to turn her back to him and cross her arms, leaving her to watch Logan Churchill try to balance a champagne glass on his forehead.

"You weren't supposed to speak," Ember said to the man, abandoning her respite to glare in his face once again.

"Miss…?"

"Woodhouse."

His eyebrows lifted at the name. The leather creaked as Mr. Knightley sat forward. He draped one arm across the back of the seat and nearly pressed his mouth to her ear. "Neither were you, Miss Woodhouse."

Her mouth dropped and she turned to confront him. The limo's inertia slammed to a halt and Ember's precarious perch collapsed, sending her plowing into Mr. Knightley. Her forehead bonked into his and her hand landed on his thigh. He caught her head, holding her cheek so she was forced to gaze into his dark, impenetrable eyes. Mr. Knightley's impudent palm swept up her waist.

"We're here," the producer said.

Ember jerked away, but the large ring on his middle finger snagged on her dress. An entire square inch of sequins plummeted to the ground. Mr. Knightley bent over to pick them up, but she beat him to it.

"Logan?" Sam said. "You're up first."

"All right!" While exiting, Logan slapped everyone on the legs as he made his escape. The second the door closed, the limo took off again.

"We'll do another circle of the building, then it's your turn, Ember."

Staring at the pile of mutilated sequins, Ember fought to tamp down the burning fuse Mr. Knightley had lit. This was her first impression and she had to make it sparkle. America hated whiners and she was going to make this work—no matter what. She put the man and his ill manners far from her mind.

Smiling wide, she declared, "Can't wait."

"No talking," Sam chastised her.

"Sorry," Ember whispered, only for Mr. Knightley to laugh and lean away.

* * * *

"Knightley, you're up next."

Finally. Time had ceased to exist while they were trapped in the never-ending loop of the darkened limo. All he knew was rolling at ten miles an hour around and around this building. Every once in a while, the limo would stop to let another person out, before beginning to circle again. Far as Booker knew, it could be the year 2055 outside and he'd step out into the AI apocalypse.

The limo jerked to a halt and skidded in the gravel. After all this time, no one had bothered to pave the road? Never mind. It was something he'd fix once this was all over.

"Ready for the next one? Yeah. Yeah, it's Knightley," the floor woman said to thin air.

Only two more people remained in the limo, both of them avoiding making eye contact as if their lives depended on it. Booker tried to stand and his entire lower half turned to watery soup. His knee screamed as he struggled to catch himself before he face-planted. So many old injuries flared up at once in anger, but he wasn't going to let them stop him now.

Squaring his shoulders, Booker reached for the door and a hand wrapped around his calf. "Hold up there, cowboy. They're not ready for you. What? Yeah, fine.

They'll let you out when it's your time. No, the second floor should be locked off. Lock it off!"

He glared at the door, trying to will it to open. The past year hung off his neck like a lead anchor. Everything he'd done, every deal he'd cut had led to this moment. He was going to see it at last. Then, all he had to do was win this stupid game and the real work could begin. *This is for you, Grandma.*

The door cracked open and a heavenly light streamed through the hole. Booker had to nearly duck in half to slip out. As he stood, he raised a hand to block the blinding light and came face to face with the assistant producer in a butler uniform.

"Uh...?" Blinking away the tears from his retinas catching fire, Booker tried to walk away, but the butler clamped onto his shoulder.

"Announcing for our mysterious donor's pleasure, Mr. Booker Knightley," the butler boomed then slammed the door behind him.

Jesus Christ, will it ever end? Booker absently adjusted his shirt that'd ridden up on their never-ending ride and finally looked to the house.

"Wait." *Where's the house? Where are the cabins?* He flipped around to look past the rolling limo. There should have been thick amber forests wafting next to a crystal lake. Instead, he glared at a sign for a Motel 6 flickering against the city skyline.

"Ah, Mr. Knightley," a voice beckoned him. "If you could please approach me."

Oh, he'd approach all right and get some damn answers. If this wasn't for the house, then he was getting in that limo and going back to un-crazy civilization. "Where the hell are we?" he thundered. A person stood next to a huge medieval door, their face impossible to make out thanks to the huge lights going nuclear just above his head.

"I see you dressed for the occasion," the stranger said with a laugh. He walked closer only to find the mystery person wore an elaborate wooden mask.

Booker looked down at the clothes he thought would be used for ripping out rotten wood and chiseling water-damaged concrete.

"You must be excited to get to work," the stranger said, staring at the cameras. He was in such a state he had damn near forgotten about them. Booker adjusted his shirt, trying to tuck it in without looking like he was tucking it in.

"Yeah, can't wait. When will we be doing that?"

A hand landed on his shoulder and he followed the long, black gloves up to an elbow. The stranger's weird getup jangled in a familiar way and Booker leaned back. What he'd chalked up as an elaborate dress of shiny bits like Miss Woodhouse wore was in fact a suit coat and skirt covered in...

"Are you wearing nails?"

"You noticed. You're the first one." The stranger did a little twirl, letting Booker get a better look.

"And nuts and bolts." *What did I walk into?* The manic twirl ended with the stranger's skirt slamming together.

"What do you think?" the masked person asked.

"It's very...heavy?"

"Quite." They laughed again, the sound familiar the way an old jingle from twenty years ago could randomly pop up in someone's mind. Booker tried to scratch it, but the stranger was already moving. "Are you, Mr. Knightley, up to the task of revitalizing my estate?"

Their estate? What the hell?

"Um, yeah, okay. Who are you?"

"Me? Doesn't the mask give it away? I'm your mysterious benefactor. Now please, darling, enter my luxurious party."

The nailed stranger stepped aside and the butler pulled open the huge door. Before walking through, Booker looked back. Far in the distance, he could just make out the headlights whizzing past on the interstate. If he ran fast enough, he might be able to find a Waffle House before morning.

Thoughts of his grandma, trapped in that small, filthy bed while machines beeped uselessly for hours, turned him back around. *For the family*, Booker thought while stepping into total darkness. The door closed behind him and he braced himself.

Hands grabbed him by the shoulder and a light burst in his eyes. "Okay, bring out the next one," a voice shouted and he groaned when he recognized Ash. "Put this tool belt on." As he kept ordering Booker, Ash dragged him down the dark hallway and through a small kitchen before shoving him out the side door.

He came to a stumbling halt, clinging to the useless belt. Ten other people in fancy outfits with tool belts slung on their hips all stared at him. Most turned back to stare through the hedges where they could all see the road and the front of the house. Only one kept looking at him, her pink fingernail perched next to her lips.

"Red?"

The question bypassed all parts of his brain and dove straight to his libido. In the dark limo, it had been easy to ignore her and the other women. But by the stars and the single light off of the producer's clipboard, that little red dress swerved down every one of Miss Woodhouse's curves without a care for safety regs. All those stupid sequins curved over her tits and crumbled together down her cleavage. She kept toying with a single curl of hair against her neck, something he knew women did just to screw with men's heads. The worst part was it always worked.

"What's red?" Booker asked, mesmerized beyond all sense. She was the kind of hot where beer companies would pay her tons of money to stand around being hot. Her eyes were huge with a poisonous mix of brown and green while her nose was thin and lips plumped to the nines. It could be filler, but the way they stayed sculpted even as she smirked told him they were real.

Miss Woodhouse pointed a finger to his shoulder. Dumbfounded, Booker looked to the tool belt. Enough sense cracked through his rampaging libido. Green, blue, pink, gray—everyone wore a different-colored tool belt around their waists. She'd cinched a sunny yellow one to hers, which dangled off her hip like an old gunslinger. Placing a hand to her waist, she stared him up and down and said, "Statistically, the people with the red belt don't last past the first episode."

Jerking away, Booker glared at the belt. Pleased with herself, Miss Woodhouse turned back to the front where the limo had once again stopped. The last man got out and the butler called, "Presenting Mr. Brent Reeva."

So he got the red tool belt? So what? Swinging it around, Booker pinched the clasp together and let the belt hang off his thin hips. "What difference does a color make?" he whispered next to Miss Woodhouse.

"Wait a moment." The butler clamped a hand to Brent, keeping him pinned in place as the limo sped off.

"What's going on? Camera three's not working? For how long?"

The producers' chatter faded away as Booker stared down at her. His lower half kept trying to direct him down her cleavage, but his erected ire claimed his attention more. "You think you have this all figured out," he said.

"Do I...? Do I go?" Brent called, his mike carrying through the speakers above them, only for the butler to push him back.

Miss Woodhouse tossed her shoulders back. Small goosebumps ran down her exposed skin. "Of course I do. I wouldn't be here otherwise. You'll be lucky to get more than five minutes on screen."

"I'd never heard of a girl being gifted with total omnipotence. You'd think that would have made the news." Booker folded his arms and stared past her.

"You wear jealousy as horribly as those stained jeans. Facts are on my side, not yours. The producers are already shuffling you off in favor of the real contestants. Did you even do an interview in the dining room?"

An interview... Booker frowned but refused to stoop to her level.

"They've written you off. You're cannon fodder, a body to pad out the numbers before the real competition begins. I'd almost feel sorry for you." She dug her elbow into Booker's side, pushing him back so she could get a better view of poor Brent left standing alone.

"Get the limo back here, now!"

"Now?"

"Now!"

Roaring, the limo bounded around the side of the house. The headlights were off, only the sound of the engine telling them it was coming.

Booker bent closer and whispered in her ear, "Do you really believe you can predict everything that will happen?"

She smugly raised her shoulders. "Of course."

The limo took the turn too fast. The back end whiplashed around, wheels squealing on the slip of pavement. "I'm coming!" the driver shouted over the loudspeaker just as Brent turned and stared into the grill.

His body hit the hood and was flung up into the air. Every head and every camera swiveled to watch as Brent crashed to earth directly onto his femur.

Chapter Three

Brent's screams peaked the microphones as the last girl, Augusta, stepped out of the limo and into a pool of his blood. She clung tight to her skirt, her body shaking as the producers kept shouting orders from all sides.

"Get her into frame."

"Will someone kill his mike already?"

"I've got the lawyers on the phone."

A producer in a ball cap ran past the contestants huddled together, staring in horrified wonder. Ember kept waiting for the flashing red and blue lights to blanket away the dark horizon. Surely they had called for an ambulance.

"Look, we'll just fix it with ADR later," the producer said before glancing over his shoulder. "Hey, should all the contestants be on the lawn?"

"What? Get them the fuck out of there."

"Where?"

"Inside. Jesus!"

Raising his arms wide, as if that could block the horror of Augusta dragging her train through Brent's blood puddle, the producer said, "Everything's fine. Why don't you all head into the ballroom?"

"No! We're not ready for them in here."

"Um." He stood up and flapped a hand for the attention of someone. A jangle of glasses and bottles rattled behind her but Ember kept watching, certain the ambulance would be rolling up soon. "Why don't you all...enjoy a drink before we move on to the next stage?"

A warm glass was pushed into Ember's palm. She clenched her hand around it without thinking and took what was supposed to be a sip. But as the limo with the dented grill and red-stained hood drove by, half the whiskey slipped down her throat. The others did the same, Logan finishing his off like a shot then asking for seconds. Only Mr. Knightley refused, crossing his arms so the insistent producer had to move on to Harriet.

"I don't drink much," the girl squeaked, pointing at the neon pink martini. She raised it to her lips, then leaned over to Ember. "Will I like this?"

Looking back, Ember noticed the bartender was quickly mixing up various drinks without once asking what everyone preferred. No doubt they'd already gleaned every contestant's favorite drink, as well as blood type, sexual history and current STI status. "Yes," she said. Harriet slurped from the lip of the glass, her eyes lighting up as all the sugar hit. But the poor girl was trembling down to her toes. Reaching over, Ember wrapped her up in her arms and tried to rub them comfortingly.

"All right. Why don't we all move in?" The producer waved everyone toward the side door and they had no choice but to follow. Logan was first, snatching a champagne bottle off of the cart and racing for the light. The others were more careful.

The frumpy fellow lingered beside Harriet, a beer in hand. "Are you…do you? Need any —?"

"We're fine," Ember interrupted. The man's intentions were as clear as was how quickly he'd be cut from the show. Forgettable face, no style and a bumbling stance that came across as pathetic instead of charming. He wouldn't make it past two weeks.

He shuffled back as if she had struck him and roughed his fifteen-dollar haircut, then stumbled away. "I'm Robert," he said over his shoulder.

"He seems nice —" Harriet began before Ember caught her eye.

"Nice is boring. We only have a few hours to form a connection. Don't waste your time on nice."

"Oh." She slurped at her martini, draining the glass.

It was the craggy, exhausting laugh from beside her that caused Ember's impeccable posture to sag. "You know everything about a man before even learning his name? That chip on your shoulder's got its own zip code."

"Yet here you are, Mr. Knightley, presuming to know the inner workings of my mind with only a handful of words exchanged between us." Ember looked over to him, then had to keep trailing up. In the limo he'd seemed small, almost insignificant, but he stood at such a height his hair nearly scraped into the trellis above. She swallowed the momentary surprise when he caught her eye. "Perhaps you should familiarize yourself with pots and kettles. Good day."

He snorted and rolled his eyes, but Ember bundled Harriet safe in her arms and pulled her for the door. Poor Harriet pointed back to the producers quickly dumping a bucket of bleach onto the blood pool. "What about Brent? Is he okay?"

"I'm sure they have it well in hand. He'll be right as rain. Don't worry." Even as Ember assured her, she kept looking for the ambulance. Nary a siren cut through the still air, the sky black as pitch.

Normally, on *Constructing Love*, there would be a big to-do made as all of the contestants were escorted one by one into the ballroom. Instead, Ember and the rest were shoved through a single open door and left awkwardly next to a fake staircase on wheels. A single bare bulb lit a corner of the large room, leaving them all pressing close to it like cave people fearing a tiger in the dark.

Ember held a comforting hand around Harriet while she guided her away from not only the dull Robert, but the infuriating Mr. Knightley. Robert kept raising his head and smiling at Harriet, who was too pure of heart to know not to return it. The last thing she needed was to be accused of leading him on. Ember would have to explain that all to her once they had a chance to slip away. Every glance and small sigh mattered here.

"Hey." Logan fell in on her right, facing the darkness with his champagne bottle in one hand. "What's your name?"

"Ember," she said, trying to keep her tone even.

"Ember?" Logan tapped his chin in thought before turning his million-dollar smile on her. "Is that because you're pretty enough to set a man's heart on fire?"

Her stomach fluttered at the compliment, or perhaps the face delivering it. Logan had the kind of looks that'd get him three feature films regardless of his acting talent, and possibly the charm to score another ten after. It required further testing on her part.

"How could you tell in this dark room?"

He leaned closer, a hand almost cupping her cheek. "Because your eyes pierce through the deepest darkness."

Whew. Ember realized her hand was raising to wave her face, when Logan caught it. He interlocked his fingers with hers and pulled her closer. His lips brushed against her ear as he whispered, "Why don't we ditch—?"

The lights burst to life, blinding everyone. After the chorus of groans, Ember turned back so Logan could finish, but he'd slipped away. Everyone was spinning to face the ballroom doors and the crew rushing through the hall. Cords trailed behind massive cameras and lighting fixtures, and an assistant was trying to put down rugs so no one tripped. Ember gulped, flashing to poor Brent and his leg cracked at a forty-five-degree angle.

She shook it off when the doors parted as if royalty were about to stride through. A woman with dyed black hair in a red pantsuit entered. "Hello everyone. I am London Goddard, executive producer. Things got a little complicated tonight."

"Is Brent okay?" Harriet asked.

The woman smiled with only her lips, the rest of her face static. "He's fine. Don't worry about him. This night is for you to celebrate your arrival at the *Constructing Love* mansion!" London brought her palms together, each rhythmic slap jarring Ember's teeth. As the producers and crew clapped in time, the rest of the contestants joined in.

"All right. Now that we've got that out of the way, we're going to change things around this season."

Ember sat up higher. She'd anticipated this possibility but had hoped it wouldn't happen. It didn't matter what twist the network threw their way. Even if they turned this show into a *Survivor* clone, or wanted them all to fall in love by smell alone, she was ready for whatever they'd schemed.

Ms. Goddard clapped her hands once more, then announced, "Here to explain the new rules is Mr. Elton Brown."

* * * *

These people were insane. For all they knew, they had just watched a man die right before their eyes, but they were lining up and doing exactly as told by the people driving the limo. There weren't any cliffs around, right?

Booker was shoved to the back of the group. That displeasing woman had somehow finagled herself and the quiet mousy one to the front. Miss Woodhouse was everything wrong with the younger generation. High on her own farts, she put her faith in the people most likely to stab her in the back. He'd almost feel sorry for her when the world inevitably bit her in the ass.

Logan approached from behind Miss Woodhouse and latched a protective hand to the small of her back. She flinched, and instinctively Booker dropped his crossed arms. Then her smooth cheeks went all pink below that born-in tan and she demurred to the obnoxious jackass.

This has nothing to do with you. Drunken idiots hooking up on camera were so far from Booker's concerns he shouldn't care. Shrugging his shoulders, he crossed his arms tight and clung to his biceps because he didn't care. At all.

One of the producers leaped onto the first step of the fake stairs. "Everyone, over here." Ash waved his hands to catch their attention, but the door opened and a man in a white suit walked in.

Two of the women full-on squealed and the rest began to clap. Booker looked again, struggling to place the face. It had that pleasing but not too attractive look one would find selling dental surgery or a law firm.

"You got any idea who this is?" The guy in the green belt approached.

"Not a damn clue," Booker said, staring above the heads of everyone else running to the smiling guy.

"I knew this was stupid. I told my sister it didn't matter how many houses I built after the hurricane, no one was gonna look twice at me."

He built houses? At last, someone with potential skills. Everyone else wouldn't last two minutes with a miter saw before losing a body part. "Booker," he said, extending his hand to him.

"Robert. Martin. I know, two first names. It's... Oh, I must sound like a fool."

"At least you aren't drooling over a guy wearing a dead tribble on his head," Booker said. His potential ally laughed, but two assistants gave him a withering glare and the shush of death. Seemed pointing out the stranger's bad rug was bad for business.

Ash took the stranger by the arm and led him away. "Mr. Brown, if you could..."

"Of course, of course." He gave one last wave to the others, then strode up the portable staircase.

"Okay, everyone, places. We good to start rolling? I need you all to clap and cheer as if meeting him for the first time," Ash ordered.

They gathered two feet away from the staircase as told, hands at the ready. Booker kept his crossed, watching.

"Introducing the acclaimed host of *Constructing Love*, Mr. Elton Brown!"

So that was who he was—another clown come to join the circus. All the others were entranced, clapping and staring wide-eyed as Elton descended the fake staircase with a fake smile below his fake hair.

"Welcome, welcome to my humble abode. I am so pleased to—"

"Wait."

Mr. Brown froze on the stairs and glared to the producer who stopped him. "What now?"

"We've got two nonparticipants. Why aren't you clapping?" Ash glared past all the enthusiastic heads right to Booker and Robert. The latter quickly slapped his hands together as if he just remembered what he was supposed to be doing. Booker, however, kept his arms crossed and stared back. He wasn't about to act the fool for these people. "Reset and run it again."

Elton trudged back up the stairs that rolled below him—because of course they hadn't secured it. Watching in anticipation of another broken leg, Booker missed when a woman tapped him on the shoulder. "We need you to be a team player."

"Did I sign a contract saying that I had to participate in every inane requirement of this show?"

"Uh..." The girl pulled up her sheet, flashing the schedule that was detailed until seven in the morning. "I don't think so."

"Then I don't think I shall."

The girl skittered over to Miss Goddard, who directed the camera off of Booker as they ran through the scenario once again. Elton began his descent. "Welcome to my pleasing... Fuck!" He jogged up the stairs and rolled his fingers. "Keep going."

In the end, it took them five takes before he got his line out. Everyone else was sporting red palms from all the clapping while Booker felt refreshed. They wheeled the stairs of doom away and picked up as if they were in a different part of this rather small ballroom. If it weren't for all the cameras and equipment, it'd be a nice place for a wedding. Thanks to the crew, the basketball-court-sized room was reduced to fifteen square feet.

Booker kept getting pushed to the side, which was where he preferred to be. Even Robert abandoned him to slink closer to the mousy girl while their host introduced the weird nail person who'd greeted them on the lawn.

"Your mysterious patron for this season, the Artist."

"Hello, hello," the host said, pressing a hand to the slipping mask. "I have invited you all here to create something spectacular, something never before seen, something sensual and also welcoming, rustic and regal, deep in the woods. Do you think you can handle that?"

Everyone shouted yes with coached enthusiasm... everyone but Booker. He didn't care what this masked weirdo wanted. In the end, it didn't matter.

"*Fantastico!*" the Artist said, tossing out a trail of ribbons. "May the best builder win." Turning, the Artist took a step before saying over their shoulder. "But beware you don't lose your heart in the process."

The group clapped like trained seals. Their 'hosts' both hustled for the door as if to escape to a real hotel away from this bullshit, when Logan pushed forward. "Are you a boy or a girl?" he shouted at the Artist.

A handful of careful laughs broke from the others and some of the assistants. The Artist spun, all of the bolts and nails clinking like a dying dryer, before giving a little curtsey. "Yes," they said, then waltzed out of the door.

"What the shit does that mean?" Logan complained loudly, but the team was already onto their next humiliation.

"Get the dance floor ready, clear off the couches." The flurry of teamsters hefting up an old velvet couch to dump everything off of it distracted Booker.

"That was stupid."

Dear God, he was never escaping this woman. Only six weeks of filming, maybe less if her smug attitude got her kicked off early. Swallowing down his vitriol, he turned to her, expecting to feel a kick of exhaustion. But the soft chandelier light caught on her glistening lips perched in a half-smile, her face unfairly beautiful. Booker's tongue caught as he realized he was staring instead of talking. All that came out was mush. "Was what?"

She stared him up and down. Nervously, Booker stuck out his chest as if he cared what she thought of his frame. Miss Woodhouse took a moment to dab the side of her mouth with a kerchief before folding it in her clutch. "Refusing to clap."

"I will not play their stupid games. You can waste your time and energy if you want. There's no point."

Her little scoff was a sandblaster to his soul. She shook back her hair and accepted a glass of champagne from the staff. Raising it to him, she said, oddly sweetly, "If you're not on camera, you might as well be dead." With a little wiggle, she walked away.

An assistant pushed a glass at Booker but he shook it off and chased after her. "How sad your life must be. How tiny and one-dimensional to think that all that matters is..."

Before he could finish, Miss Woodhouse was swept up by a producer and guided over to talk to Elton with Logan quick on her heel. Almost all of the dolly cameras followed, leaving Booker standing in the dark. Watching her sparkling with wit and shining in the light, Booker grabbed a glass off of the passing booze trolley and took a drink.

Chapter Four

"Ember?"

She paused in dancing, her drink sloshing over the side. Cupping a hand to catch the sticky syrup, Ember weaved her way around the cords to the producer. Sam waved her closer and just to the side of the camera zooming in on Logan twirling Augusta.

"You're doing great."

Logan leaned closer to Augusta, nearly pressing his lips to her cheek as she blushed to her receding hairline. *What is he saying to her?*

"The camera loves you. Look, we're not supposed to play favorites…"

Seductively, Logan slipped his fingers down Augusta's forearm. She turned her hand until he traced over her palm, then tugged her tight to his chest.

"…but I think, no, I know you could go all the way."

Ember jerked, her heart pounding as if she'd finished a half marathon. For a moment, the world streaked past and her head sloshed more than her drink. "Whoa." She tried to catch herself, but Sam did first.

The producer eyed her up, closely watching the drink in her hand. It was only her third, not including the whiskey after the accident. Or the champagne they kept having to sip for more takes. "I shouldn't be this tipsy," Ember said as an excuse.

"It's the lights. They make it so hot in here, it's a wonder I don't faint dead on my feet. Here." She waved over the wandering drink cart and picked up a glass half filled with ice.

Ember missed whatever liquid went in there as she tried to follow Logan who was being asked to do a backflip on camera. His smile was the sun to the damp fog snarl of Mr. Knightley just beyond. He didn't watch Logan steady his arms and bunch his legs, only kept glaring right past the throngs of people to Ember. What was his problem? Why was he even here to begin with?

"This should help," a voice said. The familiar clink of ice and cool water dripping against her palm barely paused Ember as she took a drink. Cherry and grenadine plummeted down her throat just as Logan launched himself up into the air. He came down hard, one foot sticking the landing but the other slipping on a cord.

The next thing Ember knew, a palm slapped against her naked upper arm and nearly tugged her to the ground. She dug her heels in, keeping herself upright, but her new drink splashed down the entirety of Logan's white shirt. The punch-pink color dripped from his beachy blond hair down to his belt buckle.

"Oh my goodness, I'm so sorry." Ember looked to find a towel on the drink cart, but it was already gone. In a flustered panic, she tried to squeegee off the liquid with her bare hands. A rare heat burst in her chest from the tight muscles rolling against her skin.

"Don't worry about it," Logan said with a laugh. He tossed his head back, shaking the liquid onto the cameras rolling in closer. "It's not the first time a beautiful woman's thrown a drink at me."

"Whatever could you have done to deserve such an end?" Ember asked playfully.

Logan drew his eyes down her body like the tip of a sword slicing away her dress. She shivered, her heart thumping as fear and excitement tumbled together in her veins. Biting his lip, Logan took a step back. "This," he declared then unbuttoned his shirt lighting quick. The edges fell apart to reveal what she'd felt while trying to clean him off — marvelous pecs, six hills of abs, a narrow waist and nary a trace of hair anywhere.

With a laugh, Logan stripped off his shirt and tossed it to the side where Augusta was quick to catch it. Raising his arms wide, Logan shouted, "Don't let the party stop on my account!"

Everyone else surged around him, dancing on their pinching heels as if they hadn't been walking in them for the past five hours. Well, everyone save Captain Killjoy and that bland man. Where in the devil was he…?

Dear, sweet Harriet was pinned in by Robert. She clutched tight to a glass, her cheeks so bright her freckles looked like pepper. That wouldn't do at all. "Excuse me," Ember said, walking crisply and carefully to Harriet's side.

"You've built how many hou—?"

Ember scooped in, cutting off whatever pleasantry Harriet was forced to make. "We should dance," she said, tugging the girl on.

"Um, sure. Sounds fun. It was nice meeting you," Harriet said.

"I could dance too. Not great, but I can..." Robert tried to call out, but Ember interrupted.

"Sorry, girls only." Smiling wide, she paced around Harriet like a lioness while watching Robert accept his lot in life.

"He's really nice and talented. Did you know that he—"

"Ooh, look." Ember pointed to a gap in the bodies where Elton Brown sat on a couch alone. "We should introduce ourselves."

"Why? He already knows us."

Holding her hand extended above the shoulders of all the dancers, Ember led Harriet over while explaining, "He knows our names, not us. You need to present yourself as authentic and as charming as possible in all corners and at all times. Hello!"

Mr. Brown was a veteran of not only this show but two other less successful reality shows, and dabbled in standup comedy. His face lit up as Ember approached with Harriet in hand and guided the girl closer.

"Mr. Brown, I am such a huge fan," Ember said.

"Please." He rose to his feet and took Ember's palm. "Call me Elton." Holding her hand safe and warm, he gave it a steady shake, then clenched his fingers once before letting go. "I have to say, this season is already off to an exciting start."

"I ain't never seen a man get hit so hard and survive in all my life," Harriet said nervously. Elton stared overlong at her and she dropped her head. "Assuming he does survive, I mean."

Ember had to step in quickly. "Mr....Elton." She blushed at her faux pas, but he beamed at her and

Ember wanted to squeal. She had this. "I wanted to introduce myself, I'm — "

"Ember Woodhouse. It's impossible to miss you."

That was sweet of him.

"You're the exotic orchid in a hothouse of daisies."

She fought to keep her lips from dipping into a frown. Better to be noticed for being exotic than forgotten. Wrapping her arms around her protégée, Ember said, "And this is Miss Harriet Smith. She's studying English at Georgia University."

Elton turned to her and smiled. "Swooning over all the silly love stories of Jane Austen and the Brontës?"

"It's a lot more complicated than that. They're full of period satire. I mean satire for the time, not jokes about periods, and…" Harriet's words faded under the house music, the poor girl working her fingers in and out. She was adorably charming in her bumbling way, but Ember would have to file down the edges.

"We should return to the spotlights, Mr. Elton," Ember said. "It was a pleasure meeting you."

He shifted from watching a half-naked Logan spin in a circle. Just as Ember tried to guide Harriet away, he took Ember's hand and pulled her to him. With his hot breath slipping over her ear, he whispered, "You're not supposed to hear this yet, but there's a very good chance that I might be more than just a host this year."

Ember's eyes shot open. He couldn't be serious. Elton placed a finger to his lips, then to hers and he smiled wide. Nodding, she stepped back and took Harriet by the arm. "Come on." Ignoring the cameras and spotlights, Ember pulled her to a small nook where only the light of the moon strained through the window.

"What are we doing? Shouldn't we go back to — "

Placing a hand to her lav mike and Harriet's, Ember leaned closer. "Did you hear what Elton Brown said?"

"About Jane Austen?"

"He's going to be a contestant, no doubt as a fix to the current Brent situation."

"Oh, that's… Is that bad?" Harriet asked.

It'd never been done before, but if that was their big twist, it was massive. Poor Harriet had gone wide-eyed, but she didn't understand. "Whoever winds up with him as a partner is guaranteed to reach the end and possibly win this."

"And that's good?"

"It's fantastic for you. If we can get him to pick you, then you'll win it all."

Harriet leaped on her little kitten heels, then gulped. "But I don't think he likes me."

"Nonsense. He doesn't even know you. But I know everything about him. All of his past girlfriends, his scandals, his interests. With my help, he'll fall so madly in love with you, he might even propose."

The girl nodded while watching Elton watch Logan. This was perfect. She couldn't have hoped for a better eventuality to this game. Her first task would be turning Harriet into the perfect distressed damsel just in time for Elton to save her. The audience would love him, they'd love her, and most of all, they'd love the woman who had brought them together.

"I have to get to work," Ember said. "You're going to be the one, I can feel it."

Harriet gave a little wave and stayed in the dark as Ember dashed into the light. Just before she got into the shot, a hand pressed a flute into her palm. She downed the celebratory champagne with one quick toss.

Everything was coming up orchids.

* * * *

He was done. From the half-naked jackass trying to stick his tongue to the dripping ice sculpture to the bland assault of royalty-free music, Booker had to get out of there. "Where's the bedrooms?" he demanded of one of the producers leaning against a wall so it didn't look like she was leaning.

The woman gave him a slow blink, then pushed off of the wall as if the boss was about to rain hell down on her. "What for? The night's young."

Only twelve hours had passed since they'd been thrown into this torture regimen turned reality show, but Booker had caught on. Whenever they asked a question, it was their way of telling him what to do and say, and he wasn't having any of it.

"Because it is nearly four in the morning and letting sleep-deprived people near power tools is a recipe for accidental amputations."

"It's not that late," the producer insisted.

"Your Fitbit says otherwise." He jerked his head to her wrist, which she quickly clamped a hand over. In truth, he'd caught the time from the reflection in her black tablet, but no reason for him to give away all of his secrets.

She couldn't outright call him a liar, so she mumbled a bit before suddenly snapping her fingers as if a wave of energy sparked inside. "I know. Why don't I get you a drink." It wasn't a question — the woman was already trying to flag down the half-empty cart.

"No, thank you. I'd rather get sleep instead of a hangover."

"Oh. Is he raining all over your parade too?"

Wonderful. Booker's ability to put up with bullshit was beaten thinner than gold leaf, so of course Miss Woodhouse had to insert herself into the equation. Last he had seen of her, she had been exuberantly shouting into a camera whatever the producers fed her. That seemed more her style than construction or hardware.

"I'm merely trying to get some sleep," Booker said when Miss Woodhouse weaved toward him. Her bare feet—slapping the ground—serpentined back and forth while her body tipped to the right. "Perhaps you should as well."

"Psh. I'm fine." She reached a hand out to him, but forgot about the drink in it. A handful of ice cubes smacked him in the chest and landed in a crunch on the floor. "Oops. I'll get that."

The woman so drunk it was a wonder she could stand bent over to pick them up. Without thinking, Booker caught her by the arm and pinned her in place. "I will get them." He bent his knees while still clinging to her arm, worried she might stumble into the equipment and accidentally electrocute herself. After tonight, anything seemed possible.

She watched, peering below her peeling eyelashes as Booker scooped the ice cubes into his hand and dumped them in the potted plant. "It won't work," she said, her words surprisingly unslurred despite her state.

"They'll be fine. A little water never killed them," Booker said, wiping his palms off on his pants.

"Not that." She giggled as if he'd said the funniest joke in the world, her cheeks brightening as she pitched backward. He almost reached out to catch her, but she bowed back in time. "Picking up ice cubes isn't gonna win them over, Mr. Kni... Night... You!"

"Win over who?"

She opened her mouth, teeth stained with bright red lipstick, then slammed it shut. "Do you not know where you are?"

"A ridiculous hotel ballroom masquerading as a mansion surrounded by frivolous people drunk out of their gourds."

Giggling, Miss Woodhouse attempted a quarter turn but snagged a toe on her ankle. As she slipped, she draped her arm across his shoulders. Booker tightened instantly, bracing himself for the stench of alcohol. Miss Woodhouse seemed to be distracted by Churchill egging the other men into a push-up contest.

"See Logan—he's playing the game. But you, Mr. Grouchy Face." She pressed a finger to his cheek, trying to lift it. Booker leaned his head back and her hand tumbled to his chest. Cupping over his sternum, Miss Woodhouse placed her cheek to his pec and beamed up at him. "Would you die if you smiled?"

"Yes," he answered, his hands hanging limply at his side.

Her chuckles only jostled the woman half hanging off of him closer. Against his better judgment, Booker breathed in. It wasn't pure-grade ethanol that struck his nose but sun-warmed apples and flowers. His hand began to rise, his fingers nearly skirting against the small of her back. The flick of a sequin shocked sense into him.

Taking her by the shoulders, Booker heaved Miss Woodhouse back to her feet. She lazily blinked her eyes, then stared up at him. In the dark of the limo he'd assumed her to be on the back-half of thirty from her sharp tongue. But by the strong camera lights, her makeup smudged away to reveal innocence below. Her youth struck him like a hard slap.

"Are you old enough to drink?"

She snorted and pushed him away. "Yes. I'm twenty-four and a half. An adult."

"Oh yes, nothing screams adult like measuring your birthdays by halves."

"I've got two degrees. Two of them." She held up the corresponding fingers, but had trouble keeping them steady.

"Let me guess…a bachelor's in *The Bachelor*?"

"Ha." She turned to shout to everyone. "He thinks he's funny. Mr. Knightley here shall be the clown of the season. For your information." She stopped and shook her head. "No, you don't deserve to know. You don't deserve to know anything, and do you know why?"

"I imagine you will tell me."

Miss Woodhouse tried to drink her empty glass then sighed. "Because you won't make it to episode two. Hey, two!" She giggled at the number, but sounded so confident in her prediction that Booker's stomach dropped.

He had to make it not just through every demoralizing challenge and elimination, but to the very end. If he didn't win this then…then he'd failed the whole family. "Why not?" he demanded, his tone sharper than he meant.

If she noticed, she gave no sign. Instead, Miss Woodhouse slapped him in the chest as she brayed, "Because you're boring. And no one wants to watch boring. No one wants to fall in love with boring."

"I am not…" Booker tried to defend himself, when her words struck him. "What about falling in love? This is a construction show. About remodeling houses."

Miss Woodhouse's shoulder jerked and a single, cute hiccup escaped. She placed the tips of her fingers to her lips, said, "Excuse me," and hiccupped again.

"Here you go." The producer returned with an open IPA in hand. She pressed it to Booker, who shook his head. Miss Woodhouse intercepted it.

"See, boring," she declared, lifting the bottle up to her shaking lips.

Booker tugged the bottle from her limp fingers. "How many have you had tonight?"

"I am... I'm being social, and exciting."

"You're drunk. No wonder. They've been feeding you drinks all night and you're not even a hundred pounds soaking wet."

She barked a laugh at him and tried to slick back her hair. "I hope you nail better than you weight guess, Mr. Knightley."

He blinked, waiting for her to realize what she'd said, but the girl was so far gone she seemed to forget it the second it left her mouth. A soft whirring caught his attention just as a camera zoomed away. No doubt Miss Woodhouse would be quite surprised at all the lines broadcast around the world.

"I've had my fill of...boring. Let's do something fun." She tried to spin in place, but her feet tangled in the many extension cords. Either she was in brown-out already or damn near. Given how the producers had filled this room with alcohol, it'd be a full blackout soon. He couldn't leave her like this.

Bending down, Booker caught Miss Woodhouse and pressed her waist to his shoulder. She bent over his back as he hefted her into the air. With one steadying hand on her knees, Booker tried to ignore the joints jabbing into his solar plexus as he turned to the enabling producer. "Where are the bedrooms?" he thundered.

"Um... Out that door and up the stairs. There's a sign for the contestants," she squeaked.

"Thank you," he said. Dodging around the cameras and walking as fast as he could with a wiggling woman over his shoulder, Booker exited the room out the back door. Free of the ever-present black lenses, he took a breath, but not for long. No doubt the producers would rebound and try to drag the both of them back to the ballroom.

Spotting the stairs, he made a beeline when Miss Woodhouse squealed. "Wait. The choosing. Where are we going?"

"You are going to sleep," he insisted, clinging to the railing to work the both of them up the stairs. She wasn't any heavier than a few bags of concrete. His problem was how she wiggled. A pert ass constantly pressing into his cheek and hands digging into the back of his pants proved a challenging distraction. "And I am going to need a long shower."

By the time he managed to reach the second floor, Booker was ready to drop. He spotted the first piece of paper taped to a door and shoved it open. Harsh light lit up a tiny motel room with a single queen-sized bed. Hopefully that was good enough for Miss Woodhouse.

"Here" — Booker heaved her off his shoulder, where she landed with a loud plop — "you go."

Miss Woodhouse's tiny body stretched out across the bed, her head resting just below the pillows while her feet didn't even reach the edge. She ran the back of her arms over the duvet before trying to sit up on her elbows. "What are you doing? I don't want to go to bed."

"You're drunk. Sleep it off," he said, massaging life back into his arm.

"No." She began to wiggle to the edge, but stopped to clutch her head.

Sighing, Booker placed a hand to her shoulder, pinning her in place. "You're going to sleep. Now."

"You can't order me around. Do you think you're my father?"

"God, I hope not."

Miss Woodhouse seemed to abandon her escape plan and slunk back for the bed. "I love my dad," she murmured, struggling to pull down the blankets.

Of course she did. Everything about her screamed 'Daddy's little girl.' Doubtful she'd worked a real day in her life.

"Everything he does is for…" Her eyes opened wide in a panic and he braced himself for all that alcohol to come back up, when she got ahold of herself. "Love," she burped out. Booker was about to leave her, when her thrashing against her tool belt paused him. Taking pity, he pushed her hands away and unbuckled it for her.

She paused and stared at him, her brown eyes flecked with dots of green damn near mesmerizing. Booker gulped, the back of his neck heating as he clung to the cheap tool belt. A single breath slipped past her luscious lips. "You won't last the week, Mr. Knightley." With that, she slumped back, falling into her drunken stupor in an instant.

Shaking off all the biting responses on his tongue, Booker placed her tool belt beside the bed and stood. "And you are a lamb to the slaughter, Miss Woodhouse," he said. Running a hand over his eyes, he fought to keep from falling dead on his feet as well. He wasn't built for these late nights anymore. At least he could get a few hours in before this hell started anew.

Booker flipped off the light and reached for the door. The knob turned, but as he tugged it back, the door stuck. *No, that is not happening.* Booker tried again, twisting the knob. He knocked hard. "Hello!" Shit, the microphone. He tipped his chin down to shout into the little lapel. "Can anyone hear me? I'm trapped in one of the rooms."

Only static answered him. Was he too far away from the signal, or were the producers ignoring him on purpose? How did the door lock in the first place? "Hello?"

"Can you be quiet?" she mumbled from the bed and rolled to her side. "Some of us are trying to sleep."

Exhausted, Booker smacked his forehead against the door. Locked in a room with one bed and a drunk Miss Woodhouse was his living nightmare. Flipping over, he let his knees give out and sank to the floor. With a hard cross to his arms, Booker leaned back and did his best to ignore the soft snoring from the comfortable mattress three feet away.

Chapter Five

"So...about last night."

Ember flinched, only to be rewarded with the stabbing of a thousand chainsaws into her cerebellum. She forced on a smile and tried to make putting a hand to her head look natural instead of necessary to keep it from falling off.

"What about last night?" she asked as naïvely as possible.

Rising in the middle of the night and stumbling for the bathroom in serious need only to kick the legs of a man splayed out by the door had not been the wake-up call she'd hoped for. Though, as the rest of the contestants blearily stumbled around with massive coffee mugs in hand, she doubted anyone had wanted the wake-up call at nine this morning.

"You vanished from the party fairly early," Sam said as if she were reading off her tablet. "With Booker."

Ember frowned and a flash of lighting struck through the haze. It involved her ass to the world, dangling off of a man's shoulders. Judging by the smirk on the producer's face, that actually happened. That would explain why he was in her room and also that it was probably a good thing that she hadn't beaned him with the lamp.

"We couldn't find him until early this morning when he walked out of your room. Care to elaborate?"

"Nothing happened," she said, then groaned. That was exactly what people said when something did happen. "Mr. Knightley decided that he'd had enough of the fun and also that I should no longer enjoy myself. So he..." A panic clenched around her heart and she dug her nails into the chair's arms. *Trapped. A man standing at the door refusing to let her out. Insisting they were just having a good time. Would it kill her to loosen up and live a little?*

Smiling so hard her eyes teared up, Ember stared into the camera. "He was kind enough to carry me to my bed. A gentleman in that respect."

"And he, what, spent the night on the floor?"

That was precisely what happened. Or what Booker had shouted before claiming the door was locked, only for it to open right up. It didn't matter. She couldn't be the victim. They'd either send her home or...or make it worse.

"Like I said, a complete gentleman," she said, assuring herself. She couldn't remember anything, but that was her fault. She'd do better to judge her tolerance in the future. Bowing her head, Ember tried to calm her voice before she asked, "Did I...miss everyone picking partners?"

Sam stopped waving to the executive producer and glanced her way. "No. You're lucky. We've moved it to today, so...choose wisely."

Ember glanced to the moaning group scattered around the small conference room. Most sat on the floor, but Logan Churchill in a pair of fancy sunglasses stood with mug in hand. "I will," she said, smiling in Logan's direction. He raised his mug to her and the camera swiveled around just as...

Damn it.

Mr. Knightley pushed him aside and stood directly in her light of sight. Ember's assured smile crashed into a scowl. "Don't even think for two seconds..." she said in a fluster.

"Think what?"

"That I wish to spend one more minute with Booker Knightley."

Sam grinned and dotted her tablet. "Got it."

* * * *

"Mr. Knightley..."

"No." He didn't even glance at the chair the producer was beckoning him to. Booker walked through the automatic glass doors of the mega-hotel toward the bus. Everyone else had already been ushered there after their interviews. He'd been forced to wait, watching Miss Woodhouse charm the camera while doing her best to look anywhere but him.

As if he'd wanted to spend the night sleeping on the floor like a rag doll. Booker groaned and tried to rub the knot at the small of his back, when that grating, know-it-all tone carried on the wind. With one hand hooked to the bus's railing, he spotted Miss Woodhouse smiling as bright as the sun. She'd put on a huge hat that wouldn't look out of place at church and kept pressing it tight to her head against the rising autumn winds. He couldn't make out what she was saying, but her exuberance with a full hangover and three hours of sleep could only be chalked up to youth.

Feeling like ten-week-old soup crusted at the bottom of a bowl, Booker ignored the girl and hustled onto the bus. The place was packed, not so much with people but boxes. Hard plastic cases filled every seat from the back up to the midway point where Mr. Churchill sat with his legs on the seat next to him. He'd pushed his sunglasses up and rested his head on the window.

Booker spotted the only man with any sense, but as he raised his hand to wave to Robert, the freckled girl scooted over and sat beside him. He could only guess that she was asking if she could sit there, but Robert's bright red face and unexpected scream of "Yes!" told Booker tales.

Shaking his head at the fool falling for a lie, Booker slipped into the only empty row. He took the window seat, hoping to finally spot the road to King's Retreat. Perhaps he could finally relax. Nervous habit caused him to reach for his pocket, as if he'd find either a cigarette or his phone. The former he'd kicked five years ago, while the latter they had taken the second he'd landed in Boston.

Hopefully his brother was getting on okay. He'd left as detailed instructions as possible, but the way things were going, he wouldn't be surprised if James set the whole place on fire. All he had to do was get through this stupid game, then he could get back to the real world where shit actually mattered.

The bus's door burst open and Miss Woodhouse had enough grace to join them. Wind blew her skirt forward Marilyn Monroe style and she raced to catch it. Logan woke up enough to give out a low wolf whistle as she blushed and asked the producer where to sit.

"I believe there's a seat back there," she said to Miss Woodhouse, before turning to the driver. "Get going. We're already an hour behind."

Being behind seemed to be the norm. If they were smart, they'd schedule for that eventuality. Booker leaned back in his chair, hoping to catch up on lost sleep. The bright blue hat passed him, then it turned and walked back. He watched it from the side of his vision like a little bird on a sunny morning. But as it sat there waiting, realization sank into his gut.

"There are no more seats left," she said.

Booker sat up and stared not at her, but the producers directing a small handheld camera at the two. He fought to keep his face neutral and stared out the window. "Then you better sit down."

She was careful to keep her knees turned away from him as she gazed toward the rest of the bus. The hotel gave way to the interstate soon enough and he began to hope that they might finally be on their way.

"I have to say, Ember—" It seemed Logan wasn't as passed out as Booker had assumed. He shoved his head over the seats and gripped behind both. "You're the best cure to a hangover I've ever seen."

Oh, brother.

Booker could barely hide his disgust, but his eyes rolled over to find her blushing and waving a hand in front of her face. Grumbling, he pulled his arms in tighter and turned forty-five degrees in his chair. The two could flirt to their heart's content as far as he was concerned. Real love didn't exist. Doubly so on a reality show.

Chapter Six

Trees of fiery amber penned in the bus as it bucked on graveled roads. Ember had to grip to the back of the seat in front of her to keep from bouncing to the floor…or into Mr. Knightley's lap. As for him, he'd kept his face glued to the window since they'd turned off at a sleepy little town. After the past hour of nothing to do, the rest of the company looked bored — except for the boringest man here.

"Ladies, gentlemen and everyone in between." Elton rose from his seat and strode backward to the front of the bus. "Welcome to the Dower Estates."

The bus took a sharp right turn and the pressing foliage opened up to reveal a grand house nestled among the autumnal trees. Everyone crowded to their windows trying to catch a glimpse of the Tudoresque building tucked away in the woods. Steepled roofs and walls painted white with black lines running down the length and across put Ember more in mind of Shakespeare than roughing it in the outdoors. Though the river stone building attached at the right with a massive chimney pulled her into a frontiersman trekking out into the wild west on his own.

As they drew closer, people pointed to small cabins hidden deeper in the woods. Tiny trails led up to cute A-frames in whites and greens. They looked more modern in comparison, but their paint was peeling off of every board. A songbird flitted straight out through a gap in a roof. At another, the door hung at an angle, revealing far too much sunlight streaming inside.

Ember focused on the main house and spotted the same disrepair. Stones were missing, almost all of the black shutters were gone, windows smashed and even the iron lattice protecting them bent or cut.

"What the…?" Mr. Knightley clenched a fist and sat up higher. "Are you seeing this? No chance there isn't water damage. The roofs are practically ripped off."

Why was he so agitated? It wasn't like they'd be working on a fully functioning house for the show.

The bus came to a stop beside what would have been a beautiful courtyard if it weren't overrun with weeds. A fountain sat in the center, marked with death. Vines sprouted through the cracks to clench around the neck of the cherub at the top.

Everyone stood.

"Please stay seated until we get the cameras set up," a producer shouted, running past with the first of the crew.

It was another half hour before they were given the go-ahead, everyone exhausted and needing to stretch their legs. "All right, you can get off of the bus, but remember to be amazed. This is your first time seeing the place," Sam shouted.

They filed off fast, the way no one who used a bus would, but it made for better television. Ember paused at the bottom of the stairs and gazed up at the building with wonder. "This grand lady's seen quite a few winters," she said.

"Oh, that's good." Sam cheered her on as she walked up to join the others who were circled around the mysterious Artist. Whoever it was had traded their nail outfit for a suit cut like a flapper dress. Small beads and fringe of glittering black swung off of the lapels sewn into the bust. Was that a clue to their first task? Did they need to set up a roaring twenties party?

"Are we all here?" the Artist asked.

"One, two, three," Ash counted before frowning. "We're missing one more. Where's...?"

He didn't finish because he had no doubt forgotten Mr. Knightley's name. While everyone else waited patiently, he was glaring up at the manor like it had left him a bad review. Ash pointed to the line, then pushed Harriet away from Ember so Mr. Knightley wound up standing right next to her. Of course.

"This is a disaster," he whispered again. "I hope the bones are salvageable."

"They wouldn't give us a lemon to work on," Ember tried to assure him, but he only stared at her as if she were the dumbest person alive.

"Quiet, please," Ms. Goddard commanded from her console of monitors. "All right, Artist."

"Welcome, welcome one and all to my little escape from the rigors of fame. Would you believe that this beautiful manor dates back to nineteen-fifteen? I wonder if there's a rum runner tunnel hidden on the property, and if I could get a snifter for a nightcap."

Everyone laughed politely, but Ember's eyes lit up. Imagine if they did find an old hidden speakeasy. It'd make this season unforgettable.

"But you are not here for a history lesson — you're here for one reason. One or two, anyway." This season's guest host was magnificent, playing both mysterious stranger and coy charmer in rapid succession. It was a welcome relief after that basketball player who had talked in monotone.

"Before we get to that—" Elton walked forward to stand beside the Artist. "The rules are changing."

"I hope you all like Mr. Brown here," the Artist said, wrapping an arm around his shoulders. "Because after the unfortunate exit of Brent... Sorry?"

Everyone stopped and the producers waved their hands before one galloped over to whisper in the Artist's ear. "Ah, right. Running it again? I hope you all enjoy Mr. Brown, because after Brent chose to leave, we're down a man."

"Chose to leave?" Mr. Knightley said. "Funny way of saying 'after we ran him over.'"

The producers glared at him, but no one shushed him. Ember did her best to sidle farther away, accidentally pressing her hand against Mr. Churchill. She winced, but he caught her fingers and held them tight.

"For good luck," he whispered in her ear.

The Artist coughed to get their attention. "Who better to fill that role than the man who's been with *Constructing Love* since the very beginning!"

There'd have been crickets if it wasn't noon.

"Clap now," Sam said, and brought her hands together, jostling her clipboard.

Everyone raised their palms, eyes darting back and forth as if uncertain about this change. Elton Brown was the wildest card of them all, but Ember peered past the grump to catch Harriet's eye. She smiled wide and jerked her head in that direction only for dear, sweet Harriet to blush and hide behind her hair.

"If you would please join the contestants as one of them, Mr. Brown," the Artist said, waving a hand out.

Elton paced down the line, skipping over everyone until he stopped before Ember. She took a tiny step back, hoping his eye would swivel to Harriet, but he kept staring at her, which was when Logan raised their clasped hands. Half-smiling, Elton nodded and turned around.

"With that dreadful business taken care of, let's get to the fun. No doubt you noticed the adorable cabins scattered across the grounds. I need you to get to one, now. One man, one woman. And you only have fifteen minutes." The Artist turned over a glittering hourglass and smiled at the camera. "Better start running."

Pandemonium broke, feet sprinting back and forth for the cabins. Ember spotted Logan sauntering for the biggest cabin in all green. She almost took off in pursuit before noticing Harriet adrift between the cameras.

"I don't know what to do," she said to herself.

Taking Harriet by the hand, Ember guided her not after the darling playboy but toward the more solid Elton. He seemed to have a head start and no doubt insider knowledge into which was the best cabin. That was perfect for Harriet. "Come on." Arm in arm, both girls took off.

Running through the dappled autumn light, breathing in the tumbling leaves and the sun on the grass, it was hard to not smile. Even as the wind picked up and yanked Ember's hat clean off her head, she kept going. Though one camera broke off to follow her wayward hat as she jogged up the sagging steps and pulled on the screen door. She raised her fist to knock, and the door opened.

Elton Brown smiled at her with a gleam in his eye. "Miss Woodhouse, this is quite the surprise. Though I cannot knock your taste." He extended his hand to her as if to pull her inside, or into his arms.

"The cabin is quite lovely," she said distantly, then tugged Harriet into view. Elton's face drooped before the camera swept in, circling past them to catch their reaction.

"This is Harriet," Ember said.

"Yes, we met before. Hello." Elton didn't take Harriet's offered hand.

"I thought this cabin would be perfect for you, Harriet."

"My friends call me Ree." Her big eyes went full saucer as she stared around the cabin while clinging tight to Ember's arm.

"Ree. That's adorable. Wouldn't you agree, Mr. Brown?"

He smiled and jerked his head once, but didn't answer. Not that it was necessary. They were a good match—he the knowledgeable and connected host turned contestant, she the naïve country bumpkin whose generous heart would unlock the full Cinderella treatment this season. Ember wanted to skip.

"Five minutes down," the Artist shouted from not only the lawn but speakers hanging from the rafters. "If you don't find a cabin, you're out of the game."

Patting Harriet once more on the arm, Ember said, "I need to find my cabin. Good luck, Ree."

"You..." Elton jerked, reaching for Ember as she held the door. "Why don't you stay here? There's plenty of...space."

"Uh-uh, you heard the rules. One man and one woman. Excuse me." Bowing her head, Ember ducked out of the cabin.

Just before she made it down the stairs she heard Elton ask, "So where are you from?"

"Georgia."

Oh, they were already adorable. Certain to be the It couple of the season, no doubt, once Ree got over her jitters thanks to Elton's calm demeanor. They'd fit together like a glove.

Excited, Ember dashed in Logan's direction. The rest of the cabins were quickly being claimed. She caught Robert standing next to one with blue trim, nervously fidgeting while talking to a girl Ember had missed the name of. They could both be forgettable together.

"Ten minutes have passed. You've got five minutes to go."

After jogging across the lawns and up the stairs, Ember paused to collect herself. She adjusted her dress and her hair, took a deep breath then pushed open the door. "Hello, is anyone in...?"

Her attempt at seeming meek and cute smashed into Augusta's back. She had a death grip on Logan's arm, her smile painted wider than a harlequin's as she kept laughing at his jokes.

"Hey, Ember."

Her legs numbed from the knees down. She almost walked out, then back in, expecting to change this reality for another. "Logan. I thought..." Her voice slipped out of its confident stride to abject confusion. "Didn't you, on the bus—?"

"Ah." Logan pried Augusta's fingernails off of him, then patted her hand. "Excuse me a moment, dear." Without a second thought, he draped a hand over Ember's shoulders and pulled her close.

Her heart pounded as she tapped each finger together. "I thought you said that we'd partner up."

"I did. I do. I mean..." He broke away and stared over at Augusta happily sizing up the cabin like it was her new dream home. "Listen, she just popped in here after me and started crying. I couldn't say no without looking like the bad guy, you know."

Ember nodded, her throat too dry to respond.

"So I said she could stay for this challenge. It's just one game, right? We can partner up properly for the choosing ceremony."

"Really? You'd pick me?" Her cheeks pinked not only from the embarrassment of walking into this situation, but that someone of Logan's stature would choose her.

"The hottest girl here? I'd be an idiot not to. But...you know. Keep it between us. Don't want them all turning on the strongest team early." Logan placed a finger to his lips, then to hers.

"Right. Of course." It made sense.

Logan grinned ear to ear and slapped his hands to her upper arm. "You're the best, Miss Woodhouse."

Jerking in shock from the touch, and how quickly Logan slipped back to Augusta's side, Ember breathed slowly. In a calm voice, she said, "Sorry. I thought this cabin was empty."

"Three minutes. You've got three minutes to make your choice."

"I'd better get going. Best of luck to you, Augusta."

The girl smiled as if she'd won. Ember slyly gazed behind her shoulder to Logan. "And you too," she said in a deep tone. Before either of them could respond, Ember dashed back outside. One cabin had Ree and Elton, another Logan and Augusta. What else remained? She took off running, shoving open doors and finding two heads peeking out.

All the while, the Artist kept counting down.

"Two minutes."

"Sorry."

"One minute."

"I thought this was empty."

"Thirty seconds. Better find a cabin fast."

Damn it, if she didn't wind up somewhere, she'd wind up nowhere. They'd eliminate her before the first real challenge, before she could even show off her designer talent. But every cabin was taken. Had this been a set-up from the start? Were the numbers unbalanced? Why couldn't she think?

Scratching her head, Ember ran past a green tree, then stopped and doubled back. Tucked deep into the forest was a single cabin. It didn't matter if anyone was in there—she'd do it all alone. Anything to stay in the game.

"Ten seconds. Nine, eight..."

Running up the dirt path, leaves trying to twist her ankle, Ember willed her heart to not give out. The door was right there. All she had to do was make it up the stairs and throw herself inside.

"Six, five, four..."

There wasn't time to take them properly. Ember leaped clean up the two steps, putting her old track days to good use. The little porch creaked at her landing and she almost froze.

"Three, two…"

Yanking the screen door back so hard it slammed into the far wall, Ember ran head first into the cabin just as "One" rang out across the resort.

Holy gracious. I did it. She gulped, fighting to catch her breath while placing a hand over her heart. It thumped a thousand miles an hour, and a stitch rose up her side, but she had made it. She was in a cabin, and even if it was all to herself—

The squeak of a door thundered through her psyche. It played like the squeal of a violin before the serial killer struck. Painfully slowly, she pivoted her head as a shadow emerged from the little bathroom. Mr. Knightley crossed his flannel arms and glared at her.

The cameras zoomed in on her face and Ember groaned. "Fuck."

Chapter Seven

He should have expected this.

At least Miss Woodhouse was as sour faced as he felt. She looked about to run out the door and try again, but the barely secured Bluetooth speakers fizzed and announced, "Get your tool belts on—it's challenge time."

The door opened just behind her as a very convenient assistant handed Miss Woodhouse her belt, then raised up Booker's bright red one. "You have to wear it," he said before Booker could even scoff.

"Fine." He took the flimsy thing and belted it across his waist. It hung precariously to the side, no doubt liable to rip in half if he actually used it.

"Normally we'd have you gather on the lawn, but we're a bit crunched for time," the assistant said, handing the both of them a sheet of paper. Only a checklist of items was on it—curtains, bed, rugs, candles, shelves, plants.

"What's this?" Booker asked, turning it back and forth.

She sighed and stared upward. "It's our assignment as part of the challenge. Do you...did you watch a single episode of this show before signing up?"

His answer was a shrug and to stare up at the hole in the roof. A huge mess of tiles were missing and it looked like a raccoon had tried to house a family inside at one point.

"Unbelievable." Miss Woodhouse huffed.

It wasn't until the whir of a zoom lens broke over the still air that Booker remembered the cameras. It'd only been two days and he was already forgetting about them. As if being followed twenty-four-seven by people trying to make his life hell was normal.

"What do we do?" he asked, needing this done before he lost what sanity he had left.

"Uh..." the assistant pointed to the speaker.

"I hope you chose your cabin well," the strange Artist announced, "because your job is to make that space livable. The cabin with the most amenities on your list wins. You have one hour. Good luck."

"Oh my goodness."

Miss Woodhouse's pseudo-curse nearly caused Booker's eyes to roll into the back of his head. But as she peeled out of the door, he grew curious and followed. Two gaffers ripped off an old tarp, revealing pallets of building supplies. Most of them were still shrink-wrapped together.

While she ran to the side filled with boxes of curtains and rugs, Booker explored the plywood and fresh shingles. They weren't a perfect match for the cabin's existing ones, but it'd work for a repair job at least.

"Where's your bandsaw?" he asked one of the assistants fleeing past with coffee in hand.

"Um... You're supposed to do the things on the list."

"I'm supposed to make that cabin habitable, which requires plywood, a saw and a nail gun." Booker crossed his arms, not giving an inch. It didn't take too long for a teamster to find him a circular saw. In his digging, he noticed some two by fours already cut to fit the holes in the roof. It was doubtful they'd reach across the huge gap, but he probably didn't have time to pry out all the water damage.

With a ladder slung over one shoulder, a hammer slipped into his tool belt and the saw in hand, Booker approached the cabin from the outside and climbed onto the roof. Prying off the damaged tiles and nails was bliss compared to the past two days of enforced partying. Cool autumn winds swiped away the sweat, though he paused to roll up his sleeves. Instead of the blaring music, the sound of songbirds and a little fox rustling in the grass filled the air. Best of all, there was no obnoxious Miss Woodhouse to tell him he was constructing wrong.

"What are you doing?"

He had hoped too soon. Booker climbed higher, careful to avoid the hole as he pried off nails. He kept his back end to her, no doubt infuriating her more. "Fixing the hole." The last nail sprung free and he added it to the trash box. "In the roof."

"Stop it."

He revved up the saw, safety glasses in place. Before carving away the plywood, he stopped and finally stared down at her. Whatever she was up to inside had messed up not only her elaborate makeup but her hair as well. It hung limp to one shoulder, the rest knotted back in a quick bun. Her entire face was red from exertion and black grime had smeared across her stomach and skirt. She should have dressed for the job.

"We're not supposed to be doing that," Miss Woodhouse berated him.

"They said to fix this place up."

"No." She wafted the sheet of paper in the air. "We're supposed to be adding these to the cabin. And we only have... I don't know. But I can't move a whole bed on my own. You're supposed to help me."

Putting a mattress, curtains and rugs inside now would only get them drenched during the first rainstorm. The logical move was to repair, then she could decorate to her heart's content. Starting up the saw, Booker focused on cutting away the damaged plywood, but he shouted over his shoulder, "I'm sure you can figure it out on your own." Her scream of rage managed to cut over the whine of the saw.

Booker didn't see her again until he had to climb down for the plywood. While he measured the piece twice, nervously chewing on the pencil held between his teeth, Miss Woodhouse ran around the massive pile and grabbed the mattress. They'd given them a queen, which she fought to heft up. Her tiny arms couldn't handle that much weight, the whole thing crashing into the mud.

A twinge of pity snaked through him. She swiped a hand back across her cheek, smearing it in mud and bent over, fighting once against to lift up the mattress. For as smug of a know-it-all as she was, she didn't give up. Whether that was a redeeming trait or not was debatable.

Sighing, Booker put down his measuring tape and turned to her.

"Ten minutes until tools down!"

Only ten minutes? And these people were stupid enough to pull him off the job even if he only hammered up half the plywood. Forgetting her, he cut the section as fast as possible and dashed for the ladder. It wasn't easy climbing while carrying the huge slab of wood, but it slotted into place perfectly. Swinging around the nail gun, Booker zeroed in on his task. Far in the distance he heard more girlish grunting and no doubt the cursing of his name. But every nail he drove in meant another dry night for the original wood floor. No doubt some would have to be replaced, but if he was lucky, he might be able to save most of it.

"One minute."

Putting the nail gun on rapid fire, Booker shook off the cramps rising in his hands and forearms. He climbed onto the plywood, having to reach to get the last nail. If he didn't do this right, he was liable to crash through the hole. Straining, he pressed the button once, then twice more, securing the wood.

"All right, tools down. Step back!"

On instinct, he swung the nail gun around, pointing it to the sky, then crawled back to the ladder. One of the assistants waited and took not only the nail gun, but also his hammer. That seemed extreme, but Booker stared up at his job. It wasn't finished. He hadn't even gotten to the tar, but it'd last a night. Tomorrow he could get to work on tiling it.

"Everyone, please return to your cabins for inspection."

Pleased with himself, Booker dusted off his hands and walked around the little porch to the door. A mud-stained mattress was wedged in the threshold. "Come on, I got it to the door. That has to count."

"Sorry. It's not all the way in the cabin," an assistant said, yanking back on the mattress. Another joined him and they pulled it out, letting Booker climb over to slip inside.

He didn't know what to expect, but Miss Woodhouse with tear-streaked mascara wasn't it. She slammed a palm to her eye and turned away. "Damn it. I almost had it."

A handful of candles flickered on top of a leather book resting on a small table. Two rugs extended outward, one next to the fireplace, and the other by the window. Despite the frame being cracked and leaking wind, she'd hung up both gossamer and heavy curtains.

"This" — Miss Woodhouse panted as if she was about to charge at him — "is your fault."

"But there's no hole," Booker said, pointing to the roof.

She faced him, the panic and sorrow gone. Instead, a rabid wolverine glared at him. "You have no idea what you've done."

Chapter Eight

She wouldn't look at him. If she even caught a glimpse of that reviling countenance, there was a high probability of Ember ripping him limb from limb. That they were forced to stand in the unfinished cabin for two hours while the camera crew worked through the others did nothing to dampen her anger. This fool had no reason, no godly right to be here. What were the producers thinking?

The screen door snapped open and Ember stood up straight. "Hello," the masked voice called from the threshold, before shoving a heel through a hole in the porch. "Damn..." They yanked hard, tugging their foot clean out of their shoe.

"Let me get—" An assistant bent over to retrieve it, but the Artist waved her off.

"Forget it. I'll lose the other one, no one will notice. Starting again?" Their smile strained as they kicked their second shoe back into the shin of the assistant and strode forward. "Hello, Miss Woodhouse, looking lovely as ever." The Artist took her hand and cupped another behind while peering into her eyes. Through the slits in the mask, Ember could make out an impossible lilac color. Contacts seemed a long way to go to hide their identity.

"Thank you," she said, giving a small curtsy. Just as she started her bob back up, a derisive snort broke from her side.

The Artist was quick to turn and eye up the wooden board in the room. "And Mr. Knightley. You look...as unscalable as a sequoia." They took his hand for a hearty shake, but pulled him closer. "Which only makes the climbers try harder."

Ember was able to pick up on the whisper, though she wondered if the mikes would. Booker's face, which had been impenetrable granite for the past hour, fractured into a shock and blush. The editing suite would have a field day with that reaction.

"Now, as for your cabin." The Artist pressed a finger to their chin, slightly shifting the mask. "I must say it's one of the coziest."

"That's why I chose lighter colors, a soft orange and tan to both elongate the space and highlight the beautiful autumn foliage outside the window." Ember darted her hands to the curtains she'd specifically selected, dappled light casting a warm orange glow through the sheer fabric across the entire sleeping space. Sidling to the left, she tried to hide the crack where a little mouse was trying to join them. "And these rugs. Durable while also comfortable for weary feet after a long hike through the forests, they add a dash of red to the oranges and break up the more clustered aspects of the room."

"Hm." The Artist dug their toes into the rug. "Very springy. I quite like the candle there. It gives the place a romantic atmosphere."

"Thank you, that's what I was going for."

"But, my dear." The Artist caught her arm and pulled her closer. "Where is the bed to take that little flame into a full-on firework?"

"Um…" Ember tapped her fingers together, nervously counting each tip as she tried to find a way to claim that a bedroom didn't need a bed. If she said that, they'd think her insane. And if she said she couldn't get it in on time, they'd think her lazy. Both would cut her to the quick before she even began. "Well, what I was going for was more rustic than luxury."

"You've certainly achieved that. Stay in one of our rustic cabins, the floor can sleep up to ten. And what of you?"

Mr. Knightley flinched as if he'd been sleeping while standing.

"What did you add to this cabin?"

He didn't even bother to uncross his arms, only pointed with a single finger. "There was a hole. Now there isn't."

"I see. So no bed, no bookshelf…"

Damn. She'd hoped the little table with a book on it might count.

Ember waited for the dismissal. To be told that she'd be banished from the site along with Mr. Knightley. But the Artist only whispered with a producer, nodded then turned to walk away.

"Wait? What about the… Who won?"

The pitying look in those lilac eyes nearly sent her tumbling to her knees. "I'm sorry, darling. You'll have to wait. Oh, and prepare to head back to the front lawn."

She nodded, digging her nails into her sides to keep from screaming. Everyone, including the camera crew, hustled for the door.

"Why not tell us now?"

Both the producer and Artist swiveled around to stare aghast at Mr. Knightley. "We're all here. No reason to stretch it out."

The Artist drew a finger above the lip of the mask as if twirling a mustache that wasn't there. "It's a little thing called showmanship, darling. You might want to look it up, and quickly. Your ice is starting to crack."

As quickly as the commotion had begun, it ended, and Ember was left standing next to her worst enemy. She needed a moment before having to accept gracious defeat in front of the camera. Taking a deeper breath, she started to count back from fifty, when Mr. Knightley peered out the door to shout, "Can I get my hammer back?"

Her minute of peace broke out into war. "What are you doing?"

He sighed and pointed to the damn hole again. "It's only half-fixed. I can't leave it without shingles. Though, the tar smell's gonna be overpowering for a few days. Good thing we've got rooms back at the big house."

Calm. Clear head. Focused heart. It doesn't matter. This was a small challenge. The big ones are yet to come. I'll pick a real partner and keep going. Maybe even become a comeback. People loved an underdog. With shored steps, Ember walked past Mr. Knightley, barely pushing him aside with her pinkie as she strode out the door.

"Where are you going now?"

"Do not speak to me. Not now, or ever again. We have exhausted all that's worth being exchanged between us." Spine straight and shoulders back, Ember strode toward the front lawn. They'd transformed the place in the past few hours, putting up huge potted urns with fake maple trees, a row of hedges and a massive craft service table under the mess of tents. While the crew sat in the chairs, the contestants were forced to stand on the lawn staring toward the sun.

Harriet stood partially turned from Elton, and pumped her hand at Ember. "I've got a spot here," she shouted, pointing right beside her. While Ember wanted to talk to the girl and hear how her cabin went, she needed a sure bet now, and he stood glistening in the sun. Logan shook back his golden locks with care, the sun highlighting his square jaw and strong nose.

"Hello, Mr. Churchill," she said, breaking him from his impromptu sunbathing.

"Hey, Embie. Get over here."

She forced on a smile at the nickname, but dashed toward Logan. His gleaming eyes drifted down and he frowned. "What the shit happened to you?"

"Oh." She finally took stock of her silk dress covered in grease stains. "I'm afraid one of the boxes was covered in dirt."

Logan's inviting face twisted into a gargoyle sneer and he leaned back, just as Augusta came sprinting out of nowhere. She slotted herself into the open spot where Ember was meant to go. Fighting for breath, she bent over, but kept cooing to Logan. "I'm sure we're...gonna win...this."

Slowly, she turned her head, her eyes telling Ember novels. Logan raised his hands as if he was impotent to help, then draped an arm over Augusta's shoulder. Not wanting to look pathetic, Ember kept going until she stood at the end away from everyone. It was doubtful the camera could even see her, the girl rejected twice now and left with the worst contestant of the season. Even dishwater Robert seemed to be having an energized conversation with his partner, though his gaze kept drifting to Harriet.

"Are we ready?" Ms. Goddard strode into the center behind the cameras and looked to one of the assistants who counted them like lost ducklings.

"We're missing one still. The bl—the big one."

"Go get him."

It didn't take long for the assistant to run off and return sweating with the last of them trailing behind. "Ah, Mr. Knightley, so nice of you to join us. If you could stand next to Miss Woodhouse there."

Of course. She folded her arms and turned to the side just as he slid in next to her.

"Well"—the Artist strode before the cameras, head raised high—"what do you all think of Dower Estates?"

"When do we get to see the main house?" Mr. Exhausting shouted.

"Soon. It was a beautiful gem in its day. You'll be in for quite a treat once we get to the manor itself. In the meantime, let's discuss your cabins. Elton and Harriet. The use of color was...interesting. Perhaps a bit too much denim for my taste, and hanging your curtains off of dowels was new. But you finished. Logan and Augusta..."

One by one, the Artist went down the line, talking about the plusses and minuses of everyone's attempts at the challenge. Ember dug her thumb and forefinger into the meatiest part of her outer thigh and pinched hard. Her smile didn't waver even as the Artist and all the cameras stopped before her.

"Booker and Ember. The Ers. Your use of colors and shapes, while more rustic than avant-garde, served the space well. However, you failed to add even the most basic of furniture for a bedroom, never mind a cabin. I'm sorry, but Booker and Ember, you both have the worst design."

Even knowing it was coming did nothing to wick away the venom. Ember limply held up her hands as the assistants slotted the 'Worst Designer' sash over her chest. Of course he put up a fuss, saying he wouldn't wear it.

"You'll either put it on, Mr. Knightley, or you'll get on that bus and leave," Ms. Goddard thundered from her monitor dock.

"Fine." He yanked it back but rather than drape it across his pecs, he tied it around his waist like a belt. "There. I'm wearing it. Happy."

That caused a fluster of excitement, but after a time, they moved on as if they didn't care. He'd folded the cheap fabric in such a way only the letters "design" were visible. Ember wished she'd thought to do that. Everywhere the sash touched, her skin burned, warning that the images and videos of her as the worst designer would trail her to the end of her days.

"I hope you all enjoyed putting your cabins together," the Artist said then took a step back.

Five gaffers each carrying three or four duffle bags walked into view. They dropped the bags to the grass and Ember recognized hers nestled in the middle.

"Because you're going to be staying in them for the rest of the competition."

"What?" Eyes went wide, mouths gasped, and everyone began to mutter in worry. Ember's mind burned with a fear she could sense forming on the Artist's lips.

"And I really hope you enjoyed who you were working with, because you're going to be spending all your time with your new partner."

Dumbstruck, Ember swiveled to the man she'd sworn off, her partner for the rest of the competition.

"No!"

Miss Woodhouse's outburst barely had a chance to dissipate before the producers ran over. She looked hopeful, as if they were about to declare this a joke. Or possibly crown her the queen of reality shows and end all of this.

When the mystery host stepped forward, she clasped her hands together in a giddy prayer. Booker absently scratched his ear, bracing for the impact.

"Silly me, I almost forgot to announce the winner." They unfurled a fan painted to look like sheet metal and wafted it. "For being able to put all the pieces together in time and a bold use of accent colors, the winner of the cabin challenge is..."

All the other groups clutched hands together, often at the direction of the cameraman zooming in on them. Only he and Miss Woodhouse were left in peace. He dug his crossed arms in tighter while she kept fiddling with her fingertips.

Booker could swear he heard the drumroll as the Artist kept whipping the fan back and forth before snapping it shut. "Logan and Augusta."

"Of fucking course."

The lucky couple gasped as if in shock, then the frat bro hefted the brunette into the air and spun her around. Booker snorted and glanced to Robert, but everyone was entranced by the forced display of affection. Even as Logan put her down with more of a drop than a gentle glide, the gushing continued.

"Your prize is this beautiful king-sized bed with a form-hugging trapezoidal mattress. Made of the densest foam on the market, you'll get the best sleep of your life."

"Or die trying," Booker whispered.

"The new bed is being added to your cabin as we speak. As well as a few little romantic touches to make your first night as comfortable as possible."

Romantic?

Churchill thrust up a thumb and collapsed an arm over Augusta's shoulder. She beamed at the idea. Booker's television habits were more streaming old horror movies and zoning out to sports, but he didn't remember any of the DIY shows giving a shit about romance.

"As for the rest of you, better luck next time. It's still anyone's game to be crowned the *Constructing Love* couple. Good luck." The Artist gave one last thumbs-up to the camera then glanced over their shoulder. "How was that?"

Couple? Romance? Okay, what the hell's going on?

Producers and assistants ran around giving advice to all the contestants but him. One even pulled Ember to the side, offering her comfort. He was the only odd man out.

"What do you mean by the best couple? I thought only one person wins," Booker asked Ms. Goddard, who only peered up from her tablet before returning to it. The masked host was too busy sucking through a straw while an assistant held their diet energy drink. For a beat, he turned to Miss Woodhouse, but she had her little nose up in a snit.

Right, she'd threatened to never speak to him again. That was going to work so well if they had to share a cabin.

"Well...?" he prompted, needing an answer. This show was about rebuilding and renovating a dilapidated building. That's what Google had said.

"One person can, in theory, win by building our mystery host's dream home." The Brown guy spoke up as if he were still in charge. "Though no one's ever managed it before."

"No one's...but you've had winners. You have to have a winner."

"Of course we have, every season, except for the third when, you know, the landslide."

All the other contestants bowed their heads solemnly while Booker's mind reeled. No one had won by building? Landslide? What incompetent hell did he walk into? "How does someone win, then?"

"Like I said, either by finishing the renovations on time..." Mr. Brown turned back to the house and Booker followed.

The manor loomed, stately but worn. Even if the foundation was solid and the water damage minimal — huge ifs — it'd take months of a full crew working round the clock to fix it up. Booker's heart sank.

"Or..." The ex-host turned contestant stared right through Booker to Miss Woodhouse. "By falling in love. The best couple is awarded their dream house."

Booker's jaw dropped, along with the other shoe.

He had to fall in love. Not just with anyone. No, he was supposed to fall in love with the infuriating woman who hated him so much she cursed him to silence. And if he didn't...all of this, the past year, everything their family had fought for, would be lost forever.

"Fuck."

Chapter Nine

"Mr. Knightley is the most arrogant, infantilizing, tight-lipped bore I've ever had the grim misfortune to meet. To think that I will... That I'll have to..." Ember clenched her fists, wanting to wring them around the neck of the man that fate had turned into her partner. The way he'd dismissed her with a smugness so palpable it was a wonder it didn't seep from his feet made her insides churn. Because of him, they were in the bottom, liable to lose after one episode and there was nothing she could do.

Her producer leaned forward in her chair and tapped her tablet. *Damn it. I'm on camera.* Ember dropped her hands, hopefully before they were in view, but her glare didn't waver off of him. Just the way he stood there made her blood boil.

"You never know. Maybe you'll find out you have more in common than—"

"Allow me to set the record straight here and now. A balloon is far more likely to fall in love with a porcupine than I am to have an ounce, no, a thimbleful of feelings for Mr. Knightley. Clear?"

If she wasn't in a near fit glaring from him to Logan, who was testing out his winner's bed with Augusta, Ember might have noted the sly smile on the producer. "Isn't it true that hate, all those angry fireworks, can often lead to…"

Ember's head swiveled as she caught sight of her only hope of salvaging this mess.

"…fireworks in the bedroom?"

Leaping to her feet, Ember called with a wave, "Excuse me, Mr. Brown?"

He smiled brightly and abandoned Ree to zero in on Ember. "There's no reason to be so stuffy. I'm Elton for you."

It wasn't until she knocked over the chair and dashed across the lawn that Ember realized she'd abandoned her interview. But it didn't matter. Hopefully, all of that footage would wind up on the cutting room floor once she'd fixed this mistake.

"Mr.…Elton." She couldn't stop the blush from her boarding school upbringing. Doubtful that was something she'd have in common with Mr. Knightley. "I need your help." Her voice dropped and she glanced around the lawn before landing on *him.*

At least he'd moved on from badmouthing the tools to standing as stand-offish as possible. If a man could look like a pit of spikes, it was Mr. Knightley. Even in a tight, cream-colored sweater with the sleeves rolled up to his elbows exposing a pair of forearm muscles that… He was still a complete pillock.

"With what?" Elton whispered next to her and Ember's erratic heart tried to saw through her ribs. She felt as if she'd been caught, but doing what? Certainly not staring at *him*.

"It's this partner situation. I had no idea I'd be trapped without a chance to pick."

Elton snickered and raised his head. "They do like to throw curveballs on this show. Are you worried you won't get on with that guy?" He jerked his chin in Mr. Knightley's direction and Ember snickered.

"I'm not worried because I know I am deathly allergic to every aspect of Mr. Knightley's being. He is poison to this competition and I need to get a new partner. Do you have any idea how...?"

It isn't cheating. He is a contestant now instead of the host. Whatever he uses to help will be purely within the confines of the competition.

"I think I've got some pull," Elton said and slipped a hand around the back of her waist. Ember stood up taller, not expecting for his lips to nearly press against her cheek. "I can ask for a switch. They haven't handed them out yet, and the last thing we want is to lose you because Booker can't play along."

"Who would you trade for?" she asked. Switches were not popular, and often turned the person that called for them into the villain, but this early on... She had to try.

"Why, for you, of course." He smiled wider and traipsed his gaze down her body. "We'd make an unstoppable force."

Leaving poor Ree trapped with the dead weight known as Mr. Knightley. She'd sink like a stone, putting all of Ember's plans to the fire. Sweet Harriet was bending over to pluck a little blue flower out of the ground, only for one of the gaffers to tell her it was a weed. She couldn't be left out in the cold.

Closing her eyes, Ember had to accept the misfortune she'd been led into. "I'm sorry. I…I think I've overstepped." She tried to back up, but Elton moved with her.

"Wait," he said, reaching for her hand.

"Ree?" Ember called to the girl, doing her best to keep her palms on her sides so Mr. Brown couldn't catch them. "I think we have a few minutes to talk."

"Okay." She dropped the flower just as Ember slipped her into a half-hug, leaving Elton standing alone. Holding tight to Harriet, Ember pulled her away from the hordes to a quiet spot on the side of the house.

"I'm so excited to be doing this. We nearly got first. I think I can do better next time."

Ember stared over the girl's head to Logan, who leaned against the side of the fountain with his arms crossed. He lowered his head to peer over his sunglasses directly at her. She raised her fingers, trying to keep all avenues open, when Mr. Knightley walked in between.

Scowling, she focused on Ree's future to help her own, and left the men to figure it out themselves.

* * * *

His brother had never mentioned anything about this being a romance show. All Booker had thought he had to do was show up, swing his hammer a few times and the prize would be his.

An actual hammer, not his… An uncomfortable heat boiled just below his skin. It wasn't that he couldn't be romantic, in his own way, but this was TV romance. All that mattered were the big, stupid gestures and getting all vulnerable on camera. For the first time since he had watched Brent go ass over end, Booker wanted to run. Putting up with the potential loss of limb from these insane TV people was nothing to him having to reveal his heart to the whole world.

"Hey, bro."

Booker jerked to find he was absently swinging the hammer into his palm. The frat bro wandered closer and pointed. "Looks like your girl's trying to ditch you."

Following his finger, Booker spotted Miss Woodhouse animatedly begging the Elton guy for something. "She is not mine."

A hand slapped across his shoulder, barely shifting him. "Not if she has her way."

So Miss Woodhouse was trying to wiggle out of this arrangement. So what? She was a maddening woman with a chip on her shoulder that could land planes. If he really had to fake a romance to get through this, it was in his best interests to find someone else.

Her illogical dress fluttered in the wind. She brushed her hand down her hip and cupped her thigh, pressing the flowing fabric to her pristine skin. The dappled sunlight danced down her dangerous curves. She wasn't the typical reality stick figure, her dress failing to hide her thick ass and thighs. They'd keep the right man warm at night.

Not that that man was he. No, some other sod here could fall for all of her mind games. Whatever she was playing with the mousy girl, the frat bro and the ex-host had nothing to do with him. Which was how Booker preferred it.

She gasped as a crimson leaf landed on her chest. It fluttered, casually clinging to her breast and drawing every mammalian eye to it. Booker couldn't help himself — the movement caught him.

A man's fingers picked at the stem, lifting the leaf from its perch, but not before casually brushing her side boob. As the handsy Mr. Brown wafted the leaf before her eyes, Booker clenched around the hammer. The ex-host kept tracing the leaf around her face while she grinned with a grimace.

"Good thing you don't like her," Logan said, then slapped Booker once more on the back.

His concentration broke, turning him from Miss Woodhouse's attempted flirting. As he reached back to either flip Logan or flip him off, orange foam crumbled in his hands. Somehow, Booker had completely wrung the padding off of his hammer.

"Worthless junk," he declared, certain that a soft breeze could have peeled it away.

"Contestants!" The lead producer, Goddard, clapped her hands hard and directed their attention. "Lunch will be provided at the service tent. After that, we're going to enter the main building."

All of this could be for nothing. After lunch, Booker would learn if he had to keep fighting or walk away forever. The others ran headlong for the food, famished as the clock rounded to two. Only Miss Woodhouse took her time, arm in arm with Harriet. For a brief second, her gaze drifted across the lawn and, like a chump, he caught it.

Chapter Ten

After a delightful lunch of frittatas and mimosas, Ember had ample opportunity to talk strategy with Ree. Everyone else was far too consumed with consuming to pay them any heed. Still, she made certain to guide her around a small path. If it weren't for the stones submerged in dirt, the weeds would have fully overtaken it. No one would find them until they were needed.

"Are we supposed to be out here?" Ree asked.

They'd slipped around the main house and passed a rotting building that looked like it had once been a stable. If any steeds remained, they'd be fit for the headless horseman. Maple branches pierced through the back wall and roof, and the paddock was littered with autumn leaves. Ember breathed in, almost expecting the scent of horse to fill the air. Instead, she got a whiff of watery vegetation. They must be close to a lake or river. Ooh, a lakeside picnic would be perfect for Ree and Elton.

"If they didn't want us here, they'd have chased us away. Aren't you hoping that one day all of this will be yours?"

The girl in adorable overalls with one strap undone and a frilly blouse shrugged. All she needed were some pigtails in her strawberry blonde hair and maybe a cute bunny sleeping in her pocket to be perfect. "I suppose so," Ree said and bent down to pluck a long piece of grass from the ground. Enthralled, Ember watched her chew on the end as if in thought. "Can I tell you something, Emmy?"

Ember frowned.

"Oh, is it okay if I call you—?"

"Emmy's fine," she interrupted.

"When I first met all of you, I thought I was doomed. I ain't got the looks like you or Augusta, or the skills of Robert."

"Who?"

"Robert. Martin. He builds houses for people that lost theirs in storms. Like he can do one from a dirt lot up to a full-fledged house. All I've done is some handiwork for my uncle's business in high school."

Ember nodded while skipping past the boring man. "Yes. Robert. He's partnered with..."

"Milan," Ree said in a small squeak.

The path led through a tight squeeze of trees. No doubt this used to be where they'd lead guests on horse rides down the trails. Without horses or weed whackers to tame it, the saplings had taken over. Crab apples and berries splattered on the path, some raining as they walked past where tiny birds would swoop in for a taste.

"She's so pretty. You're all so pretty, and I just figured out how to do those fake lashes with the glue. Only poked my eye out twice last night."

"Forget about Robert. He's beneath you. He'll be gone in a day and you won't even care because you have the best partner in the game."

"Are you sure? He doesn't seem to really like talking to me. Except for ordering me to stay out of his light."

"That's because he doesn't know you. Not properly. He's put up a fence, a wall, to shield his heart from being broken again. But you're the one to melt it."

Squishing the top of her nose, Ree asked, "How do you melt a wall?"

Walking backward in order to face her, Ember took both of Ree's hands. "You are adorable, Miss Smith. Say it with me."

"You're adorable."

Ember laughed. "No, I am adorable."

"Well, yeah you are. I mean, all the guys stare at you, especially Logan."

A blush burned on her cheeks at his mention. "Logan is a wild card, no mistake. Handsome, with wealthy prospects, and the producers seem to love him even more than the camera." He was a safe bet for anyone that could shine just as bright, but poor Harriet would fade in his spotlight. She needed the steady, guiding hand of experience to keep her in play. While Ember could tame that wild stallion and make people love him even more.

But with love came envy. Smiling, she shook away the lingering thoughts of Logan's fingers caressing up her thigh. Her prescribed sex diet was wearing on her. "I'm not here for love, be it with Mr. Churchill or anyone else."

"Why then?"

"To get you to the top. And the best way to do that is by you charming Mr. Brown with your folksy wisdom." Ember slipped her arm around Ree's, the two walking in tandem through a fallen gate. The metal had rusted clean through the hinges until it had buried itself halfway into the ground.

"I don't know what to do. What do I say?"

"I'll help. After this challenge, when we've all been sent to our cabins, I'll sneak over. Perhaps whisper a few ideas to get the ball rolling. He is going to love the real you."

Ember reached over to fluff up Ree's limp hair only for her shoe to strike a rock. She jerked away before slipping. A bright sapphire glittered in the ground. Entranced, Ember bent over to pick it up, but as she reached to scoop her fingers around it, the sapphire continued. It wasn't a gem, but flat glass. Metal formed a lattice work and a yellow color emerged. Ember tried to swipe the rest of the mud off. Alas, it was too caked in by the years.

Surprised, she gazed back down the trail. There were hundreds of stones just like that one leading from the gate back to the manor. What was this place?

"Oh my goodness!" Ree squealed.

On instinct, Ember ran to protect her. Leaves bounded across the grass at the top of a hill. Ree stared down at a three-foot-tall black stone.

"It's a grave," she whispered, then looked up. "Are we in a cemetery? At a resort?"

Ember read the fading letters. "Mr. Emmet King." A hint of gold sparkled from the etched inscription. While the name was large enough to retain legibility, the dates and the epitaph after had faded to time.

"Is this a haunted hotel?" Harriet asked, her big blue eyes wide in shock.

Ember dusted a maple leaf off of the top of the stone and stood away. *What in the world is this place?* As she reached over to hug Ree tight, a snap shattered the still air. Two cameramen raced through the woods, clomping on the fallen branches. This wasn't the time for her to air her doubts or concerns. Putting on a brave face, Ember turned so the lens caught her good side. "I suppose we'll find out tonight…if anyone survives to morning."

* * * *

"Where were you?" Booker asked as Miss Woodhouse and her tagalong arrived with a camera crew.

"Could everyone pair up with their partners?" Sam asked while standing in front of the estate's doors.

The quiet one gulped and looked to Miss Woodhouse like she was her mother. "You've got this," she encouraged and gave her a thumbs-up before casting her out of the nest to Elton. She didn't really move toward Booker, only wound up next to him by the process of elimination.

"Well?" he prompted.

Miss Woodhouse barely pivoted her head so only a single gleaming eye was visible. "I was exploring the grounds with its future owner."

She… Booker fought off the sneer from her pleased voice. She tousled through her hair as if she'd just won the game, but all he saw was a pawn placed in front of a hungry knight. This was far from over.

"Now!" The masked one clapped their hands before a producer tugged them over a step. They'd changed yet again, this time to a bright red suit with a frilly pink shirt covered in white hearts. That couldn't be a good sign. "Is this the spot? Okay, going again. I bet you've all been twitterpated about this mysterious house. It is quite grand, isn't it? Has that old-fashioned Victorian feel that makes you want to curl up with some Dickens and chase after a scullery maid. Where was I going?"

Booker raised his eye line above the broken windows, the long-rotted accents, the peeling paint, and tried to take in the beauty of what once was and could be again. Would be again. Damn it, he needed to get his head in the game for this.

"Allow me to welcome you to..." Their mysterious host cut apart the hazard tape stretched across the threshold. On cue, the massive door rattled open, creaking in the wind. If it wasn't sunny out, Booker might have felt an ominous chill.

Bowing their head, the Artist took a step back and flung out their arms. "The Dower Estates."

Everyone took off running as if they were being chased by wolves. Only Booker rooted in place. All his work, all the stories, everything he wanted, everything they lost—if he walked through those doors and the place was unsalvageable, then what? How could he rebuild after everything he sacrificed to get here?

"We're supposed to head inside."

Even Miss Woodhouse's stern voice barely pierced through the throbbing in his temples and pins sticking into his lungs. A warm hand slipping over his arm pulled him out of his anxiety spiral. He gulped and stared in shock to find a welcoming smile on her lips for once. With tenderness, she patted his hand and led him toward the house.

"If you don't move, they're going to start filming without us."

Of course. All of it was just about the cameras, the fame. She needed him to seem interested in her. As if she hadn't tried to ditch him for a better model not an hour ago.

Shaking off whatever nugget of respect he'd almost had for her, Booker removed her hand and walked into the past. The three-tiered golden chandelier was still hanging. Sure, all of the candles had been replaced with light bulbs, most of which were missing, and one of the arms held a nest of bees, but it was up.

"Wow."

He focused away from the focal point of the resort to the grand foyer. Booker frowned. Instead of the quaint circular desk, a granite counter found at every upscale hotel claimed the entire back wall. The floors were hidden by some truly atrocious carpet, stained by water and other bodily fluids. But what stood out most was what wasn't there. The floor was still sun-bleached everywhere except where the baby grand should have sat. In its place were a bunch of boxes no doubt full of camera equipment.

The host directed them all toward the sitting room. Light streamed through the floor-to-ceiling windows, along with a crisp breeze whistling past the holes. A massive fireplace in an art deco style claimed the farthest wall. The outer stone was of white marble while the inner close to the fire was a beautiful splash of hunter green struck through by splinters of gold. Columns flanked it, but they were covered by two hideous stag statues completely out of place.

"The Dower Estates were built in nineteen-fifteen," the Artist said.

"That wasn't its name."

"Ah..." The eyes below the mask darted out the door and Booker winced. Damn it, how did he forget there were cameras and the cursed producers watching? "I will have to check on that. When the roaring twenties hit, this place was hopping. All the greats played here—Louis Armstrong, Duke Ellington..."

"King Oliver?"

Booker jerked in surprise to find the question came not from a producer but from Miss Woodhouse. As she drew more eyes, her cheeks pinked. "My grandpa was big into jazz," was all she said before glancing away.

The Artist splayed their hands out. "All of them. And, the scuttlebutt in the streets is this place once served as a popular speakeasy. Who knows, you might find a secret tunnel to a long-forgotten bolt hole."

"Or a case of rum!" Logan shouted, to the applause of people no doubt sobering up after lunch. Booker had been the only one to demand water instead.

"Beyond this beautiful sitting room, the estates also include a kitchen, a sunroom, a ballroom." The Artist snapped their fingers and began to shake back and forth on their hips. "Oh, and fifteen luxurious suites upstairs which you will be decorating tonight for my dear friend..."

The Artist jerked their hands to the open door behind them. Everyone spun, waiting to see who would be their next would-be torturer. Dust tumbled through the open doorway. A creak rattled above them.

"I said, my dear friend—!" the Artist shouted.

A man stumbled through the doorway as if he'd been pushed. Booker squinted, trying to see if he knew who this was. He looked like any typical forty-something white guy, thinning on top, the type of skinny that only came from genetics, dressed in a sweater vest. The only thing that made him pause were the high-beam blue eyes. Even in the shadows, those things glowed.

"Tristan Harty," their host finished explaining. Like clockwork, the fireworks shot off.

"Oh my God!" one of the girls screamed.

"Is that really…?" another gasped as if she couldn't believe her eyes. They all scampered closer, causing the man to leap for freedom, only for the producers to slam the door. He was trapped, trying to feign a smile as the women surrounded him.

"I have all your albums. You were my first ever concert," the mousy one cried out.

"Thanks. I'm glad?" Harty sounded like he was about to be ripped apart by wolverines, but he kept smiling. For a minute, he broke to shoot daggers at the Artist who'd curled up in a ripped-up armchair with a glass of champagne. "Aren't they supposed to be doing a task?"

"Yes." The Artist stood and moved to slam the drink down, before tipping back the glass and downing it like a shot. With a grand sweep, they shoved aside all the slathering girls to take Harty by the hand and guide him before the fireplace.

"Mr. Tristan Harty here has graciously taken time away from his run in the Broadway smash hit *Pride and Prejudice*. He's Mr. Collins."

"Please don't make me sing," Harty muttered.

"No? I suspect a few of the ladies here would be delighted by a serenade in your dulcet tones."

The glare Harty gave could wither an oak tree.

"Mr. Harty is affianced. He and his bride-to-be require a proper boudoir for their first night as husband and wife."

Silence fell, only the whir of zoom lenses and the hiss of mikes cutting through. "What's that mean?" Logan asked.

"That all of you have to decorate a honeymoon suite for Mr. Harty. And whoever does the worst job…" The Artist drew their finger straight across their throat and stuck out their tongue.

Chapter Eleven

"Line up, line up." The producers, plus their mystery host, pushed all of the contestants together. Ember had to squeeze around Mr. Brown. As he reached a hand out for her, she panicked and knocked her hip directly into the crotch of the man beside her. If it'd been anyone else, she could have played it off as a laugh, but of course Mr. Knightley took the brunt.

He clamped a hand to her wayward hip and pushed her to the side while glaring. Ember wanted to scoff at his overreacting, as if she'd had any intentions to pulverize his testicles for fun. His wide fingers dug in through her dress and around the line of her panties. He kept tugging, pushing her via her underwear until she'd turned perpendicular to him.

"Are you finished?" she asked, her skin burning as his palm lingered around her hip. Staring into his eyes, Ember made certain she didn't let an ounce of emotion show. She wasn't angry that he manhandled her, didn't care that he took so much offense for an accident and certainly didn't want his hand to swoop back and grab her ass.

Mr. Knightley released her hip and dropped both of his hands in front of his crotch. "Just protecting my assets," he said, then focused on the mystery host who kept darting around a bemused Mr. Harty. He looked as happy to be here as her new partner.

"The rules are simple. Each team will have one hour to create a romantic experience in the suite. You must build a structure at least four feet tall and include the following in your room." The Artist pointed to thin air, no doubt where they'd edit in a graphic. They received a plain sheet of paper with a familiar checklist—bed, lampshade, curtains, rug, candles. The bare essentials meant nothing… The real trick was pleasing the client.

Ember was vaguely aware of Tristan Harty. His songs had been in high rotation during her grade school years, but had vanished along with the boy band craze by the time she was a teen. It was his introduction on Broadway that piqued her interest. She'd been to his show once with her father and had no idea that was who played the irksome Mr. Collins. What would he like for his honeymoon? A guitar? A record player? Did he drink?

"Logan and Augusta, since you won the challenge, you get Maya here. She's talented at swinging hammers and following instructions."

Maya gave a little wave at being singled out. Usually they just called them the bonus assistant without naming them. The producers started whispering behind the contestants.

"As for Booker and Ember, the Er-Crew, I'm afraid that seeing as you lost the challenge, you'll only get half the time to finish your room."

Ember locked on her smile and nodded. She'd been fearing such. It was the man beside her who snorted. "That doesn't make a lick of sense. Because we weren't good enough before, you're gonna hamper us even more to make sure we fail?"

"Welcome to show biz," Mr. Harty said with a shrug.

Everyone else laughed but Mr. Knightley muttered, "You can keep it."

"We've set up a booth on the side here where you get to ask five questions of Tristan. Sorry, Mr. Harty. I'd suggest you think long and hard on what to ask him. He can be a prickly pear."

With that, the producers hustled both Tristan and the Artist away to a side room that looked like it was once used to house cleaning equipment. A single camera and two huge lights were crammed in there. "I need a pen," Ember said to herself while looking down at the list.

To her surprise, a pencil was pushed into her palm. She clenched around it and looked up, expecting to thank a producer, but it was Mr. Knightley with his fingertips clenched around the eraser. "Don't think anything of it. I always carry a pencil or two."

She nodded, the thanks stuck on her tongue, and stared at the blank sheet. What was Tristan known for? Aside from being as much of a stubborn pain as Mr. Knightley. Which meant he would be doubly impossible to impress and unlikely to fake it regardless of what the producers coached him to do. That could play to her advantage.

Ember kept scribbling down questions, then scratching them off as various groups were called in. At one point, Ree slipped over. "What should I ask him?"

"Leave it up to Elton. He's more likely to respond to another celeb."

"Oh. Okay?" She didn't sound certain, but they were called in next and Ember had to focus.

On TV, they made it look as if all the contestants instantly knew what to do the second they got their assignment. She hadn't expected all of this waiting around and the doubt that came seeping in.

"Booker, Ember, you're up."

Her head popped up like a startled meerkat. Taking a breath, Ember walked toward the producer who was waving Mr. Knightley closer. "Make it quick. We're behind schedule."

Ember nodded tersely and walked into the tiny closet where she nearly ran into Tristan Harty. *Holy...!* At a distance, she hadn't noticed how electric his eyes were. But nearly nose to nose, it was impossible to look anywhere else.

"Um, do you mind?" Harty said and stepped back into the low shelf holding old paint cans.

"Sorry." Ember blushed to the tip of her nose.

"She has issues with personal space," Mr. Knightley said smugly.

"I do not. I have issues with worthless partners foisted upon me by—"

Laughter cut her off. Not from Mr. Knightley, nor was it a smug chuckle. This was an uproarious giggle as Mr. Tristan Harty bounced on the balls of his feet and shook his head. "You two are screwed. Sorry, I'm not supposed to say screw on a construction show. Hit me with your best shot."

"Mr. Harty."

"Please, Tristan's fine. I don't want to be here all day."

Ember nodded and tried again. The longer she stared at her notes, the less sense they made. "What's...your...favorite color?"

He didn't bother to hide his exhausted sigh and answered as if he'd said the same thing a hundred times before, "Blue."

Ember started to write it down before pausing. Everyone would be asking about him, but this was for a honeymoon. "What do you love about your fiancée?"

His eyes went wide in surprise before his lips slipped up in a hazy smile. "She's tenacious. Nothing stops her, no matter what. Tiny. Shorter than you, which somehow makes her even more terrifying. I've watched her interview massive motorcycle gangs and they've damn near adopted her. And, well, Beth keeps me honest."

"She doesn't put up with any of your crap? Sounds exhausting," Mr. Knightley said.

"You'd think so, but it's assuring to know that whatever little problems we have won't explode into decades of resentment because she won't let them." His love haze smile faded and he stared at the camera. "Did that answer your question?"

Ember nodded, though aside from including a stuffed wolverine, she wasn't certain how to add tenacious to a room. "What would you say your shared style is?"

"I'm a bit more rustic. Lodges, wood, blankets everywhere. She's far more modern. Clean lines and the like. Though she does love color."

Okay, that was pay dirt. A modern rustic lodge look... Ember could work with that. And it'd fit beautifully with this estate. She had two more questions left. "If there was one object, one thing, one moment from your time together with Beth, what would that be?"

He didn't pause to think and blurted out, "Pancakes."

"Pancakes?" She'd expected a romantic serenade, maybe a beloved guitar or a trip to Paris, but pancakes threw her.

"I don't know what to tell you. We're a bit strange."

"It's cute," Ember tried to assure him, as if he didn't glow whenever talking about her. "I have one last question."

"Ah." The producer interrupted. "Why don't we let Booker ask a question?"

Damn it. Ember tapped the pencil against her next question, but he completely ignored her, looked Tristan in the eye, and asked, "What do you want in your room?"

One by one, every jaw dropped as they turned to first Tristan, then the producer. "You can't just ask someone what they want."

"Why not? It's how real life works."

"Because…" The producer shouted to the command center, "Yes, he just flat-out asked that. I don't know. Okay. Okay! I'm sorry, but that's against the rules."

"Since when?" Booker asked.

"Since now. Your five questions are up. Please leave."

Ember tried to fight against the shove. "Wait, he didn't answer."

"Nor will he."

"But I should still get another question. Mr. Harty, Tristan, where are you…?"

The door slammed in her face but Ember kept shouting, "Where are you planning on honeymooning?" Enraged, she turned on Mr. Knightley, who didn't seem to have a care in the world. "Why did you do that?"

"Ask the common-sense question?"

"You knew they couldn't allow that. It's cheating."

"It's a reality show. Fake. There are no rules, only what they make up in order to get the story they want. One day you could be on top, the next in the gutter thanks to their whims. They aren't the justice system. They're spiteful gods here to wreck lives." He said that directly into his microphone where every 'spiteful god' heard it. "I'm heading upstairs to this 'honeymoon suite'," Mr. Knightley declared, including the air quotes.

Ember gulped and studied the producers suddenly paying her no mind, as if she wasn't worth their attention. Was her neck on the chopping block along with his?

If she didn't win this challenge, she'd be out before the first real night.

* * * *

"They painted the walls white?" Booker didn't care that the sound-check guy and cameraman both glared at him. Did they not see this beige travesty before them? Unlike the cabins, someone must have come through to make the bedrooms 'acceptable.' They'd certainly modernized the room so it was as unwelcoming and sterile as a dental office that sold teeth on the side.

Miss Woodhouse paused beside him, her lips pinched as if she too was annoyed, but she kept it inside while pointing to the middle of the room. "At least there's a bed."

"A cheap mattress probably stuffed with asbestos on top of a fifty-dollar Walmart frame." Booker sneered at the cheap decor littered throughout the room. At least the floors weren't painted, though they were scuffed to hell and would need resurfacing. The layout of the room was beautiful with a rosette stained-glass window resting behind the headboard. Or where the headboard of a proper bed would be. A little fireplace in white and gold stone with the same art deco columns rested on the east side, while the door to the en suite took the left. God help him, but the bones of the room looked solid. Though, a bedroom or two in good shape meant nothing if the foundation was shot. He needed to get down into the basement and check for cracks.

Dark hair brushed against his shoulder and Booker stood up straighter. Miss Woodhouse nearly laid her head on him as she took in the bed, sizing up the space with her fingers. "I think it's actually a thirty-dollar frame from an overstock website. Probably plated brass too."

He snickered without trying to shift, and she rotated her head back until her hair tickled his neck. Her sparkling brown and green eyes beamed up at him, her lips perched in a smile, when she jerked away. She kept going as if she meant to inspect the window. Feeling off kilter, Booker raised his arms in a feigned stretch while watching her move about with surprising purpose.

"All right, here's what we're going to do," she said and plopped her paper onto the bed.

Dear God, she'd drawn a dozen layouts for a room she hadn't even seen. Pointing to the only assumption close to reality, she looked past him to the ceiling. "Wow, those are beautiful."

Booker craned his head to find intricate carved panels instead of popcorn bits on the ceiling.

"I guess the drapery's out," she said, and scratched at her drawing. The pencil punctured the paper, but that didn't slow her down. "We won't have much time, so we need to prioritize the requirements and something with pancakes. I don't know."

Her random scribblings froze and she stared up at him. All of the excitement drained from her face. "Or are you going to abandon me again to fix a leaking sink?"

Booker had known this was coming. Scratching the bald patch at the base of his skull, he tried to buy himself time to think. He thought that a real contractor would run circles around these idiots, but there was a lot of bullshit to wade through. And no one was better at traversing the shit swamps like her.

He settled on, "I'll follow your lead."

"Really?" She sounded surprised, as if she wanted a fight to break out.

"It's your circus," Booker said, rubbing his chin. "Point me to the monkeys."

Miss Woodhouse sat kitty-corner on the bed, her legs folded tight. She kept explaining her plan that all hinged on what they could find on the pallets below. "I may have taken a peek to get an idea of what was on offer."

"Sneaky," he said, impressed. She nodded, actually accepting his compliment.

"We're about ready to start," one of the assistants said before being berated by a producer to get a lukewarm tea.

"You both need to get back to the threshold of the door. Act surprised when we open it," the producer ordered before turning her back on them.

Miss Woodhouse wiggled to rise, enthralled with her plans, and Booker held out his hand. For a beat, she stared at his fingers like they were snakes, then she drifted her gaze upward. A little pink claimed her cheeks and she clasped her palm to his. He helped her to stand, doing his best to not cluck at her open-toed shoes. If they were really going to be doing this, she'd need to get proper work boots and no more thin, flowy dresses.

"Roll the dolly back," the producer ordered.

Miss Woodhouse clung tight to his hand and pulled herself closer until she whispered in his ear. "You know that if we don't win this challenge..." She stared over at the producer kicking the dolly track. "We're dead in the water."

It was his fault. He was man enough to admit that...to himself. But he'd come too far to roll over just because he was the only sane one in the nuthouse. Booker jerked his head, telling her he'd try.

"Okay, okay." The producer manhandled her, then gave him a light tap on the shoulder to get them in front of the door.

"Now, once we open this, we need shock and awe. Maybe a little worry about the contest. Got it?"

This was so stupid, pretending to be surprised by a room they had just been in, but he feared Miss Woodhouse was right. If he didn't play along, if he wasn't the smiling, dancing puppet, he'd lose everything.

"And open the door..."

Booker put on a smile and walked into the room for the first time.

Chapter Twelve

Ember tore through the stacks of fabrics, trying to find something modern and rustic that screamed tenacious. Mr. Knightley stood just behind her, arms outstretched as she added more possibilities to the pile.

"Is all of this really...?" he asked before she covered over the last of his face with some tchotchkes to bring the room together.

"Get that up the stairs. Go, go, go!" she shouted.

He didn't respond with his usual vitriol, but took his time trudging back to their room. That was the bare minimum of the design, but she still needed to bring it all together. Ember dug through the decor table hoping for inspiration to strike—a two-foot metal feather, a rustic sign for an apple orchard, four wavy stone lines, a baseball-sized marble. No. None of that would work.

"How long?" she asked the assistant standing beside the camera.

He flipped around his watch. "Twenty minutes."

Fuck. "You better start putting together that shelf!" Ember shouted, hoping Mr. Knightley had enough sense to hear her.

Ember was only shoving things around, hoping for a miracle, when she caught a real possibility. Shoved nearly off of the table toward the wall was an old-fashioned typewriter.

Harty said something about interviews. Could his future wife be a reporter? Or a writer? Wrapping her arms around the old typewriter, Ember nearly fell through the floor as she took the whole weight. The keys jangled and the little teeth all flipped toward her face. Tiny sprinkles of ink landed on her cheeks and lips. She pursed them tight, trying to not drink ancient ink made from outlawed chemicals.

"Are you coming back, or am I on my own?" Mr. Knightley hollered over the loud din of the camera crew. A few heads jerked, no doubt getting the full force down his mike.

"On my way," Ember said when she caught sight of the craft service table. They'd gone all out for the crew, including hot dishes. While her stomach cried out for the rich and gooey mac and cheese, she looked to the solitary hot plate and the small frying pan on top.

"I'm taking this," she announced, no one there to stop her. "Oh, and this spatula." Before the producers could try to wrangle her in place, Ember ran for the stairs.

She worked in a flurry, shoving curtains through rods, smashing her toes and fingers at the same time. The tiny room had felt pleasantly cool for an autumn day, but as she raced around trying to wrangle sheets onto the bed, her body burned. It didn't help that a huge man sat in the center of the room diligently counting out the screws before he even started.

"You know we don't exactly have a lot of... How much time?"

"Fifteen minutes."

"That. We can't do anything with a half-finished bookshelf."

Mr. Knightley grumbled like a November rainstorm. He picked up his Allen wrench and finally started screwing everything in place. "You realize this is nothing more than cheap plywood and cardboard, right? No one in their right mind would want this."

"It's about the aesthetics."

"Shouts the drowning man who ignores the rowboat in favor of a passing cruise ship."

Ember tucked the blanket in tighter than a Marine's buns and sighed. "Do you want to win or go home tonight?" He didn't answer, which was probably the best outcome, and returned to working.

Flying down the list, Ember added leather pillows to the bed, then a middle one with a moose. She kept the colors autumnal but paler, for the more modern feel. The curtains were a combination of a sheer voile grommet for early mornings, and a heavier dark green velvet for the more romantic moments. Ember tied off the larger curtains with old sailing rope and added a metal autumn leaf from a napkin ring. She risked opening the window, hoping for a calming breeze to cool her aching head.

"Eight minutes."

"How's it going?" she shouted, needing that bookshelf up. All of her knickknacks had to go somewhere other than the bed.

"Nearly there," he said. Still, she risked looking over, expecting to find half the thing built. He was bent clean over, his jeans plastered over a round and muscular ass. That was the kind of butt for holding on with both hands while he fucked from on top. The sort of ass that'd take the deepest nail gouging and flex even harder to stone.

"Hello?"

Reality interrupted, slapping away her vision of that naked ass thrusting and those bare forearms heaving her onto the bed she'd just made. Ember blinked madly, focusing on the face that came with the ass, and more specifically the personality. "Yes? What?"

"I need the hammer," he said, wiggling his fingers for the tool just beyond his reach.

Ember handed it over, doing her best to keep away from the heat of his body. He barely looked at her before turning away to resume his hammering. With the rhythmic pounding of nails and not her, she worked on her special surprise set up on the little end table. The lamp was made with a faux wood base and a clean white shade to finish it off. All that was needed was the bookshelf.

"How much time?" she asked, watching Mr. Knightley finally step back from what looked like a finished four-foot five-inch shelf.

"Three minutes."

"We need to get that into place," she said, dashing to shove it.

"But I didn't anchor it yet. If I don't—" Mr. Knightley's complaining fell on deaf ears. Ember pushed on the shelf, moving it closer to the wall.

"There isn't any time. Help me move this, then grab the stuff."

He clung to his hammer and a bag of screws, but Ember didn't have time for his nonsense. She didn't put her foot down with the hole in the roof and look at what that got them. "Help me, or we're both gone."

Mr. Knightley sneered, but shoved the hammer into the hook on the side of his jeans. With one hand, he pushed the shelf against the wall. Ember took off, snatching every little cute tchotchke she could find. She only paused to reposition the typewriter, adding a single sheet of paper should anyone want to use it.

"One minute," the producer said.

"The candles!" Ember remembered the requirement at the last second. Both she and Mr. Knightley reached for the box at the same moment. She'd have wrenched her hand away, but the clock was not on their side. Together, they carried the box to the shelf and quickly tossed the candles wherever they fit.

"Thirty seconds."

Ember staggered back and was caught by Mr. Knightley. He had a single candle in his hand.

"Fifteen, fourteen…"

Taking the candle, Ember set it next to the special treat, arranged the frying pan and looked around the room.

"Three, two, one. Tools down!"

"We did it!" Smiling wide, she almost flung her arms around Mr. Knightley in celebration. At the last second, she paused and extended her hand. He took it with a weary sigh.

The cameras zoomed in on that moment. Before they could even get a second to enjoy the fruits of their labor, they were ushered into the hallway and the door slammed in their face.

"Now what?" Mr. Knightley asked.

"Pray for a miracle," Ember whispered. The others had twice the time they did, and could actually make something other than an out-of-the-box bookshelf.

"And if God's busy?"

Ember hefted up the screwdriver she'd slipped into her tool belt. "Sabotage?" Mr. Knightley laughed in response.

* * * *

Three hours passed before they were lined up in front of their room. With no music, no phones, no TV, not even a book, all the contestants had huddled in the sitting room doing their best to not talk. Booker began to suspect the plan was to destroy them either via alcohol poisoning or madness.

"Marker. We're ready to roll."

Miss Woodhouse stood next to him, looking about to leap onto the music guy and pummel him into approving their room. Booker reached over to take her hand before she swiped at either Harty or their mystery host. But as he held her fingers, she shifted her palm, pressing its heat to his and entwining their fingers. Booker's heart fluttered as he gazed down at her adorable awkwardness.

"Are you kids ready to...?" the Artist said, clapping their hands before glancing down. "Or should we leave you alone?" They nudged Harty in the shoulder, and he rolled his eyes.

Both she and Booker stared at their clasped hands, then let go and walked a step apart. *Jesus, why's the back of my neck burning?* He hadn't been all thumbs around a girl since junior high. "Please —" Coughing to wipe away any trace that he cared about her touch, Booker said, "Get this over with."

"Onward, dear Harty. Let us see what you make of this honeymoon suite."

"It can't be any worse than the last one," he said and shuddered. "Where did they get the clowns anyway?"

"Hey!" the executive producer shouted from the far wall. "No continuity info."

Harty frowned. "Boy, I can't wait to see the first, third or last room of this competition."

The dark glower from the other producers caused Booker to chuckle, turning it on him, as well as one from Miss Woodhouse. He had to play along or suffer her cold shoulder until the end of this. Buttoning his lip, he waited for Harty to open the door.

Turning the knob with ease, he took a step, only for a producer to shout, "Cut. Out of frame. Do it again. And remember excitement or disgust. We need to see it on your face."

"No one can emote disgust quite like Mr. Harty. See. He's a natural," the mystery host said, chuckling at his sneer.

"Can I get this over with already? You said this was a couple hours, tops."

"The fickle stream of entertainment can be poled as easily as the River Styx."

Harty didn't answer, but turned the knob and shoved the door. It stuck in the frame. "Are you fu...reaking kidding me." He bounced his shoulder into it, bucking the door in the frame.

"Can someone in the room please open the door?"

"Wait, I think we have it. One, two, push!" Both Harty and the Artist rammed their all into the door and it flung open, sending both racing toward the floor. The celebrity had enough luck to catch himself, though permanently shattering a guitarist's hand seemed like a possibility for this show.

The noon sun had dropped until golden light streamed into the room. Those sheer curtains Miss Woodhouse seemed to love kept dancing on the wind, sweeping next to the head of the cameraman trying to duck down to get the shot. He kept absently swatting at them while Harty stood perfectly still.

"Emote, damn it," the producer shouted.

"Is that a moose?" Harty asked, noticing the mass of pillows first. "Because I'm from Minnesota?"

In a flurry, Miss Woodhouse pushed Booker to the side and dashed into the room. She paused just behind Harty and momentarily adjusted her hair before striking a calm pose. "It is a faux leather pillow of a majestic moose silhouette set before the modern silver and white pillows to give both the rustic and modern feel."

He smiled slightly, revealing a crooked tooth. "Right, because of what I said… Uh, the lamp's nice."

"Allow me." She took complete control of the situation, which Booker suspected Miss Woodhouse did in every facet of life. Heaven take mercy on the poor sod she'd browbeat into dating her. After showing how a table lamp worked, she explained why she chose the curtains, the rugs, the bedspread with a high thread count and Egyptian cotton. Booker's brains turned to slush at all of the fluff words being bandied about, but his eyes found a feast. The deeper she dove into explaining the flannel blanket folded into a white fur one for extra warmth, the brighter she glowed.

There was no denying Miss Woodhouse was attractive in that symmetrical, beautiful-according-to-mathematicians way. But as she spoke about all the work she put in, her cheeks flushed and eyes shining in the autumn glow, Booker couldn't say she was beautiful. She was gorgeous.

"Over here is the bookshelf, to fit the height requirement." She brushed past Booker, her eyes drifting up to his. For a beat, she gave him a private smile. "Mr. Knightley built it, and I added little knickknacks and romantic candles."

The tiny flames danced in the rising breeze rattling the windows. Sounded like they might be in for an autumn storm tonight. Harty sized up the cheap-ass bookshelf looking like he felt the same about it as Booker did. At least until he darted from the stacks of leather books and glass orbs to the middle of the shelf.

"A typewriter?" Harty exclaimed, crouching to pluck at the machine bowing the shelf from its weight. "My wife would love that." He pecked at a key or two, before noticing the sudden silence.

The mystery host came to the rescue. "Don't you mean fiancée? He's just so excited to be married, he already wants her to be his wife."

"Yes, that's it, and not that we already wed over the summer. Otherwise all of this would be completely pointless."

It shouldn't surprise him that the supposed groom was already a husband, but Booker frowned. They'd had twelve people work themselves into a froth over a lie. What else were the producers willing to lie about?

Miss Woodhouse, of course, came to the rescue. "There's one more surprise for you. I wanted to make this room represent not just you and your fiancée, but the love you share." She took his hands and guided him to a little nightstand covered in a cloth. With panache, she pulled away the flannel towel to reveal a frying pan.

Booker frowned. She'd been fussing all this time to get an outlet for a hot plate? Why? It wasn't like anyone would be sleeping here, much less eating breakfast. If she hadn't bothered with something so stupid, he might have had time to anchor the shelves and...

"Pancakes?" Tristan Harty squeaked. Booker jerked in surprise at the hint of tears building in his eyes, while the camera zoomed in closer. Harty approached the hopefully off burner to take the frying pan by the handle. After giving a little shake, he tossed the two no-doubt-frozen pancakes high into the air. "This is... Wow. I never anticipated this."

"You said they were special to you," Miss Woodhouse said with a tip of her head.

Harty laughed and wiped at his eye. "You're impressive. Everything you've done in such short time is..." He placed a hand to his hip and turned in a circle to survey the room. Booker finally did the same. It wasn't romantic in the rose petals on the bed, hanging lights, silk canopies way. There wasn't any Barry White thumping through the floorboards, or a bubbling hot tub with cold champagne in buckets in the bathroom. But it made a grown man tear up on camera and that was a magic he couldn't mimic.

Booker took a step to clasp Ember on the back both in congratulations and gratitude. She had just saved both of their asses with her weird pancakes. Harty shook her hand, asking her questions as if a dam had opened. The producers shouted for the camera crew to get more b-roll, especially on the typewriter. Everything was finally looking up. He could get through this, and win this place for his family.

A massive wind blew through the open window, catching on not just the sheer curtain but the heavy velvet one. It bounced into the lamp, shattering it to the floor. The cameraman leaped at the surprise sound and bashed his rig into the shelf. Booker twitched, watching the wood shudder, tremble then snap. The barely holding typewriter crashed through the shelf, taking all the glass balls and candles with. People raced to try to put out the tiny fires, when the wind blew once more. It blasted against the shelf, rocking it back into the wall, then sending it careening to the floor.

Everyone leaped out of the way of the tall shelf. But as it went, the little deer filigree at the top slammed into the frying pan. The pan buckled, flinging pancakes. One struck the wall above the bed, and the other splatted right onto Mr. Harty's face.

"We, uh, we can fix this," Miss Woodhouse shouted. She reached to peel the pancake away, but a glowering Harty beat her to it.

"Fire. Fire!" the Artist shouted. Hitting the floor didn't extinguish the candles. Instead, they found fuel in the cheap-ass plywood. While interns ran to get cups of water and Miss Woodhouse, the Artist and Harty slapped blankets at it, the cameramen zoomed in. They made sure to document every horrific second about to turn this room to ashes. All because he didn't have time to anchor the fucking bookshelf.

"Here." Hands shoved two cups at him. Booker didn't even stare at the flames as he dumped the water onto the floor. It was her fault. Her flightiness. Her incessant need to be in control that doomed him. The whole world would think him an incompetent contractor. Miss Woodhouse had just destroyed his business with one window and a goddamn typewriter.

"Ah, a spark," she cried.

Booker slammed his foot down, stomping it out—along with this partnership.

Chapter Thirteen

"Will you come out of there?" Ember knocked harder on their only bathroom and changing room. The girls had to huddle next to the mirror to do their makeup and hair before the first big elimination. The guys seemed to have gotten through a case of beer while doing each other's ties. They were waiting on one person, which made this all Ember's problem.

"Do you need help?" she asked.

The door flung open, before rebounding into his knee. Barely any pain flashed in Mr. Knightley's eye, which he directed like a heat-seeking missile at her. "No, I do not need help putting on my own suit."

Once the producers had announced the first elimination tonight, Ember had dived through Mr. Knightley's clothing to find anything acceptable. To her surprise, mixed in with all of the flannel and jeans was a fairly nice suit. She'd thrust it into his arms and left him to figure it out.

He hadn't said a word to her since the excitement of their room reveal, seeming to prefer to keep his communication style to scowls and grunts. Ember eyed up his shirt collar and reached in. "Your tie is loose."

The door almost slammed on her hand. "The tie is fine."

"You look like a gambler who just bet his last dollar on the penny slots," Ember chastised. "In order to win this game, you have to look —"

"No. I don't care about your rules. I don't care about your system."

"It's not a system, just logic," she said as patiently as possible and tried to push her way in. The producers were already mumbling about starting without him. If she didn't have a partner, she was certain to be cut.

An arm lashed out in front of her. Mr. Knightley dug his nails into the doorframe. His eyes glowed with rage. "You have no idea what you're talking about. You have no idea what you're doing. And just being near you is liable to ruin what scrap of dignity I have left."

Ember sighed at his dramatics. "Is this about the room?"

"What else would it be about?"

"Don't worry. We finished it on time."

"There's plastic fused to the floorboards from the fire. The entire place reeks of smoke and lavender. All because you wouldn't listen to me. I said the bookshelf needed to be anchored."

"But we didn't have any time, because of you. Because you wouldn't listen to me!" *Damn it.* Ember's cheeks flushed with anger, but she felt the black lens of the camera wandering over to her. Taking a deep breath, she stared at her toes in her high heels. She was supposed to be the calm, levelheaded one. How did this man keep getting under her skin with every sentence?

"You made me look like an idiot. Like I couldn't even put together a cheap-ass bookcase." His voice sounded wounded, as if it was her duty to protect him from any eventuality fate could throw at them.

And you did the same to me, left me crying and desperate as I fought to drag a mattress through the mud. Ember's lips parted, prepared to take the final shot, but she gulped at the stillness of the producers. They were watching for drama that'd only backfire on her.

"Tristan loved the room we gave him." Ember cheered as if trying to assure her teammate.

Booker came back with, "Before or after it burned down?" He shut the door.

She didn't care if he couldn't hear her anymore. She needed to put on a good performance for the viewers and the editing room. "I know things didn't go according to plan, but we worked well together. When we... If we survive tonight, I'm certain we'll learn to work together better. What do you say, Mr. Knightley?"

Her answer was the sound of the toilet flushing. She didn't expect him to be civil, but he could at least act like an adult. Mr. Knightley was the most unpleasant man she'd been forced to interact with in ages. Perhaps her entire life. But she could pretend to be cordial, at the very least. Ember cast a look over her shoulder. Most of the cast were gathered around Logan.

His arms pumped wildly as he told a tale that caused everyone to laugh. As he finished his joke, his gaze drifted to Ember, and he winked. Handsome, friendly and capable of playing the game — she needed to find a way to tie herself to him before everything was lost.

"Emmy, can you help…?" Poor Ree ran over to her holding a pair of ribbons that must have fallen from her hair.

"Of course. I think this will need a little re-curling." Ember bounced Harriet's cute pigtail. Taking Harriet's hand, Ember led her away from the crowd to the front desk. Old wicker baskets that'd been chewed apart by wild animals tumbled as they slipped in behind. Ember pointed Harriet to the stool and a girl dutifully sat down. Why couldn't Mr. Knightley behave like she did?

"You look so nice," Harriet said as Ember tried to hunt for an outlet. Surely there had to be one up here.

"Thank you."

"I tried to contour once, but Mickey said it made me look like a clown. So I threw a frog at him."

Ember found one hiding among a stack of waterlogged receipts and stood. "You're cute just the way you are." She played with the end of Ree's pigtail, delighted by the freckles across her slightly sunburned cheeks. Ember should make sure to give her the heavy-duty sunscreen in case they wound up working outside.

"I'm trying, but…I don't think Elton wants cute girls."

When the iron warmed enough, Ember curled Ree's little pigtail and leaned against the desk next to her. "That's nerves talking. I saw the room you two put together. It was beautiful. You must have worked together to create that elaborate canopy for the bed."

Harriet shrugged, almost burning her shoulder on the curling iron. Ember frowned at the simple sundress she'd put on. While it'd be adorable for a summer picnic under the stars, it made her stand out among all the people in exclusive evening wear. "You should stop by my cabin later. I brought far more dresses than I'll ever need. There's a peridot one with a slit that'll fit you like a dream."

"Are you sure? I don't have your boobies."

Ember chuckled as Ree slapped her palms to her chest and shifted her pair up and down. "That's what padding is for. There, all curled and ready to dazzle both the judges and Elton Brown. Have you worked out what you're going to say to him?"

"Um, hi, do you like...stuff?"

Ember flattened her lips. She had far greater work ahead of her. "Not terrible, but how about an opening line? Mr. Brown, you look dashing in the moonlight."

"What if he's not in the moonlight?"

"It doesn't matter. You compliment a man, no matter how ludicrous, and he'll buy it hook, line and sinker. After he returns the favor, you drop your biggest bomb. 'How do you imbue such realistic characters?'"

"Huh?"

"He's an actor. Get him to talk about acting and he won't be able to shut up. Which is good. You need to let men get air out of their lungs, sometimes without refilling for hours. But don't press him about his celebrity. Do not inquire who he knows, or any salacious gossip. That will only shut him down."

Ree mouthed the moonlight compliment, then scrunched up her nose. "This is so hard. I'm always putting my foot in my mouth. What if I get it wrong or say something he don't like?"

"Then giggle, and ask 'What do you think?'"

"About what?"

"Doesn't matter. They always have an opinion and are just waiting to wow a pretty girl with it."

Harriet blushed bright pink at the compliment, but it was true. Though Ember was beginning to fear she might not realize it in time to have her Cinderella moment. Maybe Ember should try to prime both pumps for this whirlwind romance. "Why don't you try this on your lips instead?" She passed over one of her bright red shades. Ree's eyes nearly bugged out as if the hue would walk the streets after the navy came into port.

Patting Ree's knee, Ember backed away, promising she'd come get the girl and they'd walk in together. "Oh, that sounds — " was the last Ember heard from her as she raced back into the sitting room. Her prey sat on the couch next to Logan. Augusta kept trying to wiggle her way to the side, nearly shoving Logan onto Elton's lap.

"Excuse me?" Ember called out.

At first it was Logan who looked her way, one palm foisting Augusta back to her feet. Ember gulped at the intense focus in his eyes nearly peeling her dress off. Fighting down a girlish giggle, she ducked her head to avoid Logan's stare and took Mr. Brown's hand. "Could I have a word with you?"

He looked over at Logan, then smiled and rose to his feet. "You can have more than that, my dear."

Ree was in the lobby, and too many ears waited in here. Holding Mr. Brown's hand, Ember guided him around the thick cables and extension cords out through the solarium's side door. A chill hit her quick. The once warm sun had crashed to a freezing autumn wind. Wrapping her hands around her bare shoulders,

Ember tried to hustle as far from the cameras as possible.

She wound up standing under a trellis where wild roses must have once grown. Most of the flowers were long since dried up, but a single bloom of wilting flowers rested above her. Mr. Brown kept glancing behind as if to make certain the door was closed before he stood directly behind her.

Here goes. "Mr—"

"Elton," he said, his voice deep.

Flushing, Ember kept staring through the holes in the trellis and the trees to the full sky of stars. She'd never seen so many. "You're such a famous and well-beloved man. There have to be dozens of fan accounts devoted to you."

"Hundreds," he bragged, his breath brushing her hair forward.

Absently, Ember reached up to stop the tickle and a hand caught hers. She tried not to shiver while composing herself. "While it's wonderful to have you join our season—"

"It's wonderful to have you too."

"I'm just thinking, and I understand that it's part of the game, but do you have any intentions to try to find love here?"

Two palms slipped against her bare shoulders. He dug his fingers in, not so much massaging as perching. "I believe I've discovered a few enticing reasons to try."

"Fantastic." Ember had been worrying that he was only going through the motions at the whims of the producers. But he seemed as embroiled in this intrigue as the rest of them. "Ree's so shy and worried about stepping over your boundaries."

His cheek almost pressed against hers and he whispered against the back of her ear, "Who?"

"Ree. The cute, freckled, adorable Harriet."

"Oh, country girl. What about her?" He tightened his fingertips, pressing into the hollow of her collarbones and pulling her back against his chest.

Ember fought the urge to push him off, but she couldn't face him. "You two make the cutest couple on the show. A famous, multi-talented Hollywood star and the simple, backwater country girl. It's perfect. You're made for each other."

"Is that really why you brought me out here?" he whispered. His right hand toyed with her hair while he cupped over her waist with his left and pulled her ass taut to his thick—

"Are you finished?"

Jerking up, Ember managed to turn in Elton's tentacle grip to spy a man of mystery standing in the shadows. All she could make out was his perfect V silhouette in a tailored black suit. Then a huge floodlight flared above and she blinked dumbfounded into the face of Mr. Knightley.

My God, he went from grungy construction worker to captivating super spy. He could rescue me from a volcano lair any time.

Ember shivered at the famished thoughts running rampant from her starved libido. She despised Mr. Knightley. It didn't matter if he cleaned up well. So did Logan, and he came with the baggage of being rich and charming.

"They said we need to get to the ballroom for the elimination round or they'd cut us all," Mr. Knightley said. He finished adjusting his cuffs and crossed his arms. The suit struggled against his biceps, no doubt built from throwing around cement blocks and two by fours. Ember forced her gaze away from his damsel-rescuing arms to find his eyes still blazing with blame.

"You brought the..." Mr. Brown took a step away and wrenched his hands off of Ember. Except, in his fondling, his finger had gotten ensnared in her hair. He yanked without care, causing her head to snap back.

She yelped, clutching tight to the roots. Rather than remove his ring, Mr. Brown kept pulling on her hair. Tears rose in Ember's eyes, threatening to streak her mascara. She bit her lip so she wouldn't cry out on camera while Mr. Brown kept fumbling to rip her hair free.

A flash of silver in the night and she was free. It wasn't until Ember held the sliced ends that she realized it was Mr. Knightley in the garden with a knife. He calmly closed up his pocket blade while staring at her.

"Thank you for that information, Miss Woodhouse. I will take it under advisement," Mr. Brown said before scurrying back inside. Ember watched him and the cameras that followed.

Harriet suddenly stepped into the room. Her ruby lips split into a welcoming grin and she boldly threw her arms around him. All the cameras focused on the two embracing and Ember cheered to herself.

Great job, Ree.

"You know, if you're into him, maybe you shouldn't be playing these five-D chess games with the country mouse."

Such cruel cuts fell so easily from Mr. Knightley. "I have no intentions with Mr. Brown."

"So you brought him out into the dark garden away from everyone and he had his hands all over you to, what, check you for ticks?"

The combination of Mr. Brown and ticks crawling across her skin caused Ember's entire body to break out in goosebumps. She huddled tighter, her teeth chattering at the idea. When a heavy woolen jacket landed over her shoulders, she jerked up in surprise. Mr. Knightley didn't even pause at draping her in his suit coat.

"What do you care what games I'm playing? You think all of my strategies are ill advised at best."

"Dumb as a brick at worst," he said and scratched his cheek. The white shirt gleamed in the darkness, barely able to contain his pectorals and wide neck. "You know he's not into her, right?"

"Of course he is. Look at how they're holding hands."

"I've never seen a man more desperate to cut off his own arm outside of one being dragged into the swamp by a croc."

Ember shuddered at the vulgar image and huffed. "You are a man who has shielded not only his hand but his heart below an impenetrable callous. It's no wonder you find the idea of love frivolous and stupid."

He caught her by the forearm and pulled her closer. "This game you're playing, this idea that if you force two people together enough times they become soulmates doesn't work. Love, real love, is…precious." His breath shivered as he finished, his eyes blazing with a fire that raced down Ember's spine.

She gasped at the ferocity in his face. "What do you know or care of real love, Mr. Knightley?"

His lips tightened and nostrils flared. Ember wasn't sure what to expect, but the burst of emotion flared out. Releasing her, he stepped back and ran a hand through his short, textured hair. "What's it matter? No one's ever found love on a reality show. It's impossible."

"Miss Woodhouse, Booker?" Sam stuck her head out and waved them inside. "We're going to start."

Booker didn't race for it. Instead, he kept staring up into the stars, or perhaps he was checking the roof for damage. Ember slipped off the suit coat he'd given her and handed it back. At first, he seemed surprised, but she raised her chin. "Only a fool balks at the impossible," Ember declared and walked for the door.

As she moved, a cologne—of autumn forests, lightning on the horizon and comfy fireplaces—radiated off of her arms. She did her best to not enjoy the scent as its source stomped in behind her.

Chapter Fourteen

Booker tugged down the knot of his tie, wishing it would bring a sense of relief. Staring around the rickety cabin he'd forced himself to stay in with the worst possible person here, he feared he wouldn't feel comfortable until he was out of this hellhole. A quiet *oomph* caused him to look back.

A massive steamer trunk stumbled through the door. Probably not on its own unless there'd been recent leaps in baggage tech. Another grunt broke from behind the black rectangle standing between him and freedom.

Knowing she could handle it, as she kept insisting she could handle everything, Booker approached the window and lifted the glass. The hasty plastic taped over the hole on the top snagged but he didn't care. He breathed in the night air, going on two AM again, and hunched against the frame.

It'd been a nightmare. Oh, he'd expected the pomp, the constant reshoots while they cultivated blisters in their dress shoes for hours. Even for the Artist to have yet another costume change, this time with a rose theme. He knew they'd wind up in the bottom. She'd set the damn room on fire.

Thank God they didn't win by some demented twist of fate or the producers. If they did, he'd have to suffer a romantic candlelit dinner with the woman who had burrowed under his skin like ringworm. Even the fates had to pretend to follow the rules they set down.

A hand smacked into his chest pocket and Booker jerked to realize it was his, searching for a pack even though he'd kept it empty for four years, seven months and some odd days. She'd pissed him off so bad he was hunting for a smoke. Digging his idle hands into the windowsill instead, Booker pressed his forehead to the cool glass and stared out. Headlights beamed from a huge truck loaded with equipment, as well as a trailer where the Artist had slunk off with their friend.

He wished they'd cut them. Sure, it'd mean he failed, but he'd also be free. Instead, they stood there praising her decorating, claiming that they'd have won if it wasn't for that brain-dead contractor that didn't bolt the bookshelf to the wall. No matter how many times Booker tried to explain the time crunch, they'd either talk over him, kill his mike or insist that it was no excuse.

"A poor man blames his tools."

Fuck, he hated that saying. *Sometimes the tools are cheap shit that'll shatter into shrapnel at no fault of the contractor.*

Why didn't they put me out of my misery?

"There. I think that's everything," she said, dropping her huge trunk to the floor and dusting off her hands. She'd been talking incessantly since they were saved by her 'skills.' "We don't have a bed."

Booker snorted. As if he'd sleep anywhere near her. He'd rather bunk in the freezing leaves and pine needles.

"But I borrowed a mess of blankets and pillows from the decorating table." She dug into her huge trunk and revealed the stolen booty.

"Isn't that breaking the rules?" he asked, shattering his own vow of silence. *Damn it.*

Her eyes widened as if he were about to drag her in front of the judges—whoever they were. No, for as much as he despised her, he wasn't going to sabotage himself just to get at her. She passed him a pillow while assuring herself, "I borrowed them. If they require the blankets for a challenge, we can easily return them."

Booker glared at her.

"I will return them." She laid out her little bed by the large lamp at the back. This room was in disrepair, the roof about to blow away and all the furnishings taken, yet the lighting was impeccable. He could read the tiny font in the contract they'd made him sign no problem.

Raising his head, Booker spotted the why. A little black lens rested just above the smoke alarm. While he doubted the latter worked, he knew the former did. And there were probably a few more, too. Shaking his head, he grabbed his lav mike and fished the battery pack up through the back of his shirt. They were still listening through other hidden mikes, but with that thing on, he felt like they could read his mind.

Miss Woodhouse carefully arranged her throw pillows on her blanket pile, as if someone would grade her design skills. Then she pulled two pins from her hair and her lush black locks tumbled to her shoulders.

She shook it back, her hair shining like a river of oil — rich and deadly at the same time. Booker turned his back on her to stare out the window.

"Are you going to be like this for the rest of the competition?" she whined as if he were being the unreasonable one. Booker answered by leaning lower on the windowsill.

"It's unbecoming for a man to pout."

"I'm not pouting."

"You're just giving me the silent treatment like a ten-year-old. Completely different from pouting."

Booker clenched his jaw and strained his neck against his shoulders. "You made a fool out of me."

"I did no such thing. I tried to defend you."

Oh, right. Her little squeak of, "Actually, it was I who..." that he doubted made it over the haranguing from every person that got the microphone. No doubt she'd have twisted it with her flowery language that no one would have understood anyway.

"I said we needed to anchor the bookshelf, you said no."

"We were out of time because you—!" She leaped to her feet and charged at him. Booker stared at her nagging finger when Miss Woodhouse paused and flung both of her hands in the air. "I'm not litigating this with you again. Can we agree that we both failed?"

"Everyone out there thinks I'm an awful contractor because of you."

"And because of you, everyone in America believes I don't know that beds go in a bedroom!" she shrieked, tears momentarily building in her eyes.

A tiny pang of guilt, no bigger than a splinter, wedged under his skin. Booker turned back to the dark night, noticing a halo of lights in the distance. Was that the monitor bank? What if he broke in and erased all the footage from the past day? Oh they'd sue him to the stone age, but it might be worth it just to watch that she-devil Ms. Goddard explode in fury.

The sound of shuffling reminded him that he wasn't alone and taking a hammer to the monitors in a truck wouldn't solve his problem. He tried to tune out the noises of a woman readying herself for bed. It was far too intimate of a setting than he'd like to ever picture from Miss Woodhouse.

She had enough sense to slip into the bathroom to change, but the walls were paper thin. He could hear everything from the pat of a wet washcloth, to her mumbling under her breath about him. Then the zipper struck, its drawn teeth climbing up his spine.

He'd done his best to avoid staring down that dress's cleavage—which ended somewhere near her navel—but he couldn't stop thinking about it now. That black dress that'd clung to her like a second skin all night finally giving in and slinking slowly to the floor. She'd have to bend over to tug it down her hips, letting her tits spill over, her nipples pointing to the floor.

"Fuck." He groaned, his cock springing up so fast the crown smacked into the wall. Booker jerked his hips back, partially worried he might put a hole through the plaster. Yes, she was attractive.

Fine, so fucking hot it made his brain seethe every time he caught one of the other guys drooling over her. Like he cared if she chased after captain sleaze or the frat boy. He wasn't her keeper. His cock just hadn't gotten the memo.

A harried intern hurled open the cabin's front door and tossed two brown bags inside. "For insurance," was all he said before leaping back into the night.

What the hell? Curious, Booker pried off the top staple and reached inside. Dozens of condoms — ribbed, thin-skinned, long-lasting and flavored — filled the bottom of the bag. Insurance? He snorted at the idea that they didn't have any preparations for running a man over, but gave them two dozen condoms each. A good pair of safety goggles were all the protection he'd need.

The creak of the bathroom door jerked Booker up as a glistening Miss Woodhouse walked into the room. He bundled the bag behind his back without thought, then turned to face the window.

"There's no hot water," she said and slunk back to her little blanket. The sounds of her head tumbling against the pillow and her tight body twisting back and forth on the ground seeped into his marrow. His fingers crumpled the bag, drawing her attention.

"What's that?"

"They threw one in for you too," was all he said. She gave a derisive snort before opening hers and gasping. He'd swear he could hear the blush on her cheeks. Shivering, Booker tossed his bag to the side — but not before pocketing a few of the better condoms.

"I can't handle this," Booker muttered to himself. After taking stock of the few tools left to them, he quickly screwed two eyelets into the walls and ran a line of rope between them.

"What are you doing?" She'd sat up to watch, the covers just high enough to obscure the proof she had a top on.

Keeping his back to her, Booker went full pre-teen and draped his blanket across the rope, cutting the cabin in half. "There. You stay on your side, and I'll stay on mine."

"You realize I have the door. Are you planning on getting out through the window?"

He'd solve that problem when it came to it. Angry at her, at this situation, at his body's betrayal, Booker slammed himself to the ground. His old knees screamed at the move, but he didn't care and stretched out on the cold, hard floor. An inch of light escaped from below his blanket, giving him the very erotic view of a few shadows, the light from her lamp and a hint of fingers. Of course the nails were painted with a soft pink.

Booker flipped to the other side, finding himself staring through a mouse hole into the dark autumn woods. A machete-wielding psychopath might be welcome at this point. He stuffed a hand under his pillow and adjusted again. Cold swept through the holes in the insulation, freezing his exposed skin. The hardness of the floor was going to be hell on his back. And deep down, he knew it was his fault.

Though, if he hadn't insisted on fixing the roof, he'd be sharing a bed with Miss Woodhouse. A single bark of laughter escaped at the thought.

"What?" she asked, sounding annoyed at his disturbing her peace.

The idea of sleeping beside her being both ludicrous and terrifying wasn't a good answer. She'd probably use both to her advantage. Booker raced to find an excuse while the shadows on her side shifted. "Why are you helping that country mouse?"

"Harriet?" She sounded annoyed, as if she didn't think the same thing of the girl in overalls and pigtails.

"Isn't this every man and woman for themselves? You can't win by helping someone else to the top."

"Maybe I'm being kind."

Booker snorted at the thought.

"Fine. Since you cannot stop prying, I have no intentions to win either this resort, the payout and certainly not love."

"Really? The way you keep romanticizing tying Elton and Harriet together no matter how hard they chew through the rope, I'd assumed you were only here for falling in love. But you don't even believe in it."

"I most certainly do believe in love. You know nothing of my heart, Mr. Knightley."

"Ah, got a boyfriend back home."

She went quiet a moment and he peered under the blanket. The tips of her nails smoothed down her blanket for a time. "I do not. Nor do I plan to for the foreseeable future. I'm focusing on my career."

"The career of being on near-death reality shows?"

"No. I'm an interior decorator, and I'm trying to get my business off the ground." She fumed as if flames were shooting from her eyeballs. He wished he could see that. Instead, Booker placed his hands behind his head and lay back.

"Is that what your degree's in?"

"I also have a BA in business management. Intend to scoff at that as well?"

"I would never. Interior design requires some skill beyond knowing how to use a spreadsheet and fire the last hired."

Her laugh was deep and from the gut, not the carefully coached giggle to get people to like her. Booker smiled at the sound and wanted to hear more. "Why aren't you fighting to win this place?" What was wrong with him? If she'd already cut herself out of the competition, that made it easier. "Imagine what it'd do for your business if you designed the interior of a whole resort?"

"You really didn't watch a single season of this show before signing up, did you?"

Booker turned to his side to stare her way. Judging by the silhouette she was leaning up in her makeshift bed, her chest rising with slow breaths. "Take a wild guess what all of the combined winners have in common," she said and turned her head to face him.

He panicked and flipped over even though she couldn't see.

"I don't plan to win, because I won't. It doesn't matter. All I have to do is make it to the top two and show off my design talents while also endearing myself to America. Or I'd thought that was all I had to do until I had the misfortune to run into you."

That she had a practical brain inside her pretty head shocked Booker. He'd assumed she only had dreams of elaborate weddings and popping out Logan babies dancing up there. No love, only business was a motto he could get behind.

"Wait, isn't your family rich? Can't Daddy finance your random flights of fancy?"

The other side of the room flash froze.

"Or is he too much of a miser?" Booker guessed.

That was wrong. "My father is a generous and wonderful man," she fumed. He half expected her to declare a blood debt against him from the tone, when she softened to a despondent sigh. "He...he believes in going one's own way. And I plan to make it all on my merit alone."

"Ignoring his money that paid for your college, housing, clothing and food," Booker muttered, laying back.

Ember's voice softened and she asked earnestly, "What about you? Why are you here?"

He opened his mouth when a red light flashed at the top of the ceiling. Narrowing his eyes, he could just make out the camera lens stashed in the dark corner of the room staring down at them. It didn't matter how many mikes he took off, or where he ran to — they were always listening. And they had the keys to the kingdom.

"Same as you," Booker lied. "Trying to get eyes on my construction business."

"And I caused the shelf to fall apart."

"Your typewriter and...the wind. Also those water-damaged, warped floors that have to be replaced." He kept talking, trying to wipe away the blame in her voice even though it was hers to suffer.

"I'm sorry. I... Can we call a truce?"

Propping his head up on his elbow he turned to face her. She did the same in silhouette. "Shoot."

"We can argue and bicker and doom both of our chances of getting what we want. Or we work together."

"You're going to listen when I say what needs to happen to build structurally sound projects?" he asked point blank.

"If you'll listen when I tell you what you need to do to make the cameras and producers keep you around."

God, she was going to turn him into one of those frou-frou dogs with ribbons on their ears. But Booker was walking blind. He'd thought that all he had to do was construct some rooms to succeed. There was so much to this he didn't understand. He hated to admit it, but he needed her. "Deal. But if you think I'm going to fall in love with you..."

Miss Woodhouse snorted. The light fell to darkness, leaving him staring into the red dot forever watching his every move.

"Good night, Mr. Knightley," was all she said. Her rapid shuffling faded to a slow breathing.

Gazing up at the patch job on the roof, Booker whispered, "Sleep tight, Miss Woodhouse."

Chapter Fifteen

"Good morning, campers!"

The groans were so palpable they fed back through the mikes. At daybreak, a massive siren had blasted, ripping Ember from her dreamless sleep. She'd been in such a start, she'd almost dashed through the blanket fort before catching her composure. The last thing she needed to learn was if Mr. Knightley slept in pajama pants, his underwear or nothing at all.

Ember flushed at the idea and held the coveted mug of coffee close to her face. The steam lit up her cheeks and she breathed deeper, wishing the caffeine could also wipe away her dark circles and pores. Perhaps it would find her a foundation that matched, too.

She took a sip of the hot brew, nearly scalding her freezing lips. The night hadn't been kind in the leaky cabin, but at least there were walls and a roof. They'd all been summoned to the frosted lawn. She fought back the shivers by wiggling her legs back and forth.

"Here."

A massive flannel jacket landed on her shoulders. She should refuse, at least politely insist that she wasn't a child in need of rescuing every time she shivered. But Mr. Knightley's coat was so damn warm, Ember slipped her arms inside. A sigh parted her lips the deeper she snuggled. His body must be a constant inferno.

The thought of his hard form bursting with steam against the freezing autumn dawn burned down Ember's spine. She risked glancing at him, all that ebony skin gleaming like polished onyx in the sunlight. "Thanks," she whispered, her voice far more throaty than she meant it to be.

He crossed his bulldozer arms and raised his chin. "At least you're dressed sensibly today." To her shock, Mr. Knightley then brazenly looked down her tight blouse tucked into a pair of hip-hugging jeans. Ember wanted to call him out for acting like her keeper once again, but they were at a truce. Plus, she hated to admit it, the jeans were smarter. She'd picked too many cockleburs off of her dress and shins yesterday.

"Is that everyone?" London Goddard asked. Unlike everyone else, bleary-eyed and barely made up, she was in a power suit with surgical-precision eyeliner, contouring and lipstick.

"Sorry, just…" Stumbling around the corner ran Bland and the poor girl saddled to him. "Here. We're all here."

"You know what today is?" London prompted.

Everyone cheered except for Mr. Knightley. Ember leaned closer to explain, but Ms. Goddard took over. "You will be handed your assignments. Each team will be given a section of the resort. You are to elevate your section into a dream hotel for modern travelers. These will be evaluated after each day and you will be given points. Of course, there will still be daily challenges that everyone must compete in or you will risk elimination. Any questions?"

"What about the cabins?" Mr. Knightley asked, but London stared over him.

"Good," she said then turned away. "Bring 'em out."

The mystery host and two makeup artists came dashing from the huge trailer, brushes at the ready. It was no wonder. The Artist had gone all out, their face painted blue with little lines down the visible sections to give the illusion of blueprints. Their suit was the same, only the lines were stitches. Ember was impressed at the decadence. Every other season, the mystery host would wear a tux and barely show up beyond elimination night.

"Darlings. I hope..." One of the makeup brushes went straight across the Artist's cheeks and deep into their mouth. They coughed out talc and waved the two away. After spitting out the last of the setting powder, they started again. "I hope you all got good sleep last night. Team Orange? How'd you get by with no bed?"

Ember glanced to her tool belt, then Mr. Knightley's. Red plus yellow, of course. He seemed to have caught on, or at least put enough pieces together as they were the only ones who had to sleep on the floor.

"Fine," he said.

"I've always found the necessity of the bed to be rather debatable myself," the Artist purred while staring Mr. Knightley right in the eye.

"What? No. Nothing like that—"

"Anyway." They clapped once. "Are we excited to get our assignments?"

Everyone gave a cheer, then a better one after the producers told them to. Ember had to elbow Mr. Knightley but even he pumped his fist and shouted, "Ya-hoo."

"You've had a tour of the grand lady and no doubt have been brewing some diabolical plans to bring her back to the days of her youth."

Every time they'd had to wait, Ember had snuck off to the various rooms. The solarium was beautiful and wouldn't need much help, the guest rooms would offer a delightful challenge, whoever got the kitchen was a sacrificial lamb, but what she really wanted was the ballroom. Elegant, stripped to its bones by time and weather, with a historical significance she couldn't wait to show off — Ember clutched her hands together, willing it to herself.

The Artist dramatically unrolled a scroll and began to dish out the assignments. Harriet and Elton got the solarium, the kitchen went to Boring Robert as she'd suspected. The guest rooms were divided up and passed out until only two teams remained.

"Miss Woodhouse and Mr. Knightley." The Artist's haunting purple eyes focused so deeply on her, Ember couldn't look away. Blindly, she hunted for anything to keep herself tethered to the ground, and found her hand wrapping around Mr. Knightley's. "You shall be renovating the..."

Her heart pounded. This was it. *I'll get the ballroom, transform it seemingly overnight. America will fall in love with me just as Elton falls in love with Ree. Everything will go to plan and people will clamber to have Miss Ember Woodhouse decorate their houses.*

"...entrance."

"The what?"

"Which means Logan and Augusta, Team Aqua, will be working on the ballroom."

Everyone politely clapped while Ember stared dumbstruck. Logan shouted, "Woo!" and ran up to take the scroll like he had won an Oscar.

"Please, come pick up your tools and blueprints. The work starts…now!"

They took off running, leaving Ember in the lurch. She was supposed to redesign and make the entrance beautiful? Who cared about the lobby of a hotel? Her heart sank, along with her dreams.

"Well." Mr. Knightley dropped her hand and picked up a power tool. "Best get to it."

* * * *

Age had walloped this place deeper than Ember remembered. Everyone had skittered off to their rooms, eager to begin, while she only had to stroll through the door and stare around the frankly small lobby.

"Behind you," Mr. Knightley announced, wheeling in a cart he must have loaded up with purpose. After stopping in front of the desk, he unrolled the cut-off blueprints they had been given and bent over to inspect them.

Ember stared at the fading paper shredding itself from the walls, the floors covered in tacky, stain-disguising carpet that belonged in a nineties movie theater, a single vinyl chair bolted to the wall and the chandelier. Only that seemed to bear any hallmarks of the original beauty of the place, though its gold had tarnished and the candles vanished due to being a fire hazard. It wasn't the work that perturbed her but the question of whether it was worth it.

"Okay, I'm going to have to take some measurements, then take them again but…" Her partner's explanation petered out and he glanced over his shoulder. "What's the matter?"

"What do I do with a hotel lobby?" Ember sputtered, feeling closer to her rope's end than ever before. At least while fighting with the mattress, she'd thought she had a chance. "No one's going to hire a designer known for sprucing up rundown lobbies."

He released the blueprints, causing them to snap back into their tight roll. Pacing around the tight space, Ember's anxiety flared. "There isn't even room for a plant!" She jabbed her hand to the corner that held a recessed window too shallow for anything interesting.

"Okay." He bent over, ignoring her, but Ember couldn't stop panicking.

"They don't even have a producer with us. Just a single camera crew and an assistant. This is the loser room, isn't it? Isn't it!" She shouted at the lone man standing behind the lens, who turned to talk to the assistant instead of bothering to film them. They didn't care. The producers had already written them off. There was no chance to come back from this, no way to prove that they were…

"Here." From his hip, Mr. Knightley swung around a huge sledgehammer. It landed in Ember's palms and the weight almost caused her to buckle. Hefting up the huge tool, Ember stared dumbfounded into his eyes.

"I don't know anything about playing politics and forming alliances, but I do know that the best solution to a freak out" — he slammed his hammer onto the desk, shattering straight through the wood — "is to break shit."

Ember eased closer as he pried wood bits off of bent nails. "Is that safe?"

He tapped the goggles on his nose, then swung again, this time breaking the lower pieces holding up the desktop. "We need to do demolition before we can build. And this desk is…"

"Awful. Positively terrible. An atrocious, dated, charmless monstrosity." Ember patted the hammer's handle, beaming her focus on the old water stains and gouges into the Formica. All the anger she'd been suppressing, not just for the past week, but her whole life, surged through her arms. It didn't matter how nicely she asked, how calmly she explained her points, how logically she laid out her solutions—the world always silenced her.

"Ah!" Screaming, Ember slammed the sledgehammer straight through the desk. The top crumbled into plywood shrapnel. A piece shot straight through, embedding itself into the wall just beside Mr. Knightley.

He looked to it, then tapped his glasses again before digging the back of his hammer into the desk. As the nails ripped away, he said, "Bet that felt good."

Ember didn't realize she was huffing until he stared up at her. She weighed the hammer in her hands and grinned. "More than I thought possible." Taking more care, Ember swung again, this time bashing a hole into the side. It lifted the desk off of the floor, taking some of the shitty carpet with.

"What are we going to replace it with?" she asked.

Dumping the pieces she'd shredded off of the desk, Booker said, "You're the designer, you tell me."

Her arms sagged and Ember stared around the small room again. The lobby wasn't just a means to get guests from point A to point B. It was the focal point, the first taste of what they were about to experience. It needed to shine, to gleam brighter than any elegant ballroom.

"I've got a few ideas," she said with a smile. "But first, we get rid of all of this tacky shit." Grunting, Ember swung the hammer, obliterating the last of the desk to dust.

* * * *

To Booker's surprise, they let them do actual work for two days. Okay, they cut the power and took all their tools after six p.m. — probably had something to do with union rules for the crew. But they'd already removed the desk, pulled out the carpets and were starting on the wallpaper. *Who puts wallpaper in an art deco lodge in the woods?*

Savages.

He stretched out his legs on the floor, then reached to increase the light on his camp lantern. Either production didn't notice when he borrowed it, or they wanted him to have it. Probably made it easier for the eye in the sky to spy on him. His eyes drifted to the red light that'd been haunting his sleep, but he shook it off. Privacy was a luxury he could crawl back into once this was over.

"What do you think about the wall?" he asked.

"Which wall?" Her voice came back from the other side of the blanket.

"The alcove shelf that used to be for the keys. We could put a sign up there instead." He'd been eyeing it, surprised to find the wood in good shape. It'd need buffing and varnishing, but it was solid oak and could be turned good as new. Except modern hotels had no need for those old key hooks. It wouldn't serve well and, as much as he wanted to keep it, they needed to win.

"Actually, I had another idea."

Booker jerked in surprise as the blanket lifted. Miss Woodhouse walked on her knees and laid down her notebook. "What if we keep the shelves?"

Taking a quick look at her sketches, he said, "A sign would be more appealing and useful."

"I don't think so. We don't care about useful, not here. It's the style that matters, and that shelf is so beautiful it'd be a crime to dismantle it."

He finally glanced up to find a wistful gaze in her eyes. She looked tired after two days of hard labor, but her cheeks burned from a smile that wouldn't leave. Her skin glowed like this was the happiest she'd ever been. "I get it, electronic keys don't need to be stored up here, but a sign, even a tasteful one seems like a waste. What if, instead we create a system where we put old keys on a slot then automate it so that if a room is taken the key vanishes. Or it gets turned around to say 'occupied' on the fob?"

Raising her head, she looked about to break into dance from excitement. Booker fought his instinct to fall back on the simple. "It would keep the shelf."

"And the speakeasy feel we're going for, with that curved desk you're carving. I am finding an old bell for the black marble and gold countertop." She seemed to spend half her time diving into the extra boxes the production would bring in every day. It was a first-come, first-served scenario and Miss Woodhouse came prepared for war.

Booker looked over her ideas to try to work the mechanisms and wires into place without damaging the shelves. "That's...you know, I think it could work. We're gonna need a way to program it, though."

"Assuming they let us have a computer. We might have to jerry-rig it for the reveal." She didn't seem worried, for once not fretting if they'd even make it past the next elimination. "I had another idea, a bit more out there. What do you think about creating a trick for guests like a button that opens a secret compartment?"

That sounded a bit gimmicky for his tastes, but Booker had agreed to leave the decorating up to her. "Where?"

"Let me show you." She reached across her page to turn it, then yelped. "Oh my goodness, I..." Launching to her feet, she stumbled halfway under the blanket. "I didn't mean to invade your side. Sorry."

Guilt stabbed him in the gut, as if he was wrong while she scampered over and dropped the blanket. He too hadn't thought anything of her popping over, almost as if he were getting used to her invasion in his life.

"It's all right," he said, trying to assure them both.

She laughed from way over on the other side of the room. It sounded like she'd shuffled off to her bed. Booker risked staring through the blanket, but with his lantern, it was hard to make out her shadow. He reached to turn it down, before shaking his hand away.

"How do you think everyone else is dealing with tight quarters?"

Booker shrugged. It wasn't his job to worry about their competition, though he did wonder—forcing two strangers to share not only a bedroom but a bed seemed dicey.

"It's probably easier for them," she said.

It was easy for him to forget he was sharing a room with a girl because they slept on the floor. Were all the other men chivalrous enough to take the hard, freezing ground every night? He doubted it. "I'd guess harder. Literally," Booker said to a surprising gasp, as if she wasn't thinking the same. She was the one pushing Harriet and Elton together after all. "That's biology."

"Biology? Do you think so little of your fellow men that they can't control their urges?"

"The producers don't."

"That's a horrible thing to say," she chastised, as if it was his idea to create a harassment nightmare for ratings. "They would never put us in harm's way."

"Would Brent say the same?"

"That was an accident, and I'm sure he's being well tended to."

Probably got a big get-better card from the show's lawyers. Booker lay back, then twisted onto his side. He stared under the gap that'd been raised another inch. Her naked toes were visible and a hint of ankle. "No one tried to stop me on that first night. Not one producer asked me where I was taking you while you were nearly blacked out. How can you think they're worrying about your best interests?"

She went silent, a sound he was coming to fear. When Miss Woodhouse wasn't talking, her devious mind was churning. He braced himself for a biting wit that could flay a man alive, but a soft, almost child-like voice asked, "You didn't...?"

The pain caused him to suck in a gasp like he'd been kicked in the balls.

"Did you sleep in the room to protect me?" Her question swerved fast, the tone cold and dismissive.

"No," he said, pushing her notebook back to her side. "They locked the door behind me and I couldn't get out."

Shaking fingers reached for her notebook, almost scooping under the gap of their divider. Just as she brushed her knuckles against the hem, she yanked them back as if they burned. Booker shoved the last of the notebook hard so she didn't have to move.

"I've never had that happen before. I should have been more careful. I...I don't want to have to thank you," she whispered.

Booker rolled over and doused his lantern. "I don't want to have to be thanked."

Chapter Sixteen

"Congratulations, Team Orange!"

Everyone clapped as Ember leaped into the air with excitement. Mr. Knightley was more constrained, only giving a perfunctory nod before he crossed his arms.

"I have to say you've surprised everyone. From dead last to winning this week's challenge," the Artist said.

Ember glanced over to her wagon she'd made the perfect level of autumnal cozy for a hayride. With Mr. Knightley's help, of course.

"What did we win?" he shouted. "An assistant?"

"That Venetian marble countertop?" Ember asked. She'd been dreaming of the premium prize list for the past two days. Whoever won the challenges would get a crack at picking first, which was probably the only reason Mr. Knightley put down his nail gun to help her.

The Artist bounced on their heels and smiled wide. "Better. You get...a romantic hayride under the stars in your wagon!"

"Oh." Ember tried to keep her voice from warbling.

Mr. Knightley showed no compunction. "That's it? Can't we have anything else? Even a bed for the damn room would be preferable to—"

"To what?" Ms. Goddard stepped forward and his eyes dropped.

"Never mind," he muttered and refused to look toward Ember. As if she hadn't been pinning her hopes on winning anything other than sitting on straw next to Mr. Knightley. She'd rather pull every nail out of every floorboard in the manor.

"Excellent. Well, you'd better get back to work. You never know when it might be elimination day."

The Artist waved them off like errant ladybugs. There was a lot less running this time. They'd all been hard at work tearing the place apart for the past five days. On the show, this part only lasted for thirty minutes. She never realized how much work had to go into getting ready for the good part.

Ember wrung her arm around, trying to work out a cramp as she walked to the lobby. While the rest of the manor was a mystery behind locked doors, everyone saw their room. There was no hiding how far ahead or behind they were. She gulped, staring around the gutted lobby. While it'd been an eyesore before, now it looked like the kind of abandoned house where a murder clown would leap out of a closet. The walls were torn to shreds, the coveted oak flooring scuffed and warped, wires dangled from the ripped-out chandelier and the only light source was a single caged bulb hanging above their heads.

They had a lot of work and no time to do it in.

"I didn't mean how it sounded."

Blinking, Ember turned as Mr. Knightley slid in around her.

"I only was hoping that we'd get help. There's...there's a lot to do. And now we have to waste perfectly good work time on a hayride."

Despite his assurances he didn't find her and the idea of spending time with her repulsive, it was difficult for Ember to shake the idea away. But she put on a smile anyway. "Don't worry." Picking up the hammer, she turned to him. "I hate our prize, too," she said then swung at a bent nail.

* * * *

The tractor stopped for a second time and Ember paused. Her gaze darted past the camera that'd been zoomed in on her face to the producer. Sam didn't answer, only gave a curt nod. With the waning sun casting an amber glow through the forest, Ember reached for the handles on the wagon.

"Allow me." Mr. Knightley interrupted her and strode up the tall incline with one long stride. He reached a hand down to her and Ember carefully placed her palm in his. Rough canvas clawed at her skin as he hauled her up into the wagon. Just as she got her footing, the tractor lurched forward.

An arm wrapped around her waist, keeping her on her feet. She'd somehow reached out for a hold and found herself clinging to his upper arm. Both blushed and flung themselves apart, landing on the straw bales he'd hauled up and she'd placed for the perfect romantic atmosphere.

At three miles an hour, they weren't exactly racing into the woods, but the manor and the horde of people outside vanished. They drifted down a forest path with a bumpy road, trees pressed in tight, leaves tumbling at just the touch. Ember gazed around her hard work and felt pleased. She'd never had to design the perfect hayride for romance, but this was wonderful.

The bales were stacked on the sides and back, giving lumbar support and creating a little love sofa out of straw. The lucky couple would find their thighs touching and hands glancing against each other on the ride. Instead of real candles, battery-operated ones cast a haunting and romantic glow from the lanterns hanging off of the sides. It made the ride feel like they were on a private boat circling a secluded island before slipping into a grotto.

It was the perfect recipe for romance...for those who were looking to fall in love.

"You're wearing your gloves," Ember said. A wind cut through the gaps in the straw and she shivered.

Mr. Knightley stared at his hands. "Sorry," he mumbled, then tried to tug them off.

"Hoping this would be over fast enough we could get back to work?" She dug into the basket she'd placed for the lovers and unfurled the heavy quilt.

While Ember tucked the quilt around her thighs, he slapped his gloves against his. "Honestly, I forgot I had them on. The work clothes don't come off until I hit the shower."

A foreign image scampered through her mind of water beading down his glistening skin, his body steaming and naked save for those rough work gloves. Ember gulped and pressed the blanket toward him. "Here. To keep warm."

"I'm fine," he insisted.

"You're not cold?"

"Nope."

"Then why are you covered in goosebumps?" She swept a finger down the exposed skin on his arms positively quivering in this chill.

He watched her finger until it slipped off his elbow. "I don't know, but I'm not cold."

"Why do men lie about the simple act of being cold? What's the point? Is it bravado or stupidity?" Ember sighed and reached over to tuck the far end of the blanket around his hips. He made a halfhearted attempt to push it aside, but gave up quickly as he no doubt realized she'd chosen the softest and heaviest of quilts.

"Why do women only wear thin shirts and tiny skirts in freezing cold weather?" he argued instead.

Ember chuckled, comfortable in her long jeans and chunky sweater. She tossed back her ponytail and closed her eyes. "Ah yes, why do women inconvenience themselves in order to please men and are rewarded for it? Truly a mystery of the ages."

The blanket stretched taut as each tried to keep to their side. It caused their hands to land on the straining quilt. Ember curled hers up while his clung to the edge.

"Men don't care what you wear," he said.

It was so preposterous a snort came from the darkness. Both of them fell silent. In the shadows of the tractor hid not only the camera and the operator but their producer as well. She'd been the one to laugh, reminding them they were never alone.

A shiver ran up Ember's spine and she reached for the other treat in her basket. Holding tight to the thermos, she asked him, "How about a cup of warm apple cider?"

She poured out a mug, thick steam filling the air as the amber liquid sloshed into the metal tin. Mr. Knightley looked askance at her offering, like he was being handed a sippy cup before a nap. She smiled and pressed it closer. "Apple cider and a little brandy."

He too looked toward the camera and took the mug. While he slung it back, chasing after the liquid courage, Ember poured her own.

"I was looking at your specs for the hideaway door. They won't work, but with a bit of tweaking—"

"Ah," Sam interrupted, her finger waggling into the light. "No talking shop, remember."

Booker sighed so loudly, it startled a tree of birds. Their wings flapped strangely and their song was more of a high-pitched squeal than... "Bats!" Ember cried out and dove for shelter.

It wasn't an adorable nest of sparrows but a colony of bats that scattered into the night air. They flew right above them, cutting across the forest before turning to silhouette against the moon. She huddled tight, only risking a look to make certain they were gone.

"Bats can't hurt you."

"What if their feet snag in my hair?"

"Sounds more like you'd hurt them instead."

It was a silly fear. She'd seen pictures of bats with their adorable mouths stuffed full of bananas, but in the dark—with only the sound of leather wings splitting the midnight air—her heart leaped. Ember reached out and placed her palm to a steel curve. Curious, she raised her chin.

Her hand was touching, no, wrapped around his chest. Jerking away, Ember nearly flung her apple cider into the woods. Without thinking, she had pressed her cheek to him and hidden in his embrace. "They're..."

She tried to shake off her move and took a long sip that became a full shot. The cider warmed her and the brandy burned. "They're all gone?"

He nodded, his smile glowing brighter than the moon. "But if I see any more bats, or baseball equipment managers or billionaire superhero vigilantes..."

"I'll be able to handle myself," she said, trying to play it off.

To her surprise, Booker raised his mug to his lips and said, "Of that I have no doubt." He took a long drink, keeping her from asking any questions.

The hayride passed out of the forest onto a new road. Trees faded to shorter saplings, then reeds as they emerged next to a lake. No doubt by dawn's light it was serene, the perfect afternoon escape to paddle a canoe across the crystal water with a sweetheart. But in the moonlight, fog crept across the surface as if heralding the arrival of the headless horseman atop a pontoon.

Ember yelped at her foolish imagination and a hand glanced against her shoulder. Booker peered next to her and asked, "What? More bats?"

"I was congratulating myself. I suspected there was a lake somewhere close by." She crinkled her nose at her dodge, but it worked.

He settled on his side and his hand drifted into the straw behind their heads. "How'd you know?"

"The geese. I heard honking every morning, but I never saw them flying away. So there had to be water somewhere close by."

Booker smiled wide as if she'd performed a magic trick. "That's Lake Promise," he said.

"So named because a young man was to meet his star-crossed sweetheart on the bridge, but he never showed because her father found out and stopped her permanently? Every night now her ghost haunts the lake, waiting for her one true love?"

He chuckled at the fairytale and leaned closer. "Or because it's fed by the River Promise and land adjusters aren't very creative."

Playfully smacking his thigh, Ember shook her head. "Do you not have an ounce of whimsy in your body?"

"I'm not certain there's room between my stubbornness and dullness," he whispered. Both their heads turned toward each other at the same moment. The wagon tipped, pushing them closer together. Booker dug his hand into the bale just behind her, his arm tensed. Lantern lights danced in his eyes like the last of the fireflies. His body hardened so tight, the heat of his solid thighs and chest caressed down hers. Nervous, Ember dropped her hand to the blanket and found Booker's hip below.

"Miss Woodhouse?" he breathed, his lips parting so her name rested across them.

"Mr. Knightley?" she responded. Her fingers clenched on the blanket, pulling her higher. He swept his arm through the straw, casting it into the midnight air like farmyard confetti. The distance between them that'd once been as wide as a gorge shortened to a single thread. His head gently curved to the right and she found hers doing the same.

The wagon struck a rock. Both bounced in place and their foreheads smashed together like a bell. Instead of a triumphant ring, a low groan and thud burst through the night air. Booker retreated to the other side while massaging his wound. She reached up, but hissed at the pain.

It shouldn't surprise her that his skull was thicker than steel. The retort clung to her tongue, aching to distract from the embarrassment thickening the fog. Ember kept it in place and nudged the bucket instead. It was meant to hold champagne for a romantic celebration, perhaps even a proposal. She'd never expected to be the one riding in this wagon. She had almost enchanted herself by mistake.

No doubt he was thinking the same. They had a job to do. Moonlit rides, snuggling under fleece blankets and trading kisses in the straw would only hinder that. Their once light banter fell to awkward silence, Ember staring out toward the lake while Mr. Knightley focused on the passing trees.

"Take us back," Sam said, shattering not only the silence, but the illusion. They weren't alone. They were never alone. *And if I'm to be the matchmaker of the season, the woman who loves love but is never lucky enough to win it, I need to keep my wits in place.*

The wagon turned, picking the trail back up in the direction of the resort. Tiny dots of lights hung through the trees. At this distance, instead of windows they looked more like fairies bunking down for the night. With a low grunt, the man put down the camera and talked quietly with the producer. They were no longer of interest to the storyline. The once magical hayride into the woods vanished. In its place were two people uncomfortably stabbed by pieces of straw.

"Do you think there's still time to take down the last of the wallpaper?" Mr. Knightley whispered.

"Possibly. If we leap off the wagon and run for it," Ember said.

He finally looked her way just as they emerged from the secluded woods onto the estate's grounds. "I don't know if that will work. You're rather short."

"I prefer fun-sized, thank you very much."

"Might be better if I carry you." He said it as if it were a simple solution to a problem, but Ember gasped at the idea. For a beat, his cheeks burned red. "This, you know, this wasn't as bad as I feared. It was nice to take a break."

"Well, well, is that Mr. Knightley daring to let himself have a moment of enjoyment? I fear I might faint from shock."

He snickered and shrugged, but his smile didn't dim. She should never admit it, but she had enjoyed herself too.

"You're not as callow or dull as I once thought."

"Thanks for noticing," he said and leaned back to gaze at the stars. Ember stared at him, waiting. Blinking, he finally glanced to her. "Oh, you're just as exhausting as the first day we met." He laughed and, God help her, she did too. "A man would have to be a fool to..."

His easy smile faded. Hunching over, he pressed his palms together in his lap and watched his fingertips touch.

"To what?" To work with her? To spend time with her? To fall for her?

He scratched the back of his neck, his elbow waggling in the air. "To even think of −"

Headlights flashed behind them. The twin beams heralded not a truck or even an RV, but a long black vehicle twisting up the path to the manor itself. Ember forgot everything as the limo came to a stop, gravel dust rising in its wake. Like a monster emerging from the fog, the door opened and a silhouette stepped out.

"Who's that?" Ember asked.

"Ah, she's early," the producer responded and Ember's throat caught.

Even before the tractor came to a stop, she leaped out of the wagon and took off for the limo. The butler was hustling around the vehicle, arms overloaded in bags, but all of Ember's attention was on the silhouette. Slim and tight, she was dressed like a femme fatale slithering into the detective's office. With hair darker than midnight and skin paler than the moon, her eyes gleamed with sapphire hunger for the manor.

Ember's breath caught at the woman, the stranger, the provocateur. The interloper offered a delicate hand out through the distance and greeted her. "Hello, I'm Jade Fairfax."

Chapter Seventeen

"Everyone, please welcome Jade."

The mystery woman stood front and center before the fireplace after being paraded around like a best-in-show poodle by the producers. Booker fought off a yawn, feeling his extra years more than the twenty-somethings glaring at the newcomer like she was about to swipe their Christmas presents. A couple gave a halfhearted attempt at clapping for her, but most went stone. And none more than Miss Woodhouse. She damn near bristled, the straw caught in her hair and clothing standing up like quills. Booker waited for her to hiss and go claws out at Jade whose crimes included standing in place and smiling.

"Why don't you tell them about yourself?" the producer prompted. Booker knew when a line of rope was being measured, but the girl ran with it.

"I'm Jade, like they already said. Um, I'm twenty-three and single. I grew up in my grandfather's woodworking shop learning how to make furniture every weekend. I'm just an amateur but..." She hefted up a drill and buzzed it twice. "I know my way around a power tool."

Interesting. He wanted to ask what furniture exactly, but a low growl paused him. Miss Woodhouse had turned fully rabid, her eyes blazing as she glared at Jade. What in the heavens was happening?

"And you were Miss Craftswoman two years in a row." The producer smiled at the men as he said it.

"Ah, that was just something fun to do."

"Shame I don't have one of your calendars here for you to sign."

The poor girl looked like she wanted to leap up the chimney. Instead, she nervously revved the drill. "I look forward to working with you all." She took a step forward, but the producer caught her by the arms.

He had barely raised his chin before the doors opened and the all-too-familiar liquor cart rolled in. That same generic house music started up as the producer called, "Why don't you all enjoy this downtime to get to know Jade?"

Absolutely no one dashed for the booze. They all perched like gargoyles about to swoop down and devour her eyeballs. Poor Jade was left to stand alone, doing her best to act like she wasn't being watched from all sides.

Feeling a glimmer of pity, Booker picked up the first champagne flute and handed it to her. She smiled wide in thanks and took a nervous sip. Despite the throbbing music, the atmosphere was a tense wreck. Booker wished he could escape out the doors, but he'd agreed to play along with whatever curveball they threw at him, which meant getting to know this new stranger. "What's your...favorite wood?"

She laughed and brushed back her long black hair. "Hm, I'd have to say oak, for its versatility."

"I've got some wood you're guaranteed to love." Logan inserted himself into the conversation and the party took off. People rushed for the drink cart. The guys crowded around Jade, and the girls slowly picked at her from afar. Booker snagged the only beer left and stumbled back to watch.

After some time where Jade seemed content to be the center of attention, Robert joined him. They stood together in silence, not needing to speak. Eventually, Miss Woodhouse must have tired of trading barbs with Jade as she caught Harriet by the arm and whisked her off.

"What's the big deal with her?" Booker asked, jerking the neck of his bottle to Jade. "Why does everyone hate her?"

"You don't know?" Robert said.

He was getting tired of people being surprised he didn't know the inner workings of every reality show.

"She's here to disrupt the teams. Most seasons they bring on a new contestant midway through. Someone talented that could win it all but rarely does. It's to kick up the hornets' nest after everyone starts working well together."

"How in the hell do you know that?" Booker asked. Did everyone take a Reality Show 101 class that he missed out on?

Robert shrugged. "This show was on every time I visited my mom. It's not hard to pick up on their tricks after binging a few seasons."

Did that mean this Jade could be a problem? Was she a plant by the producers or a talented young woman with enough beauty to make everyone act stupid? If she really did build furniture, perhaps she could make it to the top and would be a better partner for him.

A heart-wrenching sigh pulled Booker from his half-drunk scheming. Poor Robert was full moon-eye over the squeaky country girl. He practically drooled as Miss Woodhouse adjusted Harriet's dress and tied a ribbon around her waist to emphasize it.

"You like her."

Robert gulped and shook his head. "She's...she's so. We were talking a bit and she told me about this three-legged dog she had that used to chase after a one-legged squirrel. It..." He shivered as if he'd been under a spell. "It was funny. The way she did the little squirrel arms." Then he went and mimed them, squeaking with his lips pulled back to mime the teeth.

That was what love did to a person, rotted their brain until they were a drooling husk. Booker shook his head, glad he had enough sense to keep his faculties intact. Harriet managed to break away from Miss Woodhouse's grip to give a little wave to Robert. He jerked as if he'd been graced by Aphrodite and sheepishly returned it after the girl's back was turned.

"You're wasting your time."

"I know. She's got Elton Brown. How can I compete with an actual movie star?" Robert patted his stomach, then sucked in his little gut as if a few abs could compete with a rich Hollywood type.

Booker doubted that even if Robert had a secret fortune and a yacht he could win. He wasn't competing with Elton but the machinations of Miss Woodhouse. When she had a mind to something, neither heaven nor hell could stop her. The tenacity was almost impressive, if it didn't catch damn near everyone else in the hurricane. She lifted her delicate fingers and waved them to the movie star in question.

Elton drifted away from Jade, all of his attention not on the girl Ember kept forcing in between them but his other prey. The way his gaze cut down Ember, sizing her up like pieces of body parts, made Booker's skin broil. She tried to dodge out of the way, but Elton laid his slimy hand across her shoulder, trapping her in his grip.

"You okay with that?"

Robert's soft question wrenched Booker away. He opened his clenched fist, crinkling the aluminum can. A spot of blood stained his palm. He'd crushed the beer so tight, the metal had split and sliced his skin. Placing his bleeding hand to his stomach, Booker laughed. "We can barely stand each other. There's no love lost between us, I assure you."

"So you wouldn't care if she switched to Elton, then I could take Harriet?"

"No. Of course not." Booker laughed again, even his ears picking up on the force. "What do you mean switch?"

"Every season there's a switch. It's where people have the opportunity to change their partners."

A switch? Why hadn't she said anything? Had she been planning on ditching him the whole time?

"I'm hoping, I mean I haven't had a chance to talk to her much. But if things don't work out so well with Elton, maybe I could…"

Robert's self-assurances faded. Ember clearly wanted nothing to do with Elton beyond setting him up with Harriet, that he knew. But she also believed Booker to be a lost cause, too boring for the cameras and of no interest to her romantically or otherwise. She wouldn't waste her time switching him for Elton. She'd only do it for—

"Where's Logan?"

* * * *

Miss Jade Fairfax, elegant, lovely, poisonous— slipped through the crowd like a drop of belladonna in a goblet of wine. As her oh-so-emphatic fingers lanced through the air and landed on Mr. Brown, Ember snapped. She lunged for her hand, wrenching it off of Ree's fool, and found herself left hanging onto the offending digits.

"Hey, hayride girl."

"Ember, Ember Woodhouse."

She blushed with Machiavellian skill and smiled. "Sorry. There are so many names to remember."

"It's understandable. We've had nearly a week to get to know each other, learn everyone's foibles, foster private jokes. It must be rather daunting to catch up." Ember notched up her pleasant grin and clenched her fingers tighter.

Miss Fairfax brushed back one of her expert hair tendrils from her face. "Then it's a lucky thing I happen to love a challenge." She let go of their frozen handshake, so Ember had to do the same.

It was a wonder Jade's shoes weren't underwater from the incessant drooling by the men in the room. When they weren't rushing to get her a drink, a crudité or a bed, they'd brag about their building skills and challenge her to a nail off. Ember wished she could pretend the crude humor flew over Miss Fairfax's head, but she seemed entertained and quick to volley back a dirty pun.

She was the perfect bait, and every man had swallowed the line, sinker and all.

Ember's gaze drifted from Logan trying to balance a wine glass on his nose, past Mr. Brown bragging about the last A-list celebrities he'd worked with. Apart from the antics and chest beating stood Mr. Knightley. He should be in here, getting as much camera time as possible and including himself in this storyline upset.

The part of her that'd studied the minutiae of this show was annoyed at him falling back to his old ways. But relief floated in her stomach like champagne bubbles. At least she didn't have to watch her back while she guarded Harriet's.

"Mister Elton?" Ember held her hand out to him. He paused in his regurgitated tale and his gaze danced from Jade to her like a cat clock in an earthquake. The greatest parlor battle commenced, Jade flicking her hair back to strike the first blow. Ember lowered her eyelashes and nipped her bottom lip. The attack pulverized whatever move Jade planned next and Elton took Ember's hand instead.

She was quick to curl her hand around his and pull him from the couch. Logan flung himself onto it and tried to invite Jade to join him. Augusta had enough sense to leap from the side, body-blocking Jade at the last second. Certain they could handle it all, Ember guided Mr. Elton away as if he were the one leading.

"We haven't had a chance to speak. Your work here is lovely." Ember waved a hand around the solarium which was already beautiful. All it needed was an update to remove the sun-fade from the upholstery and walls.

Ellen Mint

"I'm thinking of putting a buck's head over there." He pointed to the fireplace. "Up the manliness a bit. It's like a lady's tea room in here."

"That's a…" It would destroy the delicate balance and wrench the art deco style into an eyesore of rustic cringe. Ember fought all of her instincts to keep her smile pleasing. "An interesting idea."

"I'm full of them." He leaned closer, his lips nearly pressing to her cheek, when he darted his eyes up. Sweet Ree gave a little wave from the corner where Ember had left her. Suddenly, Elton cinched tight to Ember's hand and swung her around. "Why don't we talk in private?"

"I don't know if…" She tried to go limp and strained her gaze back to Harriet, but Elton kept pulling.

"I wouldn't want the others to overhear."

Unable to offer any resistance, Ember was led out of the small side door and into a hallway. Stacks of building equipment filled the narrow walkway like giant bricks. Between two piles of sheetrock and plywood, Mr. Brown pressed her against the wall.

"It's rather dark here," she whispered, only the flicker of the party slipping under the door.

"Are you scared?" He placed his palm to the wall beside her head, his hip leaning ever closer. "Because they say this place is haunted. At night, people swear they hear the wails of an old rum runner when his barrels snapped and took out his legs."

She shivered down to her toes and Mr. Brown reached to rub her shoulders. "I'll protect you from the ghost."

"It shouldn't be too difficult. If his legs were crushed, then a slow walk would get us away from the spirit of spirits."

He snickered but didn't call out her pun. Had he even listened to her? "You are hands-down the prettiest girl we've ever had on the show."

"What of...?" Ree flashed through her mind, but she bit her tongue. Forcing him into a confrontation now would only hurt Harriet's chances. "What of Jade?"

Mr. Brown rolled his shoulder and he shifted his weight from one palm to the other. It caused his body to loom ever closer. Ember took a half step back and rammed her heels into the wall. "She's attractive enough, but doesn't have that wow, that pop, that exotic beauty that you do. You're Hawaiian, right?"

"On my mother's side." Ember gulped, her skin prickling as a thousand tiny pins stabbed her in waves. Cold sweat plummeted down her back and she hunted through the darkness. Surely a camera had to be on them, a producer watching.

Just as surely as the night Mr. Knightley had carried her to a hotel room.

"Do you want to get lei—?"

"Mr. Brown." Ember interrupted the pedestrian pickup line she'd heard since she was thirteen.

"Please, it's Elton."

"There's a matter you should be made aware of."

"Don't worry. All the cameras are busy on their twist. No one even knows we're here."

Ember swallowed deep. She clenched her fingers tight to her dress to keep from shoving him off. "I'm celibate."

The man flung his head back as if he'd been wrenched to sobriety at light speed. "You're a what? Like a...a nun?"

"No, I'm...I've chosen, at the suggestion of my life coach, to take a sex sabbatical. Which means I don't have any." Her face burned hotter as she squirmed, wishing one of those secret passages was right behind her.

"Are you telling me you're a virgin?"

"Not exactly. I… While I find you captivating, I'm afraid that you would only be wasting your energy and time on me. My work is my life, and romance doesn't fit into it."

He stared at her in disgust and horrifying curiosity. Sometimes her claiming to be celibate worked wonders at cocktail parties when needing to chase away business men with bigger bank accounts than brains. Other times, especially in bars or dark clubs, it was seen as a challenge. They all wanted to be the man to get her to change her mind. She had no way to know which a man was until the truth lay before them. Mr. Brown didn't back off. He lingered, his gaze drifting ever lower as he dug his nails into the wall.

"Hey, what are you doing out here?"

Mr. Brown flung himself away and spun to face Ember's savior. Logan, tie lost and shirt half unbuttoned, stared at the two of them while wearing a sloppy grin. Mr. Brown quickly adjusted his hair, as if he had all the control. "We were talking."

"Cool. I think that overall chick is looking for you," Logan said and sloshed his drink back in the direction of the party.

Trapped between the two, all Mr. Brown could do was make his exit. With hunched shoulders, he loped back to the party. Ember called out while hanging onto the plywood, "Good evening, Mr. Brown."

"To you as well," he said, and slipped back into the light.

Ember breathed deep and looked to her savior. Only from an awkward situation, of course. Nothing untoward could have happened in a house full of people with cameras always on. "Thank you," she said.

Logan turned from watching Mr. Brown walk away. He beamed and took a long drink. "You know what you need." Slamming his empty glass onto the stacks of wood, Logan exclaimed, "A dance. Come on."

Arm in arm, she'd expected to be returned to the party and do a little shimmy to the house music. Instead, Logan guided her deeper into the manor house. The shadows flickered, old spiderwebs dancing in an invisible breeze, and the floorboards cried out like a man with crushed legs. Her heart leaping, Ember clung tighter to Logan. He was the perfect gentleman, keeping his hands to himself as he approached the ballroom doors.

"I'm not supposed to see them yet," she said.

He placed a finger to his lips and smiled. "I won't tell if you won't." With a little flourish, Logan pushed open the doors and led her inside.

Tarps covered the stage, the chairs and the walls were stripped of all the art and the grand chandelier lay on the ground—but it was magnificent. A mezzanine sat above like the balconies of an opera house, each box decorated in gold art deco flowers. The domed ceiling was decked out in the same elaborate design. Moonlight danced through the two-story crystal windows, casting shadows of wafting trees across the floor.

"This is…" She gasped in awe as Logan guided her closer. Shuffling on her feet, Ember didn't realize she was pulled into a dance until Logan spun her. As she fell into his arms, he guided her toward the center of the room.

"Look up," he said.

"Wow!" Above them was a single stained-glass window of two champagne glasses clinking together in celebration, gold droplets tumbling away. Even in the muted starlight, the gold shone. It had to be breathtaking by day.

"You and Augusta are doing magnificent work."

Logan gave her a little turn, then draped his hand around her waist. "Mostly me. Augusta tries her heart out, but she'd paint this whole place white if I let her."

"Don't you dare!" Ember shouted.

He laughed. "See, I knew you'd get it. You can spot the luxury hiding below the rot."

"Chasing trends only dates a place," Ember said.

"But timeless is forever." He spun her out to the extension of their hands.

All this time, she'd assumed Logan to be the hot but stupid one. Every season had their himbo, and he'd seemed perfect. Yet he shared in her ideals better than any person she'd met in ages.

Logan twisted her back in close and held her tight as they danced faster around the still room. "Word on the street is the switch is coming soon."

She should have been preparing for this. No other episode was more nail biting and back stabbing than the switch.

"I have a proposition for you," Logan whispered, reminding Ember they were completely alone. "You're clearly fed up with the man you're saddled with and Augusta is, frankly, exhausting. You could keep chugging along at that pedestrian lobby, or you could restore this ballroom to its proper glory."

She wasn't in this to win. But if the producers let slip these secrets to Logan, they must expect him to go the distance — probably even take it all. If she teamed up with him, if she had the chance to prove her mettle on this beautiful ballroom, no bank could deny her a loan. And if they did it, if she won this beautiful resort to rebuild in her image, imagine the possibilities.

"Having fun?"

Ember's foot smashed into the other and she tripped. A silhouette stood in the doorway, arms crossed, with rage radiating off his form.

"Mr. Knightley, it isn't…" Ember tried to get her foot under her, but the ankle collapsed. Logan quickly scooped his arms around her, helping then holding her up. "It's not whatever you think this is."

"You know what, I don't care." Mr. Knightley flung his hands up and turned away. "I'm going to bed. Do whatever you want, Miss Woodhouse." He slammed the door, leaving her all alone in the ballroom with Logan.

He had given her freedom. She had a future with Logan. So why did Ember want to chase after the dullard stomping out of the spotlight?

Chapter Eighteen

The knife plunged through the firm flesh.

"It was one dance."

He sawed the blade back and forth, caring nothing for the guts tumbling from the hole.

"Not even a dance."

Placing both his fingers inside the cavity, Booker closed his eyes and pushed. They popped out like grapes, leaving two gaping holes staring endlessly into the void. In this case, the void was Miss Woodhouse, elbow deep in pumpkin innards. She waggled her orange goopy fist at him and flung the squash guts toward the bowl.

"How long are you going to keep on with this childish silent treatment?"

He didn't answer, as he hadn't been answering her since he'd walked away last night. Even as she'd given chase, peppering him with a combination of questions and accusations. It was a wonder she didn't sleep interrogate.

"How are things going over here?" The Artist wandered past, this time wearing a pumpkin on their head, though this one was covered in rhinestones.

Miss Woodhouse put on her biggest smile. "Just peachy!" With pumpkin staining her cheek, her eyes dark from the long night and short morning, and shouting while white-knuckling a knife, she looked positively murderous. Booker could say something, but instead he ducked down to his pumpkin and sawed at the mouth.

"Well, make sure to avoid any *pit*falls," the masked host said with a laugh before moving on to the next table.

"How're you doing?" Harriet asked. She'd claimed the spot right next to Miss Woodhouse. It was a surprise he wasn't shoved out by either Elton or Logan. Instead, it was the quiet church girl who'd taken the largest pumpkin of them all. She held a turkey carver in one hand, a fork in the other, and looked ready to slice her pumpkin to hell.

"Fine. Everything's going…" Miss Woodhouse tried to drop her guts, only for the pumpkin innards and a mess of seeds to stick to her palm. Grunting, she flung her palm back and forth. Just as Mr. Churchill walked past, in the same clothes as last night, the guts released. His bright blond hair turned a garish shade of orange.

Booker refused to hide his laugh at the rising look of horror. Running his fingers through his hair, Logan fought to get the guts free.

"Sorry, I'm so sorry." Miss Woodhouse ran over and tried to pick them out while her hands were still covered. All they needed was to trip and land face-first inside a pumpkin.

"There's water in the house. Let me help you get cleaned up."

"I can handle it." The new girl, Jade, stepped up out of nowhere. She picked Miss Woodhouse's fingers off of Logan and swept her hand around his arm. "You're only making this mess worse."

"Of course all you can do is swoop in at the last moment and pray someone gives you attention."

Jade leaned closer, practically whispering in Miss Woodhouse's ear before she shouted loud enough for everyone to hear, "You're making a fool of yourself. It's embarrassing."

Booker expected for her sharp tongue to slice through Jade better than these flimsy carving knives. But Ember's eyes opened wide and she clicked her teeth as if she didn't know what to say. "That's enough," flew from his mouth. He didn't know why, but he bounded around the table and came between the two women. "Can you save the backstabbing for after brunch?"

"I'm not the one grinding axes all across the lawn this morning." Jade barely looked at him, all of her ire on Ember.

"At least I'm doing actual work. How's all of that wandering about while carrying a pumpkin going for you?" Ember came back swinging. Booker was quickly realizing that he would either have to hold both back, or stand aside and enjoy the catfight. Honestly, at this point...

"Girls, girls, come on. We're all friends here." Harriet wiped her hands on a towel and handed it to Ember. "There's no need to be fightin' like this. It's carving pumpkins, not carving up hearts...for... surgery. You know."

The country bumpkin's bumbling managed to dissolve the tension into wet tissue paper. Both Jade and Ember took a step apart while Logan kept whining about his hair. "Here." It was Elton, who'd been keeping to himself, that walked over and took Logan by the arm. "I know a place to get you cleaned up. Can you do my pumpkin too?"

"Of course," Harriet said with pause. Booker frowned. Was she doing everything while Elton stood around talking about all the movies he'd been in?

Why did he even care?

She wasn't his pet project, she was Ember's...

Booker bit his tongue trying to get her name off of it. He opened his hands, shocked to find they were still around Miss Woodhouse. He returned to murdering his jack-o-lantern. She did the same, diligently scraping down the sides of her pumpkin while talking to Harriet. It left Jade standing around, uncertain where to go. They'd all been sent off with their partners to carve pumpkins for the challenge. But Jade wasn't a partner with anyone.

"Why don't you...?" Booker began, but Miss Woodhouse interrupted.

"We're quite full up, but maybe you can have some luck tricking your way into Robert's good graces."

"Who?" Jade asked.

She responded with a smirk and returned to her peeling. For a beat, Booker caught Jade's eye and he felt a rash of pity. The woman didn't seem to have a friend in the world, though she had come in swinging, so maybe that was how she liked it. Hoisting her little pumpkin up, Jade walked down the line of tables.

Doing his best to focus, Booker only caught snippets of Miss Woodhouse's advice to Harriet. It seemed to amount to be pleasant, but not too pleasant. Be mysterious, but also available. Be kind, but not easy. All the useless platitudes people sold for a quick buck. Dating advice was just like weight-loss diets. If it actually worked, no one would get rich selling them.

After some time, she blew back her hair and hefted up her pumpkin. "Are you ready?" she asked, marching over to the stand he'd built.

He didn't seem to have a choice as she worried her squash onto the wooden dowel. As it slipped to land on the pelvis pumpkin he'd struggled with, Booker had to admit that it was an impressive chest. She'd even managed to carve a heart below the ribcage. Their orange skeleton needed its arms next. Bending over, Booker fished up the platform he'd attached to two other dowels that would hopefully hold the butternut arms.

"Hold it still," he said, then aimed his drill for the preset wood screws.

"You didn't have to get involved."

"I did," he said, then whirred the drill to drown out her argument. "Or else you'd have torn each other's extensions out. And no one wants to have the crazy lady design their bedroom, right?" The screw fell flush and the drill jerked in his hand. Booker slid around to the other one while she stood above him.

"You'd be surprised. The crazy one can go further than being the winner sometimes."

He pushed the button, then looked away from the screw. In order to reach, he'd had to get on his knees before her. She stared down at him, nervously licking her lip and wiping away a spot of her lipstick each time. She kept drawing his eye to it, Booker self-consciously licking his own to match. No doubt hers were much softer and plumper too. Had to taste sweet with just enough give as he —

A loud whine wrenched him back. The drill screeched as he kept trying to drive the screw through the board. Wrenching it away, he looked up. Logan marched across the lawn, golden sunshine streaming through his wet but clean hair. Took them long enough. They were probably hiding, or drinking. Doing anything to avoid actual work while the women kept falling over them.

"You better get to him quickly." Booker pointed past Logan to not only Jade turning to greet him, but also Augusta bounding across the lawn. She'd either leap into his arms or bowl him ass over end.

Miss Woodhouse rolled her eyes and began to slide the squash arm up the dowel. "I have no intentions with Mr. Churchill."

"So disappearing from the party in order to dance in the dark together meant nothing?"

"That is not what happened. I didn't..." She scowled and released her grip on the hand squash. Both it and the arm flew off, cracking in half on the ground. Neither she nor Booker gave it a second look. Shooting to her feet, she rounded on him. "I'm not here for Logan."

"Really? Then why are you so angry at my accusations?"

"Because no one likes being accused. You're acting like a jilted lover for one dance. There wasn't even any music. It was hardly a dance to begin with."

"You were in his arms."

"So what?"

"So —" Booker gulped, his face flushed as the vanished world snapped back at him. Knives dropped, tongues stilled and all the eyes focused on the two of them locked in a match of wills. He shouldn't care that some other man was leering at her. He didn't. He wouldn't. What Miss Woodhouse did or did not do on her own time was her business, not his.

"We had a deal. We work together."

She waved her hand at the pumpkin man who wobbled on his platform. "What do you call that?"

"Biding your time. I know about the switch... something you never told me about."

"What? You think I'm going to leave you just because Logan invited me to dance with him?"

Booker jerked his head, more certain than ever that she was. "Isn't it best to abandon the boring, black spot for the golden goose?"

Her voice dropped and she leaned closer to him. "I'm not here for that. If I... Look, I didn't mention the switch because it's poison. Anyone who changes their partner is guaranteed to be kicked off next episode, if not that one. People don't fall in love with a backstabber. Also..." She dropped her eyes and nervously fiddled with her fingers. "I thought if I told you, you'd leap at the chance to get rid of me."

It would be in his best interests to swap her out for someone with a background in construction, who didn't rile up his blood and make him seethe every time she was pounced on by other men. He needed to focus on the competition, on his work, on anything but Miss Woodhouse and her lithe body in tight jeans. "If you weren't planning a coup with Logan, why did you go with him?"

"To see the ballroom. To see how far ahead they are in this competition."

"And...?"

She breathed deep and glanced over at Mr. Churchill adding a straw hat to his pumpkin scarecrow. "It's exquisite. I don't think anyone, no matter what they do, has a chance in hell of beating him. The fix was always in. Logan's going to win."

That couldn't be right. That wasn't fair.

"Hm, I think we have our challenge winners!" The Artist grabbed Logan's hand and hoisted it above his head.

They'd set it up from the beginning. It didn't matter how hard Booker worked, how skilled he was, how talented, how badly he needed this — it was always going to the rich pretty boy, and America would love him for it.

"But we can keep fighting for third place. That'll get you enough followers to give your business a proper shot in the arm." She cheered him on, darkening Booker's mood. He caught his wobbling gourd skeleton, a waste of time. Instead of working on rebuilding the resort, he'd lost hours elbow deep in pumpkin guts and for what? No one would see these. No one would care.

Grinding his teeth, Booker plucked the head he'd carved off of the stand. Staring into the holes that'd never see a candle, the hollowness clanged in his skull. With a loud scream, Booker hurled his pumpkin as far as he could.

Flesh and guts exploded, streaking across the delicate walkway laid over a hundred years ago. Everyone went silent, watching as Booker struggled to breathe, to let anything in other than this soul-crushing anxiety. He didn't care if the producers marched him off of the set — he was going to lose anyway. It didn't matter if every person watching wrote him off as a brute — he'd failed his family before stepping foot off of the plane.

"Yeah!"

Another pumpkin slammed to the ground behind his, this one rolling faster down the hill. Shocked, Booker turned as Ember wiped her orange hands together, a smile wide. "Come on, everyone!" she shouted.

"Uh, please don't destroy your scarecrows. We need to do pickup shots on…" The producer's orders went unheeded as eight people who'd been trapped in this hamster wheel for a week let loose. Every kind of gourd from pumpkin to acorn squash flew through the air. With each strike, the crowd cheered, smothering the stones in slimy orange guts. It smelled like Halloween on his grandma's porch.

Booker reached back for the pie pumpkin he hadn't carved, but bumped his fingers into unexpected hands. She laughed and tried to tug on the pumpkin, not about to let him have it easy. Never one to give up, even for a pretty face, he tugged it back harder. His strength easily won and he tucked the pumpkin tight to his chest. Then Miss Woodhouse dug her hand into their excess pumpkin guts and, without pause, tossed a massive glob right at his chest.

"Two can play at that," he declared, but Ember hoisted up the bowl and held it out of his reach. They darted back and forth around the table, him trying to get the guts, her trying to cover him in them.

Booker managed to get a finger hooked onto the lip of the bowl. It tumbled from her hands. She panted, staring at the mess now on the dirty ground. Booker did the same.

Both shifted. He dove first, about to get a handful, when she leaped off of the ground and latched onto him piggyback style. She wrapped one of her arms around his eyes as he spun around, trying to get at her.

"Miss Woodhouse, I think you need a bit of orange to your countenance." Booker tried to flick the glob of pumpkin guts he got, but she cried out and dodged behind him.

Her little nose dug into the back of his neck as she braided her fingers across his chest. She pressed her thighs into him like a rider on a mustang. Her giggles shivered down his skin, igniting him hotter than he ever thought possible.

Booker kept spinning, hoping to catch her, but it seemed impossible. She was too good at dodging. Abandoning his guts, he reached a hand around to cup her waist. Her silly giggling swallowed into a low gulp. Instead of slipping off of him, she drew her leg lower and traced her foot down his inner thigh.

"Wait. Augusta!"

He looked up as the woman ran for Logan. She leaped up to wrap herself around him just as Ember had to Booker. At the worst possible moment, Logan—still holding a little carving knife—turned. The force of Augusta's leap plunged the tiny blade straight through her hand.

"What the fuck!" she screamed, flinging her hand around. Blood splattered across the pumpkins. Augusta screeched, her eyes wide with madness. Then she bolted. The producers chased after her.

"Shut it down. Get them inside. Call the lawyers!"

"And an ambulance?"

"Fine, that too."

They were pushed away, Booker only catching the last moments as London Goddard tackled the panicking Augusta to the turf.

Chapter Nineteen

Ember nervously smoothed down her skirt. Light music echoed around the empty ballroom, everyone either sitting in the middle of the floor or standing while clinging to their chair. After the accident, they'd all been rushed off to small rooms and told to change for a big surprise tonight. It had to be the elimination. But after what had happened with Augusta...

Boom. The walls rattled with a burst of thunder. Jittery, Ember yanked her fingers away as a lightning bolt split the sky above them. Her palm felt heavy and she glanced down. A burst of crimson dotted her skin. She yelped, certain it was blood, but a handful of red sequins tumbled from her unmarred palm.

"It's only thunder," Logan said. He looked less concerned than everyone else. Had the producers already told him what had happened with Augusta? Spinning in his chair, he eyed up Ember. "Or do you need comforting?" He raised his arms and the back of her neck burned. Everyone was watching.

"I think I need some air." Ember stood up so haphazardly, her chair tipped over. Its landing *thunk* echoed through the ballroom. In the dark, the place had seemed mysterious and exciting. In the light, the flowers shifted to judgmental faces staring down at them all.

Picking up her skirt, Ember tried to work her way out to the garden. There was a little overhang she could stand under to collect herself. Though screaming into the unforgiving rain might soothe her better. A thousand questions burned inside of her, but everyone kept avoiding eye contact, as if they didn't want to hear them.

"Excuse me, ma'am, where are you going?" An assistant she'd never seen before who looked like he bounced for nightclubs stood in her way.

"I only need to cool down. It's rather stuffy in here." She tried to push past, but he folded his arms and stood in the way.

"Why don't you get a drink instead?"

The liquor cart had been seeing a lot of action tonight. Unlike the bombastic libations of the previous parties, this was a dirge of shots — each one tossed back with a sneer for more. Losing herself in the bliss of alcohol sounded like her only escape. She took a step for the drink cart when a shadow crept across her body. It flew over the skylight, darkening the entire room and Ember shivered.

Bypassing the offer, she walked toward the back of the room. Still remaining inside, but away from everyone. In the shadows, she picked up on harried voices cutting across an abandoned walkie-talkie.

"Do you see him?"

"Yeah. He's not going anywhere."

"Just keep your eyes open. Word is he's already got a favorite and if he vanishes, it'll be our asses on the line."

A favorite? Who were they talking about? Ember started to sway on her feet as if she was dancing and edged closer to the box of equipment.

"Does this happen a lot?"

"Every fucking season."

They must mean Mr. Brown. Her plan had worked! He'd fallen so head over heels for Ree they were sending assistants to watch him to keep from it looking like he was playing favorites.

Oh my gosh, I have to tell her.

Dashing through the floor, her heels clicking like a hammer's fall, Ember waved for Harriet. The girl looked wonderful in Ember's little black Versace. With that gold eyeliner and the necklace she'd lent her, Ree'd gone from country bumpkin to enchanting socialite. It was the perfect night for the world to learn that Elton had fallen for her.

"I've got good news," Ember whispered, curling up in the chair next to her. She looked around and spotted the man in question with the rest of the guys. He seemed to be entertaining Logan at least.

"Is Augusta going to be okay?"

"Who cares…? I don't know. It's about Elton."

"Don't tell me he went and stabbed himself too." Ree gasped and stared at the producers who'd been lecturing them on not talking about the accident in front of the cameras.

"No, he's fine. The producers are talking. They say that he's fallen for a contestant."

"Really?" It wasn't the excited squeal Ember expected, but a confused uncertainty from Ree. "Who?"

"You, of course. He's just hiding his feelings. That's what men do. They'd rather swim an ocean than confront their emotions. After this ceremony, we need to put the next plan into play. Meet me in the —"

"Ladies, gentlemen, everyone in between — you look stunning tonight." The rest of the ballroom lights dimmed as the Artist moved into the spotlight. Instead of the usual elaborate themed outfit, this time they only wore a tux...with scarlet cuffs.

"Thank you for joining me for this most unpleasant of tasks."

"Is Augusta all right?" someone called out. At first everyone turtled up, but they quickly picked up the same question, shouting at the Artist, then turning to find the producers.

They'd gone silent, unable to stop the horde. It was London Goddard who strode forward. She pulled off her headset and took place center stage. "According to the doctors, Augusta's going to be fine."

"Oh, thank goodness." Ember collapsed in her seat. She knew everything would be fine. Nothing too terrible happened on a reality show. Maybe someone sprained an ankle, or ate a cockroach or had to confront their inner demons, but they wouldn't die. This was television.

The chair beside her squealed and Ember looked over as Booker sidled in with his long legs turned to the right. She didn't know why, but she reached over to take his hand. A part of her expected him to refuse, but he clasped her fingers tight and pursed his lips.

"She'll be in surgery tomorrow, nothing major, and they're watching in case of infection. It's all very routine."

"We should do something for her," Harriet called out.

"Can we visit?" Robert asked.

"No!" London shouted, before putting on a smile. "I'm afraid that won't be possible. She's going to be very exhausted with recovery and we'd only make things difficult for the doctors. But don't worry, we have the best team working on it."

"And Brent?" Booker raised his chin, his voice carrying off of every sconce and tile in the room. "What about him?"

"He's right as rain too, resting up in his hotel."

"Why isn't he home?" Booker asked, and the teamster assistants all moved closer.

"That's enough." London clicked her nails like they were her naughty dogs. "We need to focus on the show. Tonight is an elimination. Good news, Jade, instead of having the men vote for you, you'll be partnering with Logan now."

The woman in a low-cut dress the color of her name curtsied. It drew all the eyes to her cups running over as she skittered across the chairs and perched beside Logan. Her back was straight, her posture impeccable, her midnight hair perfect. She crossed her ankles as if suddenly demure while her neckline hovered above her belly button. To all the world, it looked as if she was paying rapt attention, but Ember caught the edge of her eye drifting over and a little smirk aimed in her direction.

If she thinks she won, she's...

"Now for the painful part. Artist?" Ms. Goddard stepped aside.

Gulping, the Artist adjusted their mask, momentarily revealing a hint of cheekbone. "I'm afraid tonight won't be an enchanting evening under the—"

Thunder struck.

"—hail. Tonight we have some bitter business to attend to. One of you will be..." The cameras all zoomed in as the Artist stood still. They glanced over, watching until the producers gave a thumbs-up. Striking a pose, they declared, "Eliminated."

Lightning obliterated the sky, blinding everyone inside. A clap of thunder shook the whole house and every light fell into darkness.

* * * *

The order for them to stay put lasted a little over five minutes. It began with Logan. While the crew ran around like headless horsemen thrown from their steed, he slipped out of the door.

Jade was quick to follow him, no doubt having to keep an eye on her new investment. Booker didn't care. He leaned against one of the posts and prepared to wait for hours until they either got the power back or the sun rose.

It was when the flickering candlelight glanced off a crimson dress slipping through the door that he took off. Snatching one of the flashlights off of the computer monitors, he chased after her into the dark house. His foot touched a warped floorboard and the creak of the wood was so loud, Booker whipped his head around. He half expected a banshee to fly down the hallway.

The heaviness of silence went unnoticed when fridges hummed in the background and power lines buzzed a hundred feet away. When all of that was taken in a second of lighting, only stillness remained. The end of the hall creaked. He beamed the weak flashlight to catch a smattering of sequins before she booked it around the turn. Where in the world was she going?

A secret rendezvous with Logan, his brain tortured him. They could have planned it last night, even taken out the power to… Okay, that was a bridge too far even for his rising jealousy. Booker scoffed at himself. He wasn't jealous, not of that spoiled brat. He certainly didn't care who she wished to dally with. That was between her and her delusions of celibacy.

Taking the same turn, Booker raised his flashlight just when a strike of thunder rolled the house. Ember leaped straight off of the floor and landed on her heels with her hand clutching her heart. Her face turned pale in the harsh light, her eyes wide as she fought for breath while standing at the dead-end hallway.

"You scared the shit out of me," she said.

"What are you doing?" Booker shone his light around, half expecting to catch a stand of blond hair hiding behind a fern. There wasn't even a pair of red eyes lurking in the darkness, only an old grandfather clock trapped at midnight.

"Exploring," she explained, before peering at the doors at the end of the hallway.

"The water heater?"

"This is the…" She walked close enough to see the little utility sign above the door. "I was trying to find the kitchens."

"Why? If you're hungry, they probably have a few tiny bags of pretzels to go with a full case of vodka."

Ember laughed and shook her head. "I'm not sure which is scarier, a spooky old house in the woods, or running around a haunted mansion while everyone's drunk."

"Haunted?"

"The cemetery. Oh right, you didn't... There's a grave just past the old stables."

It was still here? Booker clung tighter to the metal base of the flashlight, doing his best to not look back to the old hill. Ember tugged open the utility closet and pushed her candle inside. She sighed at finding it as boring as he'd said. "This place is over a hundred years old. It has to have some forgotten ghosts rattling around."

Lighting struck, strobing through the far window. For a brief second, an old portrait was visible. A black man in old-fashioned attire held a top hat and cane before the estate while a little girl in pigtails sat on the fountain wall. Ember jerked away from the window, her eye line traveling in the direction of the photograph. Booker caught her hands and pulled her close.

"If you want to see the kitchens, they're this way." He pointed down the hallway toward the west side of the building before taking her hand. The halo of light swung just ahead of their feet, leaving the two of them shuffling so as not to step on any errant blades or nails. They were still scrubbing Augusta's blood off of the grass outside.

Thunder burst and the rising pelt of hail struck the roof. Booker looked up to the ceiling as a warm body pressed to his. Her fingers climbed up his biceps, wringing safety from them as she huddled tighter.

"Hail," he said to explain away the pounding above their heads.

"I...I know. It's just so loud. Are the roof tiles metal?" She drooped even lower as if about to turtle up and fall to the floor. Slipping an arm around the back of her waist, Booker slotted her in against him. He left his hand flat, hanging in the air, but his shoulders down to his hips tingled. She rushed in, clinging to his chest with her smooth palms.

Doing his best to keep her safe without thinking about how he was touching her, Booker led her toward the kitchen. Her staggered breaths and near whimpers started to sound a lot less like fear and more like...an end he shouldn't be thinking about. Picturing. Letting his imagination run wild as his palm curled around her hip.

"Do you think ghosts are real?" he asked, dragging himself back.

"No," she said fast, then bit her lip. "That is to say, I've never encountered one myself, but if I were to become a specter, I think this is the kind of place I'd haunt in my afterlife."

"Why?"

"A fancy hotel in the woods that used to be home to so many jazz legends? What isn't to love?"

He stared down at her in surprise. She risked breaking from the safety of his armpit to turn up to him. A hazy glow highlighted her face, her lips softening into a smile. Booker clung to her hip and pulled her up as he bent closer.

"Wh...where are we now?" she asked, dropping her chin and turning to stare ahead.

"This is the west side. There's a back hallway that connects the kitchen to the ballroom. See." He let go of her and slotted the flashlight in his hand. Ember naturally slipped out, as if that was what he had wanted all along.

It was what he wanted. He wasn't here for love. She'd stated the same up front. They were completely on the same page.

Ember followed the beam of light to the old swinging doors. She stretched up on her tiptoes to stare through the porthole window. "It's very dark."

"Lights are out," Booker said, feeling like an idiot.

She glanced back at him, then stepped inside.

A voice in the ballroom called for the contestants. Booker glanced back, but his feet remained rooted. If he left her alone, she might get lost and trip, hurt herself. He had to stay with her.

Easing through the door, he stepped into the old kitchens, uncertain what to find. His flashlight glanced across a hanging pot rack, bouncing a beam of light off of stainless-steel appliances. Ember placed her candle on one of the counters and ran her hand over the bottom cabinets. "This is more modern than I'd have expected."

"What would you have done?" Booker asked.

She looked up, hair falling into her eyes. He reached over to tuck it back at the same time she did. Their fingers glanced off each other, and—for a moment—she caressed her digit over his. Blushing, Ember dropped her hand, and Booker put her hair back.

"I... Honestly, I wouldn't have done anything different. It's back of house, it should be modernized. They've done a good job with what they have."

"Praise for Robert?"

"He's still terrible in front of the camera, but knows how to build a kitchen." She nodded as if imparting a dollop of wisdom and moved on to check out the oven.

"Are you here in the hopes to talk trash about his work?"

"I'm checking out the competition. They won't let us officially look, even though elimination is on the line. I need to see how..."

How screwed we are.

Their eyes caught, the candle flickering in Ember's gaze. The specks of green sparkled as she worried her frown into a smile. "How hard we need to work."

"As hard as ten men?" Booker asked.

She looked around the kitchen, then back toward the ballroom. "Harder."

"Well, I can stretch myself to seven. So you're going to have to take up the slack."

"Another seven men for me, then," she said proudly, before cringing.

Booker laughed. "Good thing they didn't get that on camera."

She nodded. The real ghosts in the hotel weren't long-lost spirits hoping for one last dance, but the ever-watching eyes and ears preserving their every word and deed. At least with ghosts, they vanished once the lights came on. The ones here could follow them to the grave.

"How did you know this was back here?" Ember asked.

"Because I...I got a look at the blueprints. It was a quick one but enough to get a sense of the layout."

"Wow. That's impressive. So you know where every room is?"

Booker nodded. He knew every pipe, every floorboard, every nail. "More or less," he said. "Why? What are you planning?"

"I'm not planning," she poorly lied.

"You are never not planning, but your plans become schemes when you get that glint in your eyes."

Ember tossed her head back. "There's no glint. You're inventing things."

"Here." Booker put down his flashlight in order to take one of the silver pots off of the rack. Holding it up to her, he said, "Look for yourself. They're like diamonds at the bottom of a bubbling green spring when you're plotting."

She pursed her lips, but reached over to take the pot.

Thunder slammed through the house. The fixtures rattled from the blast and pans struck the ground. Yelping, Ember dashed for him. She knocked the pot he'd held and kicked his flashlight deep into the kitchen. For a moment, all he knew was the rush of her body striking his, her arms wrapping around his back, her cheek flush to his chest and her quivering whimpers.

Booker breathed, hoping his steady beat would calm hers. Instead, he took in her scent of crisp leaves, autumn apples in brown sugar and a touch of spicy cinnamon to burn. "It's okay," he said. "It was just the…"

"It's thunder. It's a storm. It's not going to—" Her panicked breathing paused and she stepped back. Wide-eyed, with only the flicker of a candle to light them, she gazed at him. Booker's manic rubbing of her back slowed to a tender caress. He didn't realize she was rising on her tiptoes until his hand landed just above her ass.

"Mr. Knightley," she whispered, folding her arms around the back of his neck. His senses were on fire in the dark. Her touch, her scent, her voice—the quiver in her body shifted from fear to need.

"Miss Woodhouse?" he asked, his voice dropping to a whisper.

Thunder struck.

Lips leaped for his and the darkness exploded. The kiss almost slipped away, but Booker bent for her, chasing after the glancing touch. Heat plunged through his body, shocking him into a crimson haze. Her scent lingered in his nose and on his tongue — a spicy autumn blend that'd seep out of the bathroom while he'd pretend to not care she was showering.

Ember parted her lips and pressed her fingers to his cheek. "I thought you found me exasperating." She moaned against his mouth before sweeping her tongue across his. Booker roved his hands around her ass and up her back. The sequins flipped against his palms like ruby dragon scales.

Her lips slipped from his and Booker groaned at the loss. As his eyes peered open, Ember's crimson mouth swept across his cheek and she breathed in his ear, "Irritating." Before he could piece together what she had said, she licked her tongue around the outer edge of his ear.

"You don't do…" The hand that'd been clinging over top of his heart started to move. It swept down his chest, her fingers dancing on every button. Booker nudged his nose against the side of her cheek, breathing her in. Every finger on her delicate hand cupped then curled around his cock.

"Romance," she damn near snarled while rubbing against his aching erection.

God damn him, he couldn't think. His neurons flickered like the last fireflies of summer. Just a twinkle here and there before they faded to a ravenous black.

Booker caught her chin in his hand. Her devious eyes lifted to take him in. Tracing his thumb up her cheek, he growled. "Aren't you celibate?"

Ember gasped, and he kissed her hard, tracing his tongue across hers. He clung to her waist and pulled her flush to him, driving his cock against her belly. Moaning into her mouth, Booker finally let himself enjoy her tits. He swept his palm across the sides, lifting the sequins, before at last tracing her silken skin.

"I am." Ember groaned, nibbling on his ear as he kneaded into her flesh. Her nipples prodded from below, raising the sequins like beacons on the open sea.

"Is that so?" he asked, daring to reach down her dress and thumb her nipples.

She squealed in joy and bonked her forehead against his. Breathing heavy, Ember placed both her hands to his chest. "Yes," she gasped before going right for his zipper.

Booker shivered down to his soul when the tip of her fingers grazed his cock. *I need more time. I need...* Not thinking, Booker grabbed Ember's ass and hauled her up. He kissed her lips harder than ever, an ache building inside of him, and dropped her to the counter.

Panting, he slid his hips back from her. She frowned like she'd lost her toy. "Then what's this?" he asked, needing an answer. Needing her to tell him that he wasn't going mad, and they were about to head down this road together.

Ember smiled coyly. She brushed back her hair and raised her chin as if thinking. As her head dropped, fire burned in her eyes. "A break," she declared and pulled him to her. Such strength surged in her body, Booker slammed a knee to the counter beside her. She swung around and started to lie back, caring nothing for the candle flickering just above her head.

Aimlessly, Booker shoved it aside while he drowned in her. She tugged on his pants, trying to free his cock through the fly, caring nothing for the zipper in the way. He pulled on her dress, struggling to lift it as sequins popped off left and right. Ember fully shifted onto the counter and Booker went with.

His head banged into a low-hanging ladle, which smacked a pot and set off a kitchen drum solo. He barely even winced from the hit, all of his focus on the woman running her palms up his cock while she bit her lip. Reaching under her dress, he didn't even care to waste time removing her panties. Slipping them to the side was his only hope of surviving this. For a brief moment, his knuckles brushed against her, wet and hot.

"Hey? Who's in there?"

They both froze, eyes wide. "Fuck," Ember mouthed against him.

"You need to get back to the ballroom." The distant voice grew closer.

"What do we do?" she asked.

"Run!" Booker softly yelled. He tumbled off of the counter and offered his hand. As she fell to her feet, he struggled to zip himself back up without doing serious damage. As she slipped on her lost shoes, a light peered through the kitchen windows.

"Where do we go?"

"There's a back stairwell that leads to the rooms." He clung to her hand, certain that if he let go, she'd vanish into a puff of smoke. Ember hobbled over, one shoe in her hand, before she broke away. Booker aimlessly clenched at thin air, watching her run back.

Not to Logan, nor Elton or even to preen in front of the camera.

She grabbed the candle and, with her shoe dangling off of her pinkie, took his hand. "Let's go," she whispered as the kitchen doors swung open.

All they were going to find was his lost flashlight and a mess of sequins on the kitchen counter.

Chapter Twenty

Ember's bare foot chilled on the stripped, wooden floor as she trailed behind Booker. *Mental note — next time you want a quickie in an old hotel's kitchen, wear slippers.* "Where are we going?" she whispered.

It'd been a quick, admittedly giggly climb up the back staircase. She'd struggled to keep her footing on the twisting iron and also to keep focused while eye to ass with Mr. Knightley. They came out somewhere on the second floor — hail and rain pelting twice as loudly.

"Where they won't find us," Booker said.

That sounded perfect. She just didn't understand how he knew that staircase was there. Was he a blueprint savant? He only had to see them once and remembered the entire layout of a twenty-room hotel?

How had no one snatched up that kind of man?

"Ooh, Booker, look. It's our room." She recognized the door with the scratches from the fire extinguisher. "Do you think it still smells like smoke?"

"Probably," was his answer. He didn't seem interested in stopping to relive that moment.

Ember, daring and a little drunk without having a sip of alcohol, slipped from him and reached for the doorknob. Booker stopped to wait for her when a loud, low grunt shattered the resort's silence. On cue, the sound of squealing bed springs joined the moaning.

Her face burned as she cupped a hand over her mouth to keep from gasping. Booker took her hand again, but as they walked away, a laugh slipped free. "I guess we're not the only ones taking advantage of the blackout," he said.

"Who do you think's in there?"

He shrugged as if it wasn't his concern, but Ember kept glancing back, hoping to catch a hint through the door. Just as the love-making sounded like it was hitting its crescendo, Booker twirled her around and she walked into a huge room. He quickly closed the door behind them and slotted in the lock.

It was hard to make out the details with only the little candle to guide them. A large bed rested in the center of the room, facing a window with a view that would look spectacular any other time than tonight. A smaller stone fireplace sat at the far wall, which Booker bent over to inspect.

"You don't really believe you'll be able to —?"

Flames burst inside the black hearth, cutting off Ember's question. Heat danced up her skin. She didn't realize she was covered in goosebumps until she saw them. Rubbing her arms and shoulders, she slipped closer to the fire and the man that made it. "How did you do that?"

"It's gas."

"And you knew it'd be hooked up?"

"There were propane tanks on a truck. I'm guessing this was to be the fantasy suite for whoever won a challenge."

Curtains on the windows, blankets and pillows on the bed, a nightstand to hold a bucket of champagne — he was probably right. "Do you think there are any cameras here?" she whispered. The giddy fool who had been about to fuck on the kitchen counter began to sober up.

Booker looked around. Then he disappeared through the side door before emerging with a few towels. In two solid throws, he covered the cameras, hiding them even if the power came back on.

This is an absolutely awful idea, Ember Woodhouse. Even if no one finds you, even if the producers, the cameras, the audience never learn you want to sleep with Mr. Knightley, he'll know. And you know what happens after, every time.

To her surprise, Booker seemed to have cooled as much as she had. He paused, entranced by the fire. She did the same, willing the fire to replace the internal one burning through her. The thunder lessened, rumbling instead of striking to her marrow. An image of her standing on the roof as lightning struck set off a quake in her bones. Warmth landed on her shoulders and she huddled under it, not even thinking of the source until his arm brushed hers.

"You are a strange man, Mr. Knightley. You tell the entire world that you are a gruff, no-nonsense character, a man who disbelieves in romance, who finds love to be nothing more than a mix of brain chemicals. Yet..."

Tucked safe in his coat, Ember breathed in his scent as she turned to him. The fire danced against his skin, causing the ebony to glow with orange highlights. "Yet when no one's paying attention, you rescue every damsel in sight."

"You're the one who turns simple manners into a knight fighting off a dragon, not me."

The pelt of rain thudded in between the prolonged silences. Cinching the coat safe with one hand, Ember delicately traced the tip of her pinkie against her lip. What had happened in the kitchen felt like a dream.

"For declaring yourself off limits, you seem to be obsessed with a child's idea of romance—two pretty people tied together until they give in to their feelings. As if there's nothing more to it than that."

"I'm sorry, are you not the one who keeps saying this isn't reality? It's a television show? What makes you think I go around pairing my barista up with a handsome man I met at the gym who'd be perfect for her?"

Booker turned, the firelight catching off his rising smile. "Do you?"

Ember flushed and tipped her head. "They are married."

His laugh churned her insides. Ember hefted her shoulders, prepared to cast his jacket to the floor, when Booker landed his hand against the small of her back. He didn't gaze at her, only held her at arm's length as if he might suddenly scoop her up.

"The whole celibacy thing? Maybe it's not my place to ask."

She would have agreed with him if they hadn't gone horizontal on the butcher block five minutes ago. "I'm focusing—"

"On your career. As if you can't decorate a bathroom by day and pound the sheets at night. It's an excuse, not a reason."

Ember frowned and dipped her hands into his pockets. "If I tell you, you're going to laugh at me. You'll be mean about it."

"Me? I'm not..." Booker's hard stance softened as she stared at him. Running a hand back through his hair, he promised, "I won't laugh."

She had hoped he'd said he would. That he'd be incapable of helping himself and she was better off staying silent. "I don't date because no one wants to date me."

He scoffed, almost breaking his rule, and darted his gaze down her. "That D-level actor would leap through a fence with one word. Who wouldn't date you?"

"Dance with me, sure. Take me home for a night, that's never been a problem. But after... It's not them, it's me. They find my goals grating, my passions pathetic and my soul smothering." She'd been told she was pretty, attractive, exotic since sixth grade. Her face and body drew them in, but she could never get them to stay. "It doesn't matter how many call the shell beautiful... They want nothing to do with what's inside."

"I'm not surprised."

Ember's eyes shot open wide. She'd expected compassion, or at least a quiet nod from him. He wasn't looking at her, all of his focus on the fire.

"You are an obstinate woman, so certain you're right, you'll burn the world down to prove it. Most men will either fold or flee in the face of that lifelong fight." Booker drew his hand up her back, turning Ember to face him. She dropped her fidgeting hands and met him eye to eye.

"And?" she prompted, needing a resolution.

The edge of his lip lifted as if he wanted to smile. But his face hardened to stone and his voice dropped to a growl. "I'm not most men." Booker tightened his palm, plucked her to her tiptoes and kissed her. The slumbering coals ignited twice as hot. She slipped her hands around the nape of his neck, hanging on for dear life as he skirted his hands around her waist.

Bit by bit, he tugged her dress higher, exposing more of her thighs to the chilly air. Ember shivered, the heat of his touch burning her core. She wobbled on her lone heel, her foot lifting off of the ground in the hope he could reach farther. Booker's palm slipped under her dress, his fingers brushing her inner thigh. The touch of a man — those rough hands, the calloused pads, the talented fingers caressing and kneading her thighs — caused Ember to whimper in frustration.

She shouldn't want this.

She was supposed to be the untouchable socialite, the cultured beauty unattainable by all... especially the handsome, rugged handyman.

If the show found out, if anyone at home learned she had fucked her partner, all of this would be for nothing.

"This isn't—" Ember gasped. Her worry careened off a cliff as he glided his fingers straight across her panties.

"Go ahead," Booker whispered. He brushed his lips down her cheek and nuzzled against her neck while brushing the flat of his hand against her thigh creases. "Tell me how wrong this is." He dug his fingers under her panties and caressed her soaked flesh.

"Incredibly wrong." She moaned. Her hands fell, racing down his back. "Foolish beyond reckoning." Ember clamped onto his ass and bit his ear. "Do you even know what you're doing?" Ember laughed.

He released her and her heart sank. Her palms that'd been overflowing with his buttocks fell empty. She'd meant it to be lighthearted, but he stared down at her with only the fire dancing in his eyes. Booker raised his arm and deliberately undid the button on his cuff.

"Miss Woodhouse." He unbuttoned his other cuff. "I am going to throw you onto that bed, pin your wrists down and make you come so many times you will never question me again."

Blushing, Ember fought to keep from leaping onto him. "Is that so?" she asked, taking her time to enjoy Booker Knightley in a thin white shirt and tight-ass pants. The off-rack button-up struggled against his built chest and arms, letting her savor the wide curves. As she enjoyed him, he fastidiously rolled up his sleeves, his gaze never wavering from hers. God, those forearms. They glistened in the weaving firelight, calling to her even as he crossed his arms and waited.

The ball was in her court. "Mr. Knightley" — Ember nipped her bottom lip and quirked her head to the side — "I'd like to see you try."

Hands clamped around her ass. He kissed her hard, his lips pressing hers back even as he hefted her into the air. She wiggled her foot and her shoe tumbled to the ground. Booker parted his mouth, daring her tongue to tussle with his. Just as she licked across it, tasting more of the man than she thought possible, he hurled her through the air.

The bed rebounded, the mattress too hard for her liking, but it did put her right back in Booker's path. He leaped on top of her, his legs straddling hers. Ember sat up and kissed him, roughing her hands through his hair and down the back of his neck.

Booker reached down to unzip his fly and Ember giggled. "Aren't you going to undress the lady first?"

The light in his eyes made her gulp. "No," he declared and pulled his cock out. Ember's gaze darted to it, curiosity always getting the best of her, but Booker caught her by the chin. He held her tight, not overpowering, but safe, keeping her eyes on his as he began to spread her legs apart.

Bending down to her, Booker kissed her with a sweetness she didn't think possible from the rasping man. Her entire body tingled as if every nerve was humming *Ode to Joy*. She clung to the back of his neck, hanging on as he guided her head to the pillows.

Booker reached into a back pocket and the firelight caught on a flash of silver in his hand. "I can't fucking believe..." he muttered, tearing the foil. A banana-yellow condom fell into his hand and he sighed while sheathing himself.

"Do you want me to −?" she offered when he kissed her hard, pressing her back into the bed.

He swept his warm palms up her thighs, straining them farther and farther apart. She sucked on the tip of his tongue and he caught her panties at the hip. Booker gasped as he tugged them down over her thighs.

Ember had never been more grateful she couldn't get her Spanx on earlier.

Her panties made it to her knees before they were trapped. Booker would have to move for her to get them off. She reached down to finish the job for him.

He clamped her wrists under his calloused hands. True to his promise, he yanked both back and pressed them into the mattress. She squirmed, uncertain what to do, when he took both her wrists in one of his huge hands. With the other, he tugged her dress up, exposing her to him.

For a beat, Booker broke eye contact and looked down. A feral grunt slipped free and he clenched the base of his cock. "All of this, every headache, every argument, every near heart attack, every infuriating moment since the second we met..." He dug one hand under the small of her back, pressed her wrists deeper into the mattress and thrust inside.

"Holy fuck!" Ember cried out. His cock thundered through her like a train jumping the tracks.

Booker bent his face to her, his lips brushing against her trembling neck as he went still. "It was worth it for this," he said, then began to buck. The bed heaved, the brass frame smacking the wall with every thrust. Booker didn't start out slow, but went for hard then cranked it too fast.

Heat dripped down Ember's thighs, her legs straining to keep him inside of her. He'd jerk so far he'd almost slip out, then plunge to his base and do it again. Her body shivered, the pleasure jolting to match his manic pattern.

"Tell me what I'm doing wrong," he ordered as he thrust himself deeper than before.

"Suck my neck," Ember said, surprised at how easily the words came.

Booker didn't ignore her, but dove closer. For a breath his lips hovered above hers, their noses touching tip to tip. Then he smiled and, with the bridge of his nose, shoved her chin skyward. Teeth and tongue plunged to her slender throat. She whimpered first in shock, then need. Booker kept bouncing his ass, thrusting himself in and out while he sucked on her tender skin. Ember moaned, wanting to wrap her arm around his head and hold him close.

She moved her arm, but the hand around her wrists tightened, pinning her back. Suddenly, Booker sat up and stared at her. "That's not what you want. Tell me. Tell me!"

Lips trembling, Ember strained up to reach him. "I want…" she whispered, her breath catching as he swept his palm down her hip.

"What?" Booker hauled her up by her wrists, the two staring eye to eye. Everything went still except for his cock pulsing inside of her. His breathing strained and his gaze pierced through her. He wouldn't take another thrust until she told him what she wanted — what she needed.

Ember bent closer, her lips brushing against his. Booker's hand clenched under her ass with each accidental touch of her wet mouth. "I want you to f—"

"Who's in there?" A voice boomed and light skittered under the door.

"Fuck," Ember cursed. The assistant or producer was advancing fast, the light growing around the doorframe like a pathway to the afterlife. Booker released her hands and hunted for something.

How the hell am I going to explain this?

Will America hate me for it?

Will the producers give me, the sweet matchmaker, a debauched villain edit?

What'll my father say?

"Here."

Granite arms locked around her waist. Before Ember could squeak in surprise, Booker hefted her off of the bed. She was still impaled on him, her legs curling around his hips. On instinct, she wrapped her arms around his neck even while confused. They were in a room with one way out. There was nowhere to hide. They were done for.

"Are you in the fantasy suite?" the voice shouted from just behind the door.

Ember yelped at the close sound and Booker kissed her hard. Her body swayed back and forth as he hustled off of the bed and toward a built-in bookcase. She hadn't given it any thought until he pulled on a little crown and the bookcase swung open. Booker dashed through the secret door when the room's doorknob rattled.

Her back struck a cool wall, and Booker kicked the bookcase shut as the producer entered the room. Total darkness encased them and cold bit at her flesh. It smelled like a long-abandoned library in the ancient ruin.

"Wha...?" Ember asked when a hand clamped to her mouth. His body heat brushed against her forehead, as if he was leaning his head against hers. She opened her eyes wider, wishing to catch even a glimmer of Booker to make certain she wasn't losing her mind. But the only light seeped under the frame from the trespasser's flashlight.

"You can't hide," the producer said.

Ember began to slip and Booker jostled her up. In doing so, his cock plunged deeper. She moaned against the hand cutting her off. Heat brushed against her ear and he whispered barely above a breath, "Keep quiet."

Booker hefted her again, his hips grinding against hers. With each thrust, his chest panted, the noise growing more erratic. She clung to him, pushing back with all her might.

"Fuck." Booker moaned. His hand slipped from her mouth and slammed to the wall beside her head. The angle changed and the base of his cock pressed against her clit. Ember's steady simmer boiled to a fevered pitch. She dug her nails into his backside, demanding he drill her faster than before.

The sounds of the stranger padding around the room only made her burn hotter. Instead of just her thighs, the heat percolated up her chest and down to her toes. She burned, hanging on for dear life as Booker fucked her against the wall.

A tiny whimper slipped from his lips. "Em—"

She kissed him, silencing her name. Her moans built with no escape, threatening to devour her if she couldn't cry out. Her heart lofted higher with every thrust, her pussy trembling in anticipation of the messy end. Ember moved her lips, giving no breath to her words as she ordered, "I want you to make me cum."

A single low growl was Booker's response. He kissed her hard and thrust balls deep. The rumbling cascaded into a fractal explosion. Ember tried to fight off her whimpers, but as her climax scaled up her throat, she lost all control. She cried out against his palm. Her screams for more, for it to never end, for him to fuck her all night came out as a single long moan.

In the dark, his head crashed against hers, Booker whispering without sound as he came inside of her.

This was beyond foolish. She'd risked everything to be with a man who drove her mad while another stalked outside, and it was the hottest fucking thing she'd ever done.

His breath staggered, coming in spurts—much like his cock. Moments that could have been minutes passed before he said, "I think they're gone."

Booker leaned back and Ember peered around his shadowed head to the door. No light drifted around it. Had they pulled off the impossible?

He guided her legs to the floor, making certain she wouldn't make a sound. Her line of sight dropped until her chin brushed against his disheveled shirt. Cold warped across her heels and she fought off the shivers. Booker pushed on the secret case, barely opening it a millimeter. When no one cried out for them to stop, he did it again until even Ember could peer out into the room.

It'd gone quiet, their fire doused.

"It looks safe," he said, then eased out. After looking around, he held a hand to her. She emerged from total darkness into minimal midnight. A haze wafted through the windows, as if the clouds were studded with lightning. As she padded closer, Booker swept a protective arm around her and closed the secret bookcase.

"How did you know that was there?" she asked.

"That's personal."

"More personal than shoving your cock in me?"

Booker raised his shoulder but he wouldn't catch her eye. He pressed up his cheeks and stared at the magical door. "What I said before, what you assumed before about why I'm here."

"To get eyes on your business?" Ember prompted, her heart pounding faster.

"That isn't exactly the reason. The truth is —"

A pop then whine screamed across their microphones. Ember jerked back. She had forgotten she even had it on. Just as they started to listen in, the room lit up brighter than Christmas. She blinked wildly, struggling to see as her world went from black to white.

"Looks like they got the power back," Booker said. He kept darting his eyes to the still-covered cameras, but she understood immediately. They were listening.

"We should find the others and hope we make it through another elimination," Ember said, her voice calm even as she hunted for her lost shoes. Booker hefted up his jacket, which that producer had to have noticed.

"Miss Woodhouse?" He slung his suit coat over his shoulder and held a hand out to her. She wedged on her shoes and dashed to take it. Holding her close, he whispered in her ear, "I hope you did not take too much dissatisfaction with being tied to me tonight."

She flushed, her body remembering his touch and aching for more. Her mind raced to find an answer that gave her full deniability. "I've had worse nights," she said before purring his name. "Mr. Knightley."

Chapter Twenty-One

"Did the elimination surprise you?"

Booker shrugged.

"Could you please vocalize your thoughts?" the producer who'd grabbed him commanded. He'd been left on his own for every other interview. But suddenly this morning, bright and relatively early, Ash needed Booker in the hot seat.

"I was sad to see Robert go. He has a real head on his shoulders, unlike other people I could mention." Through the overpowering lights, Booker watched Logan trying to balance a power screwdriver on his palm. He was either going to impale his hand, or one of the women cheering him on.

"Such as?"

"Hm?"

"Who do you think doesn't belong here?"

Me. This whole experience has been like chasing after a tiger. The second I stop thinking about the prize, I catch the tiger by the tail. Now I can't let it go, but...how long can I hang on?

It'd been a whir of an elimination ceremony. All the producers were shouting to hurry it up, fearing they'd lose the lights. Their host had enough time to banish Robert and his partner before their backup generators failed once again. Whatever fried it had done a bang-up job.

He hadn't known what to say to her as they'd trekked back to their cabin, both clinging to the single flashlight production had given them. He still didn't understand what had come over him. Aside from a hot woman in his arms, panting hard and pleading for more. That part he got. But the rest was a confounding blur.

While undressing, brushing his teeth, nervously checking the roof for leaks, he kept waiting for her to say something. It wasn't until they'd both fallen asleep on their separate sides of the room that it hit him she was doing the same.

Logan's hand slipped and the screwdriver fell, striking the table so hard the battery pack split off. Booker braced for a tiny piece of shrapnel to embed itself in Jade's forehead, but nothing dramatic happened. For once, no one was maimed by sheer stupidity. He breathed a sigh of relief and heard the same from behind the huge deflector screen. Leaning out of his chair, he caught a hint of burnt orange. The sleeve was rolled up, exposing her golden forearm. He kept trailing her arm as she raised it to place a Styrofoam cup to her burgundy lips. As she pressed them to her coffee, she closed her eyes tight and breathed deep.

Every part of his brain told him last night was a mistake. Something he'd best forget happened. He wasn't here to... Romance wasn't on the table. But even by the light of day, he couldn't deny how much it turned him on to know that, as they had stood side by side at the ceremony, her panties had been soaked through because of him.

"What about Miss Woodhouse?"

Booker jerked hard, rocking the chair. He slapped a hand out, catching himself on the background scaffolding before he hit the ground.

"You had some rather acerbic thoughts about her before. How do you feel now?"

"She is..." Beautiful. Intoxicating. Stubborn. Determined. Tempestuous. Booker swallowed deep and looked directly into the camera. "Miss Woodhouse is infuriating."

* * * *

Ember reached up to massage her shoulder and caught the black tar across her glove. She had nearly ruined both her sweater and her skin in one foolish move. Grimacing, she dashed for the table where everyone was catching their breath and depositing their equipment. The sun had passed over its zenith while they were on the roof, the light catching on the tallest leaves that refused to fall. Stubborn sounded familiar.

She risked a glance over to her partner, only in the competitive sense. One moment of passion did not a relationship make—even if it was the hottest night she'd had in years. He was picking an argument with Ms. Goddard, insisting that they needed to finish tiling the roof now. She seemed to both stare at and through him at the same time.

For a brief moment, Ember felt bad for the monster that'd had them scrambling over the manor's roof for the past two hours. Tugging off her gloves and leaving them in a bin for someone else to wash, she spotted Ree sitting down for her interview.

"I can't figure out what game you're playing."

Ember's hackles hardened on instinct, but she kept her face pure while calmly washing her hands. "The same one as you, Jade."

She snickered, her tight shirt so short it showed off her lower abs and a ring through her belly button. The cameraman had been zooming in on her all day, even if Jade sat on the roof doing nothing more than thrusting out her chest. "That's interesting, because I thought the point of the challenges were to win. Weren't you two up a good ten roof tiles from them?" Jade nodded toward Elton who was sat next to a blushing Ree. The producer asked him a question. He nodded his head, then took Ree's hand in his.

Ember smiled. "I guess we lost our steam toward the end."

"Right."

It'd been an argument and a half with Booker, both having to try to cover over their words with the snap of a nail gun. In fact, it was the most they'd said to each other since they'd slipped from the secret room behind the bookcase. He wanted to win, because male and single minded. But she'd overheard that the prize was another romantic date — something neither of them needed right now. However, it was perfect for Ree and Elton to solidify their winning chemistry.

"If you two lose your steam so easily, it'll be easier for Logan and me to beat you." Jade, model thin and beautiful, scooped up half of a bagel and smeared it in peanut butter. Ember kept waiting for her to say she wasn't like other girls while wiping grease across her cheek.

"You don't belong here," Ember said.

"Pretty sure I do. I've gone through the same tests, interviews and challenges as the rest of you."

"No, you haven't. You are an outsider, Miss Fairfax." Ember caught Ree stumbling out of her chair. She needed her help. "And an outsider you shall remain," she said to Jade before joining Harriet's side. The girl was flustered, spinning in a circle and entangling herself like the country fly in the city spider's web. Her microphone cord completely wrapped around her, pinning an arm to her side.

"Help," Ree whispered. Elton had already walked off, finding himself close to Logan, who was then joined by Jade. Ember was the one to untangle Harriet, having to spin her in place before she finally emerged unscathed.

"Wow, that was...that's tricky."

"Yes," Ember said. "Why don't we perambulate around the garden?"

"Is that a kind of coffee?" Ree asked, cinching her arm with Ember's. She led her away from the interview spot and the men being entertained by the snake, but the cameras still followed them. Of course they would—Harriet would be their winner.

"I wanted to congratulate you on your win. A private rowboat picnic with Mr. Brown. You must be excited."

"Yeah, I...I guess. I keep thinking about Robert. Like, it was so unfair. He'd done his best with the kitchen. Then the lightning. It's not like he caused the power to go out."

Ember patted her hand, leading her toward the fountain. It was the perfect spot to look fabulous on screen. She guided Ree to sit on the edge, her legs turned to the side, then Ember joined her. "That is the nature of the game. It's often cruel. But you shouldn't be worrying about Robert. Like I told you—"

Harriet moaned as if the loss of the bland man crushed her spirit. "He'd be cut first."

"Well, aside from Augusta, who cut herself," Ember muttered to herself before remembering her microphone. "I hope she's doing well. And Brent, too. At least Robert isn't injured."

"Yeah. That's...that's good. I don't want him to get hurt. Did you know he has a fifteen-year-old chihuahua named Steve? It's the cutest and ugliest dog I've ever seen." Ree giggled while clapping Ember's hands, as if a geriatric dog was the most fascinating thing in her life. She was about to win the love of a famous movie star. Ember needed to keep her on track.

"We should discuss your battle plan with Elton."

Ree gulped. "I did like you said, I asked him about himself."

"And?"

"He talked for two hours straight. I don't think he even noticed when I took a little nap."

"Harriet Smith," Ember chastised her.

"I'm sorry. There was a lot about the craft...about acting, not the salad dressing. That one I know about. I make my own ranch."

Dear Lord, she had her work cut out for her. Putting on a smile and a soft tone, Ember asked, "What did you tell him about yourself?"

"Uh, nothing. He keeps walking off to hang out with...them." She pointed toward Elton speaking with Logan, but it was Jade with her hand placed to Elton's arm that caused Ember to snarl. Was she trying to disrupt every partnership?

Of course she was. That was why the producers had added her.

"You are the one who will be enjoying a romantic boat trip with him. Not Jade."

Ree absently scratched the back of her head. "I dunno. I'm thinking about passing. My stomach's not feeling great and—"

"Do not kid like that. You cannot pass up this opportunity. It is everything. This is the moment to tell him how you feel."

"Gassy?"

Ember gritted her teeth. This was a harder row to hoe than she'd anticipated, but the fruit would be worth it. "No." Taking Ree's hands, she pulled her to her feet. "You find him charming, magnetic. You cannot get him out of your thoughts." She meant to turn the girl to face Elton, but her eyes landed on the odd man out instead.

Mr. Knightley stood alone, a fact he seemed to take pride in. As if the mysterious gentleman lurking in the shadows could be dashing or romantic. So what if he was powerful and firm while also yielding in bed...and against the wall? Those were not acceptable reasons for a man to churn her mind the entire night. Nor should her breath catch as his thunderous body stood in the sunlight. It was the sour coffee twisting her stomach, not butterflies.

Raising her head, Ember walked Ree to Elton, ignoring Booker. "Mr. Brown," she said.

"Ah, you almost gave us a run for our money."

"I wanted to congratulate you and Harriet here for snatching victory."

He rolled his shoulder, shoving Jade off and focusing on Ember. "That's magnanimous of you."

She tried to guide Ree's hand into his, but he leaned closer and whispered in her ear. "If I had it my way, you'd join me for the prize."

Ember put on a smile. She'd thought this was over once she had revealed her celibacy card. Had Booker been talking? A flash lit inside her, but she tamped it down and focused on taking Elton's hand, then draping it onto Harriet's. "I pray you two have a delightful time. That basket of goodies sounds to die for."

As she stepped back, Elton laughed. He patted Ree's hand and said, "You can't win 'em all."

Chapter Twenty-Two

She wanted a nap. No, a bubble bath with one of those fizzing bombs and a glass of wine. Alas, all she had to look forward to was more work in the surprisingly warm sun. The storm had chased away the chill of autumn, bringing a nice day to the weary masses.

Men in hard hats grunted down the hallways while filling in the gaps none of them had time to get to. She'd always wondered how a house could be completed after almost the entire workforce was cut away. Seemed the answer was in picking up a new one from a hardware parking lot.

"Move." One-half of the men carrying a stove shoved Ember aside. She rebounded against the rising stacks of drywall stuffed into the hallways before walking to their little lobby. At least no one had ripped down the work they'd already put in. She still had to figure out how to get the key mechanism to work right.

Slipping on her gloves, Ember walked to the plans. Most of them were of Booker's straight, thin lines. But as she dropped the blueprints, more of her contributions appeared. He'd let her have a say on occasion, though he kept shooting down her idea for a secret liquor cabinet.

No wonder, when there could be hidden rooms stashed all across the property. Rooms that only this mysterious contractor knew about.

"There you are."

She dropped the blueprints and reached for a hammer. "Just getting back to work." Ember smacked the head into her palm while looking up at Booker. As she lost herself in his dreamy eyes, she realized her mistake and spun around. There wasn't a nail in sight, but she walked to the bare frame anyway. Pretending nothing had happened seemed to be the smartest path forward. God knew he wasn't in the mood to talk.

"Why don't we put that off?" Booker swept his hand over the back of hers, trailing up her fingers, before he took the hammer.

Ember spun around and caught her breath at how closely he stood. Of course he had to be behind her — he'd touched her. She was being silly.

"I thought a break might be a good idea."

"A break? Okay, who are you and why are you wearing the skin of Mr. Knightley?"

He laughed. "Don't we have some *projects* we needed to discuss?"

Ember narrowed her eyes in confusion.

"After last night's...um, discussion?"

He wanted to talk about — ? She wasn't even certain if she wanted to talk about, or to dwell upon, even acknowledge that they'd...

A hand brushed under hers, opening her palm until she held his fingers. "Please?"

Nodding, Ember slipped off her gloves and joined him. She had no idea where they could talk without an entire television crew watching, but Booker seemed to have an idea in mind. While holding her hand, he led her down the same winding path they'd taken in the wagon.

The day was distressingly beautiful, sweet as the juice of a ripe apple. Walking in the woods on a pleasing autumn day like this was certain to cause anyone to fall in love.

"What did you want to—?"

"Not here," he cut her off. She fell silent, walking slightly behind while watching the red zip of a cardinal through the trees. As they approached the lake, now a glittering sapphire among the fiery forest, Booker veered off and she followed. Ember kept staring across the still surface where she caught a mess of boats on the far side.

Holding her hand above her eyes, she caught a hint of two people in one boat, then clusters of camera crews circling in the rest. "Is that Ree's date?" she asked.

"They're busy filming that. No one's gonna notice we're gone." Booker led her past the dock to an old shed. Someone had broken the window panes which he reached through to unlock the door.

Propped up on old sawhorses was a wooden rowboat. He dropped her hand in order to heft up the garage door. Booker slapped the boat with a smile. "It's a lovely day for a little trip out on the lake."

She stared harder at the wood, certain that every shadow was a hole and they'd sink before getting a foot off shore. But a question burned in her heart, and he'd never answer it where a camera might catch them. Swallowing her complaints, she reached for the boat. Together, they walked it to the water and placed it halfway in the grass. Booker helped her in first. She stumbled over the seats before taking one toward the prow and facing back.

For a moment, he gazed back toward the resort, no doubt hunting for any prowling producers. When none emerged from the woods, he shoved the aft of the boat and leaped in. It rocked, Ember quick to grab the sides, but it floated onward.

Booker settled in the seat across from hers and pulled an oar off of the side. With slow, measured strokes, he paddled them away from the cameras, the producers, the whole show. Red maple leaves the size of her head floated on the water. Ember snatched one up as they went past, her fingers chilled. She twisted the leaf back and forth, trying to dry it off.

"It's huge," she said.

"The trees here are hundreds of years old," Booker narrated.

"How do you know that?" He had come into this unaware of what lodge they'd be working on, same as the rest of them. He'd been clueless about the entire show, but he knew things about the resort no one else did—not even the producers. Ember clung to her leaf as if it could protect her from whatever dark secrets Booker was hiding.

He tugged the oar back in, water dripping into the bottom of the boat. They kept drifting on the waves, gliding toward the dead center of the lake. He kept his distance, as if out of fear of a telescopic lens catching them.

Booker darted his eyes to her, then down to her hip. She blushed, thinking of his hands inching her dress up higher and higher as she squirmed below him. Was this an attempt for round two?

He patted his side and she understood — their mike packs. They couldn't shut them off without a key only the producers had. Booker edged closer and she mimicked him. They both leaned together, their noses almost touching. He raised a hand for her and Ember held her breath. She knew he was going for the lav mike. Even still her eyes slipped closed as if expecting a kiss.

A loud slap broke the air and she looked just as a spray of cold water struck her face. Her jaw dropped and Booker grinned. "Too slow, Miss Woodhouse."

"You —!" she shouted when he slapped the water again. This time it hit her chest. Oh, he was going down. Ember rolled her sweater's sleeve high, formed a scoop with her palm, and flung as much water as possible at him. As it struck his face, his skin glistened like black diamonds and his smile grew.

Pandemonium broke, both of them shoveling water at the other. Ember dug elbow deep into the lake trying to drench Booker while he splashed from both sides of the boat at once. She weaved, trying to do the same, but her butt slipped off of the seat. Her body tumbled forward and Booker caught her.

Wet hands clung to her back, his once wide smile slowly fading to a soft pout. She shivered at the heat of his forehead pressing to hers and the darkness in his eyes eclipsed by gold. Booker's hand slipped under her sweater and she had to fight off a gasp. His fingers kept trailing under, brushing against the top of her ass until…

"There." He pulled off her mike box, then unclipped the lav. As the cord slithered under Ember's sweater, she fell back to her seat. Booker did the same with his and tossed both microphones into the watery puddle at the bottom of the boat. "Hopefully, they'll believe a water fight broke out and damaged them."

Ember cupped a hand to her cheek. The water chilled her to the bone but her skin burned. Why'd she think he'd want anything more to do with her after getting what he wanted?

"I suspect you have questions," Booker said.

"A few."

"About last night?"

Why'd you fuck me? Was it just hate sex? Were we both running on adrenaline and needed to burn it off? Has nothing changed?

"The room behind the bookcase, how'd you know it was there?"

He scratched the back of his head and dropped his eyes. "I've been keeping a secret. Not just from you, from the show. I'm not who they think I am."

Ember sucked in a breath. She didn't expect that. "Who are you?"

"My name is Knightley, but my grandmother was born Irma King. Her family, my family, built the King's Retreat."

He said it with such finality, Ember expected to hear a *dun-dun-dun*, but she didn't understand. So he came from a line of contractors. That wasn't shocking either for her or the producers. Why was he…?

Ember focused behind him to the little shed, to the hill with the gravestone that marked the resting place of a Mr. King. Her eyes went wide and she clasped a hand to her mouth.

"I know about the bookcase, and other secrets not on the official blueprints because of my grandma. She used to live here as a girl. She'd tell me and my brother about the adventures she'd have in the old rum-running tunnels."

Ember braced herself for a harrowing tale of a fire and a child orphaned.

Booker's lips knotted into a sneer, and he closed his eyes. "This is the King's Retreat, not that Dower Estates bullshit. It was a place, an escape in the woods, for people like my family — like us — to get away. To not have to use the back entrance, to be able to sleep in the suites. To live without looking over our shoulders."

He started to paddle in a circle as if he needed to do something with his hands. "It was just as grand as that masked host said. Grander. The greatest musicians of the twenties and thirties played in that ballroom. My great-grandparents built this place, log by log, with their bare hands."

"What happened? Was it the Great Depression?"

"No. They survived that well. The Retreat was booming. When times were tough, they gave jobs to those who couldn't get anything, beds to those who were hopeless. It was a haven against the storm."

Booker breathed deep and wrung his hands over the oar's handle. "My great-grandfather was rich. Mansion in the gated parts of Hartfield rich. Guess how the white men reacted to a brown man with a bigger house and fatter wallet?"

"Did the K... They march?" Ember gulped.

"Didn't have to. The state seized it under eminent domain. They made up some bogus claim that the land was needed for a state project, a park or whatever, but the real reason was that our kind didn't know their place."

"They took it? They just...? But they can't do that!"

"Can and did. Eventually, they sold the land. It passed through the hands of a bunch of investors who didn't care, who thought they could make a quick buck and let the old dame rot. My family had invested everything in this resort. It ruined them for generations, a hole we're starting to climb out of."

All the walls that'd neatly box up history crumpled. She'd heard about the old laws that would have kept her parents from marrying if they'd met a decade earlier, but it was in the past, as unreachable as Mars. Yet here was a steaming asteroid that crash-landed at her feet. His family had lost everything. Not lost. Losing implied an accident, a failure, an act of God. It was theft, and the thieves enjoyed generations of prosperity without a single mote of dust marring their brows.

"You don't believe me," Booker said. "You're hardly the first."

"No, I do." Ember reached over. Booker dropped the oar in the boat, and she took both of his hands. A surge of hope rose on his face. "I'm at a loss for what to say. Can you prove it in court?"

He shrugged, tracing his thumbs over the back of her hands. "The original deed was destroyed in a fire. Anyone who remembered the King's Retreat is long dead. Even if I could find a witness, the law's on their side."

Ember frowned. If the state couldn't legally sell it, then how was it sold legally? She wanted to argue that point, to call in her father's lawyers and sic them on the problem. But Booker kept patiently massaging the back of her hands as if he was waiting for her to succumb to the same conclusion.

"You're here for the house."

He nodded, then dropped his gaze. "That hadn't been the original plan. I tried to buy it. Thanks to mismanagement and leaving it to rot, the price dropped enough I was able to scrounge up a loan, get friends to chip in, mortgage my house. I almost had it.

They were happy to get rid of it, not caring about the history baked into the bones."

"What happened?"

"The last second, just as I was flying out to sign the paperwork, the seller pulled it. No explanation. I thought, I'll find this other buyer, somehow scrounge up more money to pay him off. Then I learn that I was low-balled. The sellers took less money for the place and that made no sense. Lucky for me, my cousin's some kind of hacker guru or whatever. He figured out an LLC bought the property, and that that LLC kept purchasing land that was used on some stupid reality show."

Ember couldn't say why, but she got up and walked over to sit beside Booker. Whatever dam Booker had built to keep this secret burst.

"I was sunk. Every damn property that was on this show doubled or in some cases tripled on the market. I'd never be able to buy the lodge. It was my brother who got it in his head to try for the show. So certain one of us would have to win. It was supposed to be him." Booker turned and said with a mirthless laugh, "He doesn't have a T-square wedged up his ass."

Ember winced. "I believe I said it was a two by four."

"My mistake. When the call came in, I could hardly believe it and I regretted it instantly. Maybe I was hoping they'd suss me out and I'd get cut. The only reason I stuck out the pre-screening was in the hope that my grandma could get one last night in her home." Tears caught in his voice and he hunched over so she couldn't see his face. "She died five days before I flew out."

"Jesus. I'm...I'm so sorry." Ember leaned over and nuzzled her cheek against his head. She held tighter to his hands, tracing her fingers over his cracked knuckles.

"If production finds out why I'm really here, they'll—" Booker drew a finger across his neck fast, then took back her dropped hand.

They wouldn't want that scandal on top of everything else going wrong. They might even edit him out of the season so no one would notice, which would take her out too. "I won't tell a soul, I promise."

"Thanks. It's…it's this old family secret, ya know. No one likes to talk about it—our ghost in the attic. A reminder that no matter how hard you work chasing that American dream, it can all vanish in the stamp of a city seal."

"Here I thought we came out here so you'd tell me last night was a mistake." Ember sighed to herself, wanting to laugh, but a shocked noise caused her to look over at Booker.

He wasn't laughing along. Instead, his face was stone while his eyes thundered. "Was it? I mean, did you, are you regretting…? Wow, smooth as ever, Boo."

"Boo?"

He winced hard and tried to pull away. "Nickname I heard way too much growing up. It's stupid."

"It's cute," Ember said. She swept her hands up his and leaned closer. "Last night?"

"Yeah." Booker gulped.

Closing her eyes, she drew the tip of her nose up his cheek. "It wasn't a mistake," she whispered, then pressed her lips to his.

"Hey! You on the boat!"

Ember and Booker jerked apart so quickly, their rowboat tipped back and forth. She lashed her hands out to keep from falling and scuttled back to her original seat. As their vessel spun in the water, she spotted producer Sam waving her clipboard.

"What's the matter?" Ember called to her even as Booker started to row them back into shore.

"You're not cleared to be out on the lake!" Sam shouted as they quickly slopped back into the shore. When the boat's prow struck the grass, Sam ran forward to grab it. "What's wrong with your microphones? We've only gotten static for the last five minutes."

Ember held up the mike packs she'd rescued from the bottom of the boat. "I'm afraid they got a little wet and started kicking feedback." After handing the two destroyed lav mikes over, Ember whispered toward Sam, "He's not very good at paddling."

Booker forced a frown-smile on as he leaped from the boat. "Miss Woodhouse," he said. "It's been infuriating as always." Bowing his head, he turned to dash back to the house, but almost smacked face-first into a tree.

"Do mind the foliage, Mr. Knightley," she called out to him.

He gave a cheeky growl and slapped his palm to the tree. But when Sam's back was turned, he cast a long look toward Ember and—for a second—touched his lips with a saved kiss.

"Why did you go out onto the lake?"

"It was his idea. You know how men are, all that testosterone has to be released somehow."

Sam stared longer at her, not buying the lie. Ember never was very good at them. But the producer had bigger problems, like the two unmiked contestants. "Look, you and Mr. Knightley need to go to the equipment truck. Hopefully they'll have replacements. Then you're due for the big dinner."

"Sounds delightful," Ember said, when all she wanted was another thunderstorm and a secret room. Head high, she walked the same path Booker had taken when Sam grabbed her arm.

"You're in luck. The switch is going to be happening soon."

"Oh?" She hadn't planned on making use of it before. Now she certainly wouldn't.

"Just in time, too. That man's dead weight. They're looking to cut him as soon as possible."

What? But they'd been working so hard and he had real talent. That wasn't fair.

"Good thing you hate him, or it might be a hard sell for the audience."

"Yes." Ember's throat constricted. "I cannot stand that Mr. Knightley."

Chapter Twenty-Three

Fire danced on the tips of five candelabras spread down the long table. When they had said dinner, Booker had expected a plate of chicken and rice gobbled on folding chairs, not an elaborate place setting with gold forks and finger bowls. Everyone, except for him, was dressed to the nines. Instead of their usual suits, though, the men wore white tuxes with tails and bowties. The women were dressed in old flapper dresses and feather fascinators.

Only he hadn't been pulled aside for the roaring twenties wardrobe. Booker tried to ignore the sinking in his gut and assured himself that even if they had asked, he would've turned them down.

"And how did we find our meal?" the mysterious host asked. Thanks to the mask, they'd had to push it tight to their face while carefully hoovering soup out of a spoon. It was the best entertainment of the night.

"Delicious," rang out across the table.

"This was one of the signature dishes of the resort when it was first opened. Tonight, we're going to play a game."

"Wait!" A producer ran into frame. "The echo is still awful. Can we get some more sheets up there?" Ash jerked his hand to the mezzanine where a handful of assistants held on to a string of blankets. They'd been trying to dampen the place to keep it from sounding like the nearly empty ballroom it was.

"I guess you can talk amongst yourselves," the host said and tipped back in their chair.

Booker dropped his napkin over his half-empty plate and caught her eye. Ember's body was not designed for the svelte flapper physique, her dress failing in every way to emphasize all those curves. He ached to tear it off her. As she dabbed at her lips, her gaze never waning from his, Booker absently stroked a finger down his knife. It was for cutting pats of butter, but it'd give him a start in ripping her dress off.

She drew the tip of her teeth across her ruby lip and nodded imperceptibly. Booker shoved his chair back the same time Ember did.

"Oh my gosh, Emmy!"

Damn it. The mousy one rocketed out of her seat to Ember's side. "You're never going to believe this. He kissed me."

For a beat, she shot him an apologetic look, then turned her mega smile on Harriet. "That's delightful. Please, tell me everything that happened, but in private." She took Harriet by the hand and led her to the side where moon and production light streamed through the window.

Privacy was the problem. As long as they were snared in this reality show web, there wasn't any. It didn't matter how badly he wanted to taste those lips or suck on her tits — they were always listening.

He should be focusing on winning. At least Ember had no intentions to walk away as the owner of the resort. She just needed the world to think she was a kind and loving matchmaker who'd never get fucked in a secret room with a producer two feet away. It was all heightened emotions. *That's what reality shows do, right? Put everyone in a fish bowl, shake it up and let them go at it.*

It was best for him, for both of them, if they let whatever this was fade with the rain. Fucking shame he never got to see her tits, though.

"Who do you think's going next?"

"Isn't it obvious?"

Booker didn't have the easy escape of gossiping with a naïve girl and found himself stuck at the table. Logan rose from his chair to pick a grape out of the centerpiece. He stuffed it in his mouth and Booker watched, curious if it was rubber or real. Elton, the odd man out, returned to sawing his meat into tiny strips.

"I can tell you it won't be me," Logan bragged, his cheek stuffed with the grape.

"Why not?" Elton asked.

"Because they…" He frowned and looked past the circle of cameras to the producers sequestered at their monitors. "Because… Look at this place. It's beautiful."

"As if you've lifted a finger. Let me guess, all they have is b-roll of you carrying a saw, swinging a hammer and carrying a single beam," Elton bandied back. Booker expected there to be teeth in the comment — this was a competition after all — but the man seemed entertained that Logan was the spoiled pretty boy.

Shrugging, Logan smirked without answer. Then he turned away to face the darkness. When he spun back, his cheek was empty. Booker smiled to himself.

"Are we speculating on the outcome of this contest?" The mystery host—in a baroque dress complete with little golden gargoyles on the shoulders—hustled over. They sat in the chair next to Booker and leaned in. "I'm most intrigued by your thoughts."

"Mr. Churchill believes he has immunity," Elton said.

"And what of you, Mr. Brown? Do you think the people at home will cheer should you take the prize?"

He rolled a shoulder. "At least I've actually put in my sweat. The same can't be said for him."

"Ew, people are eating here," Logan complained. "Besides, everyone knows it's not the room that wins. It's how fucking hot you look as a couple."

Mr. Brown sighed and cast a glare in the direction of Harriet. It seemed as if everyone but Ember could read the writing on the wall. Elton had no intention of pretending he cared about the girl.

"What of you, darling?" The mystery host abandoned the two to focus on Booker. "Who do you think will win?"

"Me."

Logan broke out into laughter so loud it shook the candelabras. Elton sniggered behind his hand, though he kept pointing toward Booker and making a face at Logan.

"Why not? I've put in the most work out of you all. The lobby's looking—"

"Who cares about a stuffy old lobby? People don't watch this show to get ideas on how to decorate a hotel lobby."

Booker frowned at how much he sounded like Ember.

On a roll, Logan continued, "Your only chance at winning this was by getting that fiery hottie into bed. But she hates your guts. They're"—he made a pair of scissors with his fingers and clamped them toward Booker—"gonna cut you next."

"Logan!" Elton shouted so sharply the producers looked up. Then he reached over to his friend's weaving body, but Logan wasn't finished.

"I'm so tired of your incessant whining. Blah blah blah. So's the audience, so's the editors. You're done. You're finished. Next round, it's gonna be your head on the block." Logan worked his scissor fingers toward Booker.

"You can't know that. I'm going to win, and you'll lose."

"Psh, I got the ballroom. I got one of the hottest women here. I could get both if I wanted to," he dared in Booker's face.

"Logan! I think you've had enough." Elton tried to pry him away, but Booker didn't flinch. He didn't raise his hand or his voice.

"Go ahead. Go after the 'fiery' one." He smirked at the idea. "Who am I to stand in the way of true love?"

"True fuck more like. Am I right? Am I...?" Logan swiveled his head like a ball bearing. At first it landed on Elton, who scowled, then his bleary eyes must have focused on the lone woman remaining at the table.

Rather than say a word, Jade wadded up her napkin, threw it onto her plate and dashed out into the dark. "Oh, fuck," Logan moaned.

"Well, this has been most enlightening," the Artist declared then scampered back to the head of the table.

"Babe, come on. It was just trash talk." Logan moaned. He tried to chase after her, but got a few steps in before his body sagged to the side. Ember returned with Harriet at the worst time. She spotted the weaving man and raced to catch him.

"Oh my goodness, are you okay?"

Logan beamed at her and shouted in her face, "Never better." He glanced back to Booker with his smug grin, fully missing Ember's painful grimace.

"All right, they have enough padding above us. Everyone get to your seats," their host called. Logan plummeted into his chair, thanks to Ember's help. He reached up as if to touch her cheek, but she stepped back. Instead, Logan's hand landed on Elton, who stared dead ahead without saying anything.

Booker wanted to laugh at his drunken antics, but God save him, Logan was right. The producers were trying to wedge him out and they decided who won and who lost. He glanced over at Ember, and her cheeks pinked. Maybe she was his only chance after all.

"Ladies, gentlefolk, I brought you here tonight to issue you a challenge — do you know the haunted history of Dower Estates?"

"Crap!" One of the stagehands slipped and yanked a sheet off. The blanket fell, drifting down like a tumbling leaf until it hit the table and burst into flames.

* * * *

"What do you think of this?" Ember slid her notes under the sheet. She expected him to take them, but Booker's fingers trailed off of the paper and up hers until he clung to her hand. She flushed at the thought when she was yanked to the other side.

Laughing in shock, Ember smacked face-first into the dangling blanket. It nearly came with until Booker batted it up behind her. She found herself floating in his eyes. The serious glare he'd worn all night after dinner had vanished. Instead, he was practically smiling as he brushed his palm against her cheek.

"What are you doing?" she whispered, so softly that hopefully the mike would only pick up static. Under the covers, the cameras couldn't see their faces, but their bodies stuck out on both sides.

"Guess," Booker answered, and he pulled her close for a kiss. Ember broke into a laugh at the idea. She felt like a kid breaking curfew in order to make out with a cute boy. Which, in some ways, she was. Booker didn't give up easy, kissing her lips stuck in a permanent grin.

The touch of his tongue chased away her giddy schoolgirl antics. Melting into his mouth, she clung to the back of his head, refusing to let him vanish back into the dark. Both panted, clutching to each other while meeting at the brows.

"Is this wise?" she asked, struggling to keep her voice level. Her body screamed at her to shut up and pounce on him.

Booker drew his fingers through her hair and mused, "I've come to accept that you bring out the stupid in me." His face twisted into a sour grimace. "That's not what I mean—!"

"Believe me, Mr. Knightley." Ember scooted closer, one leg left outside their private fort. She traced from his brow down his cheek and thumbed the stubble sprouting at his jaw. "I fear I am in the same boat as you. Clearly, you despise me." Her caressing traipsed down his neck and across his chest.

"Oh, most assuredly," Booker told her as he drew his hand down her back and palmed her ass. His voice raised. "You are a trying woman." He dug his fingers into her pajama bottoms and scooted her across the floor into his arms.

Bending close, he breathed in her ear, "I want to try everything with you."

Ember snickered when Booker bit her earlobe and tugged on her pants. The tie gave in fast, letting his famished pawing reach her bare skin. Her gasp became a whimper as he kneaded into her butt cheeks. Gripping tight to her ass, Booker kissed her hard, swallowing her next moan. He had some obsession with only half undressing her, leaving her pants just below her ass before he moved to her night shirt.

Running one hand against her cheek, Booker darted his tongue with hers, then palmed her breast in the other.

"You are..." *Fuck me.* "A positively ab-*horr*-ent man."

Booker thumbed her nipples at the worst possible time in the best possible way. She clamped down on her jaw, trying to keep her moaning at bay as he lifted her shirt and touched her skin to skin.

"Am I really?" he taunted, tweaking her nipples between his hands while his impish eyes stared at her.

"Beyond. Insufferable. Vexing," she stormed at him, fighting to keep her voice level.

The edge of Booker's lush lips ticked up into a little smirk, and Ember's heart burst. "Go on, keep telling me why I'm so awful," he said then slipped down.

She swallowed, fighting to think of fresh adjectives, when he rolled his hands under her ass and tugged her pajamas and panties clean off. Then, his gaze never wavering from hers, Booker Knightley kneeled between her legs and raised her hips to him.

"Aggravating," Ember said as he circled his tongue over her clit. "Pompous." He began to lick faster, flicking the tip back and forth over the hood while he pressed his thumbs against the bottom of her pussy. Her chest kept expanding, pleading for faster breaths that she couldn't take. She ground onto him and Booker thrust both of his thumbs inside of her.

"A most dispassionate man!" she shouted, loud enough to pop the mike. Booker dove, sucking her clit between his lips.

Her mind drained to a happy little puddle while her body electrified beneath him. "You are..." Ember's breath caught, her words panting.

He broke off from pushing her closer to the climax. "I'm what?"

"You're a..."

Booker thrust two fingers as deep as possible and Ember groaned. "Please, enlighten me." He stared into her eyes while placing the tip of his tongue against her throbbing clit. "You've left me in anticipation." He traced every syllable across her hood and dotted the hard P against the full pearl.

Scrambling to keep herself sane, Ember lashed a hand out. Her fingernails dug into the hardwood floor and Booker sucked her clit into his wet mouth. The orgasm hit her harder than she'd expected. She slammed one hand to her mouth, fighting to hide the moan as her body collapsed and expanded against Booker's lips. Her nails gouged the floor as she kept herself from writhing in ecstasy.

Booker took his time, tenderly swirling his fingers inside her throbbing pussy and daring to lick her trembling clit. Ember fought for breath, fearing that if she let out a single pant, the jig was up. Losing herself in his dark eyes and knowing smile, she sighed. "You're exasperating."

With a snicker, Booker sat and climbed up to her. "Is it my turn to state how I find you, Miss Woodhouse?"

Ember kissed him hard and drew her hand up his thigh. He forwent the pajama pants and slept in boxers, making her quest so much easier. As she cupped the soft cotton around his cock, Booker groaned against her lips.

"No," she declared.

His eyes opened wide in surprise, as if he expected her to lean over and go to sleep. Ember pulled out his cock. At her touch, Booker's eyes rolled back. She said loudly, "My ego cannot take your vitriol."

"Are you certain?" Booker wound a hand under her head and pulled her up. "I've seen it withstand hard, deep blows before."

"Why, Mr. Knightley." Ember sighed, then hooked both her hands around him and flipped positions. He hit the unforgiving ground hard and tipped his head back just as she bit his bottom lip. "You are..." She kissed his jaw and ran her hands up his stomach. How was it so warm and silky? " —a most— " Needing to see him naked, she tugged on his shirt, shoving without care.

Booker took no time in prying it off over his head. He wadded it up to use as a pillow while Ember stared in wonder. Strong, with biceps to die for and pecs worthy of manslaughter, his chest made her gulp down to her toes. "Unsatisfying man," Ember moaned, dragging her nails down his skin.

He tipped his head back as she scratched her way across his brick body. A little patch of skin, like a splash of pink champagne, rested at the top of his hip. Ember wanted to trace it, to lick it, to bite her way across it, but her fingers reached the forbidden zone. Booker was softly panting and running his hands up her back and through her hair.

That all changed when she ripped his boxers clean off. A shocked gasp broke and he sat up. She met him and placed a finger to her lips. Booker's eyes burned as if he couldn't stand having to keep silent. But he barely nodded and clenched his jaw shut.

When she thumbed open her notebook, a condom tumbled free. Booker smirked at her ingenuity, before his eyes opened wide as she tore it open. Gritting his jaw, he nodded hard as she slid the thin latex over him.

In a flurry, Ember flung her knee across his hip, steadied his cock and drove herself home.

"Miss Woodhouse!" Booker shouted, throat straining and eyes rolling back.

"What?" she asked playfully, holding still.

Booker curved his hands up her hips, tensing his fingers as if to lift her himself, but he relaxed and rolled his neck. "I thought you didn't wish to hear my opinion."

Smiling, Ember grabbed the bottom of her shirt and raised it over her head. His moan was a ten-course meal to her libido. Almost absently, Ember dropped her stretched hands and carelessly cupped her breasts, even teasing a nipple. His fingers dug in, nails scraping and tips bruising into her hips. She swerved her ass, causing Booker to moan.

"Don't you know it's rude to tell a lady her faults?"

"Then, I do not find you incredibly...repulsive." He shuddered and Ember started to rock. Booker's eyes closed. He had to be fighting to keep focused on anything but her swaying tits and warm pussy. She struggled herself. His fingers were nice, but an appetizer to the main course. At least she had control while he was at her mercy.

"Do go on," she said, bending her thighs and thrusting upward.

"You are not shallow and self-centered." Booker moaned. He cupped his palms over her ass and used all of his strength to increase her speed.

Ember too was losing this fight, her body tingling from her chest down to her knees. She wanted to have him trapped below her, force him to sputter out every carefully worded compliment while she bored herself onto his cock. But judging by the breathy cursing and sweat on his brow, he wouldn't last much longer.

"Are you tired of my face?"

"I cannot stand it," he cried out. "Your lips, your eyes. They're hideous. I never want to look at them again." His sex grunts faded and he stared up at her with a softness in his face.

"Do you mean that?" Ember asked.

Booker lifted a hand off her ass and she bent for it. As he touched her cheek, he whispered, "With all my heart."

"But I'm infuriating, I'm..." The wave of emotions hurled her off of their contrary game. She didn't expect him to say that, she didn't want to hear it.

Do I?

"You are the most infuriating woman who cannot stop needling me, pressing me, forcing me to prove that I am just as capable and worthy."

Ember blinked and a small tear slid down her cheek. She shook it away and picked up her gyrating. Booker's heartfelt plea couldn't stand a chance against her fucking him hard into the ground. She didn't need a man, a boyfriend, a husband. She was her own woman and far too busy to care beyond a night here and there.

Even if this one wanted to stay, even if he might choose her should his options change, she couldn't afford to fall into this trap.

But God, did he make her feel good.

Rolling her head back, Ember took his hands and guided them up her stomach toward her breasts. When he couldn't quite reach, she leaned down. Booker got both cupfuls to barely fit his hands and he groaned so hard his cock bucked.

"Fu —!"

Ember slapped a hand over his mouth. His eyes were wild but he started tugging on her nipples and thrusting up to meet her. Air caught in her chest. She fought to not let loose a moan as his cock plunged against her G-spot. Her hand slipped off his mouth and plummeted to the floor.

She kissed him hard, trying to pour all of her knotted-up energy into that one kiss. Booker groaned against her mouth, grabbed her hips and thrust as deep as possible. His eyes rolled back and his head hit the ground as he kept flexing, thrusting over and over even as his cum spurted into the latex.

Closing her eyes, Ember let herself luxuriate in the heat of his body, the strength clutching to her, the skin wrapped around hers, the musk filling her senses and the cock pulsing one more long, slow orgasm from her. "Mr. Knightley," she whispered, her voice ragged. "I would never choose you."

With that, she collapsed to his chest. He brushed his palm against her cheek as if trying to rouse her from a hundred-year sleep, but Ember shied away from the light. It was only in the dark that she didn't have to pretend. She could be selfish. She could keep him and help him win.

All her dreams could come true.

Chapter Twenty-Four

"Contestants, I'd advise you focus on solidifying your rooms or your relationships."

The host's words rang out across the lawn, sending everyone rushing to fight over drills and sheaves of fabric. "None of this makes any sense," Ember complained while testing her code. The first two keys spun seamlessly. The third stopped halfway and all of them flipped back to occupied. Gah, she was never finishing this on time.

"Have you tried turning it off, then back on?" Booker asked.

Ember pursed her lips and faced him, a witty comeback perched on her tongue. All the blood drained from her brain at the bare shoulders straining to hold up a huge wooden beam. Every damn muscle on his sweat-dabbed back hardened as he drilled in a hole. Ember's traitorous eyes took their time enjoying the long canyon down his spine until hitting his pants hanging slightly below the top of his ass.

The snap of measuring tape shook Ember out of her fog. She jerked in her seat and caught the amused gleam in Booker's eyes. "I wasn't referring to my display piece, but why we're expected to have our work done so soon. Three couples remain and we haven't..."

She didn't have a choice. For as easy as it would be to stay on as Booker's partner, to smile wide and show off her work for the cameras, then pout when they were both inevitably kicked off tonight—it'd take him down with her. The show was a means to an end. No one had cared about keeping the property after it finished, not until him. Somehow she had to get Booker on the winning team, make him sparkle for the producers and keep from being the bad guy at the same time.

And she couldn't say a word of it to him.

"Haven't what?" Booker asked. He climbed off his ladder and reached for their jug of water. Rather than take a deep swig, he dumped the cool liquid on his head where it raced down his shoulders and pecs.

Ember returned to the unhelpful coding screen. "The switch. I'm wondering if it will even happen."

"Who's going to trade partners? We're almost finished."

That was precisely her fear.

"Son of a—!"

Ember winced at the sharp curse radiating down the hallways. Somehow it cut over the whir of drills and saws. Stepping away from the old-fashioned circular desk Booker had built with his bare hands, Ember made her way for the door. "I'm going to check on Ree."

"Don't be long. We need to get that working before nightfall." He waggled his screwdriver in the direction of her silly key idea. Did it matter? If he won this place, would he even keep it?

Ember nodded and dashed for the solarium. The hallways were stuffed with not only the usual construction bric-a-brac, but recording equipment and napping camera crew. After the long nights and early mornings, they looked more like the walking dead than any zombie movie she'd seen. Easing her way around them, she walked into the sun room and frowned.

So much of the charm had been stripped away. White paint reflected back the sun, nearly blinding her. Ember squinted, struggling to find Harriet hefting up a moose head. It missed the bracket and came tumbling down for her.

"Where in the Sam scratch is Elton?" Ree hunted around. "Oh, hi, Emmy."

"Not all is well in dead animal land?"

She snorted and kicked at the moose's antlers. Adjusting the bandana in her hair, Harriet sighed. "He keeps adding them, more and more. We were gonna put a deer over there, but the thing weighs like two hundred pounds and I can't move it on my own. Every time I turn around, he's vanished. I've done most of this."

Ember smiled internally at this opportunity. "Have a seat." She tossed a dead fish off of the couch, eased onto the plastic then patted the spot next to her. "You deserve a break."

"There's no time."

"There's always time to complain about men."

Ree laughed, then gulped and looked around. "Do you think they heard that?"

"A man only listens to a woman when the words blow, job, down, knees or daddy are mentioned. Otherwise, it's all white noise."

Falling in beside Ember, Harriet slammed her boots to the coffee table and leaned back. "Darn tootin'. I swear, it's like the second I open my mouth he turns into one o' them cave fish—blind and deaf. Is that how it's with yours, too?"

Booker's half-grunted comment came back to her, as if he—or any man for that matter—would want a woman that challenged him day in and day out. He was in the throes of passion and would have said he was a chicken if it got him over the line. There was no stock to be found.

Harriet must have read her silence as admission as she gave Ember's knee a pity tap. Putting on her best smile, Ember looked toward Ree. "But I thought things were going well with you and Mr. Brown. The kiss?"

Snorting, Ree nervously scratched her arm, her shoulders shrinking in. "It was nice, and unexpected. But he went right back to himself after. Not giving me the time of day, vanishing just when I need him. You ever wonder if they're playing it up for the cameras?"

"Are you saying you don't think Elton's in this for the right reasons?" Ember said, hitting reality gold. Everyone hated a contestant who was here for the wrong reasons, even though all of them were.

"He sure don't seem to care about love. Or romance. The way he looks through me, it's like I'm a wart on a frog's tushie."

"You're not a wart, Ree. You're beautiful." Ember's assurances that had once shored up Harriet's spine fell through the cracks. Exhaustion, stress, never being alone and never knowing when the chopping block would come had worn them all down. Only Ree had been the chipper one, happy to keep going, until Mr. Brown had crushed her spirit.

"I'm starting to think this was a huge mistake. Maybe I should go home. Turn in my tool belt, crawl under the bed and sleep for a year." She hid behind her hands and crumpled into her lap. "My pa said this was a bad idea. I didn't expect to get a guy, just wanted to try my hand at fixing something. Sometimes, I ain't even sure I like him. But it hurts so bad, like a spike through my chest, to think he don't like me. Why?"

"I'm sorry, Ree. I didn't realize how badly he was treating you."

She peered between her fingers. "You didn't?" Those two words were spat like bullets and Ember flinched. Yes, Mr. Brown seemed to be of the collecting beautiful women mindset. But she was certain, had been certain, that he'd warm to Harriet's charm. Even come to love her.

Moaning, Harriet turned and buried her face against Ember's arm. "I don't want to see him again. Just let me quit. Flee into the woods, find a shack full of cats and live there until I die of loneliness."

Tenderly, Ember combed through Ree's hair, trying to calm her. "What if I have a better solution?"

Harriet sat up and wiped her eyes. "Get dogs instead?"

"Not quite. The switch has to be happening before tonight, no doubt tied to the elimination. Whoever doesn't have a partner at the end is sent home."

"So he could dump me right now and go after Jade?"

Ember sneered at the idea. She would be so crass as to take Ree's partner. "What if you were to pair up with Mr. Knightley?"

"I thought you said he was too boring for the camera. That they'd cut him first chance they got. Even though Robert went first."

"I know what I said, and he's shown surprising legs." Those thighs in particular were scrumptious. "His skills in carpentry and construction are unmatched. With your star power and his talents drilling..." Ember coughed and wiped her forehead. "You're certain to win. All you have to do is write down Booker's name. Mr. Knightley, I mean. If you claim him for the switch, that will leave Elton out in the cold."

"But what about you? You'll be without a partner too. They might send you home. Or worse, stick you with him."

Ember smiled at her concern. "Don't worry. I'm certain Mr. Churchill is more than ready to upgrade."

All she needed to do was get Logan alone long enough to seal the deal. Ember rose to her feet and Ree did the same. The sunlight reflected off a surface, glinting in her eyes. As Ember lowered her protective hand, she caught the flash of a camera lens scurrying away.

"I should get back to my room. Good luck with yours, Ree," she called loud enough for a boom mike in the next room to pick it up.

"Uh, thanks. Are you sure about trading? It's just—"

"Have a pleasant afternoon." Ember waved to the girl as she slipped away. It wasn't a betrayal. It was strategy. Harriet was guaranteed to win, and the chances of her wanting to keep the resort seemed minuscule. No doubt she'd sign her share over to her new partner, and the Knightleys would have their land back. All of Ember's machinations would come to light in the end and she'd be revealed as willing to sacrifice her spot in the name of justice.

Everyone would be happy — even if it required her leaving tonight.

"Put out the worst of the fires?"

"There's a moose head now," Ember said to him.

Booker's face pickled in disgust. "Why don't they shove a zoo's worth of dead animals in there too? It used to have plants and flowers the guests could tend."

"A little carnation for a gentleman's breast pocket?" Ember asked as she perched on her chair and dove back into the fussy motors.

Booker dropped the last beam as he gazed down at her. "Or a rose for a lady's hair."

"That sounds..." Ember did not feel a flush in her heart. There were no butterflies to be had. She would not picture Mr. Knightley in his suit gliding her around the finished ballroom. "I need to focus," she said, zeroing in on the ones and zeros.

He nodded and looked back to the cameras, as if that were the only reason she had shut him down. Rocking the beam to his other hand, Booker hefted it onto his bare shoulders and approached the overhang.

It's for the best. If I spend one more minute around him, I'm...

Ember swallowed, her skin prickling below her sweater. Her palms began to shake as she fought to keep from catching a glance at him.

It's a minor infatuation that will pass in the night. Mr. Knightley means nothing to me.

Chapter Twenty-Five

Booker dropped the paintbrush and stepped back. "How's that looking?" he asked, his eyes bleary from the dust hanging in the air. There wasn't time to clear anything out. God only knew how much of it was now painted to the wainscoting.

"You missed a bit," she said, wiggling at the tip of her toes to reach. Her brush passed three inches below. The little frown made him laugh. Booker dropped his brush in the pan and bent down. She stopped hopping out of fear of accidentally getting the wall by mistake.

Folding his hands together, Booker made a platform of his palms. "If you may?" he asked, gazing up at her. Ember delicately laid her fingers on his shoulder, never once breaking eye contact. She eased her foot into his grip.

He shifted, prepared to take her weight, and she moved back.

"I don't know if this is wise. What if I snap a finger?"

"Do you trust me?" Booker dropped down again.

Whatever burbled behind Ember's eyes left him adrift. She pursed her lips and swept her palm over his bare shoulder. "As much as you trust me."

"Then you should be safe."

"It wasn't my safety that concerned me."

"I know." Booker smiled and she joined him.

Slipping her foot back in place, Ember gripped his shoulder and he lifted her. She didn't have to go far, but she wouldn't let go of him, shrinking her reach. Biting hard on her lip, she focused on the little relief missing its dab of amber waves. He had no choice but to rise higher. Balanced on one knee, he held Ember and she him as she swiped the brush back and forth.

Booker looked up to watch. "There's another bit to your right."

"Good catch." Ember tipped for the missing spot. Her body weaved, but he locked on to her foot, certain she wouldn't fall. "How's that...oops?"

A cold glob splattered onto the top of his head. Booker looked up just as Ember raced to catch the second drip while the other slipped back through his hair. "I assume that was done on purpose." He lowered her to the floor but remained on his knee as she protected the paintbrush.

"Of course it was, Mr. Knightley. Every action I take is done with purpose."

He gazed up at her to find delight sparkling in her eyes. She'd been distant today. He'd thought it thanks to the key mechanism, then a darker thought invaded his mind—what if it was his fault? But her smile could beat out the sun and the way her fingers curled around the brush bristles... Not too hard, not too soft, just the right amount of pressure to—to keep the paint in place.

"I am well aware of your purposeful actions, Miss Woodhouse."

Her cheeks burned. "And I've experienced the lashing of your tongue more than any here."

Booker innocently skirted his palm up her calf as if he was keeping himself from falling over. Ember stumbled against him until he planted his chin against her belly while staring up at her. "And you may suffer it again."

"What's this? Is Bo proposing?" The airhead Logan stomped into their room as if he owned the place.

Scowling, Booker released Ember the same moment she stepped back. He tried to rise without thinking and a pop wrenched his knee. Wincing, Booker struggled to massage the angry but not broken joint into working order while beating himself up. He was too old to be acting this stupid.

"My name is not Bo," he said, glaring up then down at Logan.

The man, with a drink in hand, didn't have the grace to look back. "Doing a lot of work in here, huh?"

"That is the point of this endeavor," Booker argued back. He crossed his arms, tempted to hurl Logan out on his ass, but the cameras were always watching.

"What do you want, Logan?" Ember asked point blank. She too seemed rattled by his appearance. In getting away, she had wound up next to the desk on the other side of the room. With her arms hugged tight to her chest, she watched Mr. Churchill.

"They sent me here."

"Who did?"

"Our overlord and masters. I'm to collect the sacrificial lamb. I mean, Mr. Knightley."

What the hell for?

It was Ember's gasp that froze him. She pressed both her hands to her cheeks, leaving behind a bronze paint patch. Booker winced and reached for a towel, when she said, "It's already time?"

"Time for what?" he asked, leaning closer to dab off her cheek. Before he could get close, Logan caught him by the hand.

"Time for you to hope you satisfied your partner enough she'll want to keep you." He grinned and waggled his eyebrows, causing Booker to scowl. "With that face, I'm sure you're fine."

The sarcasm was thick enough to paint the walls in two coats, but Booker ignored it. He shrugged off Logan and the aimless man drifted out of the door. This show was a quagmire of accidents, pain, anxiety and maddening twists. But he knew he'd more than satisfied Miss Woodhouse and couldn't wait for another opportunity.

"This way, Bo," Logan shouted.

* * * *

"Ladies?" Their mysterious host dramatically gestured to a wooden box with the show's logo burned at the top. "I believe we all know why we're here."

An assistant hurriedly passed out three blank postcards and a coordinating envelope. Ember took hers and looked around for a pen, but none were to be found.

"In case you don't..." The Artist winked below the half-black and half-white mask. "We've reached the part of the game when the future is in your hands. Do you keep on your steady path trusting the future of this hotel and your heart to your partner? Or do you forge a new adventure, perhaps with a nicer pair of buttocks?"

Ree giggled at the word and Ember nervously flicked the edge of the card stock. It lifted immediately, revealing a slick coating over top.

"This is your one chance to control the hands of fate. Write down your beloved and build your castle of love. Lunging Lazarus, that was cheesy. Let me try again."

"No, no, you've got it. We're good to go." The producers hustled over to adjust the lighting and check the host's wardrobe.

Ember lifted her card and asked, "What about a pen?"

"Someone's working on it. Terry!" the male producer shouted in the direction of an assistant.

The one requisite tool necessary for this ceremony was missing and no one seemed to care. Smiling wryly, Ember turned to Harriet only to find Sam clutching her arm. She whispered, pulling Ree away and leaving Ember alone with Jade.

"Do we stand here and wait until the producers stop hyping up Harriet?"

"They're doing their job," Ember said, needing a punching bag and having one step up to the plate. "Or are you fretting that Logan's already written down another name?"

"Whose? Do you think he'd pick you?" Jade snorted as if the idea was ridiculous.

What made her think he wouldn't? Ember was graceful, beautiful, smart and—unlike the tool of the year—a generous and kind soul. A sharp retort burned on her tongue, but at the last moment she swallowed it down. "Maybe he's writing down Harriet's name. Maybe they all are."

Jade's jaw dropped, her poise slipping as she spat out, "That'd cut you, too."

"It's a price to pay for love."

"Love? Do you expect me to believe you're here as some romance genie? That you're getting up at five AM, risking the loss of fingers or motor function, just to help someone else fall in love?"

How dare Jade question her intent. Squaring up, Ember stared her down and sniffed. "At least I'm not someone's sloppy seconds," she said dismissively.

She braced herself for any eventuality — for Jade to go after Harriet, to drag Booker into this, even for the Craftswoman to namedrop Ember's father. Ember was prepared for any potential blowback except one.

Tears welled in Jade's eyes. A small whimper slipped out and she slapped a hand to her mouth. "You think you're the hero. The princess or the fairy godmother. But you're the wicked witch!" Crying, Jade flung her card at the camera and dove out of the room. She struck a light stand, sending it crashing into the wall where the bulb shattered on impact.

"Jade?" Ember cried out. Shame prickled down her skin, and the heat of a million eyes judging her crawled up the back of her neck.

"Whew, that girl sure loves her drama," the producer said, sidling up to Ember.

She couldn't leave her like this. She had to explain. "Excuse me." Ember handed her card to the producer and dashed after Jade. The cameraman tried to follow, but got stuck by the tipped-over light. It didn't prove a very difficult search, Jade's heavy breathing echoing off of the halls.

Stopping in the hallway, Ember pushed on a plain door. It rattled open to reveal a closet. Hunched over, with her knees pressed to her chest, Jade struggled for breath. "Leave me alone. You, you made a fool out of me in front of everyone."

"I..." All of her Machiavellian plans of lifting Harriet to the winner's circle by helping her step on the others slammed into the wall. It'd seemed easy when the people were one-dimensional characters — the jock, the hunk, the country mouse, the spoiled rich girl, the slut. The tears on TV equaled ratings, not a sinking stone in her gut.

"I didn't mean to."

"Yes, you did. All you've done since day one is attack me. What did I do?"

"You took Augusta's place," Ember argued, as if she'd felt anything for the woman beyond annoyance.

"Do you think that was my choice?" Jade wiped at her eyes, smearing her makeup back like a crazy clown.

"It's the game. You came in late."

"They made me. I flew out the same day as everyone else, but they trapped me in my hotel room while you all were bonding."

A man grunted, asking where the two drama queens had slipped off to. Thinking fast, Ember slipped inside and closed the door. Jade glared up at her as she leaned against the back wall and slid down.

"What are you doing? Get out."

"Do you want them to film you looking like a punk raccoon? Here." Ember handed her a secret stash of wipes, always necessary should an unexpected crying moment happen.

Jade stared at the white sheet as if it was covered in anthrax. "Why should I trust you?"

"You probably shouldn't. I doubt I would in your situation."

She took the wipe and tried to smear away her marathoning mascara.

"Can you blame me for going on the offense when you arrived? You're beautiful. You know how to use a drill. The men were putty at your feet. You're a threat."

Jade pulled the tip away to stare at Ember barefaced. "I don't care about them. I didn't want Logan. He's dimwitted as hell. The only reason he hasn't cut off his own arm is because he keeps vanishing when the work begins. You're lucky. You have a partner who actually works with you. A space to work with."

"Yes, a dull hotel lobby. But you, you have that gorgeous ballroom." Ember couldn't deny the envy in her voice.

"To do what? It's done. It was refurbished by production before we arrived."

What?

Jade sniffed and wafted the sheet smeared with her face. "I came here hoping to show off my skills. I build furniture, fucking adorable and practical furniture. Tables, chairs, wine racks, cupboards—all things a ballroom doesn't need. No one's gonna care now. Every recording of me was the camera zooming in on my ass or down my shirt while they told me to squeeze the drill trigger."

Ree was the girl next door, Ember the exotic beauty and Jade was forced into the bombshell box whether she liked it or not. They'd lived full, layered lives outside of these walls with complicated problems. But trapped in here, at the encouragement of the producers, they had leaned into their stereotypes. What if she could never shake it off?

"I'm sorry," Ember said.

"Do you even know what you're apologizing for?" Jade snarled back.

"For calling you sloppy seconds. It wasn't nice."

"It wasn't nice for you, you mean." Jade struggled to her feet and glared down at Ember. "Your little mask slipped and people saw the real you underneath, every wart broadcast to millions of homes. Now you're here doing damage control. Well, I'm not going to give you the satisfaction. I don't accept your apology, Ember Woodhouse, and I hope you rot in hell!"

Shoving open the door, Jade nearly dashed into the cameraman who'd been lurking outside the whole time. She caught the black lens and froze. The hard voice that'd cursed Ember out softened to a whisper. "All I wanted when I stepped off that bus was to be welcomed, to belong. You took that away." Her hard, methodical footsteps echoed down the hall as Ember scrunched tighter into a ball.

She could fix this. She just needed to explain to Jade that...

The door swung back and the black lens poked in like a faceless serial killer hunting for its victim. Ember touched her eyes, certain they were dry but needing to be sure. Racing down the hallway and getting into yet another screaming match with Jade would turn them both into national laughingstocks.

No. There was no fixing things with Jade. She had to stay her course, get Booker and Harriet together and take her final swan song tonight. Putting on a smile, Ember tried to stand up gracefully inside the tiny closet.

"Boy," she said with a gasp of relief, "Jade loves drama."

Chapter Twenty-Six

Ember went skidding across the floor in her socks. "Wait, wait, wait!" Weaving under Booker's arms, she extended a lighter and placed it to the candles. He held his breath, at first fearing his sleeves might go up in flames. But as Ember bit her lip, focusing on the little wicks refusing to catch, Booker struggled for far more dangerous reasons.

Her eyelashes sparkled and her cheeks flushed. "Almost got it," Ember said.

Clinging to the overhang that should have been glued hours ago, he whispered, "Take all the time you need."

"Three minutes left!"

She smiled at the announcement and wafted the lighter to the next candle. Instead of the tight gowns he had come to expect for every ceremony, she'd put on the cozy baggy sweater, though the pair of ass-hugging pants kept him at attention. He knew the rolling hills hidden below that inviting expanse of cashmere and had every intention to explore them thoroughly tonight.

"There." The lighter flicked off, but Ember didn't flit away. She pressed it closer to her chest like a prayer candle.

"What's wrong?" He strained his neck, trying to see what they could have missed when Ember placed her palm to his cheek. He'd been risking little sips of her throughout the day, a glance here, a moment there. But with all of this nearly at an end, he drank her in.

"I should tell you that..." She nibbled on her lip and Booker reached for her. The beam shifted and he jerked, slamming both of his hands to it. "You need that to stick." Ember dodged out from under him and raced toward the tools they'd tossed into the hallway. There hadn't been any time to put them away.

She aimed the drill.

"Won't that ruin the aesthetic?" Booker asked. She'd been adamant they try to avoid any holes to maintain the marble illusion.

"Fuck that," Ember shouted then drilled in the support screws.

"Thirty seconds, now twenty-nine."

Both of them stepped back, Booker keeping the tips of his fingers on the beam until the absolute last second. It shifted and he almost raced to it, but it didn't fall another inch. Good enough. They kept stumbling backward, taking in the work they'd done for the past two weeks as if they'd never seen it before. Pride swelled inside of him, not only from finishing the job on time, but her talent. The room was elegant, but also cozy. It tugged on the nostalgia wound running through his soul. He never could have managed that on his own.

"I'd say we did it." He cupped his arm over her shoulders and pulled her close for a half-hug. "Miss Woodhouse." It was supposed to be celebratory, nothing more than friendly, but Ember brushed her hip against him and curled her arm around the small of his back.

"It seems so, Mr. Knightley." She smiled wider and turned toward him, which was when Booker realized he wasn't giving his business partner a pat on the back but was holding a woman who challenged and matched him in ways he had never thought possible.

His hand lifted on its own and cupped under her chin. *There are cameras everywhere. Producers are watching just down the hall. What are you doing?*

He expected to read all of that in Ember's eyes. But the little green flecks in her ocean of brown dazzled up at him. She drew her hand across his chest and he tipped her head back.

"Ten, nine..."

"Oh no!" Ember broke out and ran for a box. Holding something tight to her chest, she full-body dove for the desk as the host kept counting down.

"Three, two, that's it!"

She opened her hands to reveal an old-fashioned call bell sitting on the desk. "I can't believe I almost forgot it," Ember said. "Now it's perfect." An assistant ran over and took both of them by the hand. Without saying a word, he dragged them out of the hotel and into the late afternoon.

Lights lit up so hot Booker's sweat started to perspire. He wafted his hand before his face, and an assistant told him to stop. Dropping it to his side, he tried to not be surprised when softer fingers wrapped around his. They both stared ahead as they were told.

"Team Orange." The Artist clapped their hands and strode closer without looking them in the eye. "It's time to reveal your room to the world. Are you ready?" Glancing to their hands, they snickered, "Needing a little courage, are we?"

Booker and Ember both let go. "As ready as ever," Booker said, his chipper tone surprising himself.

"Then please, lead me on this magical journey through your hotel lobby." The Artist gripped both of the doors and pushed them open to make a glorious entrance. The camera followed next, then Booker and Ember were allowed inside.

"Wow, this is…fantastic," the Artist said, doing their best to not sound like they had seen it two minutes earlier. They still had no idea who was under the mask, but Booker doubted it was an actor. A good one, anyway.

"It has an old-fashioned feel."

"The inspiration was the history of the resort itself. We wanted to return it to the height of the ostentatious twenties." Ember was a whiz, explaining every minute detail that Booker would just point to on a job and wait to be paid. "You'll no doubt notice the wainscoting on the ceiling. The pieces were hand-carved by Mr. Knightley to duplicate a pattern used at a famous jazz club."

"I want to talk about this desk. It's adorable." The Artist skipped over the little window seat Ember managed to talk him into and the tiny reading nook with secret USB plug-ins under the table. They drew their gloved hand across the desktop, following the curve. "Almost sensual in its design."

"That, uh, that hadn't been the thought but, I guess." Booker stumbled over his words and winced.

A quick bell rang out, saving him. The Artist pressed the button one more time before looking behind to the alcove. "And what's this? Do you want your hotel to use old-fashioned keys?"

"We wanted to preserve the old design. The shelves were beautiful. I mean, look at that." Ember pointed to the brackets that were hidden behind art deco roses. "The doors will use modern keycards."

"So it's decorative?"

"Not exactly." She looked over to Booker, the worry and excitement palpable. He raised his thumb, certain it would work. Ember eased around the cute desk and sat on the red stool she'd upholstered. "Every key is wired to a motor. When a room is occupied, the manager will push a button and..." She crinkled her nose and pressed down on room number five.

Slowly, the key with a green key chain rotated to reveal the other side painted red with the word 'Occupied' stamped across it.

"Wow, that is... That's impressive and fits so well on theme. I've never wanted to spend more than two minutes in a hotel lobby, but this place is gorgeous. I'm tempted to book a stay just so I can sit in that chair and people-watch. Congratulations."

Ember bounced in place and Booker reached out to her. She kept leaping with excitement, causing her to plow into him. So he didn't plummet into the candles, he held on to her. He brushed his forehead against the side of hers and whispered, "We did it."

"Can you do that again?" a voice called, shaking both of them out of their bubble. "The angle was awful," the cameraman explained. He adjusted, focusing on Booker who awkwardly held his arms out and patted the shuffling Ember.

"We did it," he repeated, his voice drained. She nodded at elbow's length.

"That isn't—" The female producer came in and tapped her tablet before sighing. "It doesn't matter. Get out. We need to shoot b-roll of the room."

Before they could say a word, they were shooed out, along with the Artist. All three wound up next to the grand staircase. Booker stared up it, noting how the rug needed replacing, some of the railings as well, and the entire banister required a good buffing. He hadn't dared to let himself hope before that he'd be the one fixing this place up—all of it from roof to foundation. After the magic they had pulled in there, how could they not win?

"How long is that going to take?" Booker asked.

"Probably hours," the Artist said. "They need to film every nail and screw from a hundred different angles just in case."

"In case of what?"

"In case the story changes. Oh my goodness, is that a Dashwood donut?" The Artist's eyes went wide as a young woman carrying a yellow box tried to slip inside. "I'll take all of them off of your hands," they said, waving after the vanishing pastries. At the hallway, they struck a pose. "Figures are for ice skaters and mathematicians."

Just like that, the center of the hurricane moved on, leaving the both of them wind-blown but alive. "That went well," Booker said.

"At least the key moved. I was so afraid it'd stick and they'd all flip randomly again."

"Just turn on some music so they think it was done on purpose."

She snickered at his easy answer, and Booker leaned closer. All the commotion had backed her against the wall. He kept one hand pressed above her head. If that'd happened on the first day, she would have been shrinking into a ball and refusing to make eye contact. Ember boldly gazed up at him, her fingers nervously fiddling with the edge of his vest, as if her subconscious wanted to yank him to her. But they weren't alone, as badly as he wished it could be.

All they had to do was get through another two rounds of eliminations and this fishbowl would crack. A whole week in the fantasy suite without cameras zooming in on his ass, microphones peaking with every moan and producers telling him to move his arm for a better angle. Just him, Ember and the quiet of King's Retreat.

An elbow slammed into his back and Booker flexed closer. Her palms slipped to take his waist and his innocently landed on her hip. As she beamed up at him with her fiery eyes, he couldn't understand any man that'd walk away from her.

"Booker?" Ember whispered.

He cinched his hands against her hip, the rough denim enflaming him. "Yes?"

She parted her lips and a soft sigh escaped. God, he wanted to chase it back, to feel her little gasps and squeals against his mouth as he laid her on that window seat. "There's something I should tell you."

About what comes after? He hadn't let himself hope, not to win, and certainly not to see Miss Woodhouse again. But their room was spectacular and she a cozy goddess holding on to him. "What is it?" he breathed in her ear, struggling with the quiver down her body.

"Behind you!"

Booker looked back and spotted a camera. He reined himself in. Shaking his head, he walked to the other side of the hallway as if he'd always intended to lean there. Ember nodded and silently glanced to the invasion of privacy that would never end.

"What happens next?" he asked, needing to fill the void. Whatever she had to tell him could wait, once they were back in their cabin hiding between the sheets.

"Um, well, the elimination."

"What about that stupid paper we had to fill out? I put down your—"

"The switch, yes, that will play into the elimination. Anyone who doesn't have their name on a sheet is kicked out."

"And they take the partner with?"

"Not necessarily. It depends. Sometimes a wild card can hang around for an episode or two. But they probably want to get this season over with."

"At least before they actually kill someone. So then what? What should I be prepared for?" Booker asked.

"Opening night. They throw a fancy party. The two remaining teams decorate and design the divided-up mansion, or resort, for the night."

"Even if they didn't do any of the work on the kitchen or the upstairs rooms?" Booker asked.

"I supposed it's assumed they had a hand in it. That part takes weeks, with actual contractors. Then the rest of the contestants are invited back to vote for the winner."

"Wow. Well, I can't wait to have real time and real money to put into fixing this place." He had no idea the two final teams would be given such leeway. It sounded fantastic. "I imagine you have quite a few ideas yourself."

"Huh?" Ember looked confused. Perhaps she was so lost in thought about redecorating the solarium she had missed his words.

"The world is guaranteed to fall in love with your skills after they see what you can do for a party."

"Right. Yes, the...the decorating. For the party. It's a lot of work." She lowered her head and watched the passing crew members. Teamsters argued over the donuts and hurled pieces of them in protest. Booker didn't watch the sugar fight. All his focus was on Ember, who should be on as high of a cloud as he, but her face was knotted in concern. What other fresh horrors awaited the final two teams on this show?

"Elton? Hello?" The quiet girl hustled around the corner and caught Ember's eye. "Have either of you seen Elton? We're up next and he's nowhere to be found."

"Did you check the drink cart?" Booker asked.

"Yeah, twice. I don't know where he can be. What happens if he's not there? Will they eliminate me?" She clung to Ember's hands, looking like a squirrel facing down a set of headlights.

"Don't worry, the producers won't let that happen. But maybe we should find him. I'll help you look."

"Thank you. You're the best." She laid her head on Ember's shoulders and hugged her side. Ember lightly rubbed her head to calm her.

"Let's try upstairs." Harriet broke free and dashed for the staircase. "Elton!"

Ember was slower to follow and Booker caught her by the arm. "You know he's probably screwing an intern right now."

"Don't be silly. He's madly in love with Ree." She said the words with conviction and umbrage, but her eyes were as jaded as his.

"Mr. Brown," Ember shouted, trailing after the country mouse.

Chapter Twenty-Seven

"Elton, where are you?" Harriet flopped to the ground to hunt under the bed.

"I doubt he'd fit there," Ember said.

"Check the closet," she insisted, pointing to the narrow alcove missing its door. Ember only had to give a cursory glance to spot a single construction light and nothing more.

"Maybe he's back at the cabin."

"Maybe. I can't believe he'd embarrass me like this. He knows we were supposed to be in the solarium before six. I swear, if I said 'there's a ten-ton rhino coming up behind you!' he'd stand in place to spite me."

"You don't know that he's avoiding you on purpose." Ember slipped her arms around the girl and helped her back to her feet. They'd already gone through three of the guest rooms, only another nine more to go. "Perhaps production has him tied up." She frowned, thinking of Booker's insinuation. Mr. Brown was many things, but a cad could not be one of them.

"I wish I'd never been stuck with him. He does nothing. Nothing beyond drinking and flirting with anything that moves, except for me." Harriet knocked on the door, then flung it open wide. "Got yo—! Oh." Instead of the wayward man, a massive pile of coats rested on the floor. There was no bed to be found. "Why did you force us together?"

"I believed that you'd make a good match." Ember fought to defend herself. She had thought that with enough time Ree and Elton could come to an understanding. But that ship seemed to have crashed into the lighthouse.

Harriet slammed the door and stared hard at Ember. "Or were you thinking I was competition and saddled me with the worst man out of the bunch? You talked me out of Robert..."

"Who's already been eliminated."

"And every suggestion you made—flirt with him, let him talk about himself, tell him my deepest secrets — nothing works. But he keeps staring at you from across the room like a bull around a heifer in heat. It ain't fair."

"I'm... I am sorry. I promise I had no intentions to sabotage you. I want you to win, Ree. To prove to the world that even the quiet country girl, the wallflower, deserves the love of a movie star. It's the movie star who didn't want to follow the rules."

Harriet gulped and nodded. "Apology accepted. You were looking out for me. And I do like the dress you gave me."

Ember smiled with a pursed lip. It had been a loan, not a gift. But it made her happy, so perhaps it was worth losing. "Besides, at least you'll be free of him soon. With the switch coming up, and you writing down Booker's name..."

They approached the room she'd worked on with Booker, the one still singed. She should have told him her plan, but if she did, the producers would know it too. They might try to stop her. Or worse, he'd try to stop her. Whether out of some foolish sense of duty or because he...he didn't want to lose her.

That's silly. Why won't he wish to be rid of me once he has his family's property returned? Besides, her future waited outside these walls, not in a backwoods resort with a man.

"Ree?" Ember realized the girl had stopped down the hallway. "What's wrong?"

"During the switch bit, Sam was talking to me. She had a lot of good info, you know what past winners did and such."

"Do not tell me you kept Elton," Ember thundered, her heart cracking.

"No." Harriet shook her head fast. Ember breathed a sigh of relief when she heard a second gasp behind the plywood door. "It's just that, I was thinking, I want to..."

Ember brushed her knuckles against the door in a hardly-there knock, then she pushed on the knob. "Elton, are you—?"

Two bodies roiled below a coverlet.

Her first thought was to apologize for intruding and race away before either of the lovers would notice her. But Ember's escape was foiled by Harriet marching in behind her. "Elton?"

The undercover love stalled. A hand whipped back under the sheets and fought to try to pull them over the black hair, leaving a pair of men's feet exposed. "I know it's you, Elton. You've got the damn Band-Aid on," Ree fumed, reaching for the covers.

Just before she grabbed it, he popped out from below, naked down to his waist. Ember's cheeks lit hot at the idea there was a nude man with barely a duvet hiding his shame.

"What do you want?" Elton asked like they had walked in on him making a sandwich.

"You...you son of a bitch." The quiet mouse exploded into a rampaging elephant. "You're cheating on me."

"Don't be so dramatic," he whined and rolled his eyes.

"Who is it? That intern you keep staring at?" Harriet reached for the covers, trying to rip them free while Elton fought back. All the while, his partner remained hidden below.

"What in the hell is wrong with you?" It was a struggle, but Elton won. He yanked the blankets so hard, Ree stumbled and landed flat on her ass. "I'm not cheating on you. There is no us."

Ember dashed over to help while keeping her head turned from the bed. Poor Ree crumpled to the floor bawling her eyes out. "You kissed me!" she shouted.

"For the cameras! This is a show. It requires drama."

"You're giving us an eyeful now," Ember said. She offered to help Ree up, but the girl shot to her feet.

Her eyes burned red as if all of her unshed tears had transformed into rage. "Who the fuck is it?" she thundered again and reached for the blanket. Elton tried to fight back, but it was getting harder to hide whoever lay beside him. Harriet got a firm grip to the corner and began to twist, pulling Elton around. A naked leg hit the floor and he maneuvered his body.

"It's none of your concern. Will you stop acting like a child? This is pathetic."

"You're pathetic. We're supposed to be revealing my hard work to the world. But you've snuck off in order to stuff your sausage into…who? Who is it? Sam? Are you fucking a producer?"

Uh-oh. Footsteps padded down the hall. Cameras must be racing to immortalize poor Harriet losing her shit. "Ree, we should get out of here to cool off."

"I deserve to fucking know!" she cried. "Is it Jade? Are you fucking Jade?"

"What's going on?"

Ember turned to find the source of the footsteps came from the woman in question. She took one look at Ree two seconds from mauling Elton and crossed her arms. "That explains the screaming."

"I'm going to kill you!" Harriet shouted. She dug her foot in and gave one last hard yank.

Three things happened at once.

Elton tumbled from the bed, landing in a sprawling heap of naked man parts. It was so much spray-tan flesh it reminded Ember of rotting carrots.

Unable to hide, a head popped up from behind him. With a wry grin, a completely nude Logan threw out a "Hi."

An entire camera crew, with a producer in tow, barreled through Ember and Jade just as it all went down.

No one said a word. Only the heavy panting of the man who'd had to run up the stairs with the camera broke the silence. Everyone else kept staring from Elton to Logan and back again. They'd turn to each other, hoping for someone to break this stalemate.

It was Elton ripping the blanket out of Ree's numb fingers that brought reality crashing down around them. He wrapped it around his waist while Logan haplessly swung his cock and balls around as he perched on the bed. Elton didn't even look at him, all his focus on the camera and the producer grinning maniacally behind it.

"Delete that footage," Elton shouted.

"I'm sorry, but that's not possible."

"Like the fuck it's not. Where's Goddard? Get her skanky ass in here now."

Oh God, Ember wanted to escape. The tension felt like a million shards of glass dumped into a lidless blender. But, most of all, she had to tell Booker. Too bad the equipment and crew were filling the doorway, not letting anyone in or out. That included the two naked men trapped on the bed they'd just rumpled to hell and back.

"Mr. Brown, Mr. Churchill, do you want to talk about your illicit relationship?" producer Sam asked.

"No, I fucking do not," Elton cursed.

"We're in a relationship? I thought it was just sex," Logan said with a laugh.

That perked the producer right up, but Elton slapped at him to get him to shut up. Logan sighed and leaned back, his hands cushioning his head. "That's the last time I let a guy who only won a People's Choice Award suck me off."

It took some time for Ms. Goddard to arrive. Given how small the resort was and how juicy the new development would be, Ember suspected it was done on purpose. By the time she appeared, sunglasses hiding away her eyes, the past twenty minutes felt like three days. Elton kept randomly cursing as if that would stop them from showing the footage. If his full Monty wouldn't, a few bleeps sure as hell weren't protecting him.

"Mr. Brown, you've been busy."

"Cut the shit, Carol," Elton fumed, standing up.

"My name is London."

"Right, and you're also not fucking the show's creator on the side."

She tugged her glasses down slowly. "Mr. Brown, you cannot contest the footage, nor do you have any rights to delete it. Once a contestant enters our set, we own them, body and soul."

"Check my contract. I have final rights for edits, and I want this stricken. Now!"

For the first time, Ms. Goddard gulped. She looked over to Sam. "Is that true?"

Sam shrugged. "I don't know. All the contestants signed the…"

"I never did. And if you show even a second of this footage, I'll sue the show, the studio and you personally…for emotional distress."

"That's a lot of legal fees to keep people from finding out you prefer the company of—"

Elton shoved through Ember and Ree in order to get right in her face. "Legal fees you'll be paying. My contract is rock solid."

For a moment, she stared down at him like he was a fly crumpled in a tissue. "Call the lawyers."

"Mine too," Elton thundered back. "And my agent."

Both combatants scuttled back to their corners. Elton snatched the phone right out of Sam's hand and began to dial himself. *Must be a special kind of guy to know his lawyer's number by heart.* Ms. Goddard finally looked around as if seeing them for the first time. "What are you doing here? Sam, get the contestants out of this room, immediately!"

Sam, half bent over in an apology, began to hustle them out. "Come on, nothing to see here. You should be down in the lobby. Go, go, go."

"And Sam," Ms. Goddard said over her shoulder. "No one is to talk about this. Understood?"

"Yes, ma'am."

The producer kept shoving them, first out of the room as London slammed the door, then toward the staircase. Jade chuckled under her breath, "Well, who had that on their bingo card?"

"Silence!" Sam shouted like the fist of God.

Ember reached over to take Ree by the arm. The poor girl looked to still be in shock, but as she caught her hand, Ree smiled and winked at Ember. "How's that for getting their attention?"

Chapter Twenty-Eight

"Seriously? Those two?" Booker asked Ember, who rolled her shoulder back and looked over to their guard. He'd been confused when one of the larger crew members had all but shoved him into the solarium. The second the girls joined him, he learned why.

Ember tumbled onto the couch beside him and Harriet took up the spot beside her. Jade kept pacing back and forth around the room, drawing the attention of the two men filling the doorways. They were effectively locked in with only speculation to keep them company.

"How long's this been going on?" he asked Ember, then looked to Logan's and Elton's partners.

"I had no idea." Harriet gasped. She'd been fiddling with a measuring tape, tugging it out and letting it slap back in. Another two cracks caused Jade to spin around and stare at her.

"Really? Not even an inkling from all the times he'd wander off for hours?"

"I thought he was..." She frowned. "Getting more supplies?"

"That's a believable lie to use. I'm certain no one will see through it."

"Like you're one to talk. You're so frigid, Logan chased after the first warm body he could find." Harriet finished with a sharp snap of the tape.

Jade scoffed and Ember reached over to take the measuring tape from her. "Ree, that's not fair."

"Isn't it? He cheated on her just as much as Elton cheated on me."

"Cheating implies that I give a fig where Logan sticks his screwdriver."

"This is all your fault!" Harriet shouted and leaped to her feet. Jade squared up as if she was ready to go a few rounds with the manic woman. Excited for a break from the doldrums, Booker sat up higher. Then he caught the worrying frown on Ember's lips.

Sighing, he stood up and raised his hands. "Ladies." He didn't touch either of them, but kept a palm at the ready to push them back. "Are they worth this?"

Jade was the first to break, stepping back. Harriet, however, seemed unable to let it go. "It's her fault. She couldn't keep him satisfied." She dashed forward as if to rip at Jade's hair, and Booker caught her by the shoulders. "Let me go!"

"No. You need to calm down."

"Why?"

"Because none of this is right," Ember spoke. "Where are the cameras? The producers? Why did they take our mikes?"

Harriet opened her palms and took a step back. Even still, Booker stayed between the two, half certain the country mouse was about to go full mountain lion.

"This is the juiciest plot line they've ever had on this show. Two of the male contestants found love—"

"That's one word for it," Jade quipped.

"But they're not filming us. They're keeping us penned up. Why?"

"What does it matter? We're out." Harriet buried her head in her hands. "All because he couldn't keep his pants on."

Jade snickered. "The best couple of the season is the one that can't stand each other."

Wait. Booker had been entertained at the salacious gossip, but he hadn't considered that Logan and Elton fucking around and being found out would eliminate all of their competition. "Ember?" he asked.

She raised her head and met him in the eye. "It's never happened before, but…"

"Come on, Emmy. You know as well as I do, even a hint of cheating and the couple's gone. Remember Tim and Monica? And all she did was hold Eric's hand. It's over. Done. Kaput. I didn't even get to show off my room." Harriet stared eye to glassy eye with the dead deer. Snarling, she smashed her foot into its side, crumpling the fiberglass frame. With a final whoomph, she flung herself onto the couch. "I hate that thing."

Ember kept fiddling with her fingers. Booker sat down next to her and cupped her hands. She stopped and lifted her eyes to him.

Holding tighter to her, he asked, "Does that mean all of this is gonna be over?"

"I…I suppose that's possible," she said when one of the huge men stepped back.

"All right, everyone on your feet." The executive producer stomped in. Somehow she looked even more like a white grape raisin than before. Her lips moved silently like she was chewing on the bones of her enemies. Ms. Goddard stopped in the middle of the room and crossed her arms. "Get up."

They looked to each other, then stood.

"What you think happened in that bedroom upstairs, didn't. You did not open the door, you did not even go looking for Mr. Brown. He was here the entire time helping to show off the room. Do you understand, Miss Smith?" She spoke with the force of God, willing the universe to reshape itself to her words, reality be damned.

For a moment, Harriet jerked her head in a quiet nod, then she clenched her hands. "No, I don't get it, 'cause he was in bed fuck—!"

"Ah, keep it PG."

"Why? Fuck knows Elton didn't."

Booker laughed. It was a quick, sharp one, and he tried to slap his mouth to hide it, but Goddard turned on him like a snake. She didn't strike, though he'd swear she was trying to will his soul out of his body.

"Miss Smith, if you intend to continue with this competition, then it would be in your best interest to forget what you think you saw. That goes for you as well, Miss Fairfax."

"So you're saying we're not cut?" Jade asked.

"That is..." Goddard said, when the two men of the hour stepped into the room. "Come in, gentlemen."

At first, they walked in side by side, then Elton grimaced and tried to dash ahead of Logan as if he had nothing to do with the man. The bumbling was awkward for everyone—Elton and Logan refusing to make eye contact and the women refusing to look at them.

"Your fate, Miss Fairfax will be decided in the elimination ceremony. Gentlemen!" Goddard shouted like she was about to begin a race. "Take your partner's hand and lead her into the ballroom. Now!"

Logan was the first to reach for Jade. She stared at it before sighing. "I hope you washed that," she said, then took it. Elton had a harder go of it. Every time he reached for Harriet, she'd slap his hand away. Eventually, Goddard walked over, clamped onto both of their wrists and forced their hands together. The two hung on but refused to look in the other's direction.

"March," London ordered.

As Elton and Harriet walked out at mental gunpoint, Booker held out his hand. "So much for winning this tonight," he said.

"Who knows?" Ember slipped her hand into his. Unlike the others standing at opposite sides of the hallway, she leaned close to him to whisper, "Anything could happen now."

* * * *

Clearly, they hadn't had time to set up the ballroom for the proper elimination ceremony. They were too busy dealing with contract lawyers to care if the candles were dripping wax all over the construction table. The producers were missing, leaving only Ms. Goddard behind the cameras. They were rolling, capturing every excruciating second of Jade and Logan, followed by Ree and Elton walking into place.

Booker began to take a step, when Ember held him back. Sitting just to the side of the candles was the box that held their switch cards. They couldn't seriously be thinking of...? "There's something I need to tell you."

"Is now the time?" he asked.

If her plan worked, there wouldn't be another chance. "Booker, Mr. Knightley, I've strangely enjoyed our time together. For good or ill."

He chuckled and pressed his lips closer to her ear. "And I with you, Miss Woodhouse."

"I want you to know that, no matter what, I think you deserve—"

"Orange team, get into frame!" Goddard shouted, snapping Ember out of her confession.

He shrugged, patted their clasped hands and said, "I guess it'll have to wait until later under the sheet."

Ember's gaze darted to the box. There wasn't going to be a later for her.

The lights dimmed on the contestants standing in a line. A slow clap of heels echoed from the dark. Ember squinted, trying to find the source. Ree stood next to her and pointed when a gleaming high heel walked into the spotlight.

Ah! Her eyes burned and she had to look away as a flash of silver burst into the light. A chorus of grumbles rose around her, people rubbing their eyes and cursing under their breath. Through a sheet of tears, Ember was able to make out their mystery host. Their ensemble was impossible to figure out, every silver sequin and diamond catching the light. They looked like a Christmas star going nuclear. Strangest of all, their mask—which only revealed their mouth and the whites of their eyes—was pitch black. It was so black it looked like they didn't have a face, just a talking mouth.

"Good evening, contestants," the bodiless teeth spoke. Ember yelped at the image and reached out. A hand caught her, holding her safe. The urge to peel out crying became a rhythmic drumbeat. But Booker took her elbow and soothingly ran his fingers up her forearm. Taking a breath, she was able to calm herself and listen to the host.

"…they're all quite fantastic. Not a dud in the bunch. Give yourselves a round of applause."

Ember blinked, uncertain why, but she joined in with the polite and unenthusiastic clapping.

"Now, I'm afraid, comes the painful part. As you all know, earlier today you voted on the switch. A bit late in the proceedings, but you know those wily producers, always keeping us on our toes."

A low cough from Ms. Goddard caused the host to spin around. The smile in the darkness sharpened and they continued as normal. "The rules, for those just tuning in, should love have not bloomed in their secluded cabins in the woods, this is a chance to find another hand to hold." The host gestured to Booker and Ember. As the camera zoomed in closer, they both dropped their hold and stepped to the side.

"*C'est la vie*. Everyone was asked to write their preferred partner on a card, then seal it in an envelope so no one could have a little peek. Should two people write down the same name, they will be paired together. If someone's on two cards we'll have a challenge, and if a person hasn't been picked—I'm afraid they'll have to leave Dower Estates. Understand?"

They all nodded, but the energy shifted. Instead of worry, the air crackled with rebellion. Being forced to rewrite their reality was only enraging. If Logan and Elton weren't kicked off tonight, it was possible none of the producers were walking away unscathed.

The host moved to the ominous box. First, they circled their hand over the front, then hefted up the hinge. "Please, take out your envelope." They held the box to Jade first, who scooped hers out, then moved down the line to Logan.

"This is stupid," Booker whispered. "They're going to have to change the teams now after those two were caught—"

"Mr. Knightley, your baseless speculation is interfering with our microphones. Please hold your tongue." Goddard's admonition rang out through the hall. Booker did as told, but he didn't look happy about it.

"Miss Smith?" The host extended the box to Ree.

She picked up her envelope, then waved it around. "Why am I doing this? I know what I wrote down."

"Because the rest of us don't, my dear. Ah, Miss Woodhouse. Hm, no Valentino tonight?"

Ember stared down at her sweater and laughed. "I'm afraid that I didn't..." The hairs on her arms stood on end. Goddard didn't speak the warning, but cast the threat into the air. "I thought that comfort would trump elegance tonight."

"An interesting idea. And Mr. Knightley. Now you, I expected in flannel. It accompanies you like a loyal golden retriever while the suit is more of an obstinate parrot."

"Uh, thank you," Booker said and pulled out the final envelope.

"Now that you've got your cards—" the host began.

"We open 'em?" Ree asked, reaching for the flap.

"Not quite. Let's do this orderly. Miss Fairfax, if you please? Open the card, then read out the name."

She threw on a pageant smile as the cameraman rolled the dolly closer. Jade flicked open the seal and pulled out her card. In a tight hand, it revealed the name, "Elton Brown."

Ree gasped, though not with any real fire. It sounded rehearsed and as if she'd been told to do it earlier by producers.

"Interesting. Care to explain why?"

"No offense, Harriet, but I wanted to work on a real challenge. Actually get my hands dirty, and whatever they're doing in the sunroom is painful."

"So it's a professional partnership you seek?" the host asked while taking her card away and handing it to an intern off camera. Jade answered with a shrug and leaned back.

"Mr. Churchill. Shall you flag or fail?"

"What?" Logan asked.

"Never mind, please reveal your card and explain why."

He ripped the envelope to shreds and twirled his answer in his hands. "I picked Jade because she's hot. And she likes to do all of the work."

Why for a moment did Ember think that he'd be a good partner? He was arrogant, lazy and seemed to be of the mind that anything attractive belonged on his arm or sucking his dick. Ember shivered at what nearly was and whispered a prayer for dodging that bullet.

"Logan," Ash cried from the shadows.

"Er, I mean, I've enjoyed our time working together and want more to get to know her better. How's that?"

"Fine, we'll fix it in edits. Move on," Goddard ordered.

"Mr. Brown, you've had quite an exciting time here," the mystery host said and Elton choked. The others coughed to keep from laughing while the Artist calmly smiled. "From once host to contestant possibly entering the final two. How does that make you feel?"

"Grateful for the opportunity you've given me."

"And if you were to win...?"

"I'd donate the money to charity, of course," Elton said with the same smile that'd open every episode of *Constructing Love*. He slit open his envelope and held up his card. "Harriet, of course."

"Interesting. Do you want to explain why?"

Elton stared the host dead in the floating eyes, then glared into the darkness where the producers lurked. "Because we have a real connection," he said. His voice was sincere, but the camera didn't pick up on his fist crushing the card with another name scratched out and Harriet's written over top.

"Delightful. Now we come to Miss Smith. You've had quite the day as well. Eventful."

"Yes. Getting that deer inside was a challenge, but I managed it." Harriet spoke with excitement, her cheeks flushed. But she kept twisting the envelope back and forth as if she wanted to throw it onto the ground. A bit strange. Ember had rescued her from having to spend another second with Elton. They'd certainly pair her with Booker now. And while Logan's place was threatened, they'd have to get rid of Elton to save face. It was perfect.

Ree began to tug on the little sun sticker at the center of the flap, then she froze. "You said we were to put down whoever we wanted to partner with, right?"

"Yes."

She peeled the sticker off and lifted the flap, only to stop again. "And that it could be anybody we wanted to get to know better?"

"Miss Smith, we don't have all night," Goddard chastised.

"Right. Sorry. Um..." She tugged out her card and flipped it to the camera. With tears in her voice, Ree read out, "Robert."

No. Ember stared at the monitor, certain that she had misspoken. She fumbled in saying Booker. But clear as day, in large, girlish handwriting, she'd put down Robert. Ember's chest compressed. Her breaths shallowed and she tried to pull on the neck of her sweater.

"That's an interesting choice. We've never had someone write down an already eliminated contestant before."

A low pitch siren whined in her ears, Ember struggling to keep upright. The darkness circled tighter around her as every plan, every calculated move, crashed to the ground.

"I guess, I just. They said to put down someone you liked, and I liked him. Even if he got cut early, I wished, hoped that maybe—"

"How could you?" Ember fumed, turning on Harriet. The girl's eyes were wide like headlights on a Beetle. "Do you have any idea what you've done?"

"I voted for the person that I—"

"You selfish, imbecilic—" Hands caught around her waist, pulling her from Harriet before she lashed out.

"Hey, come on. Calm down," Booker said loudly. He locked her in tight, pressing her back to his chest. She tried to fight him off, but he refused to let go. He didn't understand, he had no idea what Ree's pathetic attempt at wooing a man of minimal stature meant for him. He should be backing her up.

"Emmy, I'm..."

"You're sorry. You should be. Do you have any concept of what your selfishness has cost?"

She expected Harriet to at least hang her head in shame, but the dog bit back. "Do you have any idea how exhausting it is putting up with you?"

"Excuse me?"

"Harriet, do this. Harriet, say that. Harriet, be with the man that hates you!" She waved her hand at Elton who was trying to edge away from all of this. "You keep telling me to do things. Ordering me around like I'm your personal windup toy."

"I was helping you."

"Were you? You helped me to make a fool of myself on television. You helped to break my heart. To think that I could become a movie star's girlfriend. To walk in on him fucking another man."

"Whoa. Okay." People rushed to Harriet trying to get her to shut up. Sam in particular got her attention. The producer kept whispering in her ear, assuring her she had done the right thing.

"You're a traitor, Harriet Smith," Ember snarled.

"And you were just helping yourself, Ember." Ree raised her chin and turned away.

The host approached, the only one daring enough to deal with Ember. "And then there were two," they said. "Miss Woodhouse?"

"She has no idea what she's done. This place, the...the resort, the history. The King's Retreat." Ember choked, tears gushing as all of her failures bubbled to the surface. She'd forced Ree to flirt with a man who had treated her like garbage. She'd chased after another with cotton fluff for brains. And, in trying to save him, she had doomed Booker.

"That's...interesting, but could you open your envelope?"

"No!" Ember clutched it tight to her heart and shook her head.

"Miss Woodhouse, please. Before we die of old age."

It was a good plan. It would have worked if Harriet hadn't—

"Ember? What's wrong?"

Her heart sank at the tender plea in his voice. She'd hardened it in preparation for tonight, knowing that even if she walked away at least he'd get what he needed. Now... Ember sniffled, unable to face Booker.

With shaking hands, she slit open the seal and began to pull out the card. "Booker. I need to tell you something. The plan, there was a plan to—"

"Ember?" He stared down at her fingers clutching tight to the card. Then his eyes went wide. "What did you put down?" he thundered and wrenched the little yellow card free.

"Logan?" Rage and betrayal competed in his voice. She prayed for his sake that the anger would win, but a haze of tears wobbled in his eyes. A thousand pins stuck into her chest and she fought to breathe.

"Booker, please. This wasn't supposed to happen. I was..."

"You didn't mean to write down Logan fuckboy Churchill?"

Ember pursed her lips tight, her heart fluttering like a broken-winged sparrow.

"Unbelievable." He gripped the card as if to tear it into pieces. "After everything, I thought that you... Seems I got played as bad as everyone else." With his back to her, he shoved her card at the Artist.

"Booker, I didn't mean for you to be. I never expected for Harriet... She was supposed to—"

"Stop. For fuck's sake, just stop." The wobble in his voice caused her tears to fall. Without thinking, she tried to dab them away with the cursed envelope still in her hand. Ember hurled it to the ground, then stomped it to pieces.

"Well." Their mystery host stepped into the center stage. "That's a twist. Mr. Knightley, I'm afraid that as no one has your name on their card—"

"Yeah. I get it. At least that is a stab to the front," he muttered.

"I will have to ask you to pack your bags and leave—"

Booker didn't even wait for them to finish. He yanked off his microphone pack, hurled it in the direction of an intern and walked away. Ember wanted to run after him, to explain what had happened. But she was frozen, terrified that talking to him would only make him despise her more.

"I'm afraid, Miss Woodhouse, as you also do not have your name on any card..."

She didn't care. Sniffling, Ember tried to suck in her tears. She nodded and said in a raspy voice, "Thank you for the opportunity." She'd planned a little exit speech singing the praises of Ree to help Booker achieve his dream. But none of it mattered. Two interns helped her to pull off her microphone pack, then one took her by the arm and led her out of the light into total darkness.

Far in the distance, she heard the host say, "Congratulations. You are our final two teams and will be fighting to the end with an elaborate grand opening celebration."

Ellen Mint

She expected to be guided to the cabin and watched over as she packed next to a fuming Booker. But as they pushed open the front door, Ember spotted her luggage sitting in the drizzling rain. They'd already packed it up, probably while waiting for a call from the lawyers. This wasn't a game, nor a test of skill. It was planned from the beginning. All of her machinations were nothing more than a kid playing tic-tac-toe against the producers' omnipotence.

"Please pick up your luggage and go to the second car," the intern said before heading back inside.

Ember gazed out at the grounds. A pair of muddy footprints trailed off. Lightning lit the horizon and she spotted a dark car, steam sputtering from its tailpipe. Without thinking, she ran into the rain shouting for him.

"Booker! Please, don't go. Not yet!" She slammed her palms to the back window, planning to keep at it until he responded.

Slowly, the tinted glass rolled down. He wouldn't look at her, his face in shadow. "Miss Woodhouse."

"Ember," she said.

"Miss Woodhouse! Given all that you've done to me, I think it's best if we never speak again."

"Booker?" she pleaded, needing him to understand.

He shivered and, for a moment, looked at the woman in a cashmere sweater standing in the dripping rain for him. Wordlessly, Booker handed her an envelope, then he called for the driver to get them the hell out of here. "There's nothing left for me."

Numb, Ember stumbled back, barely avoiding the mud flung off of the tires as Mr. Knightley vanished into the night. Shivering, she popped open the envelope and looked. In a steady and certain hand he'd written only one word. "Ember."

Chapter Twenty-Nine

His fist thudded against the door, every ounce of energy drained. It didn't take long to open, a wary eye peeking through the gap before his brother threw it open wide. "Bookie, what are you doing? You coulda just come in."

"I know." Booker shrugged off his jacket. Winter had hit hard in the past few weeks. He moved to place it onto the coat rack, but it slipped and landed on the shoe pile. It'd take nothing for him to pick it up, to arrange the coats so his would have somewhere to hang. But even that tiny bit of energy was too much for him. He left his jacket and stumbled into his brother's living room.

A random college basketball game ran on the TV while his niece and nephew played with two wooden Christmas ornaments. Their tree was up, the tinsel dangling by the side.

He'd missed Thanksgiving, being trapped in isolation for the show. If they'd eliminated him one episode earlier, maybe he wouldn't have had to eat a turkey sub sandwich on a hotel bed while watching *Peanuts* balloons stroll past.

"You want a beer?" James asked. Booker answered with a slow nod, and his bro cracked, "Then get it your damn self. Your legs ain't broken."

"I'm surprised they didn't take a sledgehammer to them." Booker kept talking even as he eased into the family kitchen. A stack of bills for their construction job sat on the table. His brother had to take over while he was off wasting his time and life on the show. Booker hadn't even gone back to the worksite yet.

After coming up empty in the fridge, Booker fished a lukewarm beer out of the pantry and popped the top. "You know they actually ran a — "

"Guy over. Yeah, you said. Though then you said you weren't supposed to say so. I'm waiting for a letter from their lawyers to pop up any day now."

They wouldn't let him go to the vending machines, buy a toothbrush or take a shit without signing stacks and stacks of NDAs. All to keep the truth of *Constructing Love* a secret. When Booker had landed back home, he'd done so as they'd put the fear of God into him. Not a word had fallen from him as he'd gotten in the car and rested his head against the window. Once they had hit the freeway, it had come gushing out.

From the recesses of his brain, he kept expecting someone to rush over. To cluck their tongue at his indiscretions. To tell him to repeat an action so they could get a better shot. The freedom that should have been a relief became unnerving. The worst parts of the show were when he forgot he wasn't alone. What if he wasn't even now?

"If I'm going down, I'm taking you with me," Booker said, taking a long drink of piss-warm beer. He fumbled into the armchair, his back aching as he tried to focus on the old oak tree through the window. A broken swing haphazardly spun in a circle, the chain long since snapped and never repaired.

"Look, you tried and you failed. It was a long shot anyway, thinking we could get the King's Retreat back. Nana would..." His brother's voice caught. There wasn't even a headstone on her grave because they didn't have the money for it. "You know she'd think you were a fool for trying."

"Probably," Booker admitted. He'd put up with all of that for his family. As if anyone could right an injustice in this world on their own. If it was old enough, it became 'a thing of the past, from a different time.' Bringing it up was unkind, unpleasant. And the last thing a man like him wanted to be dubbed was unkind. A fool, though, he could live with.

"I still can't get over my brother on a romance show. During the first date, did you awkwardly tell her the difference between wood screws and nails?"

He didn't think about her. Oh, her betrayal burned a hole through his brain deeper than a cigar could. He obsessed with that late at night or while walking up and down the side of the road. He'd been a damn fool to trust her, to believe for one second that Miss Woodhouse had...

Like James said, he was a bore, a man who cared only about construction. Decrepit and exhausted, he was the kind of man any vibrant, young woman would run from. Hating her was easy, but his brain couldn't keep twisting a thought over and over in the dark edges of sleep — did those scheming producers have something to do with that? Did they talk her into it? Did they hope to save their golden boy before the rest of them realized he was fucking the old host?

Or was it Miss Woodhouse yet again grasping beyond her reach?

"Hey, Bookie?"

Booker blinked and focused on his brother. "Yeah. You're right. Any woman would be a fool to want anything to do with me."

She might be infuriating, exasperating, meddlesome and stubborn, but Ember Woodhouse was no fool.

He didn't think about her, but he dreamed of her— her lips fluttering with her opinions before parting for a kiss. Her legs wrapped around his waist as she ran her fingers through his hair. Her eyes vibrating with excitement while she talked about her decor ideas. And her smile, not the pageant-ready one, but a little crooked one that only appeared when she would look at him across the room. In the world between waking and dreams, his heart pretended it wasn't broken beyond repair.

"When do you have to go back?" James asked.

Booker leaned against the headrest and closed his eyes. "Not for another month." He hoped his heart would be hardened to cement by then. Otherwise, he'd make himself an even greater fool in front of the whole world...all because of Miss Woodhouse.

* * * *

"Scoot over," her sister Bella said, shoving Ember across the couch. Ember curled up on the other side, leaving a wide gulf. She tucked her feet under her and fiddled with her phone even though she had put it in airplane mode last night and hadn't found the courage to take it off.

"You don't have to be here," Ember repeated what she'd been telling her family since she'd landed.

"Don't be silly. You're gonna be on TV. Though where's your gaggle of friends?"

Two were in Europe, one was hiking through Christmas and the rest she didn't know or care about. Inviting people to watch her downfall while she was trapped in the room with them was a level of masochism Ember couldn't handle. She messed with her phone, threatening to open any one of her social apps, then sighed. Dropping her phone to the couch's arm, Ember cuddled a pillow tight to her chest and stared blankly at the screen.

As the logo for *Constructing Love* vanished, she visibly winced. They had to start with him, of course.

"Most people can swing a hammer well into their forties," he said, his lips wavering as if he was fighting a sneer. Then he crossed his arms and declared in a finishing move, "I'll be fine."

"He's quite the charmer," Bella mused before taking a single piece of low-everything popcorn. "He certainly makes the girls want to flee to the other side of the room."

Ember didn't respond, just watched as they quick-cut through the other contestants. For a brief moment, poor Brent got to speak, far more than he ever had to them. Then it slipped into a montage, showing quick highlights—some she didn't even remember. It was nothing more than a flicker, but spliced between Logan hefting a box onto his bare shoulders and Augusta's fateful run and leap was a moment. A second, really, caught through the leaves of Ember taking Booker's hand as he helped her out of the boat.

Her breath caught and she buried her face into the pillow.

"No."

She blinked, mostly certain she didn't exclaim that, and turned. A look of disbelief and disgust stampeded across her sister's face. "He is not the one you've been moaning about."

"Well…" She wouldn't call it moaning… More a trench of depression dug by her bare fists.

"Come on, 'ber, he's so old and grouchy, like a crotchety grandpa."

Grouchy she couldn't argue with but the grandfather part… "You haven't seen him shirtless," Ember said, moving her queen into place and fully missing her sister's armed bishop.

"Shirtless? What happened to your year of celibacy? Or have you already reached enlightenment and are free to…enjoy old shirtless men?"

"He's not." She wanted to argue that Booker wasn't that much older than her, because when she thought about her life coach, a sickening sourness bubbled in her stomach. She'd tried to keep her mind free from the clouding influence of her libido, to let her hormones find balance away from the pressing force of testosterone. It had left her angsty, nervous, lonely and desperately horny.

She might call herself a failure if being in Mr. Knightley's arms wasn't the first time she'd felt whole. Moaning, Ember bent over, burying her face into the pillow. She wanted to scream into it and also sob her heart out.

"Whoa, sis, it's okay."

It wasn't until Bella started rubbing her back that Ember realized she was doing both. Tears dripped down the expensive fabric, revealing her failure to the world.

"There's plenty of fish out there."

"Mr. Knightley was stubborn beyond measure. Patronizing at the best of times and downright callow at the worst. He..."

Ember gulped as the in-couch speakers blared her own words back to her.

"You're boring. And no one wants to watch boring. No one wants to fall in love with boring," past Ember declared with drunken certainty. For his part, Booker only looked amused at her declaration, as if he didn't care what she thought. All her life, men would tell her what they thought she wanted to hear just long enough to get her in bed, then they reverted to their true form. Booker was the first man to just be — be infuriating, be challenging, be...so much more than she'd ever met.

On the surface he was boring — a quiet man who kept to himself and only wanted to talk business. But inside was a passion for creating, for justice, for fixing the wrongs of this world, and she was entranced by it.

Entranced? Was that really how she felt about Booker Knightley? So her entire body ached and she could barely get out of bed because she had accidentally hurt him. And she couldn't stop sobbing in the shower with the spray turned to jet so no one would hear. That didn't mean anything.

"Ber, what's wrong? You were hopping over the moon when you joined the show. Now you don't want to talk about it."

I fucked up. Three simple words even a parrot could repeat. But for Ember, having to admit that she had failed so badly at playing the game she had lost everything for him was a hundred knives to her heart. And it was just a ball of soggy lint in her chest.

"I don't think I came off very well in this show," Ember mumbled.

"Don't be silly. Everyone loves you. Right, Daddy?"

Ember twisted her head around as their father stopped marching across the room. He dropped the phone from his ear and glanced to the couch. "My princesses, what are you up to?"

"We're watching Ember's show. It's the premiere episode."

"Ah, my little flame." Their father abandoned his phone on the table behind the couch to sit between them. An accountant struggled to be heard from his banishment. "What did I miss?"

"Not much, just fluff mostly. Now we're at the fancy party. Oh, and some idiot got his ass ran over by the limo," Bella summed up while Ember kept fiddling with her phone.

"Dower Estates is a gorgeous manor home resort with seven private cabins deep into the forests just outside the sleepy town of Hartfield. Its past is rich with history."

That was it. They didn't mention how it used to be owned by a black family pre-Jim Crow. How they had offered people like them a refuge from hate, how jazz legends had rocked the ballroom or how they had given succor to the homeless during the Great Depression. It had history, a history no one on production wanted to talk about.

Ember glanced over to her father, an adorable man who was whiter than mayo. It was no secret that his father had cut him off when he had brought home a new wife from Hawaii, but it didn't matter. He had gone on to make his own company and build his fortune. Not too long ago, their family would have been chased from the fancy hotels they stayed at, denied entrance to the clubs they financed and their parents' love would have been outlawed.

A spark flickered inside her. It struggled against the damp rains of depression telling her this was pointless and she was worthless. She wasn't a fool—she knew she'd ruined any chance she had with Booker. But that didn't mean he couldn't get his happily ever after.

Sitting up, Ember flipped her phone off of airplane mode. It blew up with notifications. She ignored them all and went hunting. They needed the world to know what had happened to the King's Retreat, and she needed an army to make so much noise no roomful of lawyers could ignore it.

It would work. It had to work.

The show's bumper pulled her from her phone. She had three weeks until they returned for the reunion episode and the winner was crowned. Three weeks to set the world on fire.

Ember typed a quick DM to the only person from the cast she thought could help her.

What do you know about the real history of Dower Estates?

It took a minute for a response to appear.

Chapter Thirty

The limo door opened and Ember eased out one bare leg. December's chill showed no kindness, shocking her skin into instant goosebumps, but she kept her smile locked in and rose to face not just the manor but the dozens of cameras zooming in around her. Light flooded from the main house across the snowy path.

"Welcome," a dark silhouette called from the main door. Ember eased over the slippery gravel in her stilettos and a warm hand caught hers. "Miss Woodhouse, so delightful to see you again. And in a...Dior?"

"Our mysterious host." She greeted them with a smile. "Your mask is fascinating." It was made of broken pieces of a mirror set into bone-white porcelain. She could see not only her fractured reflection, but also the black lenses looming behind.

"I was inspired by this live event. Don't want to miss a second of it, do we?"

Ember's fake smile turned devious. "No, and I dare say this is going to be one reunion no one will forget."

"Well, get on inside. Grab a glass of champagne. Try the gray stuff."

"It's delicious?"

"Positively atrocious, but that's what makes it fun." The host guided her inward with a laugh, then turned to face the darkness as another limo pulled up.

Men in butler outfits stood at the ready to usher their victims into the ballroom, but Ember couldn't help but stop to look in at their lobby. The air stank of fresh carpet glue and paint, as if they'd just finished fixing this up a few hours before the cameras rolled in. She prepared herself for any eventuality. It was normal for the finalists to redo everything for their own tastes. But as she peeked around the corner, her heart sank. Someone had pulled the alcoves clean off of the wall. All of the antiqued wallpaper had been ripped down and everything painted white. The only saving grace was the desk he'd built. It remained, even if it too was covered in beige paint.

"This way, ma'am."

She offered no resistance and walked beside one of the butlers she remembered as a teamster from before. They were practically popping out of their cummerbunds, and two obviously couldn't be talked into a clean shave. Ember tried to ignore the giant guards, but her heart couldn't stop fluttering. If tonight went the way she'd been planning, there was a good chance one of those large men might toss her out on her ass.

They approached the ballroom to find the door closed and Sam sitting at a desk outside. She glanced up, then reached behind her. "If you could wear this."

She placed a corsage of a yellow and red rose on the table. The symbolism was running around bare-assed screaming at the top of its lungs. No doubt they were going to play up her cruel and callow nature.

She hadn't watched the last episode. She hadn't had time, but had heard enough from her friends that Ember was the villain of this story. After sliding the corsage onto her arm, Ember held it up next to her tight black dress and asked, "How does it look?"

"Like you're going to get your arm torn off."

Her heart plummeted. She'd expected to face him inside, or better yet with a cocktail in hand. To at least have backup. But no, behind her stood the man who couldn't leave her thoughts. *Damn.* In the interim, he'd grown a short beard with the sharpest edges outside of a razor. His tux was custom tailored to fit his frame, leaving Ember's knees wobbling.

"I half expected you to be in flannel and jeans," Ember said, doing her best to keep her jaw off of the floor.

He chuckled a moment, then frowned. "They were strict on the dress code this time."

"As if you'd listen to a few lousy producers."

"Mister Knightley, wear this." Sam pushed over the same floral arrangement as hers, only this time as a boutonnière. Booker stared at it as if in shock. No doubt the only time he'd had to wear one was to a prom or maybe while ushering for a wedding. Ember scooped it up before he could and pulled out the pin. Turning to face him, she tugged on his jacket and eased the pin through.

She was so focused on her task, she forgot about everything until he whispered through gritted teeth, "What are you doing?"

"I'm..." She shoved the pin through, adjusted the roses then stepped back. "Trying to speed this up. If you will excuse me, I have friends to greet. Mr. Knightley."

The door opened and she took a step inside. A soft voice, so quiet it was easy to ignore, said, "You look nice."

As she turned around in disbelief, certain she had imagined it, the door slammed closed. This was to be Ember's arrival, not Ember's and Mr. Knightley's. Raising her chin, she gazed out at the festivities. They'd gone all out decorating for this ball.

Instead of the pumpkins and leaves from their season, fir garlands and red baubles dangled from the mezzanine. A projection of two snowflakes danced across the floor and lights rained down from the dark sides like tumbling snow. It was a winter wonderland heated to a thousand degrees.

"Announcing Lady Woodhouse," the first butler called from the side.

All the guests' heads swiveled to take her in. Ember raised a small hand and smiled, hunting through the sea of faces. She grew concerned, not recognizing the long scowls. Had this fallen through? Had the producers caught on?

Worry bubbled inside of her, until she spotted her accomplice speaking to a face she recognized from a profile picture. Smiling, Ember scooped a champagne flute off of the tray and wandered toward them.

"Miss Fairfax," Ember said, raising her glass as if in a toast.

"Miss Woodhouse. Or, sorry, should I call you lady now?"

"Does this mean all the men are lords?"

Jade snickered. "As if they need bigger egos."

Looking around over the lip of her glass, Ember spotted the early castoffs. Poor Brent was hobbling around on crutches and it looked like Augusta was in a cast. The others were less injured but still as uncertain about this. To the other side stood Elton, boring someone with another of his brushes with celebrity tales.

Toward the stage stood Harriet in a far nicer dress than Ember had ever seen her in. The gang was all here, save one. "Where's the golden child?"

"Logan?" Jade choked on her drink a moment, then turned to her. "You didn't hear? Turns out Logan Churchill was in fact Logan Roy, of the Canadian Roys."

"Oh. How did anyone find out?"

"He stole a forklift and drove it into town. Literally, he crashed it through the town hall. I swear, Goddard was willing to bribe all of ICE to keep him here long enough to film the ending. It was quite the day."

"You've been doing all the work on your own?" Ember asked and Jade shrugged.

"It's hardly the first time. Should we pour one out for our fallen comrade?"

Ember raised her glass along with Jade. "To the end of the saga of golden boy Logan." Both women tipped their flutes so a single drop hit the floor. Then they giggled and took a long drink.

"Announcing Mister Knightley," the butler boomed. All eyes turned to the man looking ready to bolt. She'd expected him to be growling. She could handle a grumpy Booker, or an enraged one. But he looked like the last of the wind had flown from his sails, and all that waited before him was the endless, unbroken sea.

"Are you ready for this?" Ember whispered.

"The better question is if you are. I don't know if this grand gesture will do much to defrost that ice man."

Strangling her flute, Ember tried to tear her eyes off of him. "Mr. Knightley and I are nothing more than acquaintances at best. My concern is only in preserving the history of this grand hotel."

It didn't look like Jade believed her, but they both clocked the producers watching them from the side. Smiling, Jade said, "I think tonight is the best time to shed a little light on that rather dark subject."

"Speaking of, I should go say hello to Harriet. Good evening." Ember started to dash off to join Ree fussing with a solitary Christmas tree in the middle of the floor.

"Can I count on your vote?" Jade called.

Raising her voice, Ember said, "What do you think?"

"Emmy!" Harriet shouted and damn near leaped at her. Ember barely had time to move her half-full glass away before Ree nearly hurled her to the floor. "It's been so long."

"Five weeks."

"Really? Feels like forever. I've been so busy with this manor. They gave me your lobby and I tried to spruce it up a bit, make it more modern, you know."

Ember pursed her lips, but kept smiling. "I see."

"And did you see? He's here. I mean, I knew he'd be here, but I didn't. Should I talk to him? Yes? No?"

"You are supposed to be gathering up votes, aren't you?"

Harriet froze in her random explosion of energy and stomped her shoes down. They gapped at the backs of her ankles, making her look like a child playing dress up. "That's what they said to do."

"And you always do what the producers tell you to."

"Is this about the name switch thing? Emmy, I was... I had to follow my heart. If anything, I should be mad at you. Do you have any idea how humiliating it's been having to work with him and act like everything's fine?" Harriet whispered fast, tugging Ember down to her level while she jabbed directly at Elton. There was no way anyone in the room missed that.

She should be angry at her — she'd ruined Booker's best chance. She'd gotten Ember kicked out as well, and for what? A silly romantic gesture that'd amount to nothing other than making her look foolish?

"Ree." Ember took a steadying breath. "I'm sorry. I was... It was blind of me to push you into being with a man who so clearly had eyes for another." A few others, at least. "And I think you should speak with Robert. Tell him how you feel."

"Really?" she squealed, dancing closer toward him, before frowning. "But I thought you said he was boring."

Sighing deeply, Ember glanced toward Mr. Knightley, no doubt talking about the lengths of nails with Mr. Martin. "I'm coming to realize that there's an excitement in boring."

The lights dimmed and a booming voice ordered, "Ladies and gentlemen, we need you to gather on the risers as instructed. Contestants, please take your seats. The live show's about to begin." One of the interns dashed over to take Harriet by the arm.

"Good luck," Ember said before the girl was plucked away. Ree gave her one last thumbs-up and began to talk the intern's ear off about Robert. Running the lip of her glass against her mouth, Ember caught Jade. The woman gave a single cursory nod, then took her seat.

Throwing back her drink, Ember steeled her nerves for what was to come.

Chapter Thirty-One

This was a terrible plan. One he was contractually obliged to commit, but still terrible. Booker shifted, wishing he could kick off his paper-sole dress shoes, strip off the rented tux and flee into the night. He hadn't planned to talk to her, or even look at her the whole night.

But there she'd been, in a bombshell black dress with the same 'I can handle the world' smile and all those walls he'd built brick by brick for the past month had shattered to pieces. When she'd picked up that flower and pinned it to his chest, he hadn't been certain if he would slap it away or kiss her. For a moment, he had feared he might do both.

"My mom put together a watch party. Every week she'd invite more and more people over. Even when I was kicked off."

Robert's tale of woe faded as Booker did and did not watch Miss Woodhouse trade barbs with Jade. Strange she wasn't at her pupil's side, doling out her cheap wisdom in anticipation of her win. Though, he had to admit, Ember was at least right about the mousy country girl making it to the end.

Booker jerked at thinking her name. He scowled and glared at the whiskey glass someone had shoved into his hand. The sooner tonight was over, the quicker he could work himself to death to forget it all happened. Needing a burn of liquid courage, he raised his glass and his eyesight burrowed through the mass of strangers right to her. She moved like an assassin preparing to finish the job, people aware of her before she even had to say a word. Unsurprising she'd head to Harriet, but Booker couldn't look away.

So she's hot, so what? There are plenty of hot women who'd want a man pushing forty with a failing business. So there's a light about her that draws every damn person in the room to her. Just because she'd sworn off all men until you doesn't mean that there's anything special there. And maybe if in the little time you knew each other, her voice crawled inside your brain to the point you anticipated her objection before she even made it... Now you're not sure if you miss her opinions or just the sound of her making them.

She drew the tip of her finger across the petals of the red rose on her wrist. No doubt it was an involuntary action done without thought. She'd sabotaged him willingly. Used him for her game and got caught up in the same web. She probably hated him. So why didn't he hate her?

"Did you watch it?"

Booker jerked at the voice, then felt a soft flutter of petals against his finger. He'd been clutching to his chest, practically strangling the yellow rose. "No. I...what? Who?"

"Last week's episode." Robert cheered. "That was an exciting one."

The semi-finale, the one when Miss Woodhouse had played Mr. Knightley like a fiddle. He hadn't watched a single episode aside from the first his brother had tortured him with. But as hard as he had tried, the promos for the last episode were everywhere. He couldn't watch a video about caulking without having to see his heartbroken face as an ad before.

Booker spotted Elton easing around the room, then doing a one-eighty to avoid the producers. He didn't have to watch it to know the real juicy bits had been kept off of TV. "You don't know the half of it."

The lights dropped and a voice ordered them all to their seats. "I guess this is it," Booker said.

"See you on the other side, man." Robert clasped his hand and the two shared a quick pat on the back before he wandered toward the chairs in the middle of the floor. Booker hung back, trying to finish off his whiskey. Everyone else flowed toward the center of the room like obedient grains of rice.

Only Booker remained, putting his finished glass in the wash bin of the cart. He told himself he wasn't trying to psych up for this. That he had it all under control. He had to keep lying…otherwise he'd barrel through the cart and never stop running.

Taking a deep breath, Booker prepared to turn to face his future.

"I don't care which billionaire's balls you have to fondle, get that fucking hashtag off the trending page."

It hadn't been long enough for London Goddard's voice to escape his nightmares, and this time she sounded about to go full nuclear. He took pity on whoever was trying to corral her problem. "Ma'am, it's just that every call we've placed has gone ignored. We're trying to…"

"So help me God, Brian, if 'give it back' isn't gone by the time the live show starts, you won't work on another show for the rest of your life. Got it?"

As her heels clipped away into the distance, the intern squeaked, "It's Jim."

"Mr. Knightley, here you are. We need you sitting up front. The feed is about to go live." Ash found him struggling to piece together whatever had Goddard's garters in a knot. They'd told him to get on social media after leaving the estate, but Booker couldn't be bothered.

Hooking his arm around Booker's, Ash guided him to the chair that was near but not next to hers. Instead of putting them by teams, they'd separated the group down gender lines. Harriet and Jade both sat on nicer chairs at the front and slightly to the side while their masked host ruled from a throne in the spotlight. He wound up sitting next to Elton, whose puffy face and red nose couldn't be disguised by the thick pancake makeup. Booker tried to lean away from the man, fearing his breath might cause the air to combust, until he looked up to find her watching.

Choosing the drunk over heartbreak, Booker turned slightly in his chair as the lights burned above them. Straining, he looked to their mystery host who rose and said, "Welcome folk of gentle and more nefarious nature, to the season finale of *Constructing Love*."

The peanut gallery hemmed in on both sides of them began to clap. Slowly, the contestants raised their hands and began to do the same, though wary eyes darted to the puppet masters just off the side. The producers looked one hour away from popping champagne and forgetting all about the past two months and the resort.

"It's been quite an exciting ride, hasn't it?" the Artist asked. "Beginning with Brent. Poor Brent, how are you doing?"

He piped up from the back, "I've gotten back most of the feeling in my —"

"That's wonderful to hear. And Augusta. Why, you were wrenched so cruelly from the jaws of victory."

"It's her fault," Augusta called, pointing an accusing and bandaged hand in Jade's direction.

"Yes, yes, we all enjoyed the back and hand stabbing from a front-row seat. Let's reminisce about the good old days."

A small projection screen flickered and a hazy montage of moments from the show played. All the while, the host kept narrating, reminding them of Brent's accident, which was shown from three different angles and slowed down. Then Augusta's came up. When she leaped onto Logan, everyone in the audience hissed in sympathy. It'd looked even worse in real life. Booker swore they'd digitally removed some of the blood, though they did keep her panicking and running away from help.

All for the ratings.

"And of course, who could forget about" — the Artist's voice plummeted — "the romance."

In quick succession flashed Elton and Harriet on the boat, Logan trying to deadlift Augusta, Jade walking, Robert nervously talking to Harriet before Ember pulled her away. The montage ended on the first night. Not with Brent, or even the surprise of Elton joining them. It was Ember declaring he was too boring for anyone to love, then Booker hoisting her up onto his shoulder.

"They can't all be winners," their host said to moderate laughs.

A part of him wondered if he hadn't intervened and left her to the wolves, would she have wound up with Logan or Elton as a partner instead? But, as much as he wanted to wish for that outcome, deep in his heart Booker knew he'd have done the same all over again. He steeled himself for having to relive the last month in short clips and even shorter quips. Almost all of the footage of him and Miss Woodhouse involved arguing and quick glares. Some of them he didn't even remember, and others... He remembered how they had solved it away from the cameras.

"That's enough of that. Let's get to why you're here—crowning a winner. On Team Aqua we have... Sorry, we had the fair Miss Fairfax and what was to be Mr. Logan, but Logan has decided to forfeit his prize. I believe he's feeding needy penguins in the Arctic."

A single voice piped up from the balcony above, "But penguins live in the south."

"How fascinating," the host responded and stood taller.

"I have something I'd like to say." Elton stood up and the spotlights beamed on him, blinding Booker. "While it's been a blast being on this side and helping to restore this beautiful building with Harriet Jones..."

Her gritted jaws could have cut glass from him getting her surname wrong.

"I don't think it's in good taste for me to be in the running, so I too am bowing out. Thank you."

More people clapped than Booker could have ever expected, some even cheering and wiping away tears at Elton's surprising generosity. No doubt it was part of the deal that kept his little indiscretion off of TV. He waved his hand like a beauty pageant and returned to his seat.

"Well, that makes this easier. We have two sides. On one, sweet country girl Harriet Smith, who had a hand in gussying up the parlor you saw in the house tour and also decorated half of the guest rooms."

The screen flickered again as the lights dropped on them. A montage shot earlier of Harriet guiding them through her rooms played. Booker stared at his shoes. It was one thing to watch the one slip through his fingers. It was another to be tortured with the vacation photos of her honeymoon. If he couldn't fix up the manor, then it was best if he pretended no one did. Then he heard a single gasp and broke. For a brief second, he looked over to find Ember, her face twisted in horror as she held a hand above her mouth.

She must have sensed him watching as she too looked his way and mouthed, "Shiplap."

"Barn doors?" Booker asked and she held up two fingers, then laughed.

The lights rose and both jerked back into their seats, trying to pretend that didn't happen. "On the other side, we have Miss Jade Fairfax. Your Craftswoman of the year." Jade's slideshow started with the pinup image that'd graced every ad for the show before fading to the tour of her side of the building. Booker didn't watch, though he did keep darting over to Ember to see her looking more intrigued and approving.

"Jade and Harriet are the two finalists of *Constructing Love*," the Artist declared. The constant repetition was mind numbing, but Booker gave in to the clapping as the host moved in between the two of them. "Fellow contestants, will you please rise?"

Chairs squeaked as everyone stood. Brent called out for some help, then nearly face-planted into another chair reaching for his crutch. Slowly, they gathered at the front of the stage, circling Jade and Harriet like they were the monarchs and their host the jester.

"I want you to think carefully. Who of these two lovely ladies do you think has done the most exemplary job of turning this rundown resort into a hidden jewel? Who deserves to earn, if not love, a beautiful manor home in the forest? Please take a seat on her side."

Augusta was the first one to move, not even pausing as she damn near leaped into a seat on Harriet's side. "That was quick," their host remarked. "Why did you — ?"

Snatching the microphone from the intern, Augusta pointed at Jade and thundered, "That bitch stole my chance." She opened her hand to drop the mike and the intern scrambled to catch it. Crossing her arms and legs, Augusta leaned back in the creaking folding chair.

"The ice is broken. Let the backstabbing commence," the host declared, raising their arms.

Chaos ensued. People mumbled under their breaths as they circled back and forth. Booker was frozen in place. He didn't want either of them to win it. They didn't deserve it. They didn't build it. But he couldn't just stand by. They might ask questions and it'd only put the spotlight on his family. He looked to Harriet's side, quickly filling as Robert sat there — of course — and Brent hobbled over. His explanation was that he at least got to see Harriet on the limo ride. In fact, a lot of people sided with her because they had never met Jade.

The surprise to him was Ember. He thought she'd be the first on Harriet's side, cheering her on for a win. But she carefully stood dead center while staring not at the contestants or even the other winners. She was looking out at the audience in the dark. Why?

"Mr. Elton Brown!" the host squealed just as a chair did. The ex-host landed with a thud on Jade's side. "This is a surprise."

"Is it?"

"Were you and Miss Smith not growing close in your partnership?" the host asked, a Cheshire grin growing below the mask.

Elton flung his hand in exhaustion as if that could excuse the weeks of him pretending to be courting her. "The fact is, Jade's a better designer and builder. Hotter, too." He looked smug a moment, before his blotted eyes opened and he shouted, "Wait, I meant..."

"This isn't looking good for Jade," the host interrupted. "So far she's only got one vote to Harriet's three. Ah, wait, Milan's joined with Elton. Care to explain why?"

She pulled the mike closer with one finger and said, "No."

"Fair enough. I guess it's up to our remaining holdouts. Mr. Knightley, Miss Woodhouse, one of you could sit at Harriet's side and end this now. Or you could be left to cast the deciding vote."

He couldn't handle that idea. Booker looked over at Harriet and winced. If his family's place had to wind up in anyone else's hands, at least Jade's were competent. He stumbled past Ember for his original seat. But as he went, he caught her eyes and mumbled, "Sorry," just as his ass hit the chair, casting a vote for Jade.

"Three for three, this is exciting! Shame about Logan and his saving the seals."

"Penguins."

Booker braced himself to explain why he had chosen Jade without really knowing, but the host moved clean on past him to focus on Ember. The camera did as well, zooming in. Was this all planned by the producers? Had they told her to wait until the end and cast a vote for her protégée? Unease gurgled in Booker's gut at the thought of him being used, until he caught Ember. Her face was confident and cool, but she kept picking at her corsage, accidentally littering petals on the floor. She was nervous as hell and he wished he could rescue her.

"Miss Woodhouse, the fate of these two women rests in your hands."

The intern handed her the microphone and she took a deep breath. "Ree, I wanted you to win from the minute I met you. Your heart is pure in an uncaring world. You played no games and always acted as your..." Ember gulped, looking like she had to fight to get the next line out, "...acted as your true self and chose love."

Taking a breath, Ember turned to Jade. "We were not friendly. I realize now the acrimony between us was on me fearing that you could take down Harriet's chances. You are brusque in a way that I should find refreshing instead of revolting, and so talented that I should have taken it as inspiring instead of with jealousy."

A warm smile rose on Jade's face. Slowly, she nodded her head. Ember returned the nod and took a step back. Raising her hand, she stepped in between the chairs, walking closer to the camera. "The question before us is not who should win *Constructing Love*, but who deserves this beautiful, historically rich resort."

It started small, a single voice so quiet he thought it might be a passing truck or feedback. But then another joined it, and another. "Give it back," they chanted from the dark. "Give it back."

"Fucking hell," a producer cursed and directed the teamsters to go after the chanting audience. But they were too late to stop the people moving into the light. Some of them held signs, small ones bearing the hashtag they chanted.

What in the world is happening?

Booker tried to spin around, certain this had to be some twisted trick of the producers, but they were fuming. Goddard looked like her face was about to explode into a volcano of rage and filler.

Ember walked back, taking the place of the host who'd slipped off to the throne. The camera had to keep on her as she raised the mike and dropped the bomb, "This place was not always known as Dower Estates."

She wasn't...? Panic seized up Booker's legs and arms and his mind churned that his family's greatest shame was going to be revealed to the entire world. He took a step for Ember, hoping to stop her before she landed them both in hot water, but she barreled on without any concern for the consequences bubbling around them.

"Built by the King family in the early nineteenth century, the King's Retreat was to be an escape, a reprieve from the harshness of life. A place for those segregated and cast from society to revel in their fortunate lot, for the damned to find salvation, for a king to retreat."

One by one, the people who'd hustled into view of the camera turned their little signs over. Black and white images of his family greeting guests, running the old healing spa, clipping herbs and standing before the original manor house raced across the screen. Ember drew her hand below the pictures, highlighting each one.

"What the shit, Carl? You were supposed to vet the guests," Goddard shouted at an underling.

"I did. They're the attractive type of people middle America would find hot," possibly Carl said.

"Who the fuck are they?"

"Sorority girls and runners-up in the Craftswoman pageant."

Jade? Booker caught the woman leaning back in her chair like a queen enjoying the oncoming bloodbath. She had to be the one to put them up to it, but the only way she could know was if Ember...?

"This land, this beautiful resort which they built with their sweat and love was taken from them. Not by a greedy bank. No, they made it through the Great Depression unscathed. It was the state itself. The government stole it, claimed it as their own and kicked the King family out of their home without a penny to their name."

Her voice caught and for a brief second, she wobbled. Booker shifted, trying to squeeze his way closer to help. Ember snagged his eye and a hint of a smile rose on her lips. Raising her arm high, she declared, "This ballroom was built by Mr. Emmet King in nineteen twenty-one. He loved this place so much his family buried him on a hill overlooking it for eternity. That's what they stole from them. That's the injustice heaped upon the King family."

"Give it back. Give it back!" The chanters grew louder and waved their images like flags.

"If there is an ounce of decency in your bones, you will not award stolen treasure. You will give this place back to its rightful owner." She extended her hand, her eyes watering. The lights rose and a cameraman kicked over chairs and people in order to focus on Booker's face. "Mr. Knightley, the grandson of the last King."

The silence only fell for a second, a single gasp of surprise, before the chanters filled it. They stomped their feet, they clapped, they demanded without end. He gulped, staring into Ember's watering eyes. She had painted a massive bullseye on her back for no reason. There was nothing she could gain for her reputation or her business by sending not only lawyers for the show but the worst kind of people after herself.

Lowering the mike, Ember stepped away from the light. "Give it back," she shouted, pumping her fist in the air. Jade leaped up and joined in. Ember glanced over and draped a hand across her shoulders as they both kept it up. The air sizzled with the demand for justice. It circled Booker like a tornado.

He stood dead in the eye, fearing what would happen if he spoke. Outside the cries of jubilation with most of the cast joining in, the producers schemed.

"Cut the feed."

"We can't, it's live."

"Go to commercial, then."

"Can't do that either. Not for another three minutes."

"Then what the...?"

They were trapped. Either they kept up this game, threw the protestors, Booker, Ember, one of their finalists and half the cast out. Or they did the right thing.

She did it. She had made this happen...for justice?

Tears sparkled in Ember's eyes as she nervously bit her lip.

She did it for him.

"If I could say a word." A single voice cut through the cacophony, every syllable coming to a screech as their mystery host rose from the throne. With a wry smile, they reached up, and plucked the mask off of their face.

"It's legendary pop sensation Chantelle!"

"Thank you for that introduction, not an obvious plant," Chantelle said. Booker felt all of his many years as people gawped at the possibly familiar face. Everyone else looked to be in awe, ready to drop to their knees and offer up their firstborn. Even Ember seemed shocked at the reveal and he had thought she knew everything.

Chantelle plucked the mike from Ember's fingers and strode to the center of the room. "I believe there is only one path forward." They kept walking, dragging their gown's tails on the wood before coming to a stop right before Booker. With a quirk on their lips, they fluttered their eyelashes and shouted, "Give it back!"

Before he could think, Chantelle grabbed his hand and pulled him into the fray. The lines were drawn — justice versus injustice. Would the show choose fame or infamy as its legacy? The producers huddled for a quick talk, every headset and microphone ripped away so no one could hear.

"Ah, what's this?" Chantelle suddenly jerked up. They dropped Booker's hand and reached into the darkness. "After much deliberation by the judges, it has been decided that the winner of this season of *Constructing Love* is..."

They tried for a dramatic pause, but it couldn't last long. The protestors began again, shouting reasons why this was wrong, how no one deserved to win what was stolen.

"Oh for the... Of course they're giving it back," Chantelle declared and tossed a set of keys at Booker.

He caught them at the last second, in awe as the metal loops and teeth clanged against his palm. He'd done everything for this—mortgaged his business, chased down shadowy companies, signed up for a reality show, made a fool of himself on TV, let his heart break only to fail. In the end, it had taken her to make it happen.

It was always her.

"Well, give us a speech, Mr. Knightley. Or should I call you King?"

He snorted at the idea, tears falling, each one shed for the stories his grandmother would tell. The pain in her heart from losing her father to alcohol, her brothers to early graves, the shame of having everything stolen in the dead of night.

"I don't—" Booker said. He dabbed his eyes and slipped the keys into his pocket. Chantelle tried to shove the microphone into his palm, but Booker ignored it. "Miss Woodhouse," he began then reached for her hands.

She nodded, as if telling him what he already knew. She eased away from Jade and entwined her fingers with his.

"You are the most infuriating, quarrelsome, stubborn woman I have ever known." Booker gulped. Staring into her kaleidoscope eyes, he saw his future glinting back. "And I've realized I hate you."

Gasps of "What?" broke out, but he only cared about Ember. Watching the look of surprise, then joy and finally enlightenment race across her face filled his chest with hope.

"I think I hate you too," she said.

He pulled her into his arms, caring nothing for the cameras, for the people, for those who came to praise or kill him. All that mattered was her. "Miss Woodhouse," he whispered then kissed her. Those meddlesome lips melted into a sweet refrain. She wrapped her hands tight to the back of his neck and pulled herself taller, refusing to let him go, and he in turn held her without end.

"Mr. Knightley," she spoke, her mouth dancing against his with his name. "I believe I just secured you a house."

Laughing, he scooped her up off of the floor and spun her around. "You did. I don't know how. But you..."

"You were right." Her jubilation slowed and so, too, did Booker's manic spinning. They came to a stop and Ember traced her fingers down his jaw. "I did — I do — overstep, and sometimes my plans go awry in ways I never could have imagined. The last thing I wanted was to hurt you."

"I know," he said. He'd wanted to believe that she wouldn't have stabbed him in the back on purpose. That all of this, every mistake and misstep was done out of love. "Miss Woodhouse..."

"You know, I think the cat is free of the bag now," she said, jerking her head toward the camera.

Booker winced and looked over. He had forgotten about them, forgotten about everything beyond her. "Ember," he said her name, finding delight in voicing it. "I can't thank you enough for — "

"Everyone party!" a random intern shouted and barreled into Booker. A cork popped and champagne sprayed across the contestants and the happy protestors. Ember gasped, her smile infectious as he held her close and tried to shield her.

"That's never getting off of your dress," Booker said.

She stared down at her black number stained with champagne and shrugged. "As if I care." She leaped up to kiss him.

"This is the end of a shocking and winding *Constructing Love*. I've been your mystery host, Chantelle."

"And I'm Elton Brown."

"Hey, Elton," Goddard shouted from the edge of the set. "You're fired."

The party kicked into high gear once the camera lights fell. Robert asked Harriet to dance and they both stomped into the champagne puddles, laughing their heads off. Chantelle took to signing autographs and inviting everyone back for a karaoke contest.

"Congratulations." Jade slipped in next to them while watching the wild festivities. "Both of you."

"Thank you for all your help," Ember said. "She got the hashtag trending."

"I know a few people," Jade said with a modest shrug. "If you ever need a professional furniture builder for your resort..."

"You better believe I'm going to call you," Ember said and hugged Jade tight.

He had gotten the hotel and the girl. Booker thought he would return home empty handed. Instead, he was home at last.

"You know, those sconces could use an updating," Ember said, tipping her head to the side.

"Those are original. They're antiques," Booker argued back.

"They're rusting and about to fall off."

"All they need is a good refinish and they'll be good as new."

"Is that before or after they electrocute someone?"

Booker sighed. He'd just signed himself up for a potential lifetime of these arguments, and he wouldn't have it any other way. "Miss Woodhouse, shall we continue this debate in the master suite?"

She took his hand and he led them through the ballroom. "Gladly, but you should know, I always win."

"So do I," Booker said and kissed her.

Epilogue

Two years later

A light autumn breeze blew a single maple leaf through the intricate trellis on the wedding arch. Ember watched it slip past the rose thorns unscathed before landing in her hair. She had reached to pull it free when his fingers beat her to it. While she glanced her palm over his, Ember and Booker both forgot the fall foliage as she took his hand.

They stood together under the arch as the last of the sun's rays cut a scarlet path through the trees. Only the soft brush of the wind and the whisper of the falling leaves joined them. Ember gazed up into his eyes, all his armor stripped bare as she ran her fingers over his knuckles.

"Well?"

"You're right," he conceded.

Ember yelped in glee. "I told you it was just what this garden needed." She ran her hand over the curved wood, tracing the intricate designs no one would see in spring or summer as the flowers bloomed. It made it even more beautiful for a fall or winter wedding. "Jade went all out for this, don't you think?"

"Being the new face of Woodhouse Furniture, I'd say she has good reason to prove herself," Booker mused. He stopped fiddling with the roses and took her hands again. "You know, you are wearing white. No reason we couldn't test it out here."

She giggled. "I'm in a pantsuit. And you're... Who am I kidding, you would wear jeans and a flannel to your own wedding."

Booker had to drop her hands in order to pick up his tool box, though he kept close to her as they started back on the path for the front door. "And you would enjoy the hours and hours spent debating me into a tux."

Ember smiled and brushed her shoulder against his chest. "What makes you think I wouldn't be the one telling you to wear tight jeans?" She gave his ass an unladylike pinch. The tool box fell hard and he swept her up into his arms. She started to squeal in surprise before Booker lightly dipped then kissed her. Teetering on the edge of a fall, Ember's heart raced. She ran her fingers up his jaw, toying with the white flecks in his stubble. "You will be shaving, though."

"I thought shabby chic was in," Booker said.

"For rustic farmhouses and mason jar weddings, not handsome entrepreneurs rebuilding their family legacy."

He snickered. "Got it. There's just one little problem, though."

"What's that?"

"We aren't engaged." Booker loomed closer as if to kiss her, when a clopping of hooves broke them apart.

Adjusting her shirt, Ember looked up as their horse went trotting by. "Do you think the guests have taken to Bluebell?"

The rider, an exuberant man proud to be from Philadelphia, exclaimed, "Isn't this romantic, Brandy?"

The brown-haired woman clinging tightly to the back of him responded, "Yes, very. Quite romance."

"Your eyes are closed."

"Why are you looking at me and not the road? Path? Horse street? I don't know what it's called!"

"You're cute when your life's flashing before your eyes."

"And you're lucky I love you." She gulped on the horse, which was barely moving at a trot. Risking her life and limb, she peered over to find her man had turned around to face her.

"I know, and I thank God every day for it," he said, then kissed her.

Booker and Ember watched Bluebell dutifully clop back to the stable where the best hay awaited her. "I daresay they love it," Booker said. He wrapped a protective arm around Ember and the two started back toward the main house. The moment the furnace heat hit them, so too did a generous cry of jubilation from the new sitting room. All of Elton's old animal heads had been given a proper burial. Instead, the room was full of Harlem-inspired art. A painting of the first King family hung above the black marble fireplace. With the addition of a divider and one of Jade's dining tables, they were able to turn it into a private party spot.

Tonight, one of their famous guests was hosting a celebration for their friends. Still, Ember lingered close to the door. "Maybe I should peek in. See if they need anything?"

"I'm sure they've got it in hand," Booker said, before walking past her and pushing the door open. They tried to sneak in quietly, but their guest caught them right away.

"Woodhouse, Knightley," Chantelle shouted from their throne next to the fireplace. It was the same throne from the live show. Chantelle visited so often, they kept it in storage for them. "Come in, sit down. Have you tried this prime rib? It's fantastic."

"I may know the person who hired the chef," Ember said with a giggle.

"We don't want to be a bother." Booker tried to intervene, as if they had anywhere better to be.

"Tristan's insistence that he needs to be in bed by eight is a bother. You two are a delight."

"I've got an interview at five. I can't stumble into it exhausted and red-eyed without a thousand accusations being hurled at me," Tristan Harty complained. It took all of Ember's strength to not shout that she'd loved him when she was five as he'd walked through the door.

Chantelle leaned closer to the black-haired woman perched next to Harty. "My sympathies for your bother of a husband. Would you like to trade him in for another? I'm due to host yet another season of Constructing Love."

She laughed and patted Tristan on the hand. "It's all right. I think I'll keep him. I've got him broken in."

Tristan Harty, the uptight, blue-eyed teenage dreamboat, leaned closer to his wife and whispered, "That's not all we broke."

Thanks to the acoustics bouncing off of the windows overhead, every person in the room heard that. A red-haired woman coughed and took a long drink.

"Madeline, my darling, my dear, my greatest treasure," Chantelle called. "Don't worry yourself, Everett. I'm only interested in her kitten skills."

"I know," the blond man next to her said. "And I ain't worried for a second."

Madeline giggled and laid her head on Everett's wide shoulder. He swiveled to kiss her forehead. Ember couldn't help but sigh at the tender move, when Booker swept his arms around from behind. She'd never felt more safe than when he slept beside her. No fears clawed up her throat that he'd vanish into the night. More than safe, she was home in this beautiful resort tucked away in the trees.

"A toast," Chantelle shouted, raising a beer stein. The others lifted various wine and martini glasses. "To old, grouchy love." They looked to Tristan who sneered before his wife kissed it away. "To second chances." Chantelle glanced to Madeline and Everett, both of whom blushed. "And to the most perfectly mismatched couple I've ever met."

This time they raised their glass directly to Ember and Booker and gave a wink. Ember shook off the butterflies to keep it professional. "That's very sweet, Chantelle, but..."

Booker let go of her. She half expected him to return to work. There was a lot to do before they could break ground on the new honeymoon cabin. But instead of padding out the door, he slipped to her side and turned her to face him.

"Miss Woodhouse," he began and she laughed. "Ember. You are like trying to fight thunder. Impossible. Amazing. Unforgettable. Soul-quaking."

"And you are like trying to punch earth. Solid. Impenetrable. Stubborn. Safe." She drew her hand down his cheek.

"Bringing the King's Retreat back to life—not only saving it but restoring it to its original glory—is beyond anything I thought possible."

"I can't imagine a better life," she admitted.

"I can."

Ember jerked, shocked that he'd cut her down like that, then Booker slipped to his knee. "Oh my…"

"Miss Ember Woodhouse, you are the spark that keeps me running even in the darkest of days." Booker struggled to reach into his pocket. Everyone peered over, fully invested as a few curses slipped out. "This stupid, goddamn… There." Opening the box, he asked, "Will you—?"

"Yes!" she interrupted then dropped to meet him. As their lips met, a spark shot between them and they both leaned back to rub the sting away before returning for a second one. The little audience clapped and cheered, but Ember didn't care. She'd had her fill of public attention for a lifetime.

Holding her hand steady, Booker eased the ring onto her finger. "Do you like it?" he asked.

She tipped her hand back and forth, causing the ring to slide. "The band's too big and I'm worried there aren't enough prongs to hold the diamond safe." The words flew out without her thinking and she grimaced at trashing his gift. "I mean…"

Booker laughed and held her face in his hands. "That's a cheap fake from a grocery store. Do you think

I'm foolish enough to not let Miss Woodhouse pick out her own engagement ring?"

"You are adversarial," Ember said.

"And you are demanding."

"Obstinate."

"Infuriating," Booker whispered.

She wrapped her arms around him and whispered in his ear, "I love you, Mr. Knightley."

Want to see more from this author? Here's a taster for you to enjoy!

Coven of Desire: Veil
Ellen Mint

Excerpt

Layla

The box hit the floor.

The men's voices drifted in and out, bubbling with worry and confusion as the kitten batted at the flimsy brown paper. All I could do was stare, my mouth frozen as I held it up.

When the dim yellow light struck it, a rainbow burst into the air. It didn't follow the path of the light. Instead, the entire room transformed into pulsing color. The unicorn skin was more beautiful than I had ever imagined.

"He came through," I said.

"Babe?" Cal scooped a protective hand around my waist and plucked the stone from my fingers. The light died, revealing the same blotchy brown and black surface from when I'd opened the box. "It's a rock."

"It's the final ingredient," I cried in both joy and terror. A week had passed since the witch-hunter-turned-elf had vanished. I'd tried to not dwell on where he'd gone or if I'd ever see him again. None of that mattered. With this stone, I could cast Valerie's spell and bring Daniel back to life.

What if I fuck it up?

"What has you in such a state?" Ink asked, oozing into the room. "Calvin, did you place another shackle upon her finger?"

"No." He groaned, looking at my finger, where the amethyst pressed against my pinkie from the ring slipping. Taking my hand in his, he chided Ink. "Why are you an ass all the time?"

Ink shrugged with his usual cheeky grin. "It would be cruel to deny the world this perfection." He twisted like he was snapping his spine and curled a hand around his butt, then gave it a slap.

"That isn't what I—"

Cal's complaint was interrupted by Ink plucking the rock from his fingers. Once again it lit up with the rainbow, but the colors didn't fill the whole living room. Ink tossed the unicorn skin back and forth from one hand to the other. "So the stain in the rug is to become permanent. Well, fifty or so years permanent."

Ignoring his dig, I jerked my chin to the stone. "Raul came through."

Ink tossed the rock up high and ignored it to face me. "Your concern lies in defending the honor of a witch hunter and not crying out to the ghost?"

All my focus was on the falling stone. It looked like a garden rock, but for all I knew it was as fragile as glass. "Ink…"

I leaped for it when he snatched it out of the air and clenched his fist around the stone. The rainbow vanished. "Interesting."

"Daniel?" I called before remembering the other ingredients I needed. "Garavel?"

My angel arrived with a bowl in tow. "My lady?" he asked before glancing at Ink and Cal. "Are we to have another orgy?"

Ink snickered, but was cut off by the man of the hour phasing through the air. The August heat chilled to frostiest December. The blue halo around his body was unavoidable now.

"You called?" he asked, his voice echoing not like he was in the living room but in a huge, empty hall. Time was running out.

"We've got it," I said, approaching Daniel. He lifted his chin, his eyes a ghastly pale.

"Got what?"

I reached back for the stone, but Ink dug his claws in, his lip quirked into a near sneer. Smacking into his forearm, I tried again. He sighed like a fainting dowager and finally opened his hands. As I held the unicorn skin, the light show erupted, the colors shifting around in a wave. The wandering eyes of the ghost slowed and focused. As he stared, Daniel's irises darkened to a sharp brown.

"Is that...?"

"We're bringing you back." Tears choked me and I held out the stone like it was the world's biggest diamond. Daniel placed his hands just above mine, ethereal and cool. Soon they'd be warm and solid. I could touch him. I could touch all of him.

"Because raising the dead has never been an ill omen," Ink grumped.

"Babe, when are you...? When are we doing this?"

As I stared into the achingly handsome face, at his sculpted lips and chiseled cheekbones, my heart raced. Something that hot, that beautiful, needed to be brought back to this world. "Now."

* * * *

I dusted off my hands, spreading green chalk across my jeans. Out of habit, I held Valerie's spell up to Daniel. "How's it look?"

An answer didn't come. I turned, expecting him to be behind my shoulder scrutinizing every line. Instead, he lingered by the couch we'd shoved back against the fireplace.

The other guys stood at various points of the drawn ward. Not because they needed to, but because I didn't know where to send them. Cal held my spell book open for me. He kept trying to take a peek even though the pages were blank to him. None of them knew I'd opened it to a spell that'd protect us from a zombie's curse. No one but Daniel.

"It's almost ready," I said, approaching him. He should have been jumping for joy. For thirty years, he'd been trapped in this unending purgatory. I was about to free him. His head hung to the side and he peered at the circle with wariness.

"Barring the feather of an angel and blood of a demon. Two of the most powerful magics plucked from obscurity put to use to resurrect a single mortal. I can't decide if the Celestials would find this hilarious or depressing."

"Ink." I knew he'd be a pain, but I hadn't expected him to start tightening the screws before I even cast the spell.

He met me eye to eye, his lips pulled back so the demon fangs were exposed. I braced myself for a derisive snort, but he softened. His teeth flattened and his eyes drooped. With a shiver, he turned away from me to focus on Cal. "Wolf, your posture is atrocious. Shoulders back, arms straight."

"Daniel?" I eased closer, extending my palm upward. He broke from his cross to caress his hand over mine, only the cold touching me. "What's the matter? Why aren't you excited? You're going to be alive again."

He closed his eyes. "This spell is half-baked, from a witch who, for no known reason, helped you escape. What is her plan in all of this? Why did she not only send this incredibly rare and powerful spell but possess it in the first place?"

"Is it Valerie's motives that are bothering you or...?" I gulped hard, my cheeks burning. "Or is it me?"

His eyes opened wide and he jerked back. "Layla, no, it isn't—"

"I could say the wrong word, the wrong syllable. Get the letters all messed up."

"Babe, come on," Cal said. "You're not gonna do that."

"I could banish you by mistake. Or destroy the house. I don't know."

"With this level of power, you might raze the whole of the neighborhood to ash."

"For moon's sake, Ink. Shut it," Cal fought back. "Layla, you're not going to destroy my house, or all the other houses or banish Daniel. You know that."

"The wolf..." Garavel gritted his teeth at that. "Speaks truly. Your magics never waver. Only your faith in yourself does."

Their opinions, while sweet, didn't matter. They weren't the ones whose very existence rested on my fingers. "Daniel?"

"I'm...I'm scared." Panic choked him. His face flushed. He tried to clench his fingers around mine, but they sailed on through. I braced myself for a trademark cutting incubus remark, but Ink stayed silent. All of them did while watching Daniel fall apart.

"My faith in you is as strong as ever. I believe you can do it, but at what cost? What if this…if there's a trick or a trap and you're hurt? My life's not worth that."

"At last, something we agree upon," Ink said, but his signature smirk was gone. He sounded sincere as hell. The rest of the men all nodded solemnly with Daniel.

"You're wrong. All of you. You're worth it, Daniel, because…you'd do the same for me."

He gasped, hunting for the air he didn't need. "I love you."

Placing my hand over the heart at the top of my chest, I nodded. "I know, and it's time to make you whole again. Garavel?"

"Yes?"

"Bring out the feather," I said.

The angel reached behind his neck where he somehow stored a massive sword. "Ah…" He fished his hand out where the ten-pound kitten had dug her nails into his forearm. What I cared about was the massive feather pinched between the tips of his fingers. He seemed terrified to touch the reminder of his creator who he'd killed to save me.

I lightly brushed my palm over the shaft, so white it nearly blinded me. I didn't look at the feather but focused on Garavel. At first, he didn't let go. I traced my hand around the curve of his cheek and held him tight.

"Promise me…" Garavel stuttered. "That it will be for a worthy purpose."

"Daniel knew something that terrifies Conquest. We'll find it and stop him."

"Good." He opened his fingers and I caught the feather.

"Now the blood. Ink?"

Daniel scoffed. "You gave it to the demon? I thought you said you put it in a safe place."

Snickering, Ink reached into his pocket and lifted the glass vial to the light. "Clench your sphincter, ghost. There was no safer place to store the destructive power of demonic blood than in the clutches of a creature that cannot use it."

He held out the vial to me with no fuss, but as I went to take it, he had to say, "I would ask if you think it is worthwhile to expend such power, but when have you ever acted sensibly?"

"I am fucking an incubus," I said and clenched the distressingly cold vial. Ink smiled and bowed his head. As if he had nothing more to give, he stepped back.

"One feather of an angel, one drop of demon's blood, one unicorn flesh to unite the two." Holding the feather out, I tipped the vial of blood when my hands began to shake.

I'm gonna drop it. It'll shatter at my feet and I'll lose my only chance to hold him.

Warm fingers swept behind mine, steadying them to a surgeon's level. Cal pressed in tighter behind me to whisper, "You've got this," before kissing me on the nape of my neck.

With his help, a single drop of blood beaded on the lip of the glass and plummeted for the blinding white feather. The moment the blood hit the downy spines, the feather hardened to a rock. It felt like a feather fossil but was heavier than a bowling ball. I struggled to keep it upright, tears rising.

What happened? Was the angel not good enough? Did the feather lose its magic because he's dead?

The fossil crumbled first to gravel, then sand in my palm. Just as I held my breath, the angel's feather burst to dust and began floating away.

"Is it supposed to do that?" Cal voiced what I was too terrified to say. We had another feather, but who was to say the same thing wouldn't happen? "It's gone."

The heavy dust faded from the light, the feather taken as quickly as Daniel had been.

"Look again," Ink instructed. I fought to blink away the tears and stared. The air was no different than before with the house dust dancing in the sunlight. I focused on a single mote twirling like a dirty snowflake. As it spun, worlds appeared. A giant green marble with purple waters cascading off the edge. A black volcano with hissing red veins of lava exploding from its cracks. Skies of orange with blue sunsets. Every possible impossibility formed in a second, then folded into another.

"You've reduced the feather and blood to the base ingredients of creation. We are tinkering in the Celestials' toolbox now. Be wary."

Ink's warning felt like a fire alarm blaring in my head. If he was worried, shit was about to get real. But I couldn't stop, not when we were so close. "Now I add the unicorn skin."

Kissing the rock for good luck, I cupped it in my hands and threw it. Rather than rebounding off the wall and hitting the TV, the stone landed dead center in the middle of the floating bits of creation. It began to rotate as, one by one, every color peeled off. First red, then orange… the room lit up to the solitary hue tearing off the stone. The light grew brighter, burning with every falling shift until purple pierced straight through my brain — and blackness fell.

"Layla?"

"Can anyone get a light?"

"Where are you?"

"Ink? Is that your hand on my—?"

A soundless explosion and light came into being. A single, pinprick-sized ball floated in the middle of the ward, casting both light and heat.

"Did you just make a sun?" Cal asked.

"There is no life without light," Ink mused then squeezed my ass.

I fought to tear my eyes away from the source, not just of light and heat but magic. It shivered inside of me the way no other magic had—wild and young. Ink stared at the same micro-sun and rapture dawned on his face.

"Don't even think about it," I ordered.

"To sip from the dawn of creation would be a most exquisite meal," he murmured, his face slack with awe. Then he snickered. "And also my last. Shall we chuck the bones of the dead inside and see what slithers out of the universe's birth canal?"

I shivered at his metaphor and turned to Daniel. "Are you ready?"

He bowed his head. "Layla, promise me that if...if something goes wrong, if this doesn't work—"

What? Did he have a backup plan? A way to bring back a ghost that he'd found in one of the books?

Wafting his chilled fingers above my cheek, Daniel stepped closer. He placed his palm over the locket and whispered, "You do not blame yourself."

"I can't—"

"Promise. Or this ends here."

Everyone went silent save the low hum of the universe birthing itself before us. "Daniel, I..." Clenching around the locket through his hand, I gazed into his eyes. "I promise." I pulled open the golden heart and lifted the single fragment of finger bone.

Facing the storm, I held the piece of the lost. *There's a very good chance this will fail. I won't just lose the opportunity… I'll lose him. But if I don't do anything, I'll lose him anyway.*

"Daniel, I love you," I cried out. Then I tossed the bone into the primordial fire. Nothing happened. Daniel remained beside me, his cool form competing against the heat of the micro-sun.

Now for the hardest part, reading gibberish and getting it right. Shaking, I unrolled the scrap of paper we'd been working on. Daniel had written it phonetically for me.

Raising my head, I stared at the incoherent mix of vowels and consonants. I took one last look at him and spoke. "Rise."

A bong echoed through the room and I slapped a hand over my mouth. "I didn't say that. I said this…whatever this is."

"You are speaking the language of creation," Garavel explained. "Nonsense is impossible when sense does not yet exist."

"From the ashes of Celestials, the fires of their veins, I command you to rise…Daniel Lu. Return from the darkness and enter the light."

The room exploded, blinding white rays shooting out of the sun. We hit the ground as one, power rampaging above us. Daniel opened his mouth and threw his head back. The light pierced him, burrowing tiny holes in his body that began to chew him apart. He swiveled his head to me, his mouth still strained as if he was screaming.

What did I do?

I reached for him, and he smiled. "Layla," he whispered just as the light burned him to ash.

Darkness fell.

Scrambling to my feet, I fought to catch fire on my fingers, when Ink grabbed my hand. "That is most unwise right now. You might set the entire planet aflame." I pulled to get my arm back, needing to find a flashlight and a passage to bring Daniel back.

"Cal? Garavel?"

"I am here, lady witch. A cushion softened my fall."

"That'd be me." Cal moaned. Manic shuffling told me the two were trying to get untangled, no doubt uneasy in this pitch darkness. I reached for any of them, knocking my palm into an arm and trailing down to a hand. Garavel's.

"We have to fix this. Find a way to…"

"Lady witch, look."

He pointed, though he didn't have to. A single mote of dust glowed. It appeared five feet in the air, then floated down to the ground. More appeared, each taking the same path, but as they fell, they built outward as if creating something…or someone.

"Is it working?" I cried out.

"Appears to be," Cal said. In the near darkness, he held up two thumbs for me.

Ink sauntered closer to watch and mused. "A thought occurs to me. Are you certain he shall be returned to you as he had been?"

"What are you talking about?"

"Or will he be revived as a babe, and you shall have to raise your future lover from infancy? How de Sade of you."

"Ink." I groaned, really not ready to face those fucked up repercussions.

I didn't have to wait long to see if Ink was right. The magic picked up speed, forming the outline of a fully grown man. It moved like a 3D printer, laying out a layer before moving higher. I couldn't see any details, the light blinding them away, but in the shadows I spotted toes and fingers, the crook of an elbow, a person. A man. Daniel.

Holding Garavel's and Ink's hands, I watched in near silence. Hours had to pass, but I was terrified to blink. If I looked away, he could vanish. With every layer of light, it grew harder to see, my eyes watering. I couldn't fight it anymore and closed them tight just as creation vanished.

The darkness receded as the house lights took over. Blinking away my tears, I faced my creation.

My god, he's beautiful. It hit me that in my months of knowing him, I'd never seen Daniel sleep. I couldn't. There he was, his arms at the side, his soulful eyes closed, his lips parted—deep in the throes of slumber. So deep it could almost be confused for…for…?

"Is he breathing?"

"I'm not sure. Dan? Hey, Daniel?" Cal shouted.

The hands holding me fell away. I crossed the line of creation without realizing it was there and dove for his still lips. "Daniel?" I cried, my voice beating against the darkness. "Breathe. You have to breathe. Fight. Come back to me. Please."

About the Author

Ellen Mint adores the adorkable heroes who charm with their shy smiles and heroines that pack a punch. She has a needy black lab named after Granny Weatherwax from Discworld. Sadly, her dog is more of a Magrat.

When she's not writing imposing incubi or saucy aliens, she does silly things like make a tiny library full of her books. Her background is in genetics and she married a food scientist so the two of them nerd out over things like gut bacteria. She also loves gaming, particularly some of the bigger RPG titles. If you want to get her talking for hours, just bring up Dragon Age.

Ellen loves to hear from readers. You can find her contact information, website details and author profile page at https://www.totallybound.com

Home of Erotic Romance

Sign up for our newsletter and find out about all our romance book releases, eBook sales and promotions, sneak peeks and FREE romance books!

www.ingramcontent.com/pod-product-compliance
Lightning Source LLC
Chambersburg PA
CBHW030358030726
47497CB00002B/389